Inky Stevens,

For Whom
the School-Bell
Tolls

Chris Martin

Cover design Martyn Hayes.
Thanks to Bob and Andy Martin for their technical support.
Also to John Winstanley for his guidance.

Facebook: Inky Stevens
Website: www.inkystevens.com

Inky Stevens is part of the 'murderplays.com' canon.
Facebook: Murderplays Murder-Mystery Scripts.

Other books in the Inky Stevens catalogue:

Inky Stevens the Great School Detective - The Case of the Caretaker's Keys.

Disclaimer:
This novel is set in a fictitious school, in a fictitious town, somewhere in Britain.
Having taught for over 20 years in several different schools I possess a wealth of
educational experience from which to draw. In doing so, however, I have created the
'types of characters' who I believe exist in all schools throughout the world. The *Inky
Stevens* series is a work of fiction. Its characters, places, events and incidents, though
grounded in reality, are products of my imagination and only used in a fictitious
manner. On the rare occasion I've borrowed the actual name of an individual
familiar to me, this has been done solely to honour that person (or as part of an
online competition). Any actual resemblance between them and the character as it
appears within the text is purely coincidental.
Chris Martin 2015.

ISBN 978-1-78222-426-6

Book design, layout and production management by Into Print
www.intoprint.net

Printed and bound in UK and USA by Lightning Source

For Isabel and little Sammy.
For June for her patience and Geoff for his wisdom.

Online praise for:

Inky Stevens, The Case of the Caretaker's Keys
Please post a review on Amazon.co.uk/Inky Stevens

Step aside J.K.Rowling.
A brilliant read with clever plot twists throughout, and appealing and engaging characters. This tale of mystery and subterfuge keeps the reader guessing right up to its explosive end. A 'must-read' for mystery fans of all ages!
Seventynil.

Brilliant Read.
Brought loads of memories flooding back. You can tell the writer really understands what makes school kids and their teachers tick. A brilliant mystery that twists and turns right up to its conclusion. Can't wait for the next one!
Elaine D.

Cleverly Crafted.
The story is set against a background that all teenage readers will identify with. It's well paced and contains enough red herrings to keep the reader desperate to turn the page.
Geoffrey M.

Young Sherlock.
A thoroughly enjoyable read starring Inky Stevens, the 'Young Sherlock' of Blinkton Comprehensive School. The colourful and entertaining characters were a joy to follow. The reader is led along many, varied paths before the final surprising revelation!
(A good dose of witty repartee too from this talented author.)
Paul B.

Is Inky the next Harry Potter?
This is a fantastic read! It has you gripped from the very beginning and the plot is spectacular. Funny but with some serious points to make too. More from this author please!!
Dr Robin T.

Inky Rocks!
I hoped for page turning intrigue and I wasn't disappointed. Viva Inky!
Nadine R.

Cleverly crafted with an explosive end!
Set in a secondary school 'Inky Stevens' really captures the essence of what school was really like (in a comic way). An insightful whodunit that was engaging right to the end. Fantastic!
Steven H.

A Whodunit Masterclass.
This book ticks all the boxes. My family and I read it together and I found it as enthralling as my children did. I look forward to the next instalment.
Ian G-W.

A Great Read.
I bought this book for my teenage son to keep him occupied on his holiday. It had him hooked from the very first chapter. Thanks for your efforts Mr Martin.
Nick L.

Bought on the recommendation of a friend... and I'm glad that I did!
Thoroughly enjoyed this book, I couldn't put it down. Great characters and intriguing plot. Hopefully more to come.
Scott C.

Inky Makes His Mark.
My son devoured this book in a couple of days and were left wanting more. Well done Mr Martin, let's have some more!
Sean K.

Five Stars.
Fantastic read. Looking forward to more.
Mollymog.

Contents

Prologue:

Sunday 11th December (Late Evening).

As the light receded, the sea at the base of the cliffs was reduced to a swirling mass of shadow. Freezing water hammered against splintered rocks causing spray to spew upwards onto slick granite. A desolate road snaked across the clifftops up above, its surface silvered with thick frost. Unaware of this, a Citroën *chugged* along the coastal highway, headlights slicing through icy darkness. The vehicle's registration number, 1342-BS-13, indicated that the car was of French origin and, as it had journeyed all the way from the south of France, its interior was desperately untidy. Its ashtray overflowed, a dry piece of chewing gum had been stuck onto the dashboard and its footwell was littered with fast-food wrappers, crumpled maps and empty CD cases. On its back seat, two suitcases bounced around in time with the vehicle's erratic movement.

Suddenly a rabbit leapt out from the grass verge. Caught in the car's headlights, the creature sat up on its haunches, paralysed with fear. It was powerless to do anything other than watch the vehicle's rapid approach. Wide-eyed, it let out a faint whimper then braced itself for the inevitable...

The Citroën's driver, having travelled all day, was leaden-eyed. Only seeing the rabbit at the last moment, he was forced to react on instinct. Conscious of the cliff edge, the man hauled on the steering wheel and brought his foot down onto the brake pedal. Hard. This shunted the Citroën away from the sea but diverted it onto a patch of black ice lying across the road like an oil slick. The vehicle immediately surrendered all purchase on the tarmac. Its back end lurched, then spiralled out of control. Helpless, it hurtled towards a metal road-sign which loomed up out of the night.

Out of nowhere.

The giant sign was concreted into the grass verge. Rigid and immovable.

The driver watched the distance between himself and the metal plate close with alarming speed. As it did so a reflection of car's headlights skittered across its polished surface. The young man sitting in the passenger seat raised his arms for protection, convinced that the sign's lettering would be the last thing he would ever see...

YOU ARE NOW ENTERING BLINKTON-ON-SEA, HOME

OF THE CODFATHER RESTAURANT'S WORLD-FAMOUS FISH BATTER RECIPE. ENJOY YOUR STAY AND WHEN YOU LEAVE, PLEASE COME BACK AGAIN SOON. PLEASE.

Then underneath in brackets,

(BLINKTON-ON-SEA IS PROUD TO BE TWINNED WITH 'MAL-DE-MER', FRANCE.)

The Citroën's two passengers froze. Mouths open. Bodies taught. Prepared for impact...

Then, just as suddenly it had begun, the car's tyres re-connected with dry road and the slide stopped...

Dead.

The car slammed back onto its original course, an action accompanied by the harsh sound of twisting metal. Rocking on its axis, the car continued along its way, *chugging* down the deserted road as before. All that remained of the near collision was a patch of exhaust fumes which hovered over the tarmac like a small cloud. The rabbit watched the gas disperse then hopped back into the safety of the ice-coated grass, unperturbed.

The teenager sitting in the Citroën's passenger seat was handsome in a delicate way. His hair was lustrous and long and it glimmered in the moon-light. He glanced right towards his father, his expression balanced between shock and relief. Despite the hour, the young man was wearing sunglasses. These had become dislodged during the slide and hung from his face at an awkward angle. Extending a finger, he pushed them back up onto his nose then leant over to retrieve the suitcases which had fallen into the footwell. Finally, both travellers clicked their seatbelts into place.

Belatedly.

For the final section of their journey the travellers attempted to relax and mentally prepare themselves for what lay ahead. A startled rabbit and an intimidating road-sign were just the beginning of what promised to be a very bumpy ride. Thoughtful, the pair could not help but admire the panorama which presented itself at every twist of the road. In a cloudless sky a full moon hung over the horizon like a piece of overripe fruit, smearing the black water with its silvery trail.

Despite the late hour the driver, a much older man, was immaculately dressed. He wore a fawn-coloured suit complete with waistcoat. His crisp, white shirt was fully buttoned, topped off with a tie in paisley design. But the journey had taken its toll. A large man, he looked tired and bloated.

The light from the car's dashboard gave his complexion the appearance of cold porridge. He sported thick sideburns and a Mexican-style moustache, both dyed an unlikely shade of black. What little hair he possessed had been scraped back severely then twisted into a ponytail which hung down over his collar like weathered rope.

As they rounded a bend, the Citroën's passengers caught the first glimpse of their destination. A smudge of light in the distance signalled the presence of a small town. Blinkton-on-Sea appeared to be clinging onto the coast like a limpet.

Isolated and unwelcoming.

The vehicle continued to trundle towards it, now at a much safer pace. The remote town was to be their home for the following week, (possibly two, if circumstances demanded). By the end of that time, if things went according to plan, the dismal seaside town would never be quite the same again.

When the man spoke, a gold tooth glinted at the front of his mouth,

"There it is, Jacques. Blinkton-on-Sea. At last. Remember, stick to English. Only use French for effect. I hope we'll be out of here as soon as possible, but organising everything may take a little time. Just be patient and stick to our plan. We can't afford to make any mistakes."

"Of course, father," came the reply.

The teenager settled back into a tense silence thinking that, compared to what lay ahead, a hazardous journey in a defective car would be like a stroll on the beach...

Mr Mike Bennett (Deputy-Head) Blinkton Comprehensive School:

It's time to reveal a secret that I've kept for many years. It's a terrible secret, one that I'm incredibly ashamed of and one I've never spoken of before. Not to anyone.

Until now.

What began innocently enough with a battered Citroën rolling into Blinkton ended in a trail of subterfuge, danger and destruction. But the truth of what happened back then, what really happened, has remained buried ever since. Cloaked in half-truths. Shrouded in rumour. Only discussed in whispers...

Until now.

Finally, the time's right for me to explain everything. To expose the truth... and face the consequences.

I always knew that this day would come eventually. I just didn't know when. I'd put it off for so long that it became much easier to maintain the lie than face reality. Indeed, it was only a chance event one Saturday afternoon that convinced me that I could put it off no longer. What I stumbled upon that Saturday was something that shook me from my lethargy and forced me to confront what happened. I finally understood that what took place at Blinkton School so long ago wasn't about me at all. It wasn't even about the school. It was all about 'him'. The most remarkable student I ever came across...

Inky Stevens, the Great School Detective.

The person I am today, everything I've experienced, everything I've achieved, is all down to what that young man did for me during that bitterly cold winter. Back then, Inky's bravery eclipsed my own cowardice. And although it's taken a long time, I've finally come to realise that I no longer regret what happened... I only regret that I kept it hidden for so long.

So what happened that Saturday to prompt such a change of heart?

It all started with a trip into town, no different than any other. I was loitering about the High Street as I sometimes like to do. Aimlessly killing-time. When I happened to pop into my local bookshop hoping to find something to keep me entertained during those long afternoons of my retirement. I was half-heartedly scanning the shelves, when I spotted it...

A book.

A very special book.

Instantly the colour drained from my face and my heart began to knock. 'He' was gazing back at me from the book's cover...

'Inky Stevens'.

His name was written in spooky lettering and just seeing it there caused my pulse to quicken. While I'd fought to suppress his memory for so many years, there he was staring back at me from a shelf in my local bookshop...

INKY STEVENS, THE GREAT SCHOOL DETECTIVE. THE CASE OF THE CARETAKER'S KEYS.

I removed the book from its shelf, prickling with tension. With shaking hands, I turned it over in order to discover who'd written it. For the second time that day I was confronted by a familiar face, this time an ex-colleague, 'Peregrine Dukes'.

Seeing 'Perry's' black and white photograph only confirmed my suspicions, the book I'd stumbled upon was indeed all about Inky, and about Blinkton School too. Written by Peregrine Dukes, the mild-mannered History teacher.

I stood there mesmerised... like a rabbit caught in car headlights.

I was scared of what the book might contain, yet driven to read it neverthe-less. I dashed up to the counter, thrust some notes at the assistant, then sprinted all the way back to the car park with my purchase tucked under my arm. I was desperate to find out how Dukes was connected to Inky, alarm bells already ringing inside my head.

Back at my Audi, I balanced the book on the steering wheel and started to read, eyes ablur, hands clawing at the pages. I sped through the book's Prologue with all the eagerness of a teenager on a first date. On and on I read, memories stirring like sediment at the bottom of a beer bottle... the energy of Blinkton Comprehensive, its excitement, its humour... and also its stresses.

Of course, I couldn't read the entire novel sitting in my car. So when I reached the part where the school's caretaker, Fred Varley, asked for Inky's help, I set it aside and drove home as quickly as I dared. Back home, I settled into my favourite armchair for a spell of more intensive reading. And once I'd started, I couldn't put it down... I read in my chair. I read in the bath. I read in bed. I even admit that I took the book into the loo, such was its tremendous appeal. Peregrine's story was packed full of danger and excitement. (Had I not been party to some of the events myself I'd even say his account was beyond belief.)

I devoured 'Perry's' tale faster than second-year Kevin Scarry could scoff a king-sized packet of Wotzits. What impressed me most about 'Perry's' book was Inky's ingenuity, daring and bare-faced cheek. I learned all about how he'd risked his life to confront an insanely dangerous criminal, and very nearly paid the price.

I'd heard the rumours, of course, and even dealt with Inky personally. It's just that the teenage detective was so secret in his activities that I never understood the extent of his capabilities. Suffice to say, Peregrine's novel taught me that Stevens had a much greater influence over Blinkton Comprehensive than I'd ever imagined. I knew how he'd rescued me, of course, I just wasn't aware that he'd also come to the assistance of others too. But reading all about his dealings with 'Perry' convinced me of my own course of action...

Not as an option, but as a compulsion.

He turned me into a hero but I deserted him in return. I left him to battle the demons he'd unleashed on my behalf.

So, after soaking up 'Perry's' words, I took a long, hard look at myself in the mirror... and I was ashamed of what I saw. I knew, right there and then, that the time had come. As Dukes said in his book, 'There are certain stories which have to be told!'

So the moment I'd finished reading I went into my office, switched on my computer, and began to write. And I wrote... and I wrote... and I didn't stop writing until it was done. An entire book designed to unburden me of the guilt I'd been carrying around for years. I even appear in it myself as a lesser character.

And finally, here's the truth.

My Inky Stevens story... 'Inky Stevens. For Whom the School-Bell Tolls.'

My tale takes place three months after Dukes' book during the coldest December ever recorded in Blinkton. Throughout its two week timespan the temperature rarely rose above freezing. Yet it was my own state of mind I was more preoccupied with back then. I felt that I'd lost my customary sparkle. I was desperate. Dangerously desperate. Had Inky not responded to my plea then I dread to think what would have happened to me. But he did respond. He made me a solemn promise, and the Great School Detective always kept his promises. Had I known that what I asked of him would place both him and all of Blinkton in tremendous danger, I'd never have approached him at all. But then as Dukes often said in his History lessons...

'Hindsight is an interesting, but ultimately pointless, concept.'

That winter, by sheer force of will (and the good fortune of those above me having developed serious illnesses) I'd ascended the educational ladder. From Maths teacher, to Second in Maths, to Head-of-Department and then finally Deputy-Head, every promotion had fallen neatly into place.

Too neatly.

Yet having become senior management, everything started to unravel...

I recall that, that December, I was struggling at the end of a particularly long, bleak term. After the clocks had gone back, all my leisure hours seemed to have been spent in darkness. And the arrival of Advent brought with it the added stress of the fifth-year mock examinations. My workload escalated and my spare time dissolved... the assemblies, motivational speeches, timetable, data-handling, dealing with exam boards, dealing with exam results, chasing truants down corridors (and then out of the school gates), tackling irate parents... oh, and the occasional spot of teaching, too. It was endless.

Relentless. Unmanageable. Insane.

So that December I was stressed, overworked and desperate. I was losing sleep and my health was beginning to suffer. For some reason 3:47am seemed to be my daily wake up time. I came to loathe the numb greenness of my clock's numerals mocking my attempts to sleep. And although I chose to ignore it, deep down I knew that something would have to change. For my wellbeing and for my sanity.

And then, of course, there was Her... the Snake!

Blinkton's Headteacher was sly and vicious. She governed like a tyrant. Lacking all teaching commitments Herself, Her main priority was to delegate every unenviable task to someone else. Usually me.

She ruled from afar and She made up the rules as She went along.

So the responsibility for every complaint, issue, disturbance and dilemma was deflected towards me. And by the time I finally reached out to Inky, the cracks were too obvious to ignore. Had he not come to my rescue, I dread to think what would have become of me. Inky Stevens saved my life...

And to think that I repaid him by stealing his glory!

I was wrong. Very wrong.

So what follows is my way of trying to make amends. I can only apologise for my selfish arrogance back then and hope that by finally revealing the truth that some form of atonement can be made. Here's my best attempt to do justice to the most courageous young man I ever had the good fortune to meet...

Inky Stevens, the Great School Detective.

1. The Harbor Lites Guest-House:

Monday 12ᵗʰ December (Early).

The Harbor Lites guest-house (3 stars) was owned by senior citizen, Deidre Butterfield. Her property was situated at the heart of Blinkton's seafront where the Promenade met Babylon Lane, just next door to the prestigious Codfather Fish and Chip Restaurant. Located behind both police and fire stations, her guest-house held a prime spot well away from Blinkton's more raucous attractions.

Ms Butterfield had owned the property for over a decade. After the death of husband Derek in a freak combine harvester accident, she'd invested his life insurance money on the derelict building which she'd fallen in love with during a daytrip. The name 'Harbor Lites' was all her idea. She'd deliberately misspelled it thinking that the quirky American-type wording would make it stand out to tourists. Her aim worked admirably, not so much for the name in itself, more for the fact that Ms Butterfield seemed to be incapable of spelling correctly.

Deidre had painstakingly renovated the property to a cottage-style idyll over several months. The Harbor Lites now boasted thirteen en-suite rooms, a reception area, lounge and spacious dining area. Mock-Tudor beams ran throughout, the darkness of the wood contrasting with the whiteness of the plastered walls.

Weathered fishing nets hung down from the dining room ceiling. Caught up in these were plastic lobsters, crabs, seahorses and a starfish. This installation, Deidre reasoned, would highlight Blinkton's history as a fishing town and also provide her residence with a unique talking point.

Handmade furniture and watercolour paintings further added to Harbor Lites' cottagey atmosphere. Wooden beds, upcycled writing tables and bespoke wardrobes graced every room alongside ornaments which Deidre had fashioned from driftwood... ash trays, sculptures, door stops and rough-hewn bowls containing pot-pourri. Such scatter-brained attention to detail meant that the Harbor Lites reflected Deidre's personality to a tee. Adorably eccentric.

With over ten years of service to Blinkton's tourist industry Ms Butterfield had established herself as one of the town's most popular personalities. However, with falling tourist numbers, increased council rates and a decline in the British seaside industry, she found herself in a precarious position. She'd all but run out of credit with the bank and, although she tried to ignore it, the threat of bankruptcy loomed. The proud pensioner desperately needed 'a fourth star' to be added to her signage to attract more custom yet she was unwilling to go further into debt in order to achieve this. And this was the vicious circle which kept Deidre Butterfield awake at night, one which had nudged the Harbor Lites (3 stars) towards the very brink of extinction. That December, with the off season proving especially cruel, Deidre feared that her existence as an hotelier was all but over. Yet an unusual phone call which she'd taken at the start of December provided her with one last chance of survival. It was also a call, however, which filled her with great dread...

On 2nd December Solomon Carey, Blinkton's Lord Mayor, rang Deidre out of the blue. Highly agitated, Mayor Carey had informed her all about the imminent arrival of a delegation from Blinkton's twin-town, Mal-de-Mer.

'They're a tremendously important delegation,' Carey had repeatedly stressed. He then went on to explain that at short notice two dignitaries, a father and a son, had requested accommodation in Blinkton. The elder of these dignitaries was the Lord Mayor of Mal-de-Mer, a man called Jean-Pierre Asticot. His son was called Jacques. Carey went on to explain that the pair's visit was linked to, 'a significant amount of money which the French representatives hoped to invest in Blinkton-on-Sea'.

Mayor Carey, unusually flustered for one so slippery, had gone on to inform Deidre that these Europeans were quite specific about what they required in terms of accommodation. He quoted Asticot directly,

'We wish to be sited right at the heart of your community where we can experience the real Blinkton for ourselves. Our stay will last from Sunday 11th to Friday 23rd December and, as we don't want to be seen to be overly reliant on luxury, the Harbor Lites guest-house will be sufficient for our needs. This is a 'fait accompli' monsieur. It's non-negotiable. Miss Butterfield's 3 stars will be adequate for all our needs 'provided' we have the full use of her facility to ourselves during this time.'

Mayor Carey had then gone on to explain to Deidre that, as the matter was so advantageous to Blinkton, he'd confirmed their stay without bothering to consult her. Carey felt that she'd be honoured to have been selected and that she would be handsomely rewarded for her services. Carey went on to say that he'd settle the French pair's bill in advance and, 'should their stay *prove financially advantageous to Blinkton'*, then Deidre would be awarded a substantial bonus for her pains. He'd ended his call by saying, a little too forcefully,

'It's important that this visit goes smoothly, Deidre. For your future and for that of our town. This won't be a problem, will it?'

'No... no I suppose not,' she'd replied, uneasily.

'Good, that's that then. Now,' he'd added, thinking ahead, *'all that's left for me to do is to inform the Gazette of the Asticots' visit and then arrange a tour of Blinkton's many attractions for them.'*

The conversation had ended with a warning, *'You do know how important this is, don't you, Butterfield? I cannot allow any slip ups. At any cost!'*

Thus, just after midnight on 11th December, Deidre Butterfield found herself pacing the floor of her lounge waiting for the French pair to arrive. Instead of feeling flattered at being selected so personally, she actually felt queasy.

Deidre Butterfield paced... and she paced... and she paced.

Despite the late hour, she was immaculately dressed. Ready to play host. She pulled her cardigan around her, a lump forming in her throat as she reflected on the abruptness of Mayor Carey's manner.

'Well,' she sighed, *'there's nothing I can do about it now. My guests may be extremely important, but another thing's also certain, they're extremely late!'*

Deidre padded across her leopard-skin rug finding that the leopard was not good for company. It merely gawped back up at her through black, marbled-eyes, completely unconcerned at her distress.

The welcoming fire that Deidre had lit prickled her legs every time she traipsed past. The occasional *crack* of a log was only thing which interrupted the heavy silence which had settled over the Harbor Lites. Glad of any distraction, Deidre selected another piece of wood from a wicker basket and thrust it into the heart of the blaze.

Sparks flew. Bark sizzled.

And as she gazed into the dancing flames she became lost in fond recollections from her youth...

'The feel of warm sunlight on pale skin...'

Deidre smiled as the years melted away. Her eyes softened and her face assumed a youthful appearance. Yet her reverie did not last long. It was interrupted by the *chug* of a poorly maintained motor engine pulling up outside.

The Asticots were here. Finally.

Reminiscences abandoned, it was time for Deidre Butterfield to go to work...

Jean-Pierre Asticot's Citroën spluttered along the seafront. On reaching the junction between the Promenade and Babylon Lane, he saw the words, 'Harbor Lites Guest-House, 3 stars' lit up in neon letters which flashed on and off randomly. Exhausted, he turned to his passenger,

"We're here, now remember what we planned."

"Of course, papa," replied Jacques, pointing up at the sign, "That's not how you spell *harbour* is it?"

"No. *Lights* neither."

"So much for the British education system. Les Brits. Ils sont des idiots, eh?"

"Remember what I said," he snapped, "keep French to a minimum. Only use it for effect. Don't get carried away. It's crucial that we win Blinkton over. Quickly. These people may be idiots but, for the time being, let's treat them like *important idiots.*"

"Alright, relax dad," he replied, moodily.

Asticot switched off the engine, "Well Jacques, it's time."

The French teenager unbuckled his seatbelt and gestured towards the rear of the car, "What are we going to do about him?"

"Don't you worry about him. I'll take care of all the messy stuff. You just stick to your side of the plan and we'll be home and dry within the week. Hopefully."

On hearing the Citroën's arrival, Deirdre Butterfield crept over to her window. She brushed back velvet drapes and peered out into the night. By the light of the full moon she saw that Asticot's car had pulled up onto the gravel outside. She watched as two figures clambered out, stretching their legs. The son was tall and slim with a mane of glossy hair. Strangely, he appeared to be wearing sunglasses. The elder man was shorter and heavier. More rounded. Deidre watched him rub his knees, then approach the Citroën's rear door. Hauling it open, he extracted two large suitcases which he dropped onto the frozen gravel. Slamming the door, he patted the Citroën's boot as if congratulating the vehicle for making it that far. Asticot drew his son's attention towards one of the cases, while taking hold of the other himself. The travellers then dragged their luggage towards reception, blowing out clouds of frosty air into the winter night.

Asticot, finding himself beneath a metal frame where roses had once grown, raised a hand. Yet before his knuckles could make contact, the door had swung open...

"Welcome, welcome," trilled Deidre Butterfield. "Bien-venue. Come in, come in. Quick. Tout-de suite. It's perishing out there. Welcome to Blinkton-on-Sea. Welcome to the Harbor Lites guest-house." She enquired, "It's Monsieur Asticot and son Jacques, isn't it?"

"Jean-Pierre," said the man warmly, "glad to have finally arrived. We've travelled a long way today. All the way from the South of France. It's been a tough journey but hopefully things will be more straightforward from now on. Our stay in Blinkton ought to prove," he paused, "eventful."

"Indeed," replied Deidre, "you've a busy couple of weeks ahead. The town's in a bit of a tizz about your visit. Mayor Carey's talked of little else since your reservation. He's planned a big reception for you tomorrow morning at the Town Hall. But for now, please come in out of the cold. Now," she paused for breath, "I'm here to make your stay as comfortable as possible. I'm Deidre by the way. Deidre Butterfield. Come in. Don't just stand there," she added, with a flourish, "entrez!"

The visitors wiped their feet on a doormat on which the word WELCOME was written.

"Follow me, please," cried Deidre, sweeping past reception and on into the lounge. Reaching the stairs, she disappeared without looking back. While the eccentric pensioner bounded upwards, the French duo laboured in her wake, scuffing heavy cases up three flights of thickly carpeted stairs.

At the top, Deidre pushed open the door facing her. "Voilà!" she exclaimed, "Room 13. The most expensive at my guest-house. This messieurs, is my penthouse!"

Realising that her guests were still floundering below, she announced more loudly, "Gentlemen, it's my pleasure to welcome you. Mr Carey, our Lord Mayor, has paid for everything in advance, so please don't trouble yourself with silly pounds and pence."

When the visitors finally emerged, Deidre spoke conversationally, "As requested, messieurs, you're the only ones booked in. The Harbor Lites guest-house is all yours." She continued, "This suite, my penthouse, covers this entire floor. For the next two weeks all the facilities in here, and inside the whole building, will be available to you. As am I, should you need...?"

"I can assure you, miss," said Asticot, "that neither of us will..."

"No, Monsieur Asticot. Whatever you say, I shall be available twenty-four hours a day. It's my pleasure to serve." She went on, "Let me show you around your apartment. Believe me when I say that this room, c'est formidable. Now," she gestured, "this is the lounge. Note that the windows along this side of the building are all sea facing. In daylight they offer breath-taking views of the harbour to your right, the famous Codfather Fish and Chip Restaurant to your left and, of course, the sea straight ahead. These balcony doors," she pointed to a set of glass doors which acted like a mirror in the darkness, "allow access out onto the roof-terrace just out there. Look," she said, pressing her face up against the glass, "you can just about make out the metal table and chairs outside. This garden furniture provides a front row seat to the best view Blinkton has to offer," she smiled, "although perhaps at a different time of day, in a different season. Now," she continued, "this room is placed centrally within my penthouse suite. Identical double bedrooms lead off through doors on either side. Here let me show...."

"I don't wish to be rude," Asticot placed a hand gently onto Deidre's shoulder, "but my son and I have travelled far and, with such an important meeting early tomorrow, we'd appreciate time to settle. We're capable of exploring this fine apartment for ourselves. Right Jacques?"

"Yes, papa."

"So, Miss Butterfield, if you'd be so kind as to leave us to unpack?"

Deidre struggled to hide her disappointment, "Of course. But there must be something I can do for you? Perhaps you'd like a hand with your cases?" She seized hold of Jacques' case, alarmed at its weight, "That's extremely heavy. What's in it?"

"Nothing," replied Asticot, a little too quickly. He gently prised the handle from Deidre's grasp, "Nothing's in there except what we require for two weeks of intense negotiation. So, if you'd be so kind as to give us our front door key, we'd like to bid you, bonne nuit?"

A twinkle appeared in Deidre's eye, "Mayor Carey didn't tell you, did he?"

"What?"

"There is no key here at the Harbor Lites."

"What do you mean?" replied Asticot, concerned.

"Blinkton's a friendly place, monsieur. I've never needed to lock my door in the past and I won't start now. Some people say I'm crazy, but I don't listen to them. My front door has never been, and will never be, locked. I'm sorry if you weren't informed of this little," she struggled to find the word, "*peculiarity* of mine."

Colour had appeared in Asticot's cheeks, "C'est impossible! How on earth in this day and age...?"

"On that point I'm quite adamant," she said, matching his tone. "I know you're well connected but Deidre Butterfield has never been impressed by reputation or status. This is *my* guest-house and those are *my* rules. However," she reassured, "you didn't give me time to explain properly. Your individual en-suite bedrooms..."

Asticot eyed her curiously, "Can be locked?"

"Of course. This apartment too. The keys are on the inside of the doors. See? And you'll find that both bedrooms are identical to one another so there's no need to squabble. Both have been aired specially. Beds warmed. Bathrooms scrubbed. Please let me..."

"Miss," said Jean-Pierre, "I've just said that we'll find everything ourselves. Apologies for my misunderstanding regarding the keys. Ce n'est pas un problem. Please," he gestured out into the hallway, "if you'd be so good? Goodnight."

The look in Asticot's eyes suggested that the conversation was over.

"Yes, well, I'll leave you to yourselves. Please, if there's anything I can do, don't hesitate to get in touch. I'll have your breakfast ready, nice and early. Mayor Carey will be expecting you. It's a shame that you've business to attend to so early. Would you like a call?"

"That will not be necessary," said Asticot, "our itinerary does not allow for breakfast. But thank you anyway, miss. That will be all for now. Enchante!"

Asticot bowed so low that Deidre could see how severely his hair had been scraped back. He then escorted her out onto the landing and closed the door after her.

Suddenly alone, Deidre muttered, "And welcome to the Harbor Lites to you too!"

Inside, Jacques Asticot instantly became animated, "I thought you said we needed to be the model of politeness. Being rude to the first person we've met wasn't part of our plan. You couldn't have been more abrupt if you'd tried. People in small towns talk, you know?"

"That old goat?" replied Asticot, with a sneer, "she's nothing. A nonentity. Just you wait 'til the meeting tomorrow. You'll see how charming I can be when the occasion requires it. To her, and to everyone else. Relax, and for goodness sake take those sunglasses off. Now," he said, "choose which bedroom will be ours and start unpacking our equipment. Tomorrow's going to be a busy day. Tomorrow," he grinned, "is when our plan begins in earnest."

"What about the car?"

"I'll have to wait until 'Mother Shipton' down there's asleep. Until then I need time to think."

"Fair enough. I'll have a cigarette."

"Not 'til you've unpacked, you won't!"

Jacques proceeded to lug the cases into the bedroom to the right, cursing under his breath. Meanwhile, Jean-Pierre opened the door out onto the roof-terrace. Immediately crisp sea air began to flood in. Crisp and briny. Hurriedly closing the door, the Frenchman strode outside into the night. Side-stepping the rusty furniture, he approached a set of iron railings guarding against a three-storey drop. Asticot gripped hold of the barrier firmly, relishing the bite of cold metal between his fingers. Feeling alive, he leaned out and drew cold air deep into his lungs. Beginning to feel relaxed, he studied the view which presented itself to him. The moon, he noticed, had risen steeply since the Citroën's skid an hour before. It now stood high over the horizon, cloaking the sea with a glistening train which widened as it approached the shore. The Frenchman strained to see as much of the town as he could. Way up to his left, on the clifftop, was a substantial building almost lost to shadow. This, he already knew, was Blinkton Comprehensive School. Now empty of life, the building looked robust and sinister, as if it had somehow gathered the darkness towards itself. Much closer, he saw Blinkton's more modern amenities... its restaurants, arcades and fast-food outlets. He even studied the phone box directly below and tried to discern the police and fire stations to the rear of the property. As expected, at that time of night, all was deathly quiet. Shrouded in out-of-season despondency. A grin slowly cut across Asticot's face causing a single gold tooth to reveal itself to the moonlight.

It had begun. Everything had gone to plan.

So far.

Feeling an icy breeze tug his collar, he sat down on the metal seating and folded his arms. He knew that he'd have to wait for some time before Butterfield finally turned off the downstairs lights, allowing him to return to his Citroën...

Less than a mile away Inky Stevens rolled over in his sleep. Chased by formless creatures through his dreams, he let out a troubled cry. He didn't know it at that point, of course, but a powder keg had just rolled into town... and its fuse was lit...

2. BLINKTON SCHOOL HALL:

Friday 16ᵗʰ December (Afternoon).

Out of a grey-white sky snowflakes began to fall. Gently at first then, whipped up by the north wind, with frightening intensity. The snow-storm, as well as unsettling the fifth-years in the Hall, also served to highlight the temperature difference between inside and out. While snow piled up on the playground outside, inside school the temperature bordered on tropical. The school's new heating system, cranked up to full, had created a suffocating atmosphere for those about to sit the most important exam of their lives. And having the entire year-group squeezed in so tightly together only served to push the thermometer higher. Flushed pupils removed clothing or used their hands as improvised fans. Andrew Haynes, fearing the onset of his asthma, scrabbled around in his pocket for an inhaler.

A thick layer of condensation had formed along windows which stretched the length of the school building. It wasn't long before individual drops of water had joined together to form rivulets which slid down the surface of the glass. Thus, as one o'clock approached, water streamed down onto school-bags below, finally gathering in warm puddles on the parquet flooring.

Yet this stuffy atmosphere was of no consequence to the Snake. What was about to take place had been the Headmistress's priority for months. She'd very carefully orchestrated everything that was about to happen. One o'clock on Friday 16ᵗʰ December marked the starting point of Her victory. Blinkton Comprehensive's colossal triumph. And She was determined that nothing would interrupt the preparations She'd forced others to make on Her behalf... Not the snow. Not the cold. Not the condensation. Not even Andrew Haynes and his confounded asthma.

Nothing. Absolutely nothing at all.

The dates 14ᵗʰ to the 23ʳᵈ of December had been set-aside for the fifth-year mock examinations (Blinkton School's most crucial time so far that year). Although several *lesser* tests had already taken place (Textiles, Music, Drama, PE, Motor Vehicle Studies), the afternoon of Friday 16ᵗʰ December marked the first of the heavyweight exams, those involving the entire year-group in one sitting. One o'clock that Friday was 'Mathematics'.

The whole of year-five had been fed a hearty lunch then shepherded into the Hall in readiness. Thus, as the start-time approached, over two hundred fifth-years sat at wooden desks, cocooned in a tense silence. Every student was watching the second hand of a large clock tick away their final moments of freedom. Yet strangely for Blinkton, on this occasion the fifth-year exuded an air of confidence. The students were not slumped over, foreheads plonked onto graffitied wood, fast asleep as usual. Instead they were alert and, for once, totally prepared. Students gazed across at one another nodding confidently. United in composure. Year-five were more prepared for this exam than any other they'd sat. Ever. A minority was experiencing last-minute nerves, of course, but this was only natural. All part of the Snake's masterplan. Such butterflies only served to increase anticipation for what lay ahead. Nature's way of providing that extra little boost.

A school's Maths result, rightly or wrongly, is considered more important than results in other subjects. When a school's on trial it's its Maths score that's placed under the microscope. Grades from other subjects can be squashed, manipulated or dressed-up in fancy clothes to make them look nicer. More flattering. More appealing.

But not Mathematics.

Quite simply, a school stands or falls on the outcome of this single statistic. And just before 1pm on the 16th December, nobody was more acutely aware of this than the Snake. That year, more than any other during Her career, She would not tolerate failure. Under any circumstances. Blinkton's Head was on a crusade, the roots of which stemmed from the previous summer...

The annual Headteacher's Meeting had occurred during the summer holidays at County Hall in Slambrough, the largest town in the area. There, following a break in between agenda items, the Snake had wandered over to the refreshment trolley to avail Herself of some vol-au-vents. By chance, She'd bumped into Roger Rowlandson, Headmaster of rival school 'St Derek's' at Krull. Rowlandson, smoothing down the sides of his moustache with manicured fingers, relished the opportunity to gloat. He found himself unable to conceal the smugness which hovered above his head like a halo,

"Sad to see Blinkton's exam results are down again, miss," he purred. "Guess you had a bit of a stinker over there on the coast in *the town that time forgot*? 'A sea fret', eh? Can't have done your standing within the community much good. Not results of that calibre. Especially in Maths. Tut-tut," he gloried, "I'm surprised you even turned up here at all. What with the focus of this afternoon's meeting being 'maximising potential'. You see," he said, wiping crumbs from his moustache, "Mathematics is the bedrock of any *outstanding* school. St Derek's, you see, managed to score over thirty five per cent more than Blinkton. Impressive, eh? I mean, we scored as highly as ever, but who'd have thought that, by contrast, your results would end up being so dismal, so," he stretched out the phrase, "despicably, disgracefully, stinkingly awful. Takes some doing that, I imagine? You'd need to be quite good at Maths to work out a percentage so low." Rowlandson, to his cost, failed to notice vol-au-vent which the Snake had pulverised within Her fist. "Were you aware that St Derek's Mathematics result was the highest in the county. Again. While Blinkton Comp is right at the, well, you don't need me to spell it out, do you? All down to preparation, miss. Starting with a successful mock exam. Now listen carefully," he said, in a tone even more patronising, "we treat our Christmas mock exam exactly like the real thing. That way our students are fully prepared by the time it comes around. You see..."

But Roger Rowlandson found himself incapable of further speech as a squashed vol-au-vent had been stuffed so far into his mouth that he could no longer breathe.

The Snake flung the refreshment trolley aside sending it careering into a delegation of educational advisors. French Fancies cartwheeled, chocolate éclairs scattered and slices of Battenberg flew across the room like frisbees. Spitting fury, She pinned Rowlandson up against a wall, then slashed at him with razorblade-fingernails. Bile poured from Her mouth which was contorted into an expression of disgust. No-one had ever dared to address Her with such derision. Finding Herself nose to nose with Her opposite number, She assured Rowlandson in no uncertain terms that Her Maths result, by Christmas, would not only be as good as St Derek's but far, far better. Then, just as She was about to etch Her prediction in fountain pen across Rowlandson's forehead, She was tackled to the ground by a team of educational bigwigs. And as She was removed from the building, kicking and screaming, Her voice trailed off down the hallway,

"You can shove your Maths result where the grass don't grow, Rowlandson. By the time *the town that time forgot* breaks up for Christmas you'll see what my students are capable of. I guarantee you, right here, right now, that by the Feast of Stephen Blinkton Comprehensive will have dear, departed Saint Derek spinning in his wooden box. Just you see, Rowly. Just you see!"

The Snake had finally been escorted outside by security, leaving a trail of mashed confectionary behind. On the pavement She was already forming a plan of attack. She would not be humiliated in such a manner. She would become a master-strategist, a churchillian war general, and then She would conquer St Derek's at Krull. So, even before Roger Rowlandson had been whisked away citing a severe migraine, She'd made Herself a solemn pledge,

'Blinkton Comprehensive will beat St Derek's at Maths this Christmas, whatever it takes!'

The Snake's decision, of course, had a considerable impact on the day-to-day atmosphere around Blinkton School. During the Christmas term She'd used Her influence to insist on Maths success for every fifth-year student. In the days, weeks and months leading up to one o'clock on Friday December 16th, Mathematics was targeted at the expense of every other subject. She attacked students with Mathematics like a war-general, (from afar). Every student had been put through their paces, not only in their timetabled Maths lessons, but at other times too... in lessons stolen from other (less important) subjects, afterschool, at weekends, and at a specially arranged Maths boot-camp. She even threatened to cancel the Christmas disco if so much as one student fell below Her expectations. Thus, one by one, Blinkton's fifth-year had been bullied into submission, assaulted by a never-ending succession of decimals, fractions, formulae, statistics, graphs, trigonometry, geometry, sines, cosines, percentages, data, probability and angles. Then, just as each pupil had reached breaking point, She'd algebra-ed them to within an inch of their lives. No set-square left unused.

This relentless programme of Maths-destruction took its toll, of course, and not just on the students. The teachers in the Maths Department had been driven to the brink of exhaustion. Miss Wrennall had developed an unsightly rash. Miss Jenkins, an NQT, sported a twitch at one side of her face and Mr Brain hadn't slept properly in over a month. Yet these were antici-pated side-effects. There were always going to be casualties. Staff could be replaced, but the overthrow of Roger Rowlandson at St Derek's would be permanent.

For ever and ever. Amen.

Blinkton's uncompromising Head had considered other factors too... In Her weekly meeting with new caretaker, Ray Day, She'd produced detailed plans of exactly how She wanted the Hall set out. She'd nonchalantly tossed this floorplan at Day (the one She'd forced Mike Bennett to devise, then claimed as Her own). Day had then been forced to spend the majority of his weekend transforming Her blueprint into reality. By hand, the barrel chested caretaker had manoeuvred over two hundred brand new desks and chairs into their designated positions, each with individual name and number cards. Until, finally, the Hall had assumed a chessboard arrangement of precise rows and columns, only two feet separating each desk from its neighbour.

Symmetrical. Like graph paper.

Exhausted, Day had emerged from a mountain of cardboard and polystyrene muttering a succession of highly detailed biological terms. Yet as far as the Snake was concerned, what Ray Day thought was of no importance. What anyone thought about anything was of no importance. Blinkton School would dance to Her tune. She *would* beat Roger Rowlandson.

'Blinkton Comprehensive', She fantasised, 'will shine like a beacon!'

Thus, at three minutes to one, two hundred students sat in their designated places, heads swimming with mathematical data. Blinkton's fifth-year had just one chance to shine. One chance for every student to demonstrate they were worthy of the investment made on their behalf. And, as the minute hand of an enormous clock crept slowly towards vertical, an expectant hush descended over the Hall...

The Snake, relaxing inside Her office, smiled the type of smile that causes milk to curdle. Hands laced behind Her head, She leant back in Her designer-chair indulging Her fantasies...

'The result. The publicity. The nods of appreciation at County Hall, and, more importantly, the look of smugness wiped off Roger Rowlandson's waxy face. Priceless!'

As far as She was concerned, Her task was complete. All She had to do was wait for three o'clock, then apply pressure to the Maths Department to mark the papers for Her as soon as possible.

The time was nigh!

At two minutes to one the Hall's double doors flew open and Head-of-Maths, Marjorie Spiller, emerged like a boxer to a prize fight. A sea of heads span around to greet her arrival. The no-nonsense Maths mistress wrapped her cardigan around herself, then marched through the body of the room, gracefully threading in between tightly packed desks. Reaching the stage, Spiller ascended the short flight of stairs up onto the platform then stepped across the front, curtains billowing in her wake. The sharp sound her shoes made on the wooden platform underlined the importance of what was about to happen. Two hundred faces looked up at her in expectation. Miss Spiller stopped centrestage then stared down. She cut a sinister figure standing onstage all alone. Features thin and pointed. Drawn. Ignoring the heat, she opened her mouth to speak while, collectively, the Hall drew breath...

Marjorie Spiller was painfully aware of the importance of what was about to happen. The Snake had stressed to her,

'A good Maths result, will not only bolster the reputation of this school, Miss Spiller, but it could also make a significant difference to you, if you receive my meaning? If you have any ideas of rising up the educational ladder then I'd take it kindly if our mock exam reflects My craving for success. It will, won't it, Miss Spiller. Won't it!?'

Thus, for the sake of her career, Marjorie Spiller could not entertain thoughts of failure. Despite being even more nervous than her students, she managed to convey a mood of calm. She gazed over her shoulder towards the clock with measured control.

One minute to go.

With a sense of theatre, Marjorie Spiller brushed an imaginary piece of lint from her skirt then began the speech which she'd rehearsed several times at home,

"Year-five," she said, relieved at the composure in her voice, "as I'm sure you're aware Christmas is around the corner. Judging by the weather conditions outside some of you may feel that it's arrived already. But let me assure you of one thing, it hasn't!"

Despite the mention of snow, not one student broke 'Killer's' stare.

Fifty seconds to go.

"Most of you sitting here now have already sat at least one examination. As a result you may think you know what to expect. But believe me," she paused, "you don't. This, year-five, is Mathematics. Mathematics," she repeated, "is the most important subject in the world. The subject which runs the world..."

Forty seconds.

"... so for this mock exam, unlike any other, you'll need to use *all* your concentration, *all* of your energy, and *all* your brainpower. Respond to the questions exactly as you have done in your classes. Do this, my students, and you'll excel. Remember, aim for the stars! Nothing in your exam paper," she said, voice rising, "is there to catch you out. This is merely a chance for you to show off what you already know. Do not," she said, so abruptly that Adam Cook in the front row let out a slight squeal, "finish the paper early."

Twenty seconds.

"Make sure you show all your workings out and fill in all of the answers in the space provided. Go back over the exam once you've finished and use any extra time to check, then re-check, your answers. Then, if you still have time, why don't you check them once more? Just for luck."

Ten seconds.

"Now, just before we start. Raise your hand if you do not have a pen, pencil, protractor, pair of compasses, book of log tables or non-programmable calculator."

Year-five looked up blankly from their chessboard arrangement of desks not daring to speak. No-one in the Hall (other than twitchy Miss Jenkins) moved a muscle.

Exactly as rehearsed, Miss Spiller then glanced over her shoulder a final time. Timed to perfection, the second hand of the Hall's clock ticked its final beat up to twelve.

"Right year-five," she said, decisively, "it's now one o'clock precisely. You have two hours to complete your Mathematics exam. You may now pick up your pens and open your papers. Make sure to write your name and candidate number clearly on the front. No talking. If you have a problem, raise your hand and a member of the Maths Department will attend to you promptly. Good luck, year-five," she said, with finality, then added, "and Merry Christmas!"

'Killer' Spiller had worked her magic. Like a hypnotist she'd charmed a problematic year-group into a positive frame of mind. With acting skills Miss Birkin would have applauded, she'd set a group of reluctant learners off on the turbulent voyage of Mathematics. They were now surging forwards on the course plotted for them by the Snake.

Proud of herself, 'Killer' turned to write down the exam timings onto the whiteboard behind her, the tiniest sparkle in her eye the only indication of the elation she felt. Composing herself, she turned back to face the candidates with stoic indifference. Marjorie Spiller's role within the whole pantomime was now complete.

After Spiller's instructions, there'd been a brief hubbub while pens and pencils were picked up, question papers opened, and chairs scraped into position. Then a hush descended over the Hall as comfortable as Deidre Butterfield's favourite slippers. This, combined with the deepening snow outside, had the effect of cocooning year-five in an alien world of intense mathematical thought. Every face was angled down onto its test paper, grappling with the most challenging puzzles that the exam board could conjure up. Yet 'Killer' could not afford to relax. Not yet. Two challenging hours lay ahead in which every conundrum had to be approached, seized, spun around, and then slammed down onto the mathematical canvas.

Identified. Immobilised. Then slain.

But having started off so positively, Blinkton's Head-of-Maths could see nothing ahead but success. Her fledglings were beginning to fly. Only...

... that's not how things turned out!

No-one could have predicted what happened just ten minutes into the exam.

Not the students. Not the members of the Maths Department patrolling the Hall. And certainly not Miss Spiller herself...

DDDRRRRIIIINNNNNGGGG!

An alarm bell high up on the back wall leapt into life, its vibrations causing tiny particles of dust to float down onto the bewildered staff-members below.

DDDRRRRIIIINNNNNGGGG!

A mass of scraggy haired students looked up in confusion.

DDDRRRRIIIINNNNNGGGG...!

The noise continued, prolonged and deafening.

Indecision rippled through the Hall. One by one, pens which had hitherto been a blur of activity were cast aside. Debbie Womack raised her hands to her ears and closed her eyes. Delicate Dawn Foster, terrified by the bell, slid underneath her desk. Mischievous Nadine Roberts was more adventurous. She recognised an opportunity to have some *proper fun*. She discreetly leaned over to the boy next to her and before David Quinn had realised what was happening Roberts had copied his answers from questions 8 to 13.

Liam Hatch, watching Nadine's antics, came up with an entertaining scheme of his own. He extended his leg as far as it would go. Then, by pointing his toe, he was able to flip Moreno Rowena's desk over. Her desk fell to the floor with a monumental *crash*. Liam found his prank hilarious, as did those seated beside them. Moreno, however, was less impressed. Humiliated, she was forced to retaliate. On instinct she reached over, grabbed Hatch's answer paper, and ripped it in half, an action which provoked even more whoops of delight. This meant that it was now Liam's turn to react. Yet instead of attacking Moreno, he lurched in the opposite direction and grabbed hold of

Madge Monk's work instead. Despite Monk's protests, Hatch screwed her paper up and threw it across the room towards Howard Atkinson. School goalkeeper, 'Atty', caught it easily but his flamboyant dive sent even more desks tumbling. Madge Monk, who'd revised especially hard for the exam and been promised a bike if she did well, was visibly upset. This, in turn, upset her best friend, Katy Lea and, with the Hall descending into chaos, Lea attacked Atkinson in the worst way she could think of... she messed-up his hair. Vain 'Atty', who'd spent two hours gelling his hairdo to make it look as if he'd just got out of bed, flung his arms about like he was being attacked by wasps.

And so the unrest went on, and on... and on...

More papers were thrown. More desks collapsed. More students shrieked.

And still the sound of the bell continued to tear at the air...

DDDRRRRIIIINNNNNGGGG....!

The members of the Maths Department looked from one to another helplessly. *'What do we do now?'* mouthed Miss Jenkins, her twitches and ticks more pronounced than ever.

'I don't know,' came Miss Spiller's mimed response, *'I just... I just don't know!'*

DDDRRRRIIIINNNNNGGGG....!

From her raised platform, all Marjorie Spiller could see was unbridled bedlam. She watched swathes of students rushing over to the Hall windows, trampling brand new furniture underfoot. Then, when these marauders were able to see just how deep the snow was outside, total hysteria erupted.

Cheeky Joe Leather and his friend Vera Menary started to scrawl a series of rude words into the condensation. Marjorie Spiller, realising that she didn't know what some of the words meant, was horrified. She began to massage her temples desperately wanting to be somewhere else, anywhere else, all thoughts of a successful exam having long since vanished.

DDDRRRRIIIINNNNNGGGG....!

Finally, like a sheriff dispatched to sort out a lawless town, Deputy-Head Mike Bennett burst into the Hall. Enraged, he managed to yell just about loud enough to be heard,

"Right everyone, calm down! No need to panic. It's just the fire alarm. Listen up! LISTEN UP!" he repeated. "At this stage we're unsure whether it's a genuine emergency or not. Joseph Leather," he called out, distracted by a very detailed picture in the condensation, "wipe that off this minute! Now," he said, "I need you all to walk in an orderly fashion to your nearest exit. I'd then like you to make your way to the main yard and line up in your form groups in alphabetical order so that we can commence our registr..."

But the rest of Bennett's speech was drowned out by the squeals of 200 delighted teenagers. Year-five did not need telling twice to leave a Maths exam to go outside and play in the snow. Demented kids began to rampage. Such was their hurry to leave, many students fought their way through the bottleneck that had formed beside the exit. As a result, many tumbled to the ground and were trampled upon.

Within moments the Hall was virtually empty. The few who remained included Mike Bennett, a cluster of shell-shocked Maths teachers (including Miss Spiller, rigid), and young-Dawn Foster lying among the wreckage with a size seven bootprint on her forehead. A sea of question and answer papers, pens and pencils and unused mathematical equipment were strewn across the floor alongside a hall-full of upturned desks and chairs. Any hope of a positive exam result lay with them, scattered among the debris.

And worse was to follow...

Colour co-ordinated symbols painted onto the tarmac in the main yard indicated where each form group was required to assemble. Yet on December 16th these were buried beneath an ever-deepening layer of snow so no-one knew where to line up. And Blinkton's schoolkids, being schoolkids, were intent on exploiting this loophole to its full advantage.

Anarchy ensued.

Having poured out of every possible door (and a few windows), the students compressed wet snow into snowballs and immediately started pelting one another. Under the cover of the storm they felt that they could act without consequence. Nikki Saunders hurled hers at Carol Holmes but the third-year girl ducked and the snowball caught first-year Tricia Pike in the face. This resulted in Pike's glasses flying off and being trodden on by fourth-year Kathleen Flynn. Flynn, as it happened, only stepped on them because she was running away from Laura Connaughton who, in turn, was intent on shoving snow down Flynn's back. Laura Connaughton, being muscular and quick, easily caught Flynn and grappled her to the ground. She then jammed handfuls of snow down Flynn's jumper, an act which caused the unfortunate Flynn to shriek like a squirrel with its tail on fire. Connaughton then finished off her assault by rubbing ice directly into Flynn's face. Just for good measure. (Laura Connaughton found this kind of activity much more satisfying than *proper* school.)

Elsewhere, Leah Boozey was delighted to discover an enormous icicle hanging from a dustbin behind the Dining Hall. She snapped this off and crept up behind a variety of unsuspecting dupes in order to jab it deep into their ears. Boozey found her new game hilarious, until, that is, Emma Wallage became the first of her victims to retaliate. Enraged, Wallage grabbed the icicle out of Boozey's hand and proceeded to give her attacker a taste of her own medicine. She rammed it straight down Boozey's back and held on to her collar until it had completely melted. (Boozey found the damp patch lingering at the base of her spine for the rest of the day far less enjoyable.)

Over by the bike sheds Big-Sean Kennedy and Joe 'Fish-eye' Bradshaw ambushed fourth-year Science boffin Keith Mullen. Attacking Mullen from either side, the troublesome pair pulled his legs out from under him. The Chemistry geek instantly found himself face down in a thick blanket of snow. Seeing Mullen defenceless, Bradshaw leapt upon him to pin him down allowing Big-Sean to kick clumps of the white powder all over him. Repeatedly.

Kick after kick, after kick. His boots a blur of activity.

It was only when Mullen had completely disappeared under a snowdrift that Big-Sean relented. He and Bradshaw then scampered off in the direction of the Art Block, looking to repeat their routine on another unsuspecting soul.

When Mullen finally clambered to his feet he resembled an Arctic explorer.

Yet by far the most significant assault occurred outside the Languages Block. This attack was one which was to have lasting implications both for Blinkton School...

And for Inky Stevens.

Skinny fourth-year prankster Scott Cunliffe discreetly abandoned his band of raiders. On reaching Broker's Archway, he crouched down behind the school mini-bus with an agenda all of his own. Now operating solo, he used his new-found hiding place, and a significant amount of time, to create... the ultimate snowball!

The teenager produced a golfball which he dropped down into the whiteness below. Then, one coating at a time, he painstakingly fashioned his snow-weapon with the ball as its nucleus. Each layer of snow was compressed, then painstakingly smoothed off, before the next was added. In this way, slowly and surely, the ultimate snow-missile was born.

Hard, heavy and tight.

By the time Cunliffe had finished sculpting his missile his hands were so cold that he felt as though the bones in his fingers had fused together. Yet gazing at his creation, he realised that such numbness was worth it. He transferred the shot-put-sized sphere from one hand to the other, blowing life back into each hand at a time. Circulation restored, Cunliffe raised his creation aloft and gazed at it as intently as a clairvoyant might at a crystal ball. Then, after assessing the projectile's weight, he nodded to himself.

It was time for battle!

Troublemaker Cunliffe emerged out into the storm, snow whipping around his slender frame and turning his mop of thick, black hair, white.

'My creation,' he thought, *'is special. It deserves to be deployed where it can wreak maximum damage.'*

The malicious teen strode to the centre of the yard like a cowboy with a score to settle, then paused. While snow danced all around him, Cunliffe stood stock-still, legs firmly planted into virgin snow, rolling his ice-sphere from one hand to the other. Eyes narrowed, he scanned the blurry whiteness for a suitable target. He struggled initially as the Old School area by Broker's Archway was situated some distance from the main yard. But then a figure slowly appeared...

'Yes. Right there. And injured too. A sitting duck, perfect!'

Cunliffe's intended victim was Carlos Orange, an injury prone youngster who sat next to him in Biology. 'Oz' was a classmate who'd once scrawled a rude picture onto the back of Cunliffe's Science book. Although this had taken place three years before, it gave Cunliffe the excuse he needed...

Orange, free of the broken leg he'd suffered at the start of term, now sported a plaster-cast on his arm. A muslin sling knotted behind his neck added extra support for his right arm. Carrying his injury carefully, Carlos padded across fresh snow with deliberate caution.

An animal caught in the cross-hairs.

Oz had attempted to use the storm's cover to sneak out of school early, but Drama teacher Sally Birkin had redirected him back towards his assembly point. With her fierce words ringing in his ears, Oz was stumbling back across school, head angled against the storm, directly into the path of Scott Cunliffe.

'Perfect', thought Cunliffe, *'Oz always seems to miss lessons with some stupid injury or other. Probably fakes 'em too. He deserves to be pulverised. Plus, if the worst comes to the worst, he can't throw one back. This is going to be good, sooo gooood!'*

At that moment Carlos Orange stumbled. In an effort to regain his footing he just happened to look up, eyes widening as he caught sight of the blurred figure blocking his path. Realising that it was classmate Scott Cunliffe holding the most deadly snowball he'd ever seen, a lump formed at the back of his throat the size of a pebble. Oz was confused. Scott Cunliffe was his Biology partner. His *supposed* friend. Yet seeing him standing there with sure-footed determination, it was apparent that Cunliffe's intentions were anything but friendly...

Scott Cunliffe recognised that *the optimum moment* had arrived. With Oz so exposed, it was now or never. The roguish teen geared himself up with obvious intent.

Orange was in no doubt as to what was about to happen. He knew that if he didn't do something then he was *dead-meat*. In an attempt to play on Cunliffe's pity, he raised his hands into the air, normal arm vertical whereas the one encased in plaster hung askew. With his sling flapping in the blizzard, Orange tilted his head and fluttered snow-encrusted eyelashes. Yet Cunliffe was not going to succumb to such playacting. Cracking a smile, he swivelled to face his prey square on. Cunliffe, now in position, raised his throwing arm slowly.

Oz was gripped by fear yet found himself unable to take his eyes of Scott's giant snow-orb. Its magnificence matched its deadliness.

'It's time' thought Cunliffe, *'to unleash hell!'*

"No!" shouted Orange, his words ripped from his mouth by the blizzard.

Time, very briefly, stood still.

Cunliffe's movement, when it came, was explosive. With the skill of an Olympian he launched his snow-weapon with an almighty heave. Fast as a crack in ice, the sphere cut through the air.

Swift and deadly.

Directly at Orange's head.

Propelled at such a speed, gravity failed to gain even the slightest hold on the projectile. It tore across the yard like a bullet, pushing snowflakes aside then dragging them along in its wake. And as the boulder zoned in on its target, Oz could see his own terror reflected on its polished surface.

Impact was inevitable.

Unavoidable.

With gritted teeth, the injured teen attempted to take what little evasive action he could, damage limitation being the priority.

'If it's going to hit me anywhere, please don't let it be my face. I quite like my face!'

On instinct Orange reached up for protection, all thoughts of his injury forgotten. Yet with one arm in plaster he found himself unbalanced, and before he realised what was happening he'd lost his footing and was already tumbling backwards.

Ungainly and awkward. Limbs flailing.

Yet despite making a valiant attempt to avoid impact, it was always a scheme that was destined to fail...

Cunliffe's snowball piled straight into Carlos Orange. Heavy and hard, like a boxer's body blow. A perfect throw. A direct hit...

Yet...

Because Oz was off balance the missile struck his pot, not *him* at all.

This was a turn of events that was to prove incredibly lucky for Oz.

Not so lucky for Scott Cunliffe.

(Or Inky Stevens.)

Not only did Oz's plaster-cast protect him from the main force of the impact, it also acted as a mini-ski jump. Cunliffe's snow-weapon skimmed off slick plaster and surged onwards like a daredevil from a ramp. The missile was now off course. Only a few degrees. But at such a speed *just a few degrees* proved to be fatally significant. Cunliffe's missile shot off into the void on a different trajectory altogether, one certainly not intended by its creator.

Carlos Orange continued to fall backwards, feet splayed. And as he collapsed onto the carpet of snow he continued to hold his injured arm aloft. His fall was heavy, yet cushioned. Overjoyed, Oz lay smirking from a bank of snow which would retain his imprint for several days. Seeing his arm still pointing upwards like a periscope, he began to laugh...

Meanwhile the snowball continued on its journey.

Out of control. Unstoppable. Deadly.

To Scott Cunliffe, what happened next unfolded in slow-motion.

Out of the stormy void another figure emerged from underneath Broker's Arch. Sally Birkin, the intimidating Drama teacher, had decided to park her car outside the school grounds so as not to be caught out by the weather. In doing so, she'd encountered a bunch of youths attempting to escape school early (Orange included). Yet having to redirect them was a small price to pay for not having worry about being snowed in. And so it was that Miss Birkin found herself tip-toeing back towards school with the fire alarm still sounding in the background. She had one arm pressed to her stomach anchoring her coat to her body, while other clamped her beret onto her head. The Drama teacher's boots had pencil-thin heels and she was struggling to make headway across the tundra. But as she was fearful of being caught off site by the Snake, her steps were brisk and purposeful. She hustled towards her assembly point lost in a world of thought...

'What if I'm caught?'

'Will I be able to get home tonight?'

'Who should I cast in the musical show I've written?'

'Have I caught flu from Chesney Cheetham? He sneezed all over me in registration.'

Distracted, 'Flouncey' Birkin was rendered defenceless. The deflected ice-rock shot at her out of the blizzard on course for a direct hit.

Scott Cunliffe watched the inevitable happen. He opened his mouth to yell, but his warning came out slowly, like he was speaking with a mouthful of cotton wool...

"Waattccchh oouuuttt Miisssss....!"

Then...

... impact!

With the force of a comet, Cunliffe's sculpted missile embedded itself in the centre of Sally Birkin's face. Right between her eyes. The compacted ball of ice with a golfball at its nucleus, ploughed straight into her!

THWACK!!

The outcome was devastating. Utterly devastating.

The savage impact lifted 'Flouncey's' stilettoed feet off the ground and propelled her backwards, as if jerked by an invisible rope. While Birkin's beret floated gracefully to the ground like a flying saucer, she hit the ground uncharacteristically hard for someone so petite. And having hit the canvas, Birkin remained where she was without so much as a twitch. She was completely stiff.

Lifeless.

As Scott Cunliffe struggled to process what he'd just witnessed, snow collected inside his gaping mouth.

'What on earth have I just done? I can't even begin to understand how much trouble I'm going to be in!'

While Carlos Orange struggled into a sitting position, sick with fear, Sally Birkin lay immobile. *Out cold.*

Gradually, from somewhere in the distance, the sound of sirens began to compete with that of the fire alarm...

By the time that Blinkton's fire engines arrived, closely followed by the police force, the school yard was in turmoil. Rioting students pelted one other with snow. They kicked, lobbed, and hurled snowballs at one another with reckless abandon. Even the emergency services themselves came under attack.

Further chaos ensued when the ambulance service also joined them. While jeering kids formed a corridor, Miss Birkin was rolled onto a stretcher then transported away to Blinkton General Hospital. The soundtrack to her departure was the noise of frenzied cheering.

That Friday of the fire drill order was never fully restored. Fraught staff attempted to round up maniacal students, only to find that it was easier to wait for the hometime bell rather than attempting any form of registration. And once the snow had finally settled on what had been one of Blinkton's darkest days, one thing was more than apparent...

The Snake would be far from happy. There would be repercussions. And these would be severe...!

3. The Shed:

Tuesday 20ᵗʰ December (Morning Breaktime).

Tuesday breaktime saw Inky Stevens making his way to the shed in customary fashion. The noise his boots made on the Hall's parquet flooring was clean and crisp. Purposeful. He ascended the short flight of stairs onto the school's stage then strode across its front. By parting the stage curtains, he was able to slide into the blackness beyond. Lighting his torch, the detective was then able to plot a course around the assorted junk which accumulates in all unused school spaces… broken stage flats, a bicycle (minus wheel), a tombola drum, two shopping trolleys, an archery target and Peter Boyle's school-bag which Mike Sellas had hidden there the previous March.

For Inky, gaining access to his shed while the mock exams were on was problematic, but by no means impossible. That morning RE had taken place and Physics was scheduled for later that afternoon. This left a brief window for Inky to exploit his knack of being able to move around unseen.

As the young-sleuth threaded in between obstacles, his torchlight brought giant shadows to life. Spidery images twitched and danced in time with his movement.

Macabre spirits. Guardians of his domain.

Having bypassed the clutter, Inky approached the wooden shed. This was set so far back, and surrounded by so much junk, that it was virtually undetectable. No-one would know it was there… unless they already knew it was there.

On reaching the fragile structure, the detective quickly unlocked it. It was time to conduct his business, well away from prying eyes. He pushed open its door ignoring the squeal of unoiled hinges. There, just inside the opening, was his special seat. Inky's throne. A leftover piece of stage scenery from 'the King and I'. The young-investigator lowered himself onto it and switched off his torch. He placed his forearms onto the chair's armrests, took a deep breath, and began his daily ritual…

Waiting.

Waiting to offer assistance to a needy individual *if* he found their plea intriguing enough.

Tuesday 20th December was a day just like every other... to start with.

The week before Christmas is always the most fractious in any school and that year it was doubly so at Blinkton. Factors such as the impending Christmas disco and the lingering snow when added to all the chaos of the previous Friday, meant that everyone was even more unsettled than usual.

Blinkton School was a pressure-cooker of emotion waiting to explode.

So Inky had a strong inkling that his services would be required at some point that week. Not so much of *if* as *when*. As things turned out, he didn't have to wait long...

Although reaching Inky's shed was a challenge for most during the mock exams, the person who stopped by on Tuesday 20th December had no difficulty whatsoever. This man had unrestricted access to every school area.

A shaft of light briefly illuminated the blackness. Through the darkness a figure picked his way across the rubble, a succession of *bumps, bangs* and *knocks* marking his progress. This culminated in a sharp *thud*. Inky flicked on his torch and angled the light towards the disturbance. Pinpointed at the centre of his beam was a man on the floor on his knees. He looked up in surprise, squinting. This man then clambered to his feet and brushed down his trousers. He was dressed smartly in a grey business suit. Looking embarrassed, the man straightened his tie which had fallen free of his jacket.

"Forgive me," said the man, starring into the light, "I've heard the rumours, of course, but I never questioned whether they were true or not. Not until now."

Inky paused before responding, "This is an unexpected pleasure, sir. I take it that this isn't a social call? Or that you're going to attempt to evict me? I warn you that should you try to do so I'm in a position to make things very difficult for you."

"No, no, you misunderstand, Stevens. That's not my intention at all."

Inky placed the flashlight in his lap. Its beam, now angled upwards, gave the detective's features the look of a Halloween mask. His skin appeared ghostly white while dark shadows pooled at his eyes. "Can I assume then, sir, that you're here on business? That you require my help in some way?"

"Yes. Yes that's it," spluttered Blinkton's Deputy-Head.

"I can't say that I was expecting you, Mr Bennett, but I can say that your presence doesn't come as a complete surprise. Blinkton School's assumed an air that is," Inky pondered the correct phrase, "*not exactly wholesome*. It doesn't take a genius to feel the *uncertainty* surrounding this establishment. I can sense tension in the same way that animals sense natural disasters. Can I assume that your visit's connected to what happened to Miss Birkin last Friday?"

"Yes... well no... not exactly. But yes, you are right, to a degree," said Bennett. "Listen, Stevens, you know I'm taking a chance coming here, that I wouldn't be here at all if I felt I had a choice...?"

"Nobody's twisting your arm, sir. If you like, you can turn around and we can pretend that this conversation never..."

"No," said Mike Bennett a little too loudly, "that's not it at all. Look, Inky, I've always seen you as a dependable student, one full of integrity."

"I'll take that as a compliment, sir. You're very favourably thought of yourself, yet," said Inky, "this mutual appreciation doesn't explain you being here this morning. How can I help?"

To Inky, Bennett's outline was little more than a silhouette.

"Look, Stevens, I'll be brief. Rumour tells me that you've earned a reputation for being some kind of school detective. Someone who helps others. Someone who offers hope to those who seem hope-less. At least finding you here tells me that a part of that myth's true at least..."

"And?"

"Look, I can't do this here, Stevens. Not now. I can't risk being overheard. But I do need help, yes. Do you think I'd be here if I had any other option? In this... this..."

"Junkyard?"

"Exactly. Inky, I need you to come..." Mike Bennett corrected himself, "I'd take it *very kindly* if you could come... to my office at lunchtime. I do have an urgent request for you and time's running out but I can't explain it here. Not now. It's too sensitive and it would take too long. We need privacy. Please," Bennett implored, "you're my last hope. My office? Say twelve-fifteen? You're in Room 5 for English next, so you're practically next door anyway."

"Of course I'll listen to you," Inky replied, "but this goes both ways. If you haven't the courage to share your thoughts on my patch, then I get to call some of the shots. Favours need to be returned, sir. So," he said, improvising, "send a note into English requesting that I be excused. No-one need know who sent it. Mr Whittle's only doing Christmas wordsearches anyway. Nothing important."

It was the Deputy's turn to hesitate.

Backstage, silence settled like glitter inside a snow-ornament. Inky studied Bennett's silhouette carefully. His shoulders were slumped, his hair unwashed and dishevelled.

"As you wish, Stevens," Bennett finally conceded, "of course. Yes, of course that's reasonable. Thank you. Thank you so much. And please, not a word to anyone."

"Discretion's part of what I offer."

"Good. Good, thank you. I'll be in my office, then. Next lesson. See you shortly. And Stevens?"

"Sir?"

"Thanks," he said.

"I haven't agreed to anything yet."

"You've agreed to listen, and that's enough."

As Mike Bennett turned to leave, Inky aimed his torch towards the stage front. The detective watched as Blinkton's Deputy fumbled his way back through the clutter, finally disappearing through the stage curtains.

Back to reality.

Once Bennett had departed, Inky switched off his torch. Alone in the dark, he pondered the what had just happened. Could he really refuse the request of someone so influential? Bennett had taken a huge risk. But was he being incredibly brave? Or incredibly foolish?

'Could he be trusted?'

As breaktime drew to a close, Inky decided that he would weigh up what Bennett had to say for himself before determining his next course of action. He resolved that he would not be swayed by Mr Bennett's status, or his popularity. He'd listen with an open mind, the same as he listened to everyone else. A title was just a word, after all. Yet as far as Inky was concerned, whatever it was that Bennett was about to propose... it would certainly be interesting.

Inky rose, his thoughts returning to English. By torchlight he sidestepped an upended pommel horse then moved towards the opening in the curtains. His final thought before he slipped back into the real world was that whatever was troubling Mr Bennett, it was something serious. He sounded desperate...

Mr Mike Bennett (Deputy-Head):

And Indeed I was... desperate!

The Snake was always tetchy at the best of times, but when She called me in for an early morning meeting on the Monday after the fire alarm fiasco She was the devil incarnate. She'd not calmed down over the weekend. If anything, having brooded on the deliberate sabotage of Her precious exam (and it was deliberate!) She'd churned Herself up into even more of a frenzy. So when we met inside Her office that morning there was a real sense of danger lurking behind Her cold eyes.

Having welcomed me into Her office, Her hospitality immediately vanished. I was then subjected to what I can only describe as 'a volcanic stream of vitriol'. She went berserk. Completely insane. She yelled, and She screamed, and She raged. Spittle flew from Her mouth as She condemned,

'The monstrously mismanaged shambles of a Maths exam!'

At one point, attempting to be genial, I suggested that She might want to put things into perspective. Yet I'd not stuttered beyond, 'Don't you think you're over-react...?'

Before I was hit by a tidal wave of sound. Words were flung at me with such intensity that they lost all meaning. She leaned in so close that I could see tiny veins 'pop' inside Her eyes. My face turned ghostly white. I was the punchbag into which She pummelled Her anger...

Punch, after punch, after punch.

Only when Her wrath began to subside was I finally able to discern some of the things She was saying...

'Insulted', 'St Derek's', 'Get my hands on', 'Head on a plate', 'A term's work wrecked in an instant', 'County Hall', and 'Should have ripped Roger Rowlandson's prissy moustache clean off his waxy face!'

And, like a ghost ship through the mist, the reason why I'd called to Her office slowly began to drift into focus...

It was me who'd be required to resolve the situation.

My role was defined by the one word which She repeated more often, and more strongly, than all the others...

'Revenge!'

I gulped as the terrible realisation hit me....

She wanted vengeance on the person who'd set off the fire alarm. That person had robbed Her of Her precious dream and She was not going to rest until he, or she, had been identified then dealt with in a cold-hearted fashion. Her manner was that of a starving animal driven insane at the thought of fresh meat. She would have Her 'pound of flesh' at all costs!

When I left the Snake's office, I felt like a fly that had accidentally stumbled into a Venus flytrap. She'd devoured me whole then spat out the pieces. I slumped over Jinny Cartwright's desk in Reception, and I remained there for some time.

Reeling.

I must have presented a sorry sight to Miss Cartwright. She shot me a look as if to say,

'Hang on in there, Bennett. I know exactly what you're going through. I've seen many, many others in the same state as you. You certainly won't be the last.'

And as I lay face down, desperately trying to make sense of what had just happened, the thrust of what She'd demanded returned…

She wanted to know the identity of the person who'd set off the fire alarm. A lesser but no less challenging request concerned the name of the person who'd launched the snowball at Miss Birkin. (Not through any concern for Sally's welfare, of course, but because the Snake hated paying for a cover teacher while 'Flouncey' was absent.) And the person required to find these two pieces of information, before the end of term… was me.

Just me.

And the Snake had been quite specific about what would happen if I failed Her on either count. As well as being demoted and humiliated, my timetable from January would be restricted to Blinkton's 'Sparkle Group', a group made up of the very worst kids in the school… the thugs, tale-tellers, burpers, shouter-outers, uniform-refusers, nose-pickers, body-odourers, swearers and break-winders.

And as if the prospect of teaching the 'Sparkle Group' wasn't daunting enough, She also charged me to represent Her at the next Headteachers' Meeting where I'd be forced to explain to Mr Rowlandson and the rest of County Hall how poor Blinkton's Maths mock examination turned out to be.

But even worse than all of these things put together, was Her final threat…

If I didn't deliver what she asked, then on the final Friday of term I'd be required to announce the most awful message in all the various assemblies throughout the school. I would be required to tell everyone…

… that that evening's Christmas disco was cancelled!!

I was in turmoil. The Christmas disco for many students was the highlight of the school year. It offered an opportunity for everyone to unwind and celebrate together. For some it also offered the excuse to approach that 'special person' they'd admired from afar all term in the hope that young love may blossom...

And now I was faced with the very real possibility of having to cancel it!

Head spinning, I struggled to put everything in perspective. I mean, I could survive everything the Snake had thrown at me. Even battling the Sparkle Group was doable. But the one thing I couldn't do, that I wouldn't do, was cancel the Christmas disco. It went against everything I stood for. I wanted to be Santa Claus... not the Grinch. So I simply couldn't let that happen at any cost. I'd resign first. I was not going to be the person who ruined Christmas!

When I finally found the strength to peel myself off Cartwright's desk, I realised that I didn't have a choice. I simply had come up with those two names or face professional suicide. Thus I scuttled back to my office in a frenzy, hoping to formulate some kind of a plan. And as I flew down cold corridors, I scrutinised the faces of the students I passed...

'Was it you? Or you? Or you?'

I could feel one of my headaches coming on. I knew that I wouldn't be able to think straight or sleep properly until the culprits were found.

And if I couldn't find them...?

Mind whirring, I began some detective work of my own. As the damaged sensor was located in a school corridor (in Humanities) I reasoned that whoever had set it off was someone who'd been out of class at ten past one on the previous Friday. Thus my starting point was to track down every register from every teacher in school to ascertain precisely 'who was' and 'who wasn't' where they should have been that afternoon. I also called a meeting with the staff members of the Humanities Department as they were the ones closest to the damaged sensor. But my amateur sleuthing was more 'Homer Simpson' than 'Sherlock Holmes'. I charged from class to class as mad as a cat with a firework up its bottom. What I ended up collecting was over fifty registers which I was forced to sift through. Class by class. Student by student. That evening was our staff Christmas meal at Blinkton's finest (Blinkton's only) Mexican restaurant, 'Tequila Mockingbird!' But I was forced to pull out at short notice. So instead of feasting on tacos and burritos, I crunched on crackers and cheese while grappling with my self-imposed clerical work. And well beyond midnight I'd still made very little progress. I'd managed to produce a long list of possible suspects but in the process I'd uncovered more questions than found answers. For all my pains, I was only fractionally nearer to unveiling the exam wrecker. And as for the rogue snowballer, I simply hadn't a clue. I needed help. Urgently. And all the while, time continued to tick away. Just three schooldays remaining until Friday morning's round of assemblies.

I felt like a condemned man awaiting execution.

Unable to sleep, I lay in cold sheets visualising my downfall. And with the dreaded 3:47am approaching, my stomach was in knots...

(Hard as a golfball at the centre of a snowball.)

And yet the more my problems threatened to engulf me, the more straightforward the solution became. One answer continued to present itself over and over again. So many possibilities, so many unknowns, yet just one solution...

I thought, 'Maths teachers are experts in helping students to find that one, elusive answer, so shouldn't I do likewise? If what I've heard is true, and I've every reason to believe it is, then Inky Stevens is the only person who can help me. I need to find him, and I need to do so quickly. At breaktime tomorrow. Whatever the consequences, I must find out for myself whether all the rumours about him are true.

Inky Stevens... Is my only hope...

My only hope...

My only hope...'

And with that thought echoing in my mind, I finally succumbed to the solace of sleep...

4. MR. BENNETT'S OFFICE:

Tuesday 20ᵗʰ December (Morning).

Mike Bennett looked up sharply in response to the knock at his office door. Before he knew what he was doing he'd crossed over to it and pulled it open. From Inky's expression it was apparent that the young-detective meant business.

Bennett's office, though some distance from the luxury of the Snake's, was still considerably more tasteful than the *cupboards* in which the Heads-of-Year were forced to operate. His third storey room had a significant advantage over those of his colleagues, a window. Fresh, winter daylight poured in, reflecting off white-painted walls. Occupying the far wall, it gave Bennett an uninterrupted view down into the playground below. Through freshly polished glass he could see all the way across the tarmacked yard, right up to where the Gymnasium loomed up opposite, like a tombstone.

In terms of furniture, Bennett's desk dominated his office. Placed centrally, it was piled high with all manner of educational items... Maths books, an outdated computer, the third draft of the school prospectus, a telephone, the master timetable, a pot filled with paperclips and a substantial amount of paper in a variety of shapes, sizes and colours.

Sets of metal-framed chairs with orange, padded seats faced each other along opposing sides of the room. In between these was a coffee table with a fake-wood top. This was similarly cluttered with stacks of exercise books.

Mike Bennett's office mirrored his state of mind... jumbled.

Bennett's relief at Inky's arrival was obvious. Eager to proceed, he quickly ushered him in. Wary of appearing too formal, Bennet sat on the padded seating rather than behind his desk. In doing so, he accidentally caught a set of books with his heel sending them tumbling to the floor. He hastily gathered these up while gesturing for his visitor to sit opposite.

"I'd prefer to stand," said Inky.

"Yes. Yes of course," said Bennett, flustered, "can I offer you some refreshments? I've a packet of biscuits around here somewhere. Or perhaps I could ring through to Miss Cartwright to request a cup of...?"

"I think, under the circumstances, that discretion ought to be the order of the day, sir."

"Yes. Yes of course. Yes, you're right."

Inky watched Bennett as he struggled to re-position the books into yet another precariously balanced pile. The detective steepled his hands then slowly tucked them into the pockets of an overcoat which hung down to the floor like a cape. "Sir, I sense from your agitation that time is scarce. Tell me what's more important to you than my presence in Mr Whittle's English lesson."

Mike Bennett took a deep breath...

Over the course of the next few minutes I explained everything to Inky as succinctly as I could... the Maths exam fiasco, the assault on Miss Birkin and, more importantly, the threats the Snake had made to me including that of the Christmas disco being cancelled. As I spoke he stood watching me in silent contemplation. Of course I realised that I was taking a huge risk in disclosing such information to a student, but I was desperate. Plus I felt that if Inky could help me, then he deserved nothing less than total honesty. Strangely, I also felt that if I lied to him that somehow he'd know about it. (And with my predicament being what it was, I couldn't risk doing something that might result in him refusing to help me.) Besides, there was something about Inky's manner that made me want to tell the truth. I finished by explaining,

'If I can't find out these two pieces of information before Friday morning's round of assemblies, then resignation's my only option. I just can't see another way out.'

During my account Inky had stood in front of me, silent and unmoved. Thinking back, I wish I'd spoken with a little more authority. I should have been in charge of the situation when all I was doing was begging for his help. I was the one talking, but he was the one in control!

"You say, sir, that the setting off of the alarm was a hoax. This is obvious, of course, as there was no actual fire. But I need you to describe for me, as accurately as you can, the exact circumstances in which it was triggered."

"As you're aware," Bennett began, eager to help, "there are a number of fire sensors located throughout school. Mostly in corridors. The one damaged last Friday is sited in Humanities and it was the only sensor damaged at that time." He adjusted his tie, "What happened was a deliberate attack on the smooth-running of this school. Sabotage. You see, the sensor's glass was first shattered, then knocked out altogether. The glass fragments lay on the floor in shards. I swept them up myself once the fire brigade had given me the all clear."

Inky remained thoughtful, "The alarm bell sounded just after Lesson 4 had begun, at a time when all the students were in lessons..."

"Or else in the Hall sitting the Maths exam..."

"So in order to identify the culprit, assuming that the person responsible is a student, the first step is to establish who was out of class at that time..."

"That's exactly what I thought."

"... then, by a process of elimination, we need to find out which of these suspects can be placed in the Humanities block at roughly ten past one."

"Ten past one, yes."

"Were all of the fifth-year involved the Maths mock?"

"Yes. The Head was adamant. Even those feeling a little under the weather were herded into the Hall. Not one fifth-year student was missing."

"Well, that's a start," said Inky, "a whole year-group ruled out in one go. Progress. Have you met with the teachers from History and Geography? From the four classrooms along that corridor? One of them might've seen something, or someone, suspicious."

Mike Bennett rubbed his hands together, "We're thinking along the same lines, Stevens, only," he paused, "the results of this line of enquiry are a little disappointing. I called a meeting with them on Monday morning. At break-time. Mr Mountjoy was in Room 32 teaching Geography to year-one at that time. Next door in Room 33 Miss Aries was doing the same. On the other side of the corridor, in Room 34, Mr Henry was teaching History to year-three. Finally, 'Perry' Dukes was also teaching History, to the fourth-year, in Room 35."

"Four rooms. Four classes," Inky mused, "someone must've spotted something. The sensor's located in the centre of the corridor, I believe?"

"On the Geography side, yes."

"And all the classroom doors have glass panels in them?"

"Yes indeed," Bennett looked away, "but we've still drawn a blank. The Humanities teachers, it seems, were preoccupied with their lessons. Not one of them could come up with a name. 'Brylcream' Mountjoy said his room was in total darkness. Said he was showing a film about scree-slopes and ox-bow lakes. Said he'd started the Times crossword while it was on so he didn't see anything. Clive Henry said that Amanda Blunt from the third-year arrived to his lesson just after he'd started teaching. To Room 34. Mr Henry said that Blunt had produced a note requesting Tommy Woggle, who was in his class at the time, be excused to go and see Mr Charlton over in English. Both Blunt and Woggle left his room together just four or five minutes before the alarm went off. Both youngsters registered out in the yard later on so, whatever they were up to, they stayed in school."

Inky looked thoughtful, "So Blunt and Woggle left Room 34 not long before the sensor was vandalised? Did they arrive at Mr Charlton's class?"

Mike Bennett picked up a pen from the coffee table, "I'm sorry, Stevens, I... I just don't know."

"Isn't that rather negligent? Blunt and Woggle can be placed at the crime-scene and are the key suspects so far." He continued, purposeful, "Are you aware of anyone else who wasn't where they should have been last Friday at about ten past one?"

"Erm yes," stuttered Bennett, "the thing is, the thing is... that last Friday afternoon a number of students were not where they should have been. Quite a large number, actually." He began to turn the pen over in his hands, "It may be a bit of an exaggeration, but it would appear that there were more kids out of class than actually in it at that point. I've managed to produce a list."

Inky's brow furrowed, "Explain."

"Well, as you said, finding out where everyone was when the school-bell went off was the logical place to start, so last night I missed our staff Christmas meal to do precisely that."

"To trawl through every register individually?"

"Yes. A lot of donkeywork, I know. I went through every single one. Page by page, mark by mark. They revealed very precise information about who was, and who wasn't, in class at ten past one, and why."

"And?"

"And," said Bennett, feeling like a naughty schoolboy, "the thing is, the thing is, that... as it was a Friday, during a snowstorm, there were many, many students missing from class at that time. Most had excuses. Some didn't. From the evidence I documented, last Friday was utter chaos."

Inky looked disapproving, "Who runs this school, sir, you or the students?"

As no reply came, Inky continued, "You said you documented your findings. Where?"

"Here!"

Bennett hurdled several piles of books on his way back to his desk. From a drawer he removed a single piece of A4 paper. He held it out to Inky like a pupil submitting homework.

Inky stood motionless. Inclining his head to read, he saw that Bennett had scrawled the names of all those present in school on Friday Lesson 4, but who were not in their designated classrooms at ten past one. At first glance Inky guessed that there were approximately twenty-four names. Looking across, he started to read the list...

Out of Class Excuses. Lesson 4. Friday 16th December.

Brandon Lunt- Year 4- Woodwork (Foreshaw). Nosebleed.

Spikey Martin- Year 1- IT (Sheldon). Needed to go to sick-room with itchy finger.

Mike Wilson- Year 1- Music (Fazz). Felt sick after eating too much Christmas pudding.

Lottie Jones- Year 1- Music (Wally). Toilet request. (Very urgent!)

Peter Barlow- Year 2- PE (Spence) Thought he had Biology.

Paul Blowers- Year 3- Textiles (Morris) Wind. Needed to walk it off.

John Povah- Year 3- Textiles (Morris) Went with Blowers to keep him company.

Crispin Merridew- Year 2- Geography (Mountjoy) Packing away cake sale (with permission).

Big-Sean Kennedy- Year 4 Maths (Yorkshire- cover teacher) Never turned up.

Carlos Orange- Year 4 German (Deitz) Late (again) due to arm injury.

Amanda Blunt- Year 3- English (Charlton) Never turned up.

Tommy Woggle- Year 3- History (Henry) Excused because of request to see Mr Charlton.

Paul Ross- Year 2- Health Education (Moss) Spilled stuffing on jumper at lunchtime.

William Barton- Year 4- English (Tate) Never turned up.

Isabel White...

And so Bennett's list went on... and on... and on.

Then Bennett turned the paper over to reveal the full extent of the problem. If Inky was surprised to see the names continue down the reverse side, he didn't show it.

"I know, I know," admitted Bennett, "thirty-nine students out of class."

"Three times thirteen. And those are only the ones you know about."

"Yes I'm sure there'll be a couple of others too. It's like looking for..."

"... a snowflake in the Sahara?"

"Erm, yes, precisely."

"But at least we know that Mr Charlton didn't give Amanda Blunt permission to leave class to contact Tommy Woggle."

"Do we?"

"Of course. That list reveals that she never turned up to English."

"Oh yes, indeed," said Bennett, eyeing his own writing as if for the first time, "yes it does. Right..."

"So," interrupted Inky, "what do you want me to do?"

Bennett sighed, "Look Stevens," "I wouldn't have come to find you unless I was desperate. You do know that, don't you?"

Inky didn't respond.

"The thing is... the thing is," he faltered, "I can't do this on my own. I don't think I can do it at all. I'm... I'm aware that you have a *certain reputation* around school. For helping those in need. Nothing official, of course," he back-tracked, "nothing documented. It's just that when people are in difficulty they sort of, they sort of *know* that they can come to you."

"I normally receive requests about a lost spectacle case or someone copying someone else's homework," said Inky, flatly, "not something this serious."

"I understand. And I appreciate it too. Truly. The service you offer is valued and highly respected. Essential. But the thing is, if I don't find out who set that fire alarm off by Friday morning then I'm finished here at Blinkton. Can you seriously see me cancelling the Christmas disco?"

"Time moves on, sir. People forget."

Bennett's voice prickled with emotion, "But time has also run out. For me. It's now or never." His shoulders slumped, "Look, I wouldn't have come to you unless you were my last option."

"And if I decide to help, what's in it for me?"

"What's ever in it for you?" he laughed. "I've brought you the one thing you desire most, what you feed on... a mystery." He added, "And not just any old mystery. It's a deliciously tempting mystery that's completely unsolvable. Isn't that what you thrive on, Stevens? Thirty-nine names..."

"Plus the ones you've missed..."

"Plus the ones I've missed, yes."

"And that's assuming it was a student who triggered the alarm."

Standing opposite one another, Inky appeared tall and commanding whereas Bennett seemed frail by comparison. Somehow smaller.

Inky went on, "And, of course, the person who harmed Miss Birkin is a different matter altogether. Because of Friday's blizzard, it could have been anyone. The whole school was running wild at that time."

"I know," said Bennett, his voice sounding like a sigh. "The list of suspects to both crimes seems endless, but I'd hoped you'd be inspired to try nevertheless." Bennett eyed Inky expectantly, then looked away. "It's not going to happen is it? I'm going mad. Our exam results are shot and here I am scrabbling through registers after midnight then begging a fourth-year for help. I know my evidence is weak but all this detecting-stuff is new to me." A wry smile cut across his face, "I should be telling you off for your coat, Stevens, not offering you coffee, getting you off English and..."

Inky silenced Bennett by placing a finger to his lips. Without saying anything the young-sleuth stepped towards his elder and extended a hand. Before Bennett realised what was happening, Inky had removed the sheet of A4 paper from his grasp and engrossed himself in its content. He gestured for his superior to take a seat without taking his eyes from the text. Bennett did so.

Silence.

When Inky spoke, he did so in an assured tone, "You're well liked at this school, sir. Blinkton Comprehensive wouldn't be the place it is without you. You may be a little rash at times but your intentions have always been well-meaning. The students at this establishment hold you in high esteem, sir, a claim that cannot be said of every staff member."

Inky continued to inspect Bennett's list. First one side, then the other. He then folded it and slipped it into his inside pocket, "I've decided that I will help you, sir. You deserve it. You certainly don't deserve to suffer as you're suffering now. The shadow beneath your eyes tells its own story. Try to get some sleep, sir. Nobody deserves to be placed under this amount of pressure," Inky's voice softened, "and you're right, sir, I can't resist a challenge. Especially one with so little chance of success."

"*No chance of success.*" Bennett's face lit up, "I can't tell you how..."

Inky cut him short, "Listen to me very carefully, sir," he said. "Over the next couple of days things may become hectic around school. Blame it on Christmas if you like, but don't panic and don't," he stressed, "lose faith. I'm on your side and once I'm committed, I stay committed. But," he paused, "I do have certain demands."

Mike Bennett looked uncertain.

"Shortage of time is the main obstacle," Inky explained. "As things stand I have no chance of success unless I can manipulate time to my advantage, so I'll need the rest of today off..."

"Sorry?"

Inky eyed Bennett intently, "You've taken the handbrake off, sir, it's too late to stop the bus now. I'll leave you to contact Mr Sheldon and Miss Gaudet about my absence this afternoon. Leave 'Chalky' Whittle to me."

"Well, I suppose... I'll see what I can do."

"You misunderstand," said Inky, "that you do exactly as I say is non-negotiable. And as for Wednesday and Thursday. I suspect that you'll also have to be a little," Inky deliberated over the correct word, "*creative* about my attendance then too. I'll also need resources. And a base here in school." He looked around thoughtfully, "Your office will suit me fine. For the rest of the week I'll use your facilities as my own. I have my own key but you'll have to tell me your computer password."

"My office key...? Password...?"

"I'll update you on relevant progress first thing every morning. In here. Starting tomorrow."

Mike Bennett was lost for words.

"Unless you've changed your mind, sir," he ventured. "In which case...?"

"No," said Bennett, hurriedly, "No, of course not. Of course that's logical to expect, I suppose..."

"And I offer no guarantee of success. Should I fail, then I'll inform you ahead of the Friday morning deadline, the time when you're required to make a decision about the disco. If I require anything else... I'll find you."

"Of course," said Bennett, thinking aloud, "a student missing lessons is taboo, but it is the last week before Christmas, I suppose... so with a bit of luck I may be able to pull it off. Nobody does anything important this week anyway."

"Except for the mock exams," said Inky, bringing the Deputy back to reality.

"Oh yes, yes I'd forgotten about..." Bennett's voice trailed off. When he resumed, his voice was measured, "Whatever you need, Stevens, I'll find a way to provide it for you. I give you my word. And," he paused, "and thank you."

Inky nodded respectfully, then made to leave. He turned in the doorway, "As you may be aware, sir, it's customary for me to ask for some form of token from my clients when the task is complete."

"I'd heard something to that effect..."

"This will not be money, nor will it be something that you're unable to provide, but I will require *something*."

"Of course. That's reasonable. Good luck."

"I appreciate the sentiment, sir, but I don't believe in luck. Just stay calm. Get some rest. You've me fighting your corner now. You're only a victim of crimes committed by others. Don't lose faith."

Having watched Inky open the door, Bennett called out, "Erm, Stevens," he said, sheepishly, "I was at the Town Hall last Monday. As you know we've a prestigious visitor in school. From France. A Master Asticot. I'd, erm," he forced eye-contact, "appreciate it if whatever happens, could happen without his knowledge. Asticot's knowledge. If that's at all possible?" he gabbled. "It's a status thing, you understand?"

Inky's expression didn't change, "Whatever happens, happens, sir. As I'm sure you're aware by now I hold no respect for," he outstared Bennett, "status."

And with that, the school detective was on his way, striding back along the corridor towards English.

Inside his office Michael Bennett sat down with a sigh. Suddenly he felt very faint. The clean, wintery light reflecting off the walls made everything appear a little too vivid. Green around the edges.

I couldn't believe what I'd done. At thirty-four years of age I'd just begged a teenager for help. Yet, instinctively, I knew I'd made the right decision. The Great School Detective exuded such an air of confidence that I couldn't help but be reassured. All I had to do from that point on was put Friday out of my mind and carry on as normal. Perhaps there was still a chance? It was the season of goodwill after all...

Of course, I had no idea of the consequences of what I'd just set in motion. What happened as a result of our meeting was far more dangerous and far-reaching than either of us could have imagined. But I recall that as Inky left my office that morning I felt more than just a sense of relief. For the first time in a long while I actually felt... happy.

By the time Inky'd travelled the short distance back to Room 5 his mind was abuzz. He'd already reread Bennett's A4 piece of paper and memorised all thirty-nine names. His immediate priority was to cut this down. Immediately. Suspects had to be eliminated as a matter of priority.

As he strode into English, the teenage detective was greeted by a scene of *enforced relaxation*. The students, many out of their seats or sitting on desks, were completing a variety of word puzzles. (The round of Christmas lessons had begun early in English.) Inky approached 'Chalky' Whittle's desk knowing what his reply would be in advance, "Sir," he asked, "Mr Bennett's asked me to run an errand for him. This will take the rest of the lesson so I won't be coming back. He's in his office if you'd like to phone him for confirmation."

"No. No need, Stevens, you go ahead," said Whittle, concerned about the noise Bennett might hear if he did ring him up. "I'll take your word for it," he added, before taking Inky to one side. Whittle ran his hands through his mass of white hair, "Look Stevens, we're all counting down to Christmas here. It's not just me. I've got the English mock to mark this evening, so there's no way I'd set *real* work for you lot. Just don't go telling Bennett now, would you?"

A thin smile troubled Inky's face, "Wouldn't dream of it, sir."

As he exited Room 5 Inky stooped to whisper five short words into the ear of trusted classmate, Ross Berry. Then the Great School Detective was gone, the sound of the door closing after him barely audible.

It had begun...!

39 suspects, maybe more?

Amanda Blunt?

Tommy Woggle??

5. BLINKTON TOWN HALL:

Monday 12th December (Morning).

Blinkton's Lord Mayor, Solomon Carey, was a dowdy individual. Short in stature, he was more often found outside the Town Hall's back entrance smoking roll-up cigarettes than performing civic duties. It was a surprise to many that Carey, often unshaven and impolite, had been elected Mayor at all. The fact that he owned most of the town's boating fleet and its only removals firm, appeared to have swung the vote in his favour. But, for all his failings, the one thing that Mayor Carey was good at was *putting on a show*. And never had this talent been more important than on Monday 12th December...

Carey found the cross-Channel phone call he'd received less than two weeks earlier too good to be true. While Jean-Pierre Asticot had outlined his proposals, all Blinkton's Mayor could hear was the chance to make a significant amount of money and guarantee his own re-election. Solomon Carey was beside himself with glee. And with good reason, too. The charismatic Frenchman had promised substantial investment. So even before the telephone had settled in its cradle, Carey was already scheming. *'What Jean-Pierre Asticot promises,'* he'd announced to the Blinkton Gazette, *'is too monumental to ignore. With my guidance I foresee bounteous wealth for every man, woman and child in this town.'* And to publicise this glorious opportunity, Carey had called all interested parties to a meeting at the Town Hall...

Both to introduce the delegation from Mal-de-Mer... and strut like a peacock!

On the day of the meeting Mayor Carey, to his great annoyance, was unable to adjust the height of the lectern set in front of him. This meant that those sitting on the front six rows of the function room were unable to see him properly. This was frustrating, but unavoidable as no-one was able to swap seats as every chair was taken. The chamber was packed to capacity. Stuffed. Those who hadn't arrived early enough to claim a seat were forced to stand up around the sides. In fact, for the purpose of listening to a Lord Mayor, the function room had never been so full in its history. And despite it being a bitterly cold Monday morning, the atmosphere inside the chamber was expectant. Buoyant. Blinkton's community, hyped up by Carey's press release, held its breath in expectation...

Solomon Carey, on seeing the size of the gathering, felt at least a foot taller than he actually was. He was positively dizzy at the thought of making history. Ecstatic. He silenced the gathering with a gentle cough, then embarked on the most important speech of his political career. (One which his personal secretary, Miss Sandra Choudhury, had been re-drafting ever since the Asticots had first announced their arrival).

"There are many who said it couldn't be done," Carey began, with a smile wider than Blinkton's harbour-mouth, "yet here we are. *We* are doing it. All of us. And we will continue to do it, *together*. Our humble town is proud to offer a welcome to two very important guests. One a Lord Mayor, like myself. The other, his son. Our welcome, like the drystone walls which traverse our beautiful county, reaches further than the eye can see. It extends so far that the white cliffs of Dover cannot contain the munificent warmth of our heartfelt greeting..."

The audience beamed back at him joyfully secretly wondering what the word *munificent* meant.

"Ladies and gentlemen. Today. Monday the 12th December, is a chance for us all... to make history!"

(Carey had been dubious about some of the exaggerated images in his speech but Miss Choudhury had assured him that the gullible residents of Blinkton would lap it all up. And lapping-it-all-up they were, by the bucketful.)

The hall erupted in tumultuous applause. Those lucky enough to have a seat stood to register their approval.

Town grocer, George Groves, shouted, "Hurrah!"

Florist, Sharon English yelled, "Bravo!"

Even Jasper Thickett, who'd only wandered into the chamber to keep warm and eat free sandwiches, yelled, "Good one, Carey. Go and stick it up 'em!"

(Jasper Thickett was removed shortly afterwards by two bulky-looking gentlemen in dark suits.)

And as Carey's oration continued, Sandra Choudhury beamed proudly up at her boss. She muttered the speech along with him, relieved to see Carey polish his chains-of-office in exactly the places they'd rehearsed. This gave Blinkton's Mayor ample time to bask in the waves of adulation which sloshed around the chamber.

The audience cheered Carey all the way to his big climax, delirious...

"And finally may I draw your attention to the main point of this morning's gathering, its *raison d'être...*?"

He punctuated his use of French with an ironic wink.

"... I'd like to present to you the man who has imbued our humble town with a sense of optimism greater than the mighty ocean. This single Frenchman, just one man, flesh and blood like ourselves, has dared to achieve immortality. He has done this by transcending the claustrophobic restraints of convention to put his neck on the line, or rather *under the guillotine...*"

He waited for the ripple of laughter to subside.

"... for the sake of our little town. Ladies and gentlemen, what this man proposes stands to significantly boost trade links with our brothers and sisters, our *frères and soeurs*, across the Channel. He's suggesting that by sharing expertise, opening trade links, fixing the value of the exchange rate and by forming an alliance which excludes all competitors..."

"Like you do with our harbour quotas!" came an unexpected cry from the floor, one which was immediately quelled by the same dark-suited gentlemen who'd just returned from sorting out Jasper Thickett.

"... allowing both parties to share all the slices of an especially rich *gateau* between ourseves. Both Blinkton, and our twin-town, Mal-de-Mer, will thus be free to enjoy a profitable union which will not only enhance the wellbeing of both our towns today..."

Carey paused for effect.

"... but also ensure our prosperity well into the future. Indeed," he crowed, "it will guarantee Blinkton's fortune for *all our tomorrows*. The tomorrows of our children and our grand-children. So," he said, light sparkling on his chains-of-office, "the man I'm delighted to introduce to you now is the person who's made all of this possible. Ladies and gentlemen, my opposite number from Mal-de-Mer... *mon bon amie*, Lord Mayor Jean-Pierre Asticot!"

A cacophony of delighted squeals and whoops erupted. Several individuals felt so moved that they grabbed hold of one another and hugged like reunited family members. Finchy Propp, the oldest man in the room, threw his flat cap into the air as high as he could. (He instantly regretted this as it became stuck on the chandelier.)

From the back of the hall a sizeable figure burst through the wood-panelled doorway pumped up like a pro-wrestler. All heads swivelled in an attempt to catch their first glimpse of Blinkton's saviour. The man framed in the entranceway sported thick sideburns and a Mexican-style moustache far too dark to be natural. Jean-Pierre Asticot was squeezed into his customary suit, shirt buttoned up so tightly that his head looked as though it had been squeezed through the top like toothpaste from a tube. With hair pulled back into a tight ponytail, what Asticot lacked in good looks he made up for in charisma. He opened his arms as a gesture of welcome. Immediately the assembly burst into another round of applause. Only when this subsided did Asticot make his way to the front. His progress, like the winning captain on Cup-Final day, was interrupted by an army of hands demanding to be shaken. Like a whirlpool sucks water to its centre, the entire function room gravitated towards him, everyone clamouring for some form of physical contact.

It was several minutes before Asticot reached the front. Mayor Carey waited patiently for him feeling slightly upstaged. When the Frenchman finally approached, Carey instinctively recognised the photo-opportunity. While flashguns *popped* around them, he offered the Frenchman a hand, which quickly became two, then four as the pair wound all available hands into a tight knot. The Mayors' greeting reached a climax as Asticot 'the bear' enveloped Carey 'the weasel' in his tight embrace. Carey, despite having the air squeezed out of him, was able to worm his way around to face the paparazzi in his desperation to be photographed. (Better publicity than a clever campaign poster.)

"Cheese!"

The most publicised photograph that day was one taken by Simon Kench from the Blinkton Gazette. His photograph of the two Lord Mayors locked 'in concorde' was splashed across the front cover of Blinkton's weekly newspaper. Yet with the glitz of Asticot's visit dominating that weekend's edition, one item of much greater significance was relegated so far towards the middle of the paper that it was more or less totally overlooked. In retrospect, this was to pose a signifi-cant challenge to Inky Stevens... and even greater danger to Blinkton-on-Sea.

Introductions over, it was time for Asticot to begin his address. Carey gestured towards the lectern but the Frenchman refused his offer, opting to stand directly in front of the gathering instead. Now the focus of attention, Asticot paced from side to side, one hand tucked into his suit pocket. Having met Solomon Carey in person only minutes before, he'd taken an instant dislike to his *weasely* counterpart and decided to undermine him whenever possible. With no pre-written speech, Asticot relied on spontaneous wit to charm his audience...

"Good morning, mesdames, messieurs... I thank you for welcoming me, not only into this magnificent room on such a cold morning, but also into your charming seaside town and hopefully," he smiled, "your hearts. Thank you for sharing your home with me. Now," he beamed, gold tooth glinting, "I can call it my home too. As Monsieur Carry has just said, we are hoping to create a bond between ourselves, one which will bring great unity to our towns and, of course, even greater prosperity," he winked. "This fortnight will see both myself and Carry create a foundation, a cornerstone, from which our wealth can germinate and then flourish like the mighty English oak. The expansive Eiffel tower itself will lie down to create a walkway across which our mighty nations can unite in the spirit of oneness." Asticot placed a hand on his heart, "I must also thank you, most humbly, for booking me in to stay at what I believe to be the finest establishment Blinkton-on-Sea has to offer. I do, of course, refer to the Harbor Lites guest-house belonging to the charming, Miss Deidre Butterfield..."

Eccentric Deidre, seated at the centre of the gathering, flushed with embarrassment and pride.

"You see," Asticot explained, "wanting to avoid the trappings of status I deliberately selected a residence which is towards what you British call *the Asda-priced* end of the market. You see, I'm a simple man with simple tastes. The Harbor Lites guest-house has only three stars, yet I feel that this is incorrect..."

There was a collective drawing in of breath.

"... the hospitality that this magnificent lady provides is worth five stars, even more if c'est possible. She's welcomed me into her homestead as if I were her own son."

Ms Butterfield, despite her reservations about Astocit, was moved never-theless. She plucked a lace handkerchief from her sleeve and waved it at her townsfolk who, in return, congratulated her on her excellent work.

Under his breath, Mayor Carey muttered, "Asticot's only been here half a day. Who's he think he is?"

The speaker glanced over his shoulder, "I'm also indebted to Monsieur Carry your *efficient* Mayor. He's devised a full programme of events for us. These will enable me to report back to le conseil municipal in Mal-de-Mer on the vast array of amenities that your ville magnifique has to offer."

Asticot noted the effect that his scattering of French expressions were having on the gathering.

"Believe me," he continued, "I intend to take from you everything that

Blinkton has to offer. Mayor Carry's not only arranged for me to see your town for what it is now, but also what extra she'll be able to offer in the future," he straightened his tie, "when our joint revenue, like le puissant Thames, begins to flood in."

Solomon Carey, upset at having his name mispronounced so wantonly, decided to crowbar his way back into proceedings, "That is indeed the case, sir. I've personally devised an itinerary both enjoyable and extensive. Even at this insufferably cold time of year," he chuckled.

The assembly mirrored his laughter.

"I only hope that the heavy snowfall predicted later this week will not ruin this schedule. Our series of excursions includes visits to the Plastic Cutlery Museum, the 'Age of Aquarium', the magnificent lighthouse out at Coyote Point plus an evening performance of Blinkton Players' pantomime 'Babes in Boots'. Ah," said Carey, attempting to match Asticot's spontaneity, "I see we have one of our star performers here with us now..." A sea of heads turned to the back of the room where a heavily tattooed lorry driver offered a wave. Jewellery jangling. "Yes, there he is everyone. Derek Chambers. Yes, Derek," Carey beamed, "We're all looking forward to having a glimpse of your 'Widow Winky' a week on Wednesday."

Carey realised that his comment hadn't sounded quite the way he'd intended and he quickly returned to his notes, "We've... we've... we've also arranged a splendid boat trip on one of *my* many boats. Down the coast to see the wreck of the 'Lucky Lady', the pleasure cruiser which ran aground. Oh, and what else?" he fumbled, "Ah yes, it says here that you've also an afternoon at the Funshine Arcade, a tour of Blinkton's General Hospital and that your stay will end up at Blinkton Comprehensive School where, at the Christmas disco, you'll be able to say *au revoir* to all the friends that your son Jacques has made during his stay..."

"On which note," interrupted Asticot, "I'm especially proud to introduce to you tout le monde, my son, Jacques. Jacques," he bellowed. "Where are you my beautiful, beautiful boy? Don't be shy. Come here, tout-de-suite."

Blinkton's townsfolk looked from one to another uncertainly.

Three rows from the front a handsome young man rose to his feet with the type of grace rarely seen in British teenagers. Jacques Asticot was wearing a copper-coloured jacket over a black turtle-neck sweater. Around his neck hung a scarf, the stripes of which were randomly arranged. Yet despite the mish-mash of colour, the teenager possessed enough charisma to make it work. He looked dynamic.

Chic.

Even the sunglasses he persisted in wearing appeared stylish. Young-Asticot slid to the end of the row then sauntered up the central aisle, unruffled. He approached the lectern full of panache. As he faced the assembly he tilted his head and, with the self-confidence of a bronco, shook out his lustrous mane of hair. Beneath the chandelier his locks assumed the faintest tinge of blue.

'This young man,' thought tea lady, Heather Smith, *'is the epitome of style!'*

Jacques Asticot removed his sunglasses and placed them inside his jacket. In the same movement he produced a packet of cigarettes and made to remove one. While the audience recoiled in horror, his father was quick to react,

"Not here my son, this is Britain, remember?" he said, guiding Jacques' hand back inside his coat. "Our cousins this side of La Manche are a little more conservative than us."

A wave of relief surged through the room. What could have been a moment of controversy passed almost before it had begun. Indeed, Jacques' indiscretion served to endear him even further. The assembly, now able to see the teenager's face, found themselves immediately captivated by his roguish charm. His glacier eyes now uncovered, Jacques' demeanour was enthralling. Mrs Elaine Hope, who really should have known better, let out a faint gasp and fanned herself with a (mostly clean) tissue. Mr Hope, sitting beside her, tapped his wife on the knee with a disgruntled *'huff'*.

"This monsieurs et mesdames," crowed Asticot, "is my son Jacques. I'd wanted to come to Blinkton alone but who could leave a face as handsome as this behind, eh?"

The French teenager pouted and folded his arms.

"Yes," interjected Carey, returning to the words of his speech, "Jean-Pierre and I feel that *integration* will be the key to our proposed partnership. So, with that in mind, Jacques will be attending school until the end of term. Mr Bennett, Blinkton School's Deputy-Head, has kindly devised an individual programme of study for young-Jacques. Isn't that so, sir?"

Taken aback, Mike Bennett rose to his feet, "Yes, yes that's right. Erm, young Jacques has been... has been assigned to work alongside a rather pleasant young man in our, our fourth-year. Master Brandon Lunt. These two students will, erm," he babbled, "share the same timetable. Brandon's a very honourable young man. Solid and dependable. Solid, erm, yes Jacques will enjoy... if that's the right word, well yes, of course it is... two weeks in our education system. And, erm, having Master Asticot with us will be a valuable cultural lesson. Both for Jacques... and also for us."

Bennett sat back down, relieved to be anonymous once more.

"Indeed," stated Carey, annoyed by Bennett's blathering, "tell me Jacques, what are you looking forward to most about school?"

The wintry coughs and wheezes subsided as Carey, to his horror, found his meeting suddenly held to ransom by the young Adonis.

Jacques Asticot cupped his chin in thought then, with the faintest trace of an accent, said, "Why, that is easy... le Christmas disco of course."

The assembly let out a giggle which grew steadily into hearty applause, climaxing with a standing ovation.

Carey retook the limelight, relieved that Jacques had deflected any controversy, "Well, I think that concludes this morning's business. I'd like to thank you all for braving the sub-zero temperatures in order to support what promises to be a seminal moment in Blinkton's history, the outcome of which, like the spire of St Paul's Cathedral, will stand the test of time..."

Asticot pounced, "Does St Paul's have a spire?"

"Of course it does," snapped Carey, peering at Miss Choudhury for confirmation. (She shrugged.) He continued, agitated, "Well, thank you all so much for your time. I trust that I can count on your votes when I stand for re-election on June the 13th. The booths will be open as usual from 7am to 7pm. In the meantime I feel that, in partnership with Mal-de-Mer, both our communities can face a future... erm... erm..." Carey stalled, having lost his place, "face a future that will be both prosperous and... golden delicious. Ladies and gentlemen, we stand on the precipice of greatness. What you've seen... witnessed... seen... here today is the beginning of our Christmas future..."

Asticot smiled, "'Doesn't Ebenezer Scrooge see misery and desolation in the Christmas yet to come?"

"Erm... Christmas future... and that future, is bounteous. Here's to tomorrow... and all our tomorrows!"

But before Solomon Carey could receive the applause he felt he deserved, Frank Parkinson had lurched to his feet. Blinkton's most celebrated restaurateur hollered from the back of the hall, "With all due respect, *Carry*. Aren't you forgetting something?"

"Am I?"

Asticot clarified, "Quite a serious omission too, Carry. What's the most significant thing about Blinkton-on-Sea? The thing puts your *charmante* town on the map? What you promised to show Jacques and I on le tele-phone," he prompted. "Surely it hasn't escaped your attention…?"

Silence.

Finally something flickered, "Of course," Carey hit his head in comic fashion, "how silly of me. How on earth could I have neglected…? Under pressure, you see. Mind went blank. Lost my place…"

Frank Parkinson found his voice, "The Codfather Fish and Chip Restaurant, Carry! Remember? *My* restaurant? Blinkton's most famous attraction. Made famous by our top-secret fish-batter recipe. Some people say that batter is just batter…"

"But they're deluded," championed Margaret Brewster from the floor. "I agree with you Frankie, people who say that obviously haven't tasted your magnificent fare."

"Exactly, Margaret, thank you. Because, by the time I've added an exact quantity of salt, water and flour and then, on top of that, sprinkled my very specific quantity of herbs and spices…"

"Your magic dust, eh Frank?" cried Pete Preston.

"My magic dust, exactly, Pete. Passed down through four generations. It transforms ordinary fish batter into," he paused, "the ambrosia of the Gods!"

Hugo Lassetter called out, "God bless you, Frank. My wife's a Codfather junkie! Says nothing tastes quite so magnificent as your cod and chips."

"Nothing even comes close," agreed Parkinson, extending a finger, "so come on *Carry*, what about me? Nobody's visit to Blinkton would be complete without sampling a portion of my prize-winning fare in our newly refurbished restaurant. I've invested in brand new tables and chairs. Easy-wipe tablecloths too. And in pride of place I've made a feature of the sealed envelope containing my great-grandfather's recipe. I've had it framed and hung on the wall. Spot-lit for posterity. So why've you missed me off? The Harbor Lites is just next door…"

Deidre Butterfield nodded.

"… so it's hardly out of the way for the Asticots, is it?"

"Mais, non," Jean-Pierre agreed.

Parkinson was unstoppable, "My eatery's the only reason people come back to this grotty place year after year…"

Carey objected, "Now come on Frank, I wouldn't say that our town's *grotty*."

Suddenly the meeting descended into chaos with everyone desperate to share an opinion. Comments were tossed around with the ferocity of hand-grenades,

"This town *is* grotty *Carry*. Have you smelled the public toilets on King Street?!"

"I wouldn't be seen dead in those toilets."

"Plenty of other things are though."

"Come on, *Carry*, the whole of Blinkton might as well hibernate over winter."

"It's not much different in summer!"

"How come you dictate all the fishing quotas, *Carry*?"

"I opened my rock shop all last week only to sell *rock all*!"

"Can someone help me get my cap down from the chandelier," yelled Finchy Propp.

Over the course of several minutes, *'Taxes', 'Education', 'Health', 'Parking Permits' and 'Seagull droppings'* were all vehemently flung into the discussion.

"Please," said Asticot, finally spreading calm like butter on warm bread, "local politics is outside my control. For now," he smiled, "but I can assure you that a visit to the world famous Codfather Fish and Chip Restaurant is definitely on our agenda. It was the very first thing that Monsieur Carry and I discussed."

Carey, glad of the lifeline yet more than sick of the word *Carry*, added, "Of course it was. Please check as you leave if you don't believe me. A full itinerary is pinned onto the noticeboard in the foyer." Carey hastily gestured to Miss Choudhury. In response, she scampered out of the assembly in search of a computer with a printer, "And as for all your other concerns, these will be addressed in the fullness of time through the appropriate channels," he said, unsure of what the appropriate channels actually were.

"Mes amis," boomed Asticot, extending an arm towards Frank Parkinson, "The Codfather is the jewel in Blinkton's crown, Monsieur Frank. Mayor Carry just became a little muddled *reading* his notes, that's all. Quelle dommage."

Carey folded his arms and in so doing tangled his cuff links in his chains-of-office.

"I can assure you, Frank, you'll be seeing a lot of my son and I before our stay's over."

"Well," said Parkinson, seating himself, "you'd better hurry up. We close this Thursday for Christmas!"

"Which is why," Carey took on the appearance of an escapologist as he struggled to disengage his cuff, "Mr Asticot and son-Jacques, have been booked in on that very day. Thursday. They'll be served the very final meals of the year. We've saved the best 'til last," he said, wincing as he yanked his sleeve free. "Next week," he went on, "both of you will be the Codfather's guests of honour, just as my itinerary states. No offence, Frank, of course no visit to Blinkton-on-Sea would be complete without sampling your award-winning nourishment."

"Well, in that case," said the restaurateur, mostly appeased, "we'll put on a right royal spread for you. Just one, final question Mr Asticot?"

"Oui Monsieur, Frank?"

"Do you like gravy...?"

Mr Mike Bennett (Deputy-Head):

I recall being snowed under with work on the Monday of that chaotic Town Hall meeting. I'd arrived to school early and was ploughing through a stack of books when the Snake decided to 'hiss'. She decreed that a senior member of staff ought to represent the school at such a prestigious event and, of course, it was me who was 'volunteered'. Thus I skated across the yard to my Audi then sped off down Wordsworth Drive hoping to grab a seat. Stressed.

The meeting itself, despite the confusion at its end, was hailed as a great success. Blinded by the Frenchman's promises, the whole town was swept up in a (snow) cloud of optimism. Jean-Pierre Asticot, without saying an awful lot, had us all eating out of his hand. I just think that we wanted to believe what he was offering. Yet from the onset, I should have known that there was something not quite right about him. His manner was too confident, too smug. Yet Carey, firing a question at me in the way he did, caught me off guard. It plagues me now, but if I'd been more prepared I'd have chosen someone more suitable to chaperone Jacques Asticot than Brandon Lunt. I mean, young-Brandon was a student of unparalleled integrity, but he wasn't quite in the same league as someone like Jacques Asticot.

Not as streetwise. As sophisticated.

Yet despite my doubts, I still don't feel there were enough warning signs to suggest the tremendous danger we were all in... the danger I'd inadvertently placed Inky into.

The front page of that weekend's Gazette sported Simon Kench's photograph of Carey ensnared in Asticot's embrace. The headline read, 'ASTI-COR BLIMEY! A MAL-DE-MIRACLE FOR BLINKTON'. And the French theme continued inside. Page two showed Frank Parkinson dressed in a stripy jumper with a string of onions around his neck passing over a heaped plate of fish and chips to the French visitors. In fact, the Gazette's first five pages were exclusively devoted to the Asticots' activities. It even published a copy of their schedule, the one Sandra Choudhury had typed up at short notice...

Programme of events for Jean Pierre Asticot.
(Jacques Asticot to accompany when not attending Blinkton Comprehensive School.)

Sunday 11th December: Le grande arrivé, Harbor Lites Guest-House (3 stars) Welcome supplied by Deidre Butterfield.

Monday 12th December: Town Hall. Official Welcome Meeting hosted by Mayor Carey (10am).

Tuesday 13th December: Tour of Blinkton General Hospital (noon). Visit to Blinkton Post Office Depot (3pm).

Wednesday 14th December: Lunch at 'Tequila Mockingbird' (noon). Tour of Blinkton Sewage Works hosted by Thomas Lee (4pm) (Evening meal included).

Thursday 15th December: Evening meal supplied by 'The Codfather Fish and Chip Restaurant' (7pm) hosted by Frank Parkinson.

Friday 16th December: Tour of Plastic Cutlery Museum hosted by Karl Goddard (1pm).

Saturday 17th December: All day use of facilities courtesy of 'the Funshine Arcade'.

Sunday 18th December: Clifftop walk with Blinkton Ramblers (10am). Tour of 'the Pump House Working Farm' hosted by Glenda Lovelady (2pm).

Monday 19th December: Boat Trip to see wreck of 'Lucky Lady' on South Shore hosted by Mayor Carey (11am).

Tuesday 20th December: Tour of 'the Age of Aquarium' hosted by Millie Swabb (noon). Lunch included (Choose your own from the tank).

Wednesday 21st December: Tour of Blinkton Railway Station hosted by Martin Rich (10am). Evening Performance of 'Babes in Boots' Blinkton Players (7:30pm) St Hilda's Church Hall.

Thursday 22nd December: All day trip out to lighthouse at Coyote Point hosted by Mayor Carey (11am).

Friday 23rd December: Le grand départ après le disco à Blinkton School (7:30pm)!

In retrospect, the Gazette's decision to focus so heavily on the Asticots was an error. While Jean-Pierre's expensive dental work was flashed all over the first five pages, other more newsworthy events were relegated towards the middle of the newspaper. In this way significant items such as...

John Winstanley's three legged dog Rupert who'd dramatically rescued his owner when he fell through ice at Millhouse Pond (Monday).

Finchy Propp's public appeal for the recovery of his flat cap (Tuesday).

Graham Cohen's onstage frying-pan accident resulting in caravan park owner Mark Rickards taking over the part of 'Dishy Wishy' in 'Babes in Boots'. (Wednesday).

Little Kenney Chatterley who ended up in tears after his sledge was stolen as he helped vagrant Jasper Thickett cross the road (Thursday).

Vandals throwing a rock through the Codfather's door the day after it had closed for Christmas (Friday).

And of course...

The fire alarm at Blinkton School summoning fire, police and ambulance services (Friday).

... were swallowed up by several tales of 'French fancy' and adverts of dubious quality.

(Until it was much too late!)

Despite being troubled by certain aspects at the meeting, by the time I'd raced back to school all thoughts of the Asticots had been abandoned. I had other, much more pressing things on my mind... the mock exams, marking, plans for the Governors' meeting, plans for the School disco and Matty Hay who'd been caught cycling down the school corridors on Tim Gledhill's bike singing 'O Come All Ye Faithful'. And during the ensuing week it was the fire alarm and snowball incidents which consumed my every waking thought. By that time Jacques Asticot had joined us at Blinkton Comprehensive and was making sterling progress (or so I thought). So I confess that by then Mal-de-Mer had dropped off my radar altogether. By the second week of their stay I was fraught, desperate and totally self-absorbed.

But at least enlisting Inky on the Tuesday had given me a glimmer of hope. As he left my office, I could tell by his expression that the challenge I'd presented to him was already 'bubbling away' inside his overactive mind. On reaching English, Inky fed 'Chalky' Whittle a pack of lies that freed him up to go wherever his investigation led him. His whisper to Ross Berry as he left Room 5 was a signal of intent.

It had indeed begun!

(And as Inky himself predicted, 'Chalky' never did contact me about him being excused English. But that's the thing about schools... teachers won't go looking for trouble if they don't need to. If trouble's going to find you, it will do so all by itself.)

6. THE HUMANITIES CORRIDOR.

Tuesday 20ᵗʰ December (Morning).

Inky Stevens strode out of 'Chalky' Whittle's English lesson leaving his peers completing their Christmas word-puzzles. He knew that his chances of finding who'd triggered the alarm in such a short time were almost impossible, but the threat of the Christmas disco being cancelled was incentive enough to try. Plus he could never ignore the challenge of an intriguing puzzle, especially one which would help Mr Bennett.

'*The Snake is wrong,*' Inky reasoned, '*To cause the suffering of many in order to punish the few is not acceptable. School's tough enough as it is without 'management' complicating things even further.*'

So, while there was sand in the glass, the Great School Detective resolved to try to prevent the unpreventable.

'*Thirty-nine suspects is far, far too many,*' he thought.

The super-sleuth knew that if he was to succeed then his priority had to be to eliminate as many as of them as possible.

Immediately.

In terms of procedure, Inky always found the scene-of-the-crime a logical place to start. So that Tuesday his first action was to inspect the broken fire sensor. With Lesson 3 well under way, Inky found himself racing towards Humanities, leather coat billowing out behind. He sped past a series of display boards showing valuable English work... felt-tip drawings of characters from 'Of Mice and Men' and essays stemming from the title, 'What Would I do if I Won a Million Pounds?'

In order to reach Humanities Inky descended three flights of stairs then exited school through a door beside the statue of Lionel Roebuck (Blinkton's most famous ex-pupil). He then circled the perimeter of the main building, brittle ice *crunching* underfoot. He re-entered it on the far side having bypassed the RE Department and the Humanities Block toilets (the latter's windows held open by a stiff metal catch). Pushing through a set of double doors, Inky was confronted by a dimly-lit stairwell, its floor damp where ice had been carried in on thick-soled shoes then melted. Strewn across its concrete floor were discarded bun casings, soggy Christmas cards and drinks cartons. From this entranceway two sets of stairs led off. One up to IT. The other down to Humanities. Choosing not to grip the handrail (someone had dribbled a 'honey-like' substance over it) the investigator crept downwards, governed by caution. At the bottom Inky was faced by another set of double doors. He composed himself, then pushed out of the shadowy stillness into the deserted passage beyond.

The Humanities corridor was long and narrow. Its flooring comprised of a set of black and white tiles arranged in a chessboard pattern. Its walls had been painted with gloss emulsion, cream for the top half, snot-green for the bottom. A set of strip lights ran the length of the passage, the one furthest away blinking on and off like an irregular heartbeat.

Inky studied the passageway carefully. Rooms 32 and 33 on the left were Geography, while Rooms 34 and 35, the History classes, were on the right. At the far end was the caretaker's store-cupboard. Opposite this on the History side were the Senior Boys and Girls Toilets (the ones Inky'd just passed on the outside). Then at the far end was a wall onto which a noticeboard had been bolted. Inky noted that the entire corridor, just like the stairwell he'd emerged from, was also full of litter... a stray sock, a bike saddle, Lemmy Beeston's English book, a scuffed belt and a punctured football. At his feet there was also a puddle of something which looked like raspberry milkshake. The entire corridor was a mess.

Inky stepped over the milkshake then edged forwards, mind open, senses alert.

With Lesson 3 coming to an end the Christmas festivities appeared to be in full swing. Noise from all four classrooms collected in the centre of the corridor, spontaneous hoots and howls emerged first from one classroom, then another.

The fire sensor, the one from where the alarm had been activated, was situated halfway down the passage on the left. Inky approached this cautiously. He noted that the device was linked to the school's warning system by a thick wire which snaked up the wall then disappeared through a small hole in a roof tile. The sensor itself was a small, circular object, no bigger than a stack of drinks coasters. It was screwed onto the wall at shoulder height giving it the appearance of a small porthole. Normally a circular piece of glass would've been present inside its casing to create a smooth, flat surface. But because the device had been activated, its interior plane, (containing the inscription 'IN CASE OF EMERGENCY BREAK GLASS'), was now fully exposed.

Inky inspected the device carefully. Just as Bennett had said, the sensor's glass had not been cracked accidentally. Scratches on its inner section suggested that whoever had set the alarm off had done so deliberately with some degree of force, probably by hitting it with a blunt object. It appeared that, once shattered, the culprit had scooped out all the glass and let it drop down onto the tiles. Inky looked below but all he saw was dust and what looked like the top of a Smarties tube. Mr Bennett, he surmised, had been effective in cleaning up all the stray fragments.

Inky, wary of cutting himself, placed his index finger inside the broken sensor and ran it around the casing. With most of the glass missing, the metal ring was cold and smooth to the touch. Yet in places a few remaining fragments stubbornly clung on. Sharp and rough. Inky leaned in closer, one eye shut the other narrowed. It was then that he caught sight of it...

Almost microscopic. But there nevertheless.

A small piece of black material had been snagged on the inside of the casing. A tiny piece of tough fabric. From his rucksack he removed a small plastic container then delicately plucked the cloth fragment between thumb and forefinger. He then dropped it into the tube and stowed it away carefully.

Suddenly a commotion erupted.

Although the door to Room 34 remained shut, Inky could clearly hear the sound of a heated dispute. Mr Henry's music quiz did not appear to be running smoothly...

"Everyone knows that George Michael was in Duran Duran, you big spozz!"

"No he wasn't! My dad said he was in Wham."

"What, your dad was?"

"No, George Michael, you spoff. And he wore a little white glove."

"That was Prince, you dimmock!"

"There was no Prince! I think you mean Queen...

Clive Henry finally barked his frustration, "That's enough you lot. Your music questions are on the papers in front of you, so less of the brouhaha. Just shut up and read!"

"Bruhaha," sniggered Barry Doggett, "what kind word's that, sir?"

"I said... SHUT UP!"

"Ooo, touchy! Brouhaha indeed...!?"

As the disturbance settled, Inky resumed his search of the corridor. When he arrived at Ray Day's maintenance cupboard he tried its handle only to find it locked. Then, as he turned to face the toilets opposite, Inky became aware of a chemical smell. Intense, heavy and sulphurous. The strange aroma lingered at the bottom of the corridor. Intrigued, Inky pushed his way into the Senior Boys' Toilet yet a quick search revealed nothing more unpleasant than what's normally unpleasant inside a schoolboy toilet. But one thing was certain, the tiled room was not the source of the odour. With its window propped open, the boys loo was more than amply ventilated.

Inky was confused. He debated whether or not to search the Senior Girls' Toilet. After all, it appeared to be empty and was so close to the boys' that their door handles almost touched. Had it been crucial, he would certainly have done so. Yet as things stood, the young-detective couldn't justify it. Standards had to be maintained, after all. He consoled himself with the thought that if it became essential he'd ask Rose Berry to search it later on his behalf. Or come back himself afterschool.

So, finally, the investigator turned his attention to the wall at the far end. This was made of solid brick, a fact made obvious as some of the plaster at its base had been dislodged revealing the brickwork underneath. But there was nothing to suggest that this damage had occurred during the events of the previous Friday. The stonework was cool to the touch. Dry and intact. Just another example of general school decay.

Ignoring the smell which continued to linger, Inky studied the notice-board itself, a task made more difficult beneath the *twitchy bursts* of the broken strip-light. He initially took a step back to focus on everything as one. The board itself was wooden, bolted directly into the brickwork by a brass screw at each corner. Judging by its condition it had been there for some time, its wood peppered with a mass of tiny drawing-pin holes. A graveyard of bent staples stuck out at odd angles, apt to snag a trailing elbow. Yet despite the board's condition, it was covered with patchwork of printed information. Some notices were important, some trivial. Inky then read each notice individually, word by word. By doing so he found out about...

*Anthony Edmonds who'd started his campaign to be Head Boy three months early.

*The first eleven's most recent football match. (A 7-3 defeat where Blinkton's goalkeeper had been sent off for removing his shin pad and slapping the opposition number 9 with it.)

*Crispin Merridew's cake-sales which took place every Friday, all lunch-time, inside the school's back entrance.

*Miss Birkin's announcement that next term's school musical would be a self-written musical version of Dickens' Oliver story, called '*Twist*-in By the Gruel'. Auditions were scheduled for after Christmas.

And...

*The Christmas disco which, according to a poster decorated with holly, was billed as

The Highlight of the Year! Friday 23rd December at 7:30! 'Don't be a turkey. This will be your cracker of a Christmas!!' Then in brackets, *(Mr Morris will be spinning the decks!)*

And so the exchange of information went on, and on, and on...

Inky read everything as carefully as time allowed knowing that he'd already unearthed something very significant. (Something overlooked by Mr Bennett.) Satisfied, and conscious of the lunchtime bell, the detective made to leave. When suddenly, his investigation took an unexpected turn...

From nowhere, a giant hand clamped down onto his shoulder with a savage grip,

"Ink-o," boomed Ray Day, towering above the detective. The man-mountain of a caretaker wheeled him around, "Fancy seeing your batty face in this neck of the woods. Poking your nosy beak in where it shouldn't be again, eh? Naughty, naughty. I think it's time for some old fashioned retribution ...!"

As Deputy-Head I'd no idea of the ongoing feud between Ray Day and Inky Stevens. I mean, how could I? It was only after reading 'Perry's' book that I became aware of the full extent of the bad blood between them. Day used to be Head-of-Science but was demoted after 'the Case of the Caretaker's Keys' exposed him as a manipulative, self-seeking brute. But although Day had no-one to blame but himself, it was typical of him to try. Believing Inky to be responsible, the arrogant caretaker was constantly on the lookout for his chance 'get even'. And having finally grabbed hold of Inky, there was no way that Day was about to let him go without a struggle...

"Day-o," replied Inky, surprised at being caught off guard, "fancy meeting you here. Haven't you something more important to be getting on with. Shovelling grit? Mending this strip-light? Washing your hair?"

Day's bald head had assumed a waxy sheen beneath the strip-light. Almost green. A vein the size of a worm pulsed at his temple, "Stevens, I was hoping our paths would cross..."

"I'm surprised they have. I imagine the paths you lope down dragging your knuckles on the floor are very different to the ones I travel along. Tell me, Day-o. Have the zookeepers given you a tyre to swing on yet?"

"Think you're funny don't you Ink-o?"

"I think you're far funnier than me, Pay-Day. Take your jacket. It's about twenty sizes too small. But then, perhaps you like dressing up as Barbie?"

Day's neck turned the colour of a plum-tomato. On instinct the giant caretaker reached out and seized hold of Inky's lapels. In a single movement he spun Inky around, hauled him up into the air, and slammed him back against the noticeboard. Posters scattered as Inky found himself pressed into the coarse wood. Now several inches off the ground, his feet twitched uselessly. Inky could feel the metal staples piercing the leather of his coat.

Day leaned in so that he was nose to nose with his opponent, "It *was* you wasn't it, Steve-o? The one who cost me my job? Now I spend my days setting out exam desks, changing loo rolls and touching up paintwork..."

"Not very well I hasten to add. Perhaps you'd like to inspect the plaster below my feet?"

"You turned the Snake against me!"

"I think, *sir*," patronised Inky, "that you managed to do that all by yourself. Being a manipulative, meat-headed, supercilious, egotistical bully might have had something to do with it?"

"Supercili... Egotis...?"

"Sorry, *sir*, I forgot you struggle with words of more than one syllable. Let's just say that you managed to make an ass of yourself all on your little lonesome."

"Why you...!"

Spitting fury, Day heaved Inky up then flung him to the floor. The investigator landed in a heap, hard, a sharp pain exploding at his ribs. Yet despite this, he returned Day's stare, unwilling to let the oversized ogre see his distress, "That's your answer to everything isn't it, Day-o? Throw your considerable weight around. Is this what makes you tick? Ambushing schoolkids in pokey corridors?"

"Think you're smart don't you, Stevens...?"

"I'm ten laps ahead of you, lunk-head!"

Day leaned over, his shadow covering Inky like an eclipse, "Listen carefully, Stevens," he whispered, "I don't know what little *jolly* you're on down here in Humanities. But whatever you're up to I'd advise you to wind in that creepy neck of yours and stay away." A smile spread across his egg-shaped face, "When all this kicks off it would be better for you if you weren't here. Am I making myself clear?"

"Not really. Was that meant to be a threat?"

"Let's just say that I'm giving you," he paused for effect, "a... very... strong... warning."

"Well, let... me... just... say," mimicked Inky, "that despite me being half your size and a quarter your weight I'll always be one step ahead of you."

"What?"

"No, I didn't expect a plank like you to understand simple Maths. Keep looking over your shoulder, Day-o, 'cause I'm going to stick to you like tar." Despite his discomfort, Inky managed a smirk, "You may even catch me sitting on your shoulder like Jiminy Cricket on Dumbo's in that film... erm, what's it called?"

"Eh?"

Inky mimed the pressing of a stopwatch, "Too bad, time's up. I guess my clue was too obscure."

Day spluttered, "This isn't finished, Stevens. You and me."

"Grammatically speaking, Day-Break, it ought to be *you and I*, but who's quibbling?"

Day indicated his jacket, "You're responsible for me wearing this..."

"So I'm your mother, now?"

"You told the Snake..."

"I told Her, what?" he countered. "Tales? Sticks and stones? Or do you mean the truth? You just don't get it, do you? When will the smallest glimmer of reason penetrate that peanut-sized brain of yours...?"

Confused, Day resorted to being physical. With a snarl, he slammed the flat of his hand into the detective's chest. Inky found himself pressed forcefully into the tiles. Under extreme pressure, he could feel the air being squeezed out of him as he lay jammed onto the floor. Immobile. Breathless.

With his spare hand Day formed a fist the size of a cauliflower. He raised this slowly into the air, "This one's for old time's sake, Ink-o," a crooked smile creased his pumpkin-sized face, "I'm going to enjoy this..."

DDRRIINNGG!

The sound of the lunchtime bell rang out down the corridor, short, shrill and precise.

DDRRIINNGG!

An army of students immediately tumbled out of the four Humanities classrooms exploding into the corridor like firecrackers.

Running, fighting, leaping, jostling.

Day hauled Inky back to his feet. With a sigh he brushed down the crumpled leather of the detective's coat. "Saved by the bell, Ink-o," he said, with a cruel stare. "Funny how school bells can be used for good..."

"... or evil!"

Day leant in so close that Inky could smell the coffee on his breath, "I've told you that this isn't finished, Stevens."

Inky retorted, "I won't keep you from your duties, Day-o. After all, you've some plaster to sweep up."

"I haven't the faintest idea what you're talking about...?"

But before Ray Day could react, the detective had aimed a kick at the base of the wall. Loose plaster immediately came free and scattered across the floor-tiles. Day's face exploded with anger...

But Inky was no longer there.

Quick as moonlight, the investigator had joined the torrent of schoolkids pouring down the corridor. Lost in the crowd, he'd surged up the stairs and then out into the playground beyond.

Finally alone, Inky doubled over, greedily drinking in the cold winter air. The sweet taste of relief...

Once the corridor had emptied, Ray Day stood alone. Square-on, his bulk would have prevented anyone passing either side of him. He looked up at the faulty strip-light, momentarily mesmerised by its sporadic rhythm. Then, without warning, he charged at the far wall and smashed his fist directly into the centre of the noticeboard!

"Steeeevvveeennnsss!"

Having composed himself, Inky retraced his steps to Bennett's office. In relative safety he rubbed a curious hand across his stomach. The pain at his ribs was intense, but nothing appeared to be broken. He was lucky to have escaped with only minor bruising. (On this occasion.) Slowing his breathing, he began to reflect on what had just happened. Only a few minutes into his assignment things were already spiralling out of control.

'Ray Day's a troublesome abscess, one that needs to be lanced. But did he set that fire alarm off?'

Whatever the case, the odious caretaker had made the decision to reopen old wounds. Now he had to be prepared for the repercussions.

And there would be repercussions!

In terms of Inky's mission, the visit to the crime-scene had provided him with the means to narrow down Bennett's list of suspects...

'But at what cost?'

The Great School Detective was in no doubt that he was skating on extremely thin ice. But was he already in danger of falling through...?

39 suspects, maybe more?
Amanda Blunt?
Tommy Woggle?
Ray Day??

7. The Languages Department:
Tuesday 20ᵗʰ December (Afternoon).

Inky Stevens spent the remainder of lunchtime cocooned inside Bennett's office. There, he was able to collect his thoughts then plan ahead. (And take time to recover.) Having accessed Merridew's timetable on Bennett's computer, he knew that the young second-year had French Lesson 4. Thus, just after afternoon classes had begun, Inky made his way across school to initiate contact. After knocking politely, the detective pushed open Room 47's door. This action caused a cluster of faces to look up from their French books. Mademoiselle Gaudet smiled warmly,

"Ah, bonjour, Monsieur Stevens, Quelle surprise agréable. La classe," she gestured, "je vous présente Inky Stevens. Qu-est ce que je pourrais faire pour vous cet après-midi splendide?"

Without hesitation, Inky outlined the reason for his visit, "Je voudrais brièvement parler avec Crispin Meridew. D'accord? J'ai seulement besoin de lui pour quelques minutes, si c'est possible?"

"Bien sur," Gaudet agreed, "allez-y."

"Ah, vous etes très gentille, Mademoiselle," he gushed, before explaining that he'd be absent Period 5 as he was on an errand for Mr Bennett.

"Ah, oui. Il m'en a parlé," Gaudet nodded, "ça me convient."

The detective bowed politely as Crispin Merridew rose to his feet. Gaudet opened her classroom door to let them leave, clearly impressed. As they exited, she announced, "That, les enfants, is how to speak French. Très bien, Stevens. Très bien."

As she closed her door, Francoise Gaudet became aware of her class looking up at her in utter bemusement.

Blinkton's Languages Department was arranged around a square cloak-room area consisting of a number of wooden benches and metal coat-racks. Students were required to leave their belongings in this central area then enter French, German or occasionally Spanish via a series of doors leading off each side. With a gesture, Inky invited Crispin to take a seat on one of the benches. Merridew beamed with excitement and hunkered down among racks of soggy bags and steaming coats.

Young-Crispin, whose father was Chair of Governors, was also the only student at Blinkton to wear short trousers. The young brainbox perched on the bench's wooden slats, bare legs swinging with excitement, "This is a pleasant surprise, Inky," he chirped. "What's this all about? I bet you've taken me out of French because of something terribly exciting. Is this one of your, you know," he looked around sneakily, "missions?" Crispin removed his wire-rimmed spectacles to clean them on the tail of his shirt.

Inky sat next to him, "The less you know the better," he commented, "I'm actually here to ask you about your cake-sales."

"Cakes?" asked Crispin.

"I saw a poster advertising them. *Every Friday* it said, *all lunchtime*. May I ask whether you hosted one last week?"

"Of course."

"Just inside the back entrance to the school?"

"That's right. Same every week."

"That's very unselfish."

"I suppose. All the proceeds go to help Mr Charlton's reading group. Wednesdays afterschool. There are so many exciting books that he wants us to read. He's interested us all in Shakespeare. More modern books too. 'Nineteen Eighty Four', 'Treasure Island', 'Lord of the Rings', or 'Flies', whichever you prefer. But, as you and I both know Inky," he added, "schools don't have much money. Mr Charlton can't afford to buy class copies of all the titles he'd like. So I racked my brain to see if there was something I could do," Crispin smiled, "and finally I came up with the notion of a cake-sale. We all have to eat and everyone loves a good cake. *Edible treats, for reading feats.* Good slogan, eh?"

"What type of cakes do you make?"

"Every kind that schoolkids like."

"Schoolkids like all cakes."

"Indeed," said Merridew, eagerly, "if they'll buy it, I'll bake it... butterfly buns, lemon fingers, flapjacks, brownies, cherry bakewells, lemon curd tarts, chocolate fudge cake, key lime pie, strawberry cheesecake, Battenberg and, for the festive season, mince pies and chocolate logs. Costs me a fortune in ingredients but I factor in a four hundred percent mark-up on each item. That's after subtracting my overheads."

"Sounds thorough?"

"If I can provide Mr Charlton with a class-set of 'Coriolanus', then it'll all be worth it."

Clearly impressed, Inky began to steer the conversation, "Crispin, I need to ask you about what happened when you packed away last Friday."

"Last Friday? You mean when the fire alarm went off?"

Inky kept his voice low, "That's exactly what I mean. What you tell me could be significant, so think carefully. I need to know everything that happened in the few minutes between the start of Lesson 4 and when the alarm sounded at ten past one. Were you still packing away? According to Mr Mountjoy's register you had permission to be late to Geography."

Crispin's eyes appeared unnaturally large through his spectacles, "Oh yes, Mr Mountjoy knows all about my sales. He's very supportive. Thinks it's all *charitably unselfish*. His lesson's just downstairs in Room 32 anyway, so he's not too worried about the Snake stumbling upon me. We only watch films on Fridays anyway," he added, "and Mountjoy's easy to bribe with a slab of Battenberg. How come you know all this?"

"You know better than to ask," said Inky, "I just need to find out a little more about last Friday, that's all."

"Fair enough, you've always been good to me."

Inky's silence invited Merridew to continue.

"Well," Crispin began, "on Friday it was..."

Suddenly the sound of a school bag being dropped onto the floor caused a disturbance. Inky discreetly turned around. Peering in between a fish-tailed parka and a ski-jacket, he spotted Carlos Orange arriving to German. Late again. Oz removed a wristwatch from his pocket with his left hand, the one not encased in plaster. Inky and Merridew both spied him use his fingers to count up how many minutes he'd managed to waste. His fundamental use of arithmetic was halted when Mr Deitz flung open his classroom door. Scowling, the stern German teacher ushered Carlos inside.

"Sorry," whispered Inky, turning his attention back to Merridew, "you were about to tell me about Friday...?"

"Oh yes," said Crispin, gathering his thoughts, "now let me think. Friday. If I remember correctly, my sales were a little down that day. Perhaps it was the weather...?"

"And because year-five were sitting their mocks?"

"Of course," replied Crispin, reassured, "I knew there had to be a reason. Anyway, on Friday I had quite a bit of produce left over. Took me a while to pack it all away. You see," he explained, "I sell any leftovers at church while they're still reasonably fresh. At St Hilda's. On Sunday. It's never locked so I can take all my stuff over on Friday night and set my stall out there."

"So, last Friday. Describe exactly what happened when the end-of-lunch bell sounded."

"Well," Crispin smiled, "It was just like any normal Friday. Total chaos. Packs of kids surged past, even more demented than usual..."

"Because of the snow?"

"I suppose. Yes," he recalled, "the snow had just about started by then, and it was beginning to settle too, which turns everyone bonkers."

"Where was your stall?"

"Are you testing me, Inky, you already know? It was inside the back entrance. Just behind the double-doors separating IT and Humanities."

"So your stall was right at the heart everything?"

"Of course," said Crispin, "that way I can catch anyone going to Geography, History *or* IT. More customers, you see? But you have to be alert. Light fingers often try to grab a doughnut or snaffle one of my buns. Plus, that day," he confided, "snowballs were beginning to fly so I had to be extra vigilant."

"What I need to know, Crispin," said Inky, suddenly serious, "are the names of anyone who went down to Humanities that day, late. Specifically, between the time that Lesson 4 began and when the alarm went off ten minutes later." Inky leaned in close, "In particular, I need you to identify anyone who didn't have an official reason for being on that corridor at that time. I mean, I know that there were lots of kids going to their Geography and History lessons. Four classrooms full, in fact. One hundred and thirteen students. And that's ignoring the twenty-six going up to IT. Yet I can account for each and every one of those. But what's important for me to find out is whether anyone down there was unaccounted for. So think hard and tell me if you saw anyone going down to Humanities *after* classes had begun. Possibly alone? Or in a pair? Did you see anything suspicious at all?"

Inky watched Crispin closely.

A pause.

Merridew removed his glasses and pinched the bridge of his nose.

"Yes," he said, eventually, "yes I think there was someone." Nodding as if to convince himself, he added, "More than one person if I remember correctly. Now let me see," Crispin paused, then went on, "on the bell there was the usual stampede. I recall Harrison Webster trying to get his hands on one of my coconut macaroons, but I told him to *beggar-off*!"

"Then?"

"Then, after a couple of minutes, things quietened down so I started to tidy away. Lessons in both Humanities and IT began as normal and school settled into its Friday afternoon rhythm."

"Lively?"

"It was Friday afternoon," Crispin replied, the answer sufficient in itself. "But things seemed to calm down quickly. I think it was because the Humanities staff were just showing films or doing quizzes or something."

"What happened next?"

"Yes, yes, that's her," said Merridew, lost in recollection, "yes, it was that *human tornado* from year-three who came along first. Amanda Blunt. She charged past me first. In a huff. Swept clean past then tumbled down to Humanities like a bowling ball. Nose in the air, piece of paper in her hand. She didn't even look at me. But that's Amanda Blunt for you she's... she's..."

"Blunt?" offered Inky.

"Exactly."

"Tell me Crispin, and this is very important. Did Blunt retrace her steps before the alarm went off? Perhaps with someone else? Or did she stay downstairs?"

"Someone else?" Merridew scratched his head. "No, no, there was no-one else. She didn't re-appear at all. Not that I saw, anyway. Alone or otherwise."

"And you're sure?"

"Positive."

"So she must have remained down in Humanities until the alarm went off and everyone emerged together."

"I suppose."

"Do you know who Tommy Woggle is?"

"Sorry Inky, I'm not sure I do."

Inky prompted, "Stick thin. Not an ounce of meat on him? 'Oggy' Woggle."

"Oh 'Oggy'," Crispin exclaimed, "Of course I know Oggy. Nice lad. Mop of sandy hair. Kiss-curl at the front."

"That's him."

"Just didn't know his real name, that's all."

Inky asked, "So, do you remember Oggy Woggle passing you?"

"Of course. He bought a lemon finger from me before History. He often does, he's a good customer. He's a third-year too, yes?"

"Yes."

"Then he went down to Mr Henry's class for the start of Lesson 4 with everyone else. Blunt came past minutes later on her own."

Inky rubbed his chin, "And did you see him re-appear? Oggy? Either on his own or with Blunt?"

Crispin smiled, "You're trying to trick me again aren't you? I've already told you I didn't see Blunt re-emerge. No," he added, "I don't recall seeing either of them come back up. But once the fire alarm had started all Hell broke loose. It was like one of them Christmas sales off the telly when the staff open the doors and a stampede of *crazy-people* gush in trying to save ten pounds off a microwave. Good job I'd finished packing away or my stall would have looked like the Cookery Room after the Sparkle Group's been in."

Crispin took a moment to reflect. Inky chose not interrupt.

"No," said young-Merridew, finally, "I can say with all certainty that Oggy went down to Room 34 in plenty of time for his lesson. Blunt arrived later, descending the stairs carrying a note. Alone. I never saw either of them again that afternoon. Individually or together."

Inky took time to process what he'd heard. "So tell me, Crispin," he added, "was anyone else late to Humanities that afternoon?"

"Two others, actually. It's all starting to come back to me now," he replied, proud to be useful, "Spikey Martin was next. No wait," he exclaimed. "Sorry, Inky. Spikey went upstairs to IT. Had a small bandage wrapped around his finger. He was holding it up in a strange manner, like he was testing the wind direction. Looked like he'd been to the Sick Room."

"He had."

"Inky, why do you keep asking me things you already know?"

"Cross-referencing. Just keep going, it's perspective that's important. So," he stated, "just one more person other than Amanda Blunt went down those stairs late last Friday? Who?"

"Just one person, yeah. Now, there's no mistaking him. You're going to love this Inky!"

Inky's expression suggested the opposite.

"The only other person to go down onto the Humanities corridor was... that new kid who's just joined your year."

Inky's eyes narrowed.

"You know," said Crispin, "au juste la personne auquelle tu réfères, Inky. Le gars français!"

"Quel gars français?"

"Stop playing devil's advocate, you know very well who I'm talking about. He's the talk of the school... Jacques Asticot!"

Inky sighed, "That puts a very different perspective on things."

Oblivious to Inky's mood-change, Crispin remained upbeat, "Everyone's talking about Jacques Asticot. Everyone. That guy's just so cool. His dad's the Lord the Mayor of Mal-de-Mer, Blinkton's twin-town. The Snake's given him special permission not to wear school uniform, but that guy takes the biscuit. Coat, gloves, stripy scarf. He even wears sunglasses. In winter." He went on, "Robin Armstrong says Jacques' a semi-professional footballer in France..."

"Has Robin Armstrong ever seen Jacques Asticot play football?"

"No, but that's not the point. Everyone around school loves him. *Everyone.* Brandon Lunt's showing him around. Lucky Brandon, that's what I say."

"So," said Inky, unimpressed, "Jacques Asticot travelled down to Humanities on Friday at the start of Lesson 4. Was that before or after Amanda Blunt?"

"A couple of minutes after."

"What happened? Did you speak to him? Was he alone?"

"No and yes," said Crispin, with a smile. "Lunt was nowhere to be seen. I saw Jacques approach my stall. He even walks kinda *cool*. To impress him, I thought offer a French fancy, but as I held it out he swept past so quick that I never had chance. He appeared distracted."

"You're aware that French fancies aren't really French, Crispin?"

"Of course," he replied, impatiently, "he just caught me off guard, that's all. Seems everyone in school feels a little self-conscious around Jacques Asticot. I waited to see if I could catch him on his way back up but he must have stayed downstairs too. Anyway, I never saw him return. He's amazing, isn't he? I read all about him in last weekend's Gazette. Half the paper was dedicated to him and his dad. Loads of Simon Kench's photographs. Those two are going to revolutionise our town."

"A liaison with Mal-de-Mer could anyway," Inky corrected.

The teenage-detective's features clouded over. He stood up, paced to the end of the bench then leaned against a coat-peg, deep in thought. Crispin looked around nervously.

Finally, Inky returned to Merridew, "Your assistance has been very important Crispin, but it's time for you to return to class. Just before you go, allow me to recap on what you've told me..."

"OK," said Crispin, obediently.

"Last Friday you hosted a lunchtime cake-sale inside the staircase which divides Humanities from IT. Your sale, as usual, ran into the start of Lesson 4 and, as you packed away, you encountered a large number of students scrambling to class..."

"Including Oggy Woggle who bought a lemon-finger."

"And once this initial rush had died down, only two students, neither of whom had any discernible reason for being there, went down to Humanities..."

"Because Spikey Martin who also passed me..."

"Went upstairs to IT."

"Exactly."

"First it was Amanda Blunt from year-three who trooped past brandishing a note."

"Correct."

"Then a couple of minutes later our French visitor, Jacques Asticot, also made his way downstairs..."

"Hair shimmering," said Crispin, smiling, "he looked brilliant. He even smells good too. Lemony!"

Inky was visibly unmoved, "And neither Blunt nor Asticot communicated with one another?"

"Not that I'm aware."

"And by the time the school-bell sounded neither Amanda, nor Oggy Woggle, nor Jacques had re-emerged."

Crispin nodded, "That's it in a nutshell, Inky. I just presumed that they joined everyone else fleeing for their lives at the thought of a fire."

Glancing over his shoulder, Inky noticed Miss Gaudet peering at them through her classroom door. Having caught his eye, she pointed at her wrist. Inky nodded, then turned back to Merridew. "Time to go, Crispin. Thanks for your time. Your responses have been invaluable."

Merridew placed bony hands onto red knees and pushed himself up. "My pleasure, Inky. It all sounds very exciting. Good luck with whatever it is you're involved in this time." He tucked his hands into the pockets of his shorts and bounced back to Room 47. Just before opening the door, he added, "I'm guessing that if you've only two or three suspects to go on then you'll have everything wrapped up in no time." Then, as an afterthought, he added, "Unless you count the caretaker."

Inky felt the colour drain from his cheeks,

"Caretaker?" The investigator covered the short distance between himself and Merridew in three strides, "Explain. Quickly!"

"Oh yes," said Crispin, startled, "I guess I forgot to mention him. Didn't think a staff-member counted. Well, yes," he said, unaware of Inky's unease, "after everyone else had swept past me Mr Day came up to help me with my trestle table. Wasn't that kind of him?"

"Yes," replied Inky, deadpan. In silence he let Merridew return to French.

Left alone in the Languages' cloakroom, a dark shadow passed across the detective's face. His case had just become considerably more complicated.

Amanda Blunt?

Tommy Woggle?

Jacques Asticot??

Ray Day??

8. INKY'S HEADQUARTERS 13 HORROBIN LANE:

Tuesday 20ᵗʰ December (Evening).

A number of candles flickered from wall-mounted holders, their light struggling to make an impression against the predominant colour. Black. Three teenagers looked across from one to another, faces distorted by shadow. Suddenly the door opened and a shaft of brightness sliced the room...

"Your room's so dark and dreary, Inky," said Mrs Stevens, bustling in with a tea tray. "Why do you insist on lighting your bedroom like this, Inky? I know candles create atmosphere but the wax dribbles down onto the floor-boards and I can hardly see well enough to set down my tray."

"I told you not to disturb us," said Inky.

"I know, love, but I just couldn't help myself. It's been ages since you two called, hasn't it?"

Twins Ross and Rose looked up and nodded in unison.

"I was beginning to think the three of you had fallen out. Nice to see you both looking so well."

"Thanks Mrs Stevens," they replied.

"I mean, look at you," she exclaimed, "you two must be at least an inch taller than, when was it? Last September? You must call on us much more often. It would cheer Inky up no end."

"Mother!"

"Anyway," Alice Stevens went on, "just so you know, there's always a nice pot of tea for you here. Inky could always use a bit more company, anyway. I've no idea what he gets up to up here for hours on end. It's not normal to be so reclusive. I mean, it wouldn't harm to..."

Inky took the tray from his mother and set it down on his desk-top, causing tea to slop, "Now mother, if you don't mind, I've business to attend to."

"More important than tea and biscuits?"

"Yes," said Inky, firmly. "Your kindness is endearing but please don't disturb us again. We won't be long."

"Very well, dearie, I know when I'm not wanted." Alice Stevens left the room yet before the door had closed, her head suddenly re-appeared, "I'll be downstairs watching the News with Eric if you need me. Although," she laughed, "what's happening in Blinkton these days is far more exciting than the telly, isn't it? What with those French chaps and what-not? It's ever so thrilling. Today Mayor Carey took Jean-Pierre Asticot to 'the Age of Aquarium'. Millie Swabb, its owner, was beside herself. And that lad, the teenager, he's at your school isn't he? How's he settling in? Handsome young fellah."

Inky's response was terse, "Mother, we have work to do."

"Alright, I get the message. Just call if you need either of us."

"Thanks Mrs Stevens," the twins replied.

With Alice finally gone the darkness gradually reasserted itself.

In his book Peregrine Dukes highlighted that Inky Stevens didn't have any friends, not in the conventional sense. Twins Ross and Rose Berry were as close as it's possible to be to someone so isolated. The Great School Detective, when relevant, turned to these two for assistance. In return, his classmates were honoured to support him. Yet that was the extent of their relationship... to undertake 'donkeywork' if required. Inky led the charge while the twins were happy to tag along as foot-soldiers.

As Inky left English earlier that morning the five words he'd whispered into Ross' ear were, 'Meet me tonight. Bring Rose.'

As requested, the pair had made their way to Inky's house at the customary time (six o'clock). By the time the Berrys had turned away from the seafront, December's natural light had long been swallowed up. Along their route, splashes of colour from Christmas lights directed them towards number 13 Horrobin Lane, Inky's semi-detached house. In appearance it was little different to all the others on the street and indeed the whole of his estate. It was there, after a warm doorstep welcome, that the twins had been whisked through the bright, cheeriness of the Stevens' home into the gothic blackness of Inky's room...

Hands behind his back, Inky paced bare floorboards, "I'll not keep you. What I ask is both straightforward and specific, so listen carefully."

Ross was seated in customary fashion, leant back against the wrought-iron headboard of Inky's bed. At the other side of the room his sister sat straight-backed on Inky's office chair. She reached out for the cup set in front of her.

"Not yet," stated Inky, "I'll have explained everything before that's had time to go cold."

Rose withdrew her hand.

"On this occasion what I'm asking is deliciously straightforward. Last Friday, as I'm sure you're aware Miss Birkin was hospitalised by a snowball which was thrown at her with excessive force. Either deliberately or otherwise. She's recovering well, but will not be returning to class 'til after Christmas."

Ross was unable to control his eagerness, "Is that what this is all about? I saw 'Flouncey' being stretchered across the yard. The whole school did."

Rose said, in disgust, "A lot of people seemed to find her predicament funny."

"I laughed," Ross confessed, "but only under my breath. It's difficult not to when everyone else's in hysterics."

"It would appear," stated Inky, "that last Friday's blizzard caused everyone to behave a little, bizarrely. Well that's it," he said, with finality, "that's what I require. As Miss Birkin has no recollection of who threw that snowball at her, I want you to find out who did."

"Us?" chimed the Berrys.

"You," confirmed Inky. "And, Rose?"

"Yes."

"I have an additional task for you. You know the Senior Girls' Toilet at the end of the Humanities corridor?"

"Yes?"

"I need you to go inside before school starts tomorrow and look for anything suspicious."

"Suspicious? Before school?" she complained, "You know we're not allowed in the building before the bell..."

"More specifically," Inky explained, "I'm looking for a note. A single piece of paper, probably, which, if found, may contain nonsensical information. Probably handwritten. Possibly inside the bin. Possibly with Tommy Woggle's name on it. I can't be more precise at this stage. If you do find something of that nature I need you to pass it over to me in registration tomorrow. Understood?"

"I suppose," said Rose, uncertainly. "I'll do my best."

"Good."

Silence.

The detective looked down at his visitors then gestured towards the door,

"You may go. I need to be left alone with my thoughts. You can finish your drinks on the way out."

Silence.

Brother and sister looked from one to another.

"Now hang on, Inky," complained Ross, "we've just run all the way here, risking our necks on black-ice, just for that? You normally give us a little more, more..." he faltered,

"direction."

Rose said, "Searching the Senior Girls' Toilet is possible, I suppose, provided I can sneak into school early. But we're going to need more guidance if you expect us to find out who threw that snowball at Miss Birkin. The whole school was involved in a snowball fight once the Maths exam had been suspended. I wouldn't even know where to start."

"Me neither," Ross added, "it's impossible."

Inky steepled his hands, "Time's valuable, so use your initiative. Have you learned so little from me?"

Rose said, "I appreciate your point, Inky, but let's just review the facts. Miss Birkin, was injured during the fire drill last Friday..."

"Correct."

"... by a snowball launched with some force judging by the size of the bump which had formed on her forehead by the time that the ambulance..."

Ross interrupted, "And all the other emergency vehicles..."

"... had ploughed through the school gates."

"But nobody knows who threw it," Ross complained. "It happened in the middle of a snowstorm, somewhere near Broker's Arch. That's by the Old School, one of the quietest areas in school..."

"And there *were* no witnesses, Inky. If somebody'd seen something, well," Rose explained, "you know what schools are like? Somebody would have said something. Gossip that good would have spread like wild fire. Nobody knows anything."

"But somebody does know something," said Inky, tone direct, "the person who threw it, for one. Which is why I've said that you'll need to be creative."

"But," said Rose, "that line of enquiry's dangerous. The type of person who flings a ball of ice at a teacher's head is likely to, how do I put this...?"

"I think, sis, you mean to say they're not going to be especially *saintly*."

"Exactly bruv. What if whoever lobbed it turns out to be dangerous? What then?"

"Nothing," Inky levelled. "Just lie-low and pass the information on to me.

I'll take things from there. If anything turns nasty, I'll step in. So," he turned away, "if there's nothing else…?"

"Now come on, Inky," said Rose, rising, "give us a few pointers. A bit of help…"

Inky moved over to his window and, ignoring the fact that his curtains were closed, gazed down as if into the garden. When he spoke, he did so dispassionately, "Ask questions *diplomatically*. Listen to responses *carefully*. Proceed with caution. I find that a visit to the crime-scene's essential. So take a stroll over to Broker's Archway. Poke about by the mini-bus to see what's there. And bear in mind," he stressed, deliberate, "that because the weather since Friday has rarely climbed above freezing, there will be clues still etched into the frozen ground. If you look carefully enough you'll find them. But don't waste time. I'd hate everything to have melted before you've managed to put your thinking caps on." He concluded, "There's no time for any more meetings like this one. I'll see you in registration tomorrow, and from then on, if I need you, I'll come to find you. Or vice-versa. But by the time I come to you for a progress report," he turned around, eyes alive, "make sure that you've some progress to report."

"Now hang on, Inky" said Ross, also rising, "what will you be doing while we're out playing in the snow?"

Inky's response was matter of fact, "Believe me Ross, my time's not spent idly. You're aware that I didn't attend class today, nor do I anticipate doing so tomorrow. Or the day after if necessity demands it. I have a separate agenda about which you need not concern yourself."

"How come you're allowed to skip classes?"

Inky grimaced, "It's Christmas, Ross. No one cares!" The detective turned his back once more, "Let's just say that I have a special dispensation. Trust me when I say that you don't need to trouble yourself with what I'm involved in. What I require from you," he said, simply, "is only a small piece in a much larger jigsaw. Make sure you conduct yourselves with integrity."

Ross asked, "Has this anything to do with Mr Bennett? You were in his office this morning instead of 'Chalky's' English lesson, weren't you?"

In the ensuing silence the candles flickered as though touched by a gentle breath.

"As I said Ross, it's best not to know." Inky linked his hands behind his head, "Goodbye!"

The twins looked at one another, then at the back of Inky's head. When it became apparent that their classmate didn't intend to speak further, Rose nodded towards the door. Unable to help themselves, Rose grabbed two cups of tea while Ross snatched a bourbon each.

As the door closed the candle flames momentarily turned horizontal.

Inky stood alone. Motionless.

Thinking.

Downstairs he heard the twins bid muffled *goodbyes*. Once they'd left, the young-detective laid down upon his bed. Beneath his mattress was the Stevens' copy of the Blinkton Gazette. From this, Inky had already memorised all the relevant details of the Asticots' visit. Placing his hands over one another on his chest, he slowly shut his eyes. Deathly still, he allowed his thoughts to roam like a bird released. Swooping. Banking. Soaring.

'*Who, last Friday afternoon, on that corridor, deliberately triggered that alarm?*'

'*Who? Who?*'

'*And why?*'

And while the remaining cup of tea turned cold and candles burned away to columns of wax, a number of different possibilities took shape. Some were straightforward, fresh as first light on a cobweb. Others, however, were much more sinister, mutating into beasts capable of tremendous harm...

'*Crispin Merridew's evidence was vital, yet what he revealed also places him at the crime-scene. Merridew, Amanda Blunt, Tommy Woggle and Jacques Asticot. All out of class on 'that' corridor at 'that' time. Along with Ray Day...*'

'*Is that the final list of suspects, or could there be someone else? And what of the snowball...?*'

Inky closed his eyes, delighting in the feel of cold blackness. To an onlooker he looked as though he was asleep, yet this was far from the truth. In reality, it would be some time before Inky Stevens would allow himself the luxury of slumber...

Mr Mike Bennett (Deputy-Head):

My Friday morning assembly started off in customary fashion. I waited patiently omstage while rows of students snaked past me, giddy and jostling. Then, when everyone had finally seated, I opened my mouth to speak...

When, in an instant, everything changed!

To my horror, I found all that emerged from my mouth was an incoherent rattle. Hundreds of pairs of eyes looked up only to see me clutching my throat in panic. Gasping and spluttering. Even the simplest of words seemed beyond me. I simply... could... not... speak...

Then everything went black.

The Hall was seized by the fiercest chill.

The deepest freeze.

The blackest night.

The harshest winter.

I sank to my knees, sensing rather than seeing the ice-sculpture students before me. I tried to scream but an invisible fist had grabbed me by the throat. Hard and heavy. And as it squeezed, my eyelids slowly slid shut.

Slumped onstage, surrender came quickly. All too soon I felt myself drifting away, shocked at how quick I was willing to accept the cold relief of inevitability...

Then I felt Her presence.

Her!

The Snake was there!

I could sense Her hidden away at the back of the Hall where the shadows were deepest.

My eyes snapped open, an action which caused the glitterball hanging from the ceiling to whir into life. Yet light which should have been silvery and bright emerged the colour of blood. Immediately the Hall was enveloped within a crimson snowstorm.

Terrifying in its thickness.

I scanned the red mist, desperate for understanding, desperate to find Her. Until finally Her loathsome form decided to reveal itself to me...

With terrifying slowness She slithered out of the blizzard, like a serpent through undergrowth...

The Snake, and yet not the Snake.

Her, yet not Her.

What I saw was not human. She'd become a hellish creature, gnarled and unformed with skin the texture of dried mud. She threaded Her way through the Hall until finally She rose up at its centre. Abhorrent in majesty. Oblivious to the students surrounding Her. From behind Her a pair of black, leathery wings unlatched. Coarse like tree-bark. Veined with an intricate network of capillaries. I watched on in horror as Her misshapen limbs extended with terrifying slowness.

Then Her rubbery eyelids peeled back... and She stared directly at me.

Into my very soul.

And at that same moment, Her eye-sockets sparked, ignited, then flared. Fiery beams of hatred leapt from Her skull, slicing the Hall's cold vacuum.

I tried to turn away... but I was trapped within Her Medusa stare...

Petrified.

Ensnared.

She threw back Her head and dredged up a sound belonging to the swamps of pre-history. A black-tongued 'screech' which boomed all around the Hall. Primitive and raw. An inhuman cry of pain.

Gulping in terror, I realised that the splintered light of the disco-ball had synchronised with my own heartbeat. Pulsing, it matched the tempo of my fear beat for beat.

Deep, red and terrible.

Tiny pricks of light sliced through the air with scalpel-sharpness. Faster and faster they flared until the entire Hall was drenched in light. Saturated. And at the centre of this swirling cloud of crimson I saw Her features contort in agony. Her festering mouth-hole opened once again but this time She began to 'speak', each loathsome word punctuated by jets of fire,

"TELL THEM," She screeched.

"What?" I replied, struggling to find voice.

"TELL THEM."

"I... I can't," I said, realisation dawning.

"YOU... HAVE... NO... CHOICE. I HAVE DECREED THAT YOU WILL TELL THEM AND TELL THEM YOU WILL!"

"I, I can't... I'm scared. If I tell them... if I tell them... then... then..."

The force of Her voice caused the windows to vibrate, "STOP MUTTERING YOU PATHETIC LITTLE SLUG! DO AS I ASK. NOW. IF YOU FAIL I WILL CREMATE YOU HERE AND NOW. MY FIRE-EYES WILL STRIP THE FLESH FROM YOUR BONES!"

"No!"

Her voice continued, part-human, "THEY'RE WAITING FOR YOU,

LOOK! LOOK AT THEM. TELL THEM RIGHT NOW. TELL THEM," She screeched, tongue lolling, "THAT THE CHRISTMAS DISCO IS CANCELLED. TELL THEM THAT IT'S ALL YOUR FAULT BECAUSE YOU FAILED THE TASK I SET YOU. TELL THEM NOW!"

"I can't... I simply can't..." I stuttered, tears streaming, "Forgive me, miss. But I can't..."

"IT'S YOUR CHOICE, BENNETT. BUT YOU KNOW THE CONSEQUENCES. SO I'LL ASK YOU ONE, FINAL TIME, ARE YOU GOING TO TELL EVERYONE THAT THE DISCO IS CANCELLED?"

Unable to avert my eyes from Her eye-sockets, I mumbled half-heartedly.

"SPEAK UP YOU MISERABLE LITTLE WORM. ARE YOU GOING TO TELL THEM OR NOT!?"

In desperation I summoned up every ounce of resistance I possessed, "NO! NO I AM NOT GOING TO TELL THEM. I will not be the one who ruins Christmas for so many of our..."

"THEN YOU HAVE MADE YOUR CHOICE," She interrupted, the savagery of Her tone propelling me backwards, "PREPARE TO SUFFER!"

The last thing I heard was the rush of the flames which spewed from Her eye-sockets. The twin columns of death shot across the Hall and slammed into my defenceless body. Hot air ran at me, then through me, causing my skin to blister and split. Finally my flesh was incinerated and I was erased from existence.

"NOOOOOOOOO!!!"

And then I woke up.

Gasping for breath, I sat upright in bed. Dripping with sweat.

Scared out of my senses.

Struggling for composure, I propped myself up on my pillow, alarmingly hot on such an icy morning. In semi-darkness I focussed on slowing a heartbeat which hammered against the wet cotton of my pyjamas. I leaned back against the head-board and reassured myself that the vision which had felt so real moments before was nothing but a dream. A terrifying nightmare, but a dream nevertheless. But although I was awake and it had ended, a sense of foreboding lingered like the smell of cigarette smoke on clothing.

A sense of normality slowly shuffled back through the gloom. The sweat which had soaked my nightwear began to dry leaving me cold and clammy. Bleary-eyed, I looked at the clock on my bedside cabinet. Its sickly-green numerals told me that it was 3:47. Again. Just three more hours before I'd be forced to emerge from my sanctuary to face the torture of yet another school day.

Having had sleep wrenched from me, I swung my feet out of bed and scrabbled around for my slippers. I switched my bedside light on, recoiling at its brightness. I then plodded through to my study and plonked myself down at my desk. On autopilot, I pulled a set of Maths books towards me and started marking. As it happened it was Michael Porter's exercise book on the top of the pile that morning. Not a good omen for the day ahead. Without thinking, I began daubing it with red crosses.

And as I sat there suffocated beneath a blanket of depression, it was to my shame that I never spared Inky Stevens a second thought. He was my greatest hope, (my only hope), yet somehow I'd underestimated what he was capable of. Thinking back on what he went on to face that Wednesday, I ought to have given him more credit. Much more credit. If I'd have fully appreciated his ability at the time, then maybe instead of marking Maths books in the dead of night, I'd have managed to have a refreshing sleep instead...?

As it was, I resigned myself to slapping a barrage of red crosses onto Mick Porter's inept work, tortured by thoughts of what dawn would bring...

9. Mr. Bennett's Office:

Wednesday 21th December (Morning).

For Mike Bennett the day of the winter solstice began with a loud knock at his door. Answering it, the Deputy spluttered, "Inky, great to see you. I'd almost forgotten... Have there been any...?"

But the young-detective had already pushed past and stationed himself at Bennett's window. The detective scanned the playground, watching curiously as an army of students slipped and slid towards their first lesson of the day. From such a height, it appeared as if all Blinkton Comprehensive was within his grasp, a microcosm of activity governed by rules which made sense of the apparently senseless pattern below. Like the workings of a giant clock.

Inky, like a raven on its perch, sought his prey with silent intensity. Looking down, he caught his first meaningful glimpse of Jacques Asticot. The French-teen was easy to identify despite only being just one individual among many. Wherever Asticot went, others followed. His disciples scurried around him like piglets around a sow at feeding time. Inky noted with interest that Big Sean-Kennedy and Joe 'Fish-eye' Bradshaw, two of Blinkton's most notorious trouble-makers, had already made Asticot's acquaintance. His self-appointed henchmen flanked him wherever he went. It was apparent to Inky that the French-enigma possessed the power to pull others towards him by sheer presence alone. His *mystique*. Not the most moral of individuals either. Trouble, it seemed, was always a pace or two behind Jacques Asticot.

Inky also watched Jacques' hapless chaperone, Brandon Lunt. The diligent fourth-year laboured a pace or two behind his charge, struggling to keep up. Lacking Asticot's charisma, Lunt looked confused and lost. Out of his depth.

Hunched and steely, Inky thought ahead to their encounter, *'How events will play out, only time will tell...?'*

Bennett tentatively approached, "Stevens, how good... how refreshing to see you. Is there... has there... been news?"

"Sit down," Inky replied, gesturing towards the seating.

Once Bennett had complied, Inky sat opposite.

"Inky, it's such a relief. I've been a little distracted. A little tired. Can't seem to, to get my mind in gear. Had a terrible nightmare last night. Have you... I mean... has there been progress? Are you," he ventured, "any nearer...?"

"Sleep has to be a priority, sir. You're weary. And, yes," he admitted, "progress has been made."

Bennett's shoulders relaxed, "I gave you a list of names. Thirty-nine. Were they of any...?"

"As a starting point, undoubtedly. Yet as a starting point only. Refinement is ongoing."

"I see," said Bennett, without really seeing at all. "Have you managed to whittle the list down?"

"Of course, but now's not the time for explanation, there's still too much to do. What I need right now, amongst other things, is information. So don't ask questions, just answer. I take it you've ten minutes to spare?"

"Yes... yes, I suppose, I was just about to..."

"Right," said Inky, handing over a piece of A4 paper, "then I'd like you to take a look at this. It's a note. You teach Amanda Blunt, don't you?"

"I'm afraid so."

"Then could you confirm, briefly, whether what's written on that paper *could be* her handwriting."

"Well," replied Bennett, "although I don't actually take Miss Blunt for Maths myself our paths have crossed. Due to her behaviour. She's often in the Isolation Unit. And yet," he paused, scrutinising the paper, "whatever work she's given to do, she usually only scrawls just two words over and over again. In bold capitals. Page, after page, after page..."

"Would those two words be 'TOMMY WOGGLE' by any chance?"

"I'm impressed, Stevens."

Bennett scrutinised the paper carefully. His reply, when it came, was considered, "Now, I can't be one hundred per cent sure without a matching sample, but based on a quick glance, I'd say it was her handwriting, yes." He eyed Inky curiously, "Blunt's name was on the list I passed on to you, wasn't it? Mr Henry said she'd asked to see Oggy Woggle just before the alarm went off. He let them both leave his class not knowing her note was forged. Was it Blunt who set the alarm off? It wouldn't surprise me. Or even the pair of them. They did leave Room 34 together, I believe?"

Inky sidestepped Bennett's questions and retrieved the note, "Sir, according to last weekend's Gazette you attended a meeting on Monday 12th December. At the Town Hall. At this meeting Mayor Carey presented Jean-Pierre and Jacques Asticot to Blinkton."

"I still can't believe Blinkton's good fortune..."

"I need you to outline everything that happened at that meeting. Everything," he repeated. "I need you to tell me exactly what was said, the atmosphere in the room and how the French pair came across. Don't confuse fact with opinion, I need as much detail as possible..."

So I told Inky everything I could remember. As I ran through my account, I can still picture him sitting opposite, head bowed in silent concentration. I'm ashamed to say that I tended to 'meander' as different things occurred at different times. But overall, I'm pretty sure I explained everything as accurately as I could. It was only when I'd finished that he looked up. What I'd said obviously made sense as he concluded our meeting purposefully. I, on the other hand, was more sceptical...

Bennett's features clouded over, "Does that mean that you think that somehow Jacques Asticot could be mixed up in all this? His name wasn't on the list I gave you."

"That's because he's not officially registered here."

"Yes, I suppose that's true," said Bennett, rubbing his chin, "but I'd urge you to tread lightly with that line of enquiry. Young-Asticot's presence here at Blinkton School is of great cultural significance. As I've just explained, the financial input offered by Mal-de-Mer is crucial for..."

Inky pulled Bennett up short, "With all due respect, sir, you asked me to supply you with the names of two individuals who have wronged this school and that's what I intend to do. No matter who they turn out to be. Did you expect me to do otherwise?"

"No, no of course not," Bennett spluttered. "I didn't mean, no what I meant... it's just that..."

"Leave everything to me," Inky insisted. "You wanted answers and that's what I'll provide. *The truth will out*, as Shakespeare wrote, whatever the truth turns out to be."

Bennett laughed, "You speak with such wisdom for one so young. I do believe you're the only person I can trust in this establishment."

Inky continued, "And as for Jacques Asticot, it's time to hear what he has to say for himself. From what you've just told me, I know exactly where I'll be able to intercept him."

"My pleasure," said Bennett, unaware of what he'd actually said.

"Right," said Inky, rising, "I need you to call Ray Day for me. On your telephone, right now. Summon him to this office."

"Ray Day? Our caretaker, Ray Day?" Bennett's brow furrowed, "Why on earth would I...?"

"As I've explained," said Inky, "it's best not to ask too many questions."

"But, as far as I know he's busy. He's reapplying plaster to the Humanities corridor."

"Then it's doubly important you distract him. I want you to detain him in here for as long as possible."

"But how do I get hold of him? What should I say when he gets here?"

"Use you initiative. Miss Cartwright can contact him on his radio. From Reception. Phone her and summon him here straight away. I need him well away from that corridor for at least ten minutes. More if possible," he stressed. "That should give me enough time for what I have to do." Inky elicited eye-contact, "Just make sure you keep him occupied. Ten minutes."

Bennett clambered to his feet, "But what should I say?"

"You'll think of something, sir... alternative seating for the mocks, gritting the staff car-park, ordering more water for the cooler in the staffroom..."

"How do you know there's a water cooler in...?

"Anything. Say whatever you like, but make it convincing. And like yesterday, I need you to excuse my absence from class. The next phase of my mission will take me the rest of the day. Say I'm working on a school magazine article with you."

"What article? Look Inky, I need you to be a little more honest..."

"I haven't said anything dishonest."

"No, no of course not, it's just... it's just that I need to know what to do about the Christmas disco. Will I have to cancel it? What's your gut feeling? Are you any nearer to...?"

But Bennett's words tapered off as the Great School Detective left his office. With the sound of the door ringing in his ears, Inky was already on his way back to Humanities. To pry into the activities of certain caretaker.

Feeling queasy, Mike Bennett picked up the phone, "Hello Jinny? Could you pass a message on to Ray Day for me please? It's important that he receives it straight away, I need to see him urgently..."

10. THE HUMANITIES CORRIDOR:
Wednesday 21ᵗʰ December (Morning).

As Inky looped around the perimeter of the main building once more, he felt the sub-zero temperature catch at the back of his throat. As before, he re-entered school by the double-doors to its rear. This time however, instead of going down to Humanities, he took a few paces upwards towards IT. There, he paused inside the gloomy stairwell, hidden among the shadows. Motionless and alert.

Waiting.

He didn't have to wait long. Within seconds he heard the heavy plod of workbooks and the grunt of an irritable caretaker. Ray Day, upset at being disturbed, huffed his way up the stairs, then trudged out into the icy playground. As he departed, Inky was momentarily illuminated by a shaft of winter light. Had the egg-headed lunk looked up he would have seen Inky standing above. Resolute. Yet Day was too distracted. He simply barrelled onwards, flinging the door shut behind him with a meaty paw.

Inky, hearing the *scuff* of Day's boots subside, slid out of hiding. Silent as nightfall he descended the short flight of stairs onto the Humanities corridor.

The previous night Inky'd spent a considerable amount of time thinking about Ray Day, more specifically, how he'd been able to creep up on him so unexpectedly. The super-sleuth was always alert to danger, yet somehow the meat-headed Neanderthal had managed to grab him undetected. Day's enormity should have meant that his presence was telegraphed in advance. The fact that it hadn't been wasn't meant that something wasn't right. And that 'something' needed an explanation...

From his mission the previous September, Inky'd acquired a large bunch of keys which unlocked every door on the school premises. Finding the one which fit Day's maintenance cupboard hadn't been easy. A school the size of Blinkton Comprehensive had many such cupboards. Yet by a process of elimination, Inky'd been able to identify seven 'potentials'. He'd removed these from the main bunch and brought them into school in readiness.

'Ray Day', the detective reasoned, 'hadn't tip-toed the length of the corridor in silence. He'd been there all along. Hidden inside his maintenance cupboard.'

Inky Stevens had no idea what Day was up to in there, but he knew that he was up to something. And he'd just engineered himself a ten minute window to find out...

As before, the Humanities corridor channelled the commotion from the four classrooms along its length. Registers complete, the latest round of Christmas lessons were in full swing. 'Brylcream' Mountjoy was showing another one of his semi-educational videos, this time something to do with the Geological features of North America. On the opposite side, Mr Henry was repeating his music quiz,

"Shut up you lot," barked Clive Henry, "and concentrate on your papers. No, Steven McClean, 'Gringo' was not a member of the Beatles, and yes, Armstrong-Ball, surprisingly enough, there were four members of the 'Fab Four'!"

"What about the Jackson Five, sir?"

"Shut up. Less of the brouhaha... I mean, less of the noise!"

Inky continued along the corridor. On reaching Day's maintenance cupboard, he produced the seven keys and proceeded to try these one at a time. As he did so he was again hit by an overpowering chemical smell.

The law of averages said that the lock should have yielded by the fourth key. On this occasion, however, Inky had to wait slightly longer. It wasn't until the sixth of the seven keys had been tried that the door finally yielded. It swung slowly outwards. If Inky was surprised by what he saw within, his expression did not convey it...

Day's cupboard was similar to all non-priority areas in a building where room was scarce, it was small. A square, brick-built space, it measured little more than six feet by six. To Inky, it seemed inconceivable that a man of Ray Day's size could fit inside it at all, let alone customise it. Yet, customise it he had. The scheming caretaker had not wasted an inch of space during his *very specific* renovation, one which explained the intense smell...

The storeroom was lit by a pull-string attachment. Inky pulled this on and Day's secret closet was instantly bathed in soft, ruby light. The room which had once held mops, buckets and cleaning fluids had now been redesigned as a photographic darkroom. Ray Day, it seemed, had been developing photographs.

Personal photographs.

Hundreds of them.

Ones of a very specific nature.

Inky checked that he hadn't been seen then slid inside and closed the door after himself. The teen-detective was immediately assaulted by an intense smell which settled at the back of his throat and caused him to gag. In response, he removed a handkerchief from his backpack and placed it over his mouth. By controlling his breathing, he found that he was able to inspect the room with a degree of composure...

Beneath the soft red light, Inky saw that not an inch of space had been wasted. Firstly, the cupboard had been light-proofed. Long plastic strips had been glued around the doorframe and under the door to prevent light seeping in. Shelving erected on three sides of the room contained all manner of photographic equipment. There were a number of differently-sized chemical containers. As well as these Inky saw developer, photographic paper, an enlarging easel, printing tongs, chemical trays, a timer and a small basket of rubber gloves. On the back of the door a lab-coat (presumably stolen from Science) was hung.

Wedged in at the centre of the tight space was the enlarger itself, a cubed-shaped piece of equipment with an adjustable head. It was from here that light shone down through the negatives onto light-sensitive paper beneath. Timing his efforts carefully, Day had been able to generate a substantial amount of black and white prints. The final stage of his process was to allow the enlargements to dry. This was achieved by hanging them on a number of specially adapted washing lines, several of which criss-crossed the room giving it the appearance of a kind of miniature laundry. Inky only needed a brief glance at Day's macabre bunting to understand what he was up to... he was amassing a collection of Blinkton School's flaws. The meat-headed lunk appeared to be intent on damaging Blinkton School's reputation.

Seriously damaging it.

The collection of photographs, many blurred or taken at jaunty angles, depicted Blinkton at its worst... students smoking behind the bike sheds, rotten food in the canteen's freezer, students operating machinery in Metalwork without safety equipment, the tangle of rubble backstage in the school Hall, the heap of horse manure which constituted the Rural Studies garden, the statue of Lionel Roebuck with a pair of underpants placed onto his head, various examples of graffiti, a snarl of exposed wiring in the Computer Room, students engaging in snow-related horseplay whilst lining up to be registered after the fire alarm... and so his sinister exhibition went on, and on, and on.

Other prints were of a more statistical nature... examination results, complaint letters from parents, examples of poor lesson planning from teacher-files and evidence from the school's financial report indicating a significant deficit. But the most controversial pictures of all related to the Snake Herself. Several showed Her office, gleaming and new, with nothing of any educational relevance inside it whatsoever. Day had snapped Her half-finished cup of cappuccino and 'Celebrity Pap!' magazine. He'd also photographed Her diary which documented several visits to a masseuse during school time. Other than such appointments, Her diary was completely blank except for the words 'Roger Rowlandson' carved into the back cover in black ink, again, and again, and again. Inky was left in no doubt that Day was compiling a damning account of how Blinkton Comprehensive School was run. Starting at the very top. In the wrong hands such evidence would cause an outcry.

'So whose hands are they designed for? For who have such prints been taken?'
(Five minutes remaining?)

Careful to disturb as little as possible, Inky decided to leave. His opinion of Ray Day had just sunk to a level even lower than he'd thought possible. Then, without warning, the investigator realised he wasn't alone...

There was a sharp *bang* on the outside of the cupboard door.

Inky froze.

'Perhaps Bennett failed to detain Day after all?'

Bang. The noise came again, only inches away from his confined position.

Durff, durff, durff!

Inky was entombed in a brick-built cell six foot by six. He looked from side to side knowing that either escape or concealment were impossible. He remained calm, readying himself for what was to follow...

What did follow was a muffled shout.

"Ian Turnbull, you asked permission to go to the toilet. Now *go* to the toilet and stop banging on Mr Day's cupboard door."

Even through thick wood there was no escaping the shrill voice Miss Aries, her instructions made more sinister by her Scott's accent,

"But, miss, it's fun!"

"But... miss... it's fun," she mocked, then changed tone, "you're not here to have fun, Turnbull, you're in school! Now, you have one minute, and then I want you back in your seat!"

"One minute? That's not fair. What if I want a...?"

"You have fifty-five seconds left!"

The pad of Turnbull's footsteps faded and silence settled once more. Inky exhaled, aware of the strong tang of sulphur at the back of his mouth. He decided to give Ian Turnbull twice the time Miss Aries had allotted him. Just to be on the safe side.

(Three minutes remaining?)

Stranded, the investigator decided to make use of the gained time. Beneath the glow of the safelight he re-read what was scrawled onto the piece of paper Rose Berry had passed over in registration, the one Bennett had just confirmed *could have been* written by Amanda Blunt...

"I believe this is what you wanted," Rose had grinned, placing the single piece of paper onto Inky's desk. "It's lucky that the bin in the Girls' Toilet hadn't been changed this week. But unlucky in the sense that it was also full of goodness only knows what else." She brushed the palms of her hands on her school skirt, "I had to sift through sweet wrappers, deodorant cans, paper-towels and a half-eaten scotch egg before I found what you'd described. It's a note just as you said. Quite a strange one, actually. Handwritten. And you were right, Inky, it does have Tommy Woggle's name written on it. As well as Mr Henry's. I found it crumpled in a tight ball near the top but it'd still been in the bin long enough to have some kind of sticky fluid dribbled all over it. Probably hair gel? I hope it was hair gel!"

Inky had slid the paper across his desk to read it.

Rose went on, "I hope you appreciate me doing this, Inky? You know we're not allowed in school before the morning bell. Lucky there were no teachers around. Just the caretaker knocking about down there. He shot me one of his dirty looks, but I ignored him and ran off."

Inky had folded the paper on its original creases and placed it inside his pocket, "You've done well, Rose."

Inky used Turnbull's ablution break to thoroughly scrutinise the note which Rose had managed to locate. It was Blunt's handwritten request which she'd carried into Room 34. On the outside was written...

'Mr Henry. Room 34.'

'Re. Tommy Woggle'

The writing inside, however, was less ordered...

'Do not react Tommy. Look at this peece of paper seriously. Nod your head. Then ask Mr Henry if you can leeve the room. Say that Mr Charlton needs to see you immediately. DO IT NOW!'

Inky nodded to himself, his features appearing demonic beneath the red light. The investigator had been unsure of how to approach Amanda Blunt. But he wasn't any more...

'So, Miss Blunt. What's so important about Tommy Woggle that you need to fake an excuse to steal him away from History?'

Aware that Turnbull's allotted time had passed, Inky slipped out of the maintenance cupboard relieved to find nothing more threatening than a blinking strip-light waiting for him outside. He noted that the plaster at the bottom of the corridor had been attended to. Half-heartedly.

Inky quickly retraced his steps, eager to distance himself from his alarming discovery. Relishing the fresh December air outside, Inky chose to watch Day's return from a distance. At the far side of the yard the detective shrank into the covered doorway which led into the Gym. Thus concealed, he had to wait several minutes before Day heaved his way back into view. Whatever excuse Mike Bennett had found to delay him had been effective. The detective watched the oversized oaf appear, thick-jawed and frowning, a bobble hat crammed so tightly onto his head that its stitching was strained.

As Day trudged back to his lair, Inky wondered if he had his secret camera hidden about him at that very moment. Whatever the case, one thing was sure... Ray Day had involved himself in something rather ugly. Whether this was connected to the attack on the fire alarm was still to be determined. But one thing was for sure, Day's moment of reckoning was coming. The bullish caretaker needed to be exposed for what he really was, a deed, Inky realised, that would be as dangerous as it would be enjoyable.

Ray Day?
Jacques Asticot?
Amanda Blunt?
Tommy Woggle?
(Crispin Merridew?)
(Someone else?)

11. THE RE DEPARTMENT:

Wednesday 21th December (Morning).

As Ross Berry left Maths at the end of Period 1 Inky was already there waiting for him. The investigator quickly steered his classmate away from a line of stampeding students, "I need your assistance, Ross. Come with me."

Young-Berry was intrigued, "What do you want?"

"I need you to follow me to RE2. Right now. And when we get there I want you to show this note to Mr Passaretto." Inky passed over a folded piece of A4 paper he'd taken five minutes to scrawl inside Bennett's office. "It's a note requesting Amanda Blunt be excused from class. All I want you to do is to pass it over to her then escort her outside. It's as simple as that."

"What if Passaretto wants to read the note?" asked Ross. "Or worse, what if he won't let her leave?"

"He won't read the note and he will let her leave," Inky stated. "Passaretto'll be glad to see the back of Amanda Blunt, every other teacher is. In fact, he'll be disappointed that she'll only be missing a short time."

"She's in the third-year, isn't she? Blunt? Bit of a battle-axe?" He eyed Inky curiously, "And what will you be doing while I'm running this little errand? I don't want to be stranded with her. Rumour has it that Amanda Blunt can be quite *feisty*."

"Don't panic, Ross, I'll be waiting just outside RE2. As soon as she's joined me your job's done and you'll be free to go. Your Music lesson's just along the corridor so you won't even be late."

Ross started to turn the note over in his hands, "So, is your mission getting serious?"

Inky raised an eyebrow.

"You are going to be alright, aren't you, Inky?" he asked. "You're not in danger are you?"

"Let's just say that at the moment I'm one step ahead of the game. If things stay that way, I'll be fine."

"Anyway," said Ross, curious, "if you're coming with me, why can't you pass the note to Passaretto yourself?"

"And ruin the element of surprise?" he replied, "I'm afraid not. The less my face keeps popping up the better. Better for my chance of success. Anyway, this pleasant interlude gives you a chance to tell me everything you've learned about the snowball attack. I take it you and Rose have started your homework?"

Ross's face lit up, "I've some good news to tell you about that, actually. Very good news."

"I'll be the judge of that. Come on, let's go."

The detective set off towards RE with Ross struggling to keep up, impeded by general school traffic.

"The first thing I did this morning," said Ross, side-stepping a group of first-year girls with tinsel in their hair, "was to act as lookout while Rose ventured into the Senior Girls' Toilet. Down in Humanities. Before school. We managed to evade Ray Day who was lurking around. You have the note we found, don't you?"

"I do."

"Was it any use?"

"Time will tell," said Inky, stepping over Heather Edkins' bag without breaking stride, "but it's what you've been up to that I'm more interested in. Did the frozen ground reveal its secrets?"

"Well," said Ross, swerving a cluster of third-years playing Top Trumps, "as you suggested, Rose and I took a detour after registration. We inspected all around Broker's Arch where the school minibus is parked. By the old part of the school. And you were right, Inky. There were clues engraved in the ice. Tons of them. Everything that happened last Friday could be seen clearly."

The teen-detective darted behind the statue of Lionel Roebuck and beckoned Ross to do likewise. Sheltered from the stream of traffic, Ross was able to explain himself without interruption, "Strangely," he said, "the footprint-evidence indicates that there were *three* people involved in the attack, not two. It would appear that the perpetrator, wearing size-nine shoes, emerged from behind the minibus. Rose and I could see where he'd scooped up handfuls of snow to form his weapon. Oh yes," Ross stated, "I forgot to mention that the style of shoe would suggest it's a male you're after. That's why I said *he*."

"Continue."

"Anyway," Ross went on, animated, "judging by the footprints, this boy emerged from behind the school bus, planted himself in the snow, then *let rip*! Miss Birkin was some thirty feet away across the yard. Her stiletto heels were easy to identify. As was the area where she fell. Her outline's still imprinted into the frozen ground. She didn't struggle," he confirmed. "There was no twitching or shuffling. She simply keeled over and lay in the snow, immobile. A 'dead-weight' if you can use that expression of someone so dainty? Now, here's the interesting thing." Ross dropped his voice, "There was also someone else involved. A third person standing in between the attacker and victim. This extra person also had a size nine shoe. Or perhaps a ten at a push. But it was definitely another male. Anyway, now here's the odd part, this person also seems to have been hit and fallen over. Or," Ross struggled to disguise his excitement, "more likely, he slipped over trying to get out of the way."

After some thought, Inky clarified, "So you're saying that Miss Birkin was not the only person involved?"

"That's what the evidence suggests. The imprint of this other boy's body was also visible on the floor, only," said Ross, "his outline was much less distinct than miss'. It was fuzzy at the edges. Like he'd squirmed around on the floor for a bit."

"Interesting."

"I know. Well anyway, after a bit of a shuffle, it would appear that this other boy got up and charged off in a hurry. You can still see his footprints leading towards the main yard." Ross enquired, "Do you want to know what I think?"

"I think I'm about to find out."

"I think that this boy ducked, then fell over. But," Ross peered around the statue before continuing, "the state of the ground beside Broker's Arch suggests that both miss and this mystery boy were *both* floored during the same attack."

"You're saying that one snowball caused two people to tumble?"

Ross tilted his head, "Yeah, Inky, I know it sounds odd. But the evidence is right there in the ice. I mean, the obvious thing to say is that there were two snowballs but," Ross announced, "Rose and I were actually able to find it, *the actual murder weapon* as they say in the movies."

Inky's eyes narrowed.

"Yeah," Ross nodded, "I thought that'd impress you. We located this lad's snowball. It lay only a few feet away from Miss Birkin's imprint but close to the wall so that it lay undisturbed. Rose and I picked it up and I have to say… it was 'a beauty.'"

Inky frowned.

"Alright, a little disrespectful, I know, but trust me, it really was a magnificent piece of sculpture. Destructive, polished and deadly. It would have taken our attacker quite some time to make it. Layer after layer of compacted snow. And get this, right at its core was this!" Ross put his hand into his pocket and produced a fist. "Ta-dah!" he exclaimed, opening his hand to reveal a golfball. The young-investigator took it and held it up. Inscribed on the ball's surface was the word, *'Drivesure'*, but more importantly, it had also been branded. The initials *'C.C.'* had been stamped onto its dimpled surface.

"What about that, Inky?" Ross beamed, "Have Rose and I done well?"

"On this occasion, you appear to have surpassed yourselves."

Inky slid the ball into his pocket then led his classmate out to re-join the general surge towards class. Together they progressed along the Performing Arts corridor to RE. They arrived just as lessons were beginning, narrowly avoiding cluster of girls who were brandishing a sprig of mistletoe in a threatening manner.

Ross tugged Inky's sleeve, halting his progress, "I've just remembered something else. Something strange and probably important..."

"Go on."

"This second boy," Ross whispered, "the one in between the attacker and Miss Birkin, had strange patterns on the soles of his shoes."

"*Strange patterns?*"

"Well, his shoes were different."

"He was wearing different shoes?"

"No, I mean, yes," Ross stuttered, "I mean, the footprint from each of his shoes was different. Noticeably different. The boy's left footprint was very distinct, like he was wearing a brand new shoe with deep ridges in the tread. While his other shoe, the right, had almost no markings on it at all. It was worn completely flat as if the wearer, our witness," Ross paused for effect, "was wearing an odd pair of shoes."

For a moment the detective appeared to be very far away. Finally, he said, "You've done well, Ross. Both of you have. The evidence you've uncovered is even better than expected."

"Do you know who's involved?"

"Don't you?"

Ross looked away.

Inky stated, "Good work, Ross. The net's definitely closing in. Now, RE2's right there. It's time for you to complete your task. Do so quickly..."

Grinning, Ross turned to knock on the door.

"Enter," came the voice of Brian Passaretto from within.

While Ross stepped inside, Inky loitered in the corridor reflecting on what he'd just heard.

Electricity was beginning to flow.

As predicted, Brain Passaretto was happy to let Amanda Blunt leave his class without even reading the note. The RE teacher, (and Head-of-Year Three), actually breathed a sigh of relief as the spirited young-lady paraded out of his classroom. Under his breath Passaretto prayed to the God he taught all about that she'd be gone for as long as possible.

The words Inky'd written onto Ross's note were very specific. On the outside, in biro, he'd written...

'Mr Passaretto. Room RE2.'

'Re. Amanda Blunt'

While on the reverse, he'd scrawled...

'Do not react Amanda. Look at this peece of paper seriously. Nod your head. Then ask Mr Passaretto if you can leeve the room. Say that Mr Charlton needs to see you immediately. DO IT NOW!'

As Amanda Blunt left class her expression was thunderous. She emerged red-faced and snarling, visibly unnerved by the note.

Inky stepped into her path, "Miss Blunt, a pleasure indeed."

Blunt looked at Ross Berry in confusion, "What? What's going on? What are you doing here, Stevens? What's...?"

Inky dismissed his classmate with a wave of his hand. "Amanda," he stated, "it's actually me who wants to see you. I was hoping to have a quiet word." While Blunt gulped, Inky pressed his advantage, "Did you recognise the note I sent?"

"Should I have?" she swallowed.

"Of course. It's virtually identical to the one you used to excuse Tommy Woggle from Humanities last Friday. At approximately five minutes past one. Just after it had started to snow. Remember?"

"I've no idea what you're talking about," she said, voice gruff.

"Then perhaps you need a recap." Inky stepped into her personal space, "Last Friday afternoon, just after lunch, instead of attending English with Mr Charlton, you arrived at Humanities instead. Late. Once there, you produced a forged note claiming that Mr Charlton needed to speak with Tommy Woggle. You and Oggy then left class together. The next thing we know about either of you is that you registered outside in the yard during the blizzard." Inky moved behind Blunt to whisper into her ear, "What I'm chiefly concerned about, Amanda, is what happened to you and friend-Tommy during those missing ten or fifteen minutes. What were you up to down on that corridor?"

Blunt started to recover her composure, "I don't know nothing, Stevens. That note in Henry's History lesson can't be traced back to me..."

"Oh, but it can, you see. It's in your handwriting. I've had it verified by a number of sources." Inky tapped his pocket, "I have it with me now, Amanda. And," he said, feigning surprise, "what was that? A moment ago you said that you didn't *know nothing* yet you've just said that it was presented in Mr Henry's lesson. I never mentioned anything about Mr Henry, or History." He folded his arms, "I'm going to ask you again, Amanda, what did you do with Tommy Woggle once you excused him from Mr Henry's lesson? And just so you know, Mr Henry's confirmed that you left Room 34 with Tommy. So, instead of *knowing nothing*, how about telling the truth."

Blunt wheeled around, "Is this about the fire alarm going off?"

Inky responded sharply, "Funny you should mention that. I haven't said anything about the alarm going off... but an alarm bell's certainly ringing now. Loud and clear. So, seeing as you've introduced it, would you care to tell me about that as well?"

"I never did it."

"I never suggested that you did."

"The sensor was in the corridor though, wasn't it?"

"Which sensor?"

"The one from where the siren was set off."

"Was it?"

"Yes," she stuttered, "but I only know about that 'cause Joe Kelly's in my class. His dad's a fireman and he told Joe all about it. It's no secret. Everyone knows."

"Everyone?"

"Yes!"

"But you were right there."

"I don't know nothing."

"So you keep saying but I don't believe you. Tell me what you do know."

Inky hoped the ensuing silence would provoke a response yet he could already sense the ground shifting.

Blunt launched her retaliation, "Who do you think you are, Stevens?" She folded her arms, "I have human rights, you know? I don't have to tell you nothing. You're violating my right to education." She extended her index finger and punctuated her words with a series of prods aimed at the detective's chest, "You've-got-a-cheek-turning-up-here-pointing-the-finger..."

"And-yet-an-onlooker-would-see-exactly-the-opposite," Inky replied ironically, attempting to stand his ground.

"You've dragged me out of RE on false pretences. This is nothing to do with my educational right. I don't have to say a Scooby-Doo to you. You're just some freaky spozz who likes to poke his beak into other people's business." She planted herself in front of him, "I've only been in your company for a minute and I've had enough of you already. You're a weirdo, Stevens. A nosey-parker. You get some kind of thrill out of sifting through other people's dirty laundry, don't you?" Blunt suddenly made her way back to RE, deliberately barging the detective out of the way. As Inky regained his balance Blunt reached the doorway. She turned to face him, ruddy-cheeked, "The Education Authority's decreed that I'm entitled to receive RE. The Government's decreed that I'm entitled to RE. So if you'll excuse me," she reached for the handle, "I'd like to receive RE!"

Inky, doubting that Amanda Blunt had ever felt quite so passionate about RE in her life, saw his advantage disappearing, "You're aware that I'll be talking to Tommy in about ten minutes?" he blurted.

Amanda Blunt froze.

Silence.

Her failure to carry out her threat indicated that Inky's comment had hit home.

Seconds passed.

"So what?" she muttered quietly.

Inky pressed on, "There are a number of different players in this drama, Amanda. You're one of them, undoubtedly. Tommy Woggle's another. But don't get carried away in thinking that you're the lead. Not yet. At this moment the pair of you are just extras caught up in an elaborate end-of-term pantomime. But I can assure you," his tone sharpened, "that if you choose to exercise your *educational right for RE* at the expense of my request, then I'll be forced to take a much harder line with young-Oggy. Fragile, delicate Tommy. All freckles and curls. You know," he said, drawing out the pathos, "I'm not sure he'll be as resilient as you're pretending to be right now, Amanda. And believe me, I will be hard on Woggle. He's not like you, you see. He'll not snarl like a bulldog. Oh no! Gentle Tommy will sing like a canary in a cage." Inky dropped his voice, "Tommy will tell me everything I need to know. He'll also learn about how obstinate and uncooperative you've been. Disruptive. A pain in the neck. And I'll tell him everything in return. That's how it works, Amanda. A decent question deserves a decent answer. So what's it to be? Are we playing this my way? Or yours? 'Cause it's all the same to me. It's just that the outcome might be very different, for you... and for poor Tommy, of course, if you choose to exercise this supposed right of yours?"

A pause.

Very slowly Blunt's grip on the door handle relaxed, then her arm dropped. Without looking at Inky, she spun on her heels and headed past him down the corridor.

"Not here, Stevens," she uttered, grabbing hold of the detective's coat-sleeve.

Amanda Blunt drew Inky the length of the passage like a naughty child. On reaching the Reflection Room, she flung open the door and bundled him inside.

Blinkton School's Reflection Room was a special area focused on student wellbeing. Because of its unconventional nature the room was unlike any other in school... pure white walls, deep red carpet and different coloured floor lamps to create *ambience*. Cushions scattered across the floor provided seating. The room's only desk was situated up against the far wall. From there, a CD player pumped out relaxing music on a loop.

Dominating the room was a large canvas tent named the Harmony Tent. Inside this, vulnerable students could zip themselves away from the pressures of the world. And it was into the Harmony Tent that Amanda Blunt steered the Great School Detective that Wednesday morning...

"Make this quick," she bellowed, face the colour of a grilled tomato. She zipped the tent up and plonked herself down onto an oversized cushion.

Inside the tent it was dark and spooky. Patches of different coloured light pooled on its canvas walls, creating an otherworldly atmosphere. While Inky struggled to adopt a comfortable position he became aware of the Beatles' song 'Something (in the way she moves)' being played on panpipes in the background.

Attempting to assert himself, he asked, "Are you always this awkward, Amanda?"

"If you don't want to get knocked out it helps to land the first punch."

"So why the change of heart? Why didn't you re-join RE as you threat-ened? What's happened to make you pass up on learning all about the journey of the Magi? Was it possibly," Inky leaned forwards awkwardly, "Thomas Woggle who's brought about this sudden change of heart?"

Blunt's nostrils flared, "I don't want to talk about Oggy. Direct your comments to me and I'll decide whether I'll answer. And I warn you, I am going back to Passaretto's lesson."

"Because you want to?"

"Because I have to. But I warn you, Stevens," Blunt revealed a clenched fist, "one false move and that's it!" She leant back, arms splayed to take her weight.

"Well, seeing as I have your attention, I'll be brief." Inky readjusted himself, ribs still sore from his encounter the previous day, "Let's start again," he said softly, "may I remind you of my original question?"

"By all means. Whether I choose to answer it or not's another matter."

"Last Friday you and Tommy Woggle left Mr Henry's History lesson..."

"Sounds more like a statement than a question."

"... and I need you to tell me what happened next. What's so interesting about Tommy that you were prepared to excuse him from History using a false note?"

Blunt's face softened, "I needed to talk to him, that's all. Urgently. So I took him somewhere. My ground. My terms." Inky noted that Amanda's tone had lightened, "I had something I needed to ask him. Something important," she paused, "to me."

"Where did you take him?"

"Nowhere."

Assertive rather than harsh, Inky asked, "You bundled him into the Senior Girls' Toilet didn't you? Once inside, you crumpled up your note and threw it into the bin..."

"So that's how you...?"

"I'm guessing you pulled Oggy Woggle into the toilets in the same way you've just dragged me in here. Was it against his will?"

"No."

"Do you consider manhandling people acceptable? Are all your relation-ships a physical battle?"

"No!" Blunt shot Inky a stern look. "You don't understand, do you, Stevens? You'll never understand. It's not easy, not for someone like me. When you behave a certain way, for reasons I'll never explain to you, people assume that that's what you're really like. And because that's what people think, you start to behave that way. It's a vicious circle, Stevens. Can't you see? And," she said, folding her arms, "before long you find you've *become* this other person, this stereotype, even though it isn't who you are at all. It's just easier to keep up the facade rather than reveal that, that... inside, you may be quite... quite different." Inky noticed that a small tear had formed in the corner Blunt's eye. She wiped it away as though it had betrayed her. "Alright, Stevens, yes. I dragged Oggy into the Girls' Toilet because I needed to talk to him. He'd been expecting me to confront him. I needed to ask him something that wouldn't wait. Something secret. Away from everyone else."

Inky timed his response carefully, "So, when both of you left Henry's lesson, was there anyone else in the corridor? Is that why you dragged...?"

"That's not the point at all," she interrupted, "getting Tommy alone, somewhere private, was all I cared about. There are ears everywhere in school, you of all people should know that. It could have been anywhere, though. The toilet at the bottom of the corridor just happened to be close at hand so, once I'd discovered Day's maintenance cupboard was locked..."

"Could you have knocked up against the alarm sensor by accident as you passed?"

Blunt's expression told Inky everything he needed to know.

"So," he continued, "did you see anyone else in the corridor?"

"No."

"Are you sure?"

"As Tommy and I disappeared I was dimly aware of the double-doors opening at the far end. Possibly? But then again," she added wearily, "it might've been my imagination. Oggy was my priority at that point in time."

"So what was this thing, Amanda? The thing that it was so important to talk to Tommy about?"

But Blunt's mood had changed. She clambered to her feet, head brushing against the tent's canvas roof. Staring at Inky sitting cross-legged below, her tone was such that it drowned out the sound of panpipes, "Ask Tom yourself. You said that you're going to speak to him anyway. I'm sure he'd love to tell you all about what we discussed. Go on," she threatened, "tell him all about this conversation too. I'm sure you'll both have a good laugh." Her face flushed once again, "I hate it when others judge you. Who isn't entitled to a little happiness, eh? Tell me that, Stevens? All I'll say is that, whatever else happens, Tommy Woggle saved me."

"What?"

"He came back to save me."

"From where, Amanda? Look," said Inky, desperate to keep her talking, "I need to know where you were when the fire alarm went off. Were you were both together...?"

But Blunt had spun around. She yanked up the tent's zipper then disappeared. Then, to Inky's surprise, she suddenly reappeared. Head thrust back through the gap, she stated, "When the fire alarm sounded Tom left me. He had to. But he came back. Tommy Woggle came back, for me. Whatever I have, or don't have. Whatever people think, or don't think, I still have that thought to cling on to... *he came back for me.* If you'd be so kind, tell Tommy I said 'hi, and thank you'."

Amanda Blunt disappeared for good. On leaving the Reflection Room she shut the door so forcefully that 'Take Me Home Country Roads' skipped three tracks up to 'Eidelweiss'.

Inky decided that pursuing her was pointless. Instead he decided to stay inside the Harmony Tent and allow the gentle sound of panpipes to accompany his thoughts. He rued the fact that that many of his questions had lacked direction or been unanswered. Yet Blunt had certainly revealed enough to make him think...

As 'Eidelweiss' segued into 'Careless Whisper' Jacques Asticot drifted into the Inky's mind. The teenage detective wasn't sure how to approach his upcoming meeting with the French upstart, but at least he knew where he'd find him. With Amanda Blunt (presumably) having returned to RE, Inky decided to wait for breaktime. Rearranging the cushions, Inky laced his hands behind his head and laid back to rest. With Blunt's responses still crashing around in his mind, he managed to slow his breathing. Then, in silent contemplation, he sifted through everything that had happened so far. The truth of what had happened the previous Friday was still out of reach, tucked away beyond the fringes of understanding... but he could just about sense the jigsaw pieces slowly locking together.

Just about...

12. The Bike Sheds:
Wednesday 21th December (Morning).

At 11 o'clock the bell rang to signal the start of morning breaktime. For a number of minutes Inky remained inside the Harmony Tent suspended in a trance-like state. He'd found the Reflection Room a much more effective environment to process thought than Mr Bennett's office. He was now more than ready for an encounter with a certain young-Frenchman.

Inky remained in self-enforced isolation a while longer, knowing that Jacques would take a few minutes to reach his destination. He used the gained time to listen in on what the student population had to say. With the tent's zipper fastened up tight, he was able to eavesdrop on discussions taking place only inches away. From the moment the room started to fill up, Inky was immediately reminded of the impact Jacques Asticot was having on Blinkton Comprehensive School. Prissy Townsend and Carla Watts were closest to him...

"I'm going to ask him to the Christmas disco."

"Who?"

"Jacques Asticot."

"Jacques Asticot? You?"

"Yeah, isn't he a dream. A complete dreamboat."

"A dream-*bateau* you mean?"

"That hair, those sunglasses, and those pale, blue eyes. When he looks at me he makes me feel all, all *pphhhwwwwuuuurrr*!"

"All what?" scoffed Townsend.

"All *pphhhwwwwuuuurrr*!"

"That's not even a real word. And he's never even looked at you."

"He has."

"Hasn't."

"He smells nice too. Have you got a whiff of him yet?"

"No. Aren't the French supposed to smell all garlicy?"

"I dunno but he doesn't. He smells all gorgeous, like, like... like the subtle hint of jasmine drifting along a cobble lane."

"Stop showing off, Carla. Just 'cause you're studying *similes* in English.

What's more worrying is that you actually *sniff* Jacques Asticot?"

"It's true. I went up behind him to sniff him. When he wasn't looking."

"Well there's no chance he'd go to the disco with you anyway."

"Why not?"

"Well," said Townsend, disapproving, "not only are you a phantom-sniffer but you're also in the first-year while he's in year-four. He looks even older than that, too. Someone that old's not interested in girls like us..."

"He might be."

"... and you don't even speak French."

"I do."

"Don't."

"Do."

"Go on then..."

"Erm," stuttered Watts, "Paris, Grand Prix, Lacoste... Stella Artois..."

"Stella Artois is Belgian."

"Yes, I know. I was just testing. Erm, Tour de France and Eric Cantona. Told you!"

Inky shook his head in disbelief. Listening further afield, it was apparent that Townsend and Watts weren't the only ones under Asticot's spell...

"I saw Jacques Asticot in the Dining Hall. He ordered a tuna sandwich and a yoghurt. Black-cherry. He looked so gorgeous that I thought I was going to faint. I'm not going to eat anything else but black-cherry yoghurt for the rest of my life."

"I can't wait for the Christmas disco. I can't wait. I just can't wait. I'm so excited, so very excited. I really can't wait!"

"Jacques is stopping at the Harbor Lites Guest House, you know? It's only got 3 stars. Deidre Butterfield, its landlady, is as mad as cat-nip. She's not looking after him properly. She's not been seen nowhere recently. My dad's hotel, the Belvedere, has 4 stars so Asticot should be stopping with us. I'd be more attentive. Much more attentive!"

"In History I learned that Archduke Franz Ferdinand was shot in the Balkans. That must have hurt. I was caught in the Balkans by a football once and had to sit down for half an hour."

"Je suis a un rock star. Je avais un residence. Je habiter la. A la south de France."

"Have you been to see 'Babes in Boots' yet? You simply must see Derek Chambers' Widow Winky. He's amazing."

"Everyone says that Mayor Asticot's really special and that we should treat him nice 'cause he's going to bring in lots of money. Well my mum, disagrees. She runs 'the Age of Aquarium' on Wimple Street. She says that Jean-Pierre Asticot was rude during his tour. Said he was all twitchy and that he smelled a bit too. Didn't even stay to see the seahorse show and that's the best bit!"

"I think I'm going to move to France when I'm older. What really appeals to me is the way they wear their hats."

Inky unzipped the Harmony Tent deep in thought. Silent as snowfall, he left the room in full view of several youngsters busily munching king-size bags of Monster Munch. Yet strangely, no-one saw him leave beneath the subdued lighting. Not fully. To them, Inky was little more than a passing shadow. One moment he was there. The next he was gone, already on his way to confront the French Adonis who'd clearly whipped up quite a storm.

From Mike Bennett's account of the Town Hall meeting, Inky knew exactly where he'd find Jacques Asticot. The bike-sheds were sandwiched between the outside of RE and the Rural Studies garden. It was there, beside a brick-built structure, that Blinkton's smokers congregated every breaktime.

Having left the pleasant warmth of the school building, Inky first decided to study his quarry from afar. Despite the freezing conditions, the area around the bike-sheds was packed full of pasty-faced youths. Cold breath and warm cigarette smoke mingled in the crisp, winter sunshine. Seeing everyone packed so together tightly together, Inky was reminded of Emperor penguins he'd seen on a television documentary. And right at the heart of the cluster was Jacques Asticot.

Confident and aloof. Winter sun reflecting off olive skin.

The young-Frenchman was seated on the backrest of a wooden bench using its seat as his footrest. This position raised him up and also endowed him with a look of casual arrogance.

A King perched on his throne.

Asticot's henchmen were in attendance. Big-Sean Kennedy perched to one side of him. Joe 'Fish-eye' Bradshaw at the other. The rest of his entourage remained at floor level, hopping from foot to foot in an effort to keep warm, clapping their hands together like seals at feeding time.

Inky approached cautiously. As he neared, it became apparent that Jacques was telling some kind of story. Holding court. Smoking. All eyes on him. He delivered his performance with the skill of the music conductor. Cigarette in hand, he embellished his tale with an exaggerated series of actions and gestures. Throughout his rendition Jacques' audience listened intently. Hanging off his every word.

Inky noted that there were as many females as males who'd braved the cold that morning. In response to his tale, Blinkton's schoolboys grinned inanely and cuffed one another manfully. The girls, by contrast, twisted hair through shivering fingers and pouted lips that were forbidden to wear lipstick... but did anyway.

As Inky approached he caught the climax of Jacques' tale...

"And then, you see," said Asticot, his accent adorning his speech with a musical quality, "it all came crashing down around me. The lunch was completely ruined, but as for the afternoon, well," he went on, tossing back glossy hair, "that was only just beginning!"

The males erupted in deep guffaws while the females released high pitched giggles. A volley of comments erupted,

"What did you do then?"

"I don't believe you got away with it."

"Didn't it hurt?"

"You really make me laugh, you do."

"You could get arrested for that in Britain."

"What a guy, what an absolute guy. He is, isn't he everyone? He's an absolute guy!"

As if in acknowledgement, Asticot raised his cigarette theatrically. He then brought it down and received it greedily between full lips. As he inhaled its embers glowed bright. Asticot's elaborate routine climaxed with him releasing of a dense cloud of smoke which curled upwards only to melt in the sharp December sunshine.

"Gauloises," he announced, nodding, "one hundred percent French. No filter. Full flavour. Magnifique!"

Inky couldn't help noticing the only person not captivated by Asticot's commanding performance. Positioned beyond the edge of the congregation, set apart, was Brandon Lunt. Inky imperceptibly slid through the crowd to accompany him.

"Must be difficult," Inky whispered.

"What?" replied Brandon Lunt, startled.

"Being in charge of him. Asticot?"

Lunt's response was uncertain, testy, "It's, it's not so bad. Not really. Not all bad, I mean."

Inky pulled up the collar of his coat, "I see you and he have been drawing quite a lot of attention. There must be, what, at least forty people out here? Must be nice to be so popular?"

"I suppose," replied Lunt, flatly, "but it's Jacques who attracts it all, not me. He's the one at the centre of everything. I'm only recognised 'cause I'm with him. I don't necessarily want to be, I just have to be, that's all. Mr Bennett's put me in charge of him. Thinks I'm a *steadying influence*. Jacques is sharing my timetable. As if Jacques Asticot could learn anything from me."

Inky glanced at his companion, "Come on, Brandon, I'm sure he's learned a lot from you."

Lunt shrugged.

"Surely, it's an opportunity for both of you, eh? A French exchange," Inky dropped his voice, "one that'll be over all too soon, eh?"

"Yeah, thank goodness. I need a rest. I mean," Lunt confided, "Jacques was quite subdued at first, when he arrived. I enjoyed it then, while I felt I was helping him to settle in. But lately he's become more disconcerted, more," he searched for the word, "*unpredictable*. This chaperoning business has become hard work. *He's* become hard work. No, Inky, I want to go back to being anonymous so I can just get on with my work. It's safer that way."

Inky noticed that his companion had started to shiver. Aware that Asticot had launched into another anecdote, the teen detective took the opportunity to lead young-Brandon away from the main group. Backs pressed up against the brickwork of the bike-sheds, Inky began to probe more freely, "I just can't see what all these people find so fascinating about Asticot."

Brandon nodded, teeth chattering.

Inky went on, "I guess that being one of his disciples is not all *Can-Can at the Moulin Rouge*, eh?"

"Something like that."

"How bad is it?"

Lunt, now segregated, became animated, "Well, take now for instance. I'm freezing. I'd prefer to be the Library studying but he," a thumb was extended, "doesn't. I tried to engage him in educational stuff as Mr Bennett suggested and he seemed interested, at first. But these days all Jacques wants to do is give me the slip."

"Get rid of you?" said Inky, knowingly. "So that he can do whatever he wants?"

"I guess so. He knows the rules. He just chooses not to follow them."

"So what does he do?"

"Spends most of his time telling stories," Lunt looked around warily, "to that lot. To Big-Sean and 'Fish-eye'. He likes smoking too. And running his hands through his hair. Playing about with his stupid sunglasses. Running off. I spend all of my time trying to find him. Freezing cold and stinking of cigarettes." He tutted, "No Inky, being in the spotlight's nice for a short while…"

"But not permanently?"

"No," said Lunt, lips blue.

"It must be difficult keeping track of someone like that?"

"Tell me about it."

Inky measured his words carefully, "What about last Friday afternoon?"

"Last Friday afternoon?"

"When the fire alarm went off."

For a moment Brandon Lunt looked unsure, "How did you know?"

"Know what?"

"About Friday."

"I'm not sure that I do. But tell me anyway?"

Lunt exhaled, "Well I suppose Friday's a prime example. I had Woodwork straight after lunch. With Mr Foreshaw in D3. Before this I was in the Dining Hall with Jacques. I sat across from him because he was surrounded by his gang of admirers. Well," he continued, "just before the bell went I made my way over to tell him we needed to go to class. I like to arrive early, you see. There's a lot to do. So I squeezed through everyone and said, 'Time to go.' But it was obvious that Asticot didn't share my eagerness, 'What's with the serious face, Lunty?' he replied. I said, 'We've got Woodwork up in D3.' But Jacques just ran a hand through his hair and said, 'But what if I don't feel like making a stupid bird-table today? Are the police going to come and smack my derriere? Will they come and shoot me? Oh no they won't will they, 'cause they don't carry guns in this country.' Then he laughed, and because he laughed, all his friends laughed too. Then he stood up and, without warning, grabbed me in a head-lock. With his free hand he made the shape of a gun and pressed it into my temple, 'Cause you know, Lunty,' he went on, 'I think bird-tables are for, how you say *birdie-brains*! Now why don't you put a chaussette in it while I go buy a milkshake?' Then he mimed pulling the trigger and making a *bang* sound." Lunt's voice wavered, "For some reason his gaggle of followers found this hysterical."

"What did you do?" asked Inky.

"What could I do? I sat back in my seat and waited for him."

"What did he do?"

"Dunno. But the one thing he didn't do was buy a milkshake. When he didn't come back, I started to look for him but he wasn't in the Dining Hall at all. He'd cleared off. I've no idea where to."

"So you don't know where he was at the start of Lesson 4 last Friday?"

"Not a clue."

"And you searched for him?"

"All over," Brandon blew onto his hands, "the yard, Broker's Arch, the Maths and English corridors. I even sneaked up to Woodwork to see if he was playing a game and had arrived early to fool me. But I couldn't find him anywhere and by then I was late myself. Everyone came charging past in the opposite direction 'cause of the fire alarm. I had to tell Foreshaw that I'd had a nosebleed."

"So you weren't with Jacques when the alarm went off and you don't know where he was either?"

"He wasn't where I've just mentioned, but other than that I haven't a clue. The next time I saw him was when he registered during the snowstorm. As far as I'm concerned," Lunt confessed, "trying to look after Jacques Asticot is all a bit," he made his fingers into the shape of a gun, aimed it at his head, and mimed pulling the trigger.

Then, suddenly, the atmosphere changed.

Horribly.

"LUNTY!"

The cry came slicing through the air like a blade, "Lunty, what are you and your weirdo friend talking about? Are you mimicking me?"

"Erm... erm, no," came a reply, which stuck like a pebble in Lunt's throat.

Yet Asticot had leapt down from his perch. Cigarette in hand, hitching up his trousers, he pushed his way through the throng. In no time he'd arrived at the brick wall, hot with anger. He planted directly himself in front of young-Brandon. Blocking off his escape.

Inky stepped to the side leaving Lunt cornered.

For the moment.

Asticot positioned himself square on, "Well now, Lunty. Call me a little, how do you say, *paranoid*, but for a moment there I thought you might have been talking about me?"

"Erm, no, no I wasn't, Jacques," he mumbled, "honest."

"Sorry Lunty, you're going to have to speak louder than that. For the benefit of those in the cheap seats. You appear to have forgotten the most important French lesson of all, *sit tight and ferme ta bouche*. And that, mon amie, is quite unforgivable."

Asticot gave a final pull on his cigarette and then flicked it into Lunt's chest, tab-end bouncing off in an explosion of sparks. Crushing it beneath his boot, Asticot then leaned forward and blew a lungful of smoke into Lunt's face. When it cleared young-Brandon was obviously upset, "You see, Lunty, you distracted me mid-sentence, meaning that my audience missed out on the end of mon petite histoire. And now they feel short changed. So I feel some sort of encore is needed, don't you?"

Lunt spluttered, "Well, yes, I suppose, that would be..."

"Don't suppose, Lunty, because it's all for your benefit. Trust me." Asticot flung an arm around the youngster's neck, forcefully steering him away from the wall. As he did so the crowd filled in the space behind him. Young-Brandon suddenly found himself at the centre of a heaving circle, "You see, Lunty, *you are the encore*. I want you to bask in my sunshine. For a while, at least. So what I'd like you to do," Asticot removed his arm and stroked the thin layer of stubble at his chin, "now let me think carefully. Yes, that's it. I have a task for you. Quite a simple task, even for you." He pointed, "You see that cigarette-butt, the one I've just squashed onto the ground?"

"Yes."

"Eat it!"

The intake of breath was audible.

Lunt's eyes widened, "What?"

"You're not telling me you don't know what eating is, are you, Lunty?" said Asticot, his accent both charming and sinister.

"Erm, no."

The French teen leaned in so close that Lunt could see his own terror reflected in Asticot's sunglasses, "Why the confusion? We both speak the same language," he laughed. "Now, you heard what I said. Pick up that tab-end and eat it."

To excite the crowd, Asticot circled his victim, arms extended, bellowing, "Who would like to see my good friend Lunty eat what's left of my cigarette?"

The gathering immediately found its voice. While Inky watched on, a sea of spotty faces called out,

"I would!" "Do it!" "Yes!" "Yes indeedy!"

Jacques Asticot cupped a hand to his ear, basking in the role of pantomime villain, "If he's going to do it then he'll need much more encouragement than that. I'll ask you again, do you think Lunty should eat my fag-end?"

This time the crowd's reaction emerged as a savage roar. Individual comments spewed out from the heart of the cacophony...

"Eat it, Lunty!"

"Get it swallowed."

"Shove it in your gob!"

"Suck out all the juice!"

"It'll count as one of your five a day."

"I think," said Asticot theatrically, "that your audience, they say oui. So Lunty, your stage debut awaits. Enjoy the limelight Monsieur Lunt." He gestured, "Now pick up that cig-end."

As Brandon Lunt looked down at the squashed tab, tears formed in the corners of his eyes.

"I'll tell you what, Lunty," said Asticot, "we'll all give you some encouragement. Not for Dutch, but for *French*, courage!"

The bully extended his arms and began to clap. Slowly at first, then he picked up the pace. And once the horde had adopted his rhythm, they clapped without inhibition. Louder and louder. Stiff hands turning red. Faster and faster. Until each clap became indistinct, just a blur of noise. And as the wall of sound adopted an energy of its own, Asticot hooked his thumbs into his belt-loops, overjoyed to hear a two-syllable chant materialise...

"LUN-TEE! LUN-TEE!"

Fast as forest fire, each student passed the chant on to their neighbour until the crowd became as one. A single heaving beast squealing, full-throated. The bike-shed area rang out with the single cry. Loud, clear and incessant...

"LUN-TEE! LUN-TEE! LUN-TEE!"

Brandon Lunt, looking from one pimple-encrusted face to the next, realised that he was trapped. Fear churned inside him like acid. Feeling like a character in his own nightmare, he bent down and levered the rancid tab-end off the ice. Holding it between thumb and forefinger, he saw that it had been reduced to a mixture of ash and soggy tobacco. Casing torn and damp. Brandon Lunt began to gag. Convulsions shook his body until finally, one hand over his mouth, he managed to regain a sense of control. Through a stream of tears he looked across at Asticot.

"LUN-TEE! LUN-TEE! LUN-TEE! LUN-TEE!"

The French teen, with a sudden movement, snatched the cig-end and proceeded to check it like a jeweller might inspect the quality of a diamond, "What's the matter, Lunty?"

Brandon's reply was inaudible.

"Sorry what was that? Your little *aperitif's* a little too dry for your discerning palate? Well let's see what we can do to, how you say... liven things up a bit."

With the cig-butt cupped at the centre of his gloved hand, Asticot snorted, then, in a movement which shook his entire body, *hacked* forwards. The resulting gob of phlegm flew into his palm, covering both fag and glove in saliva.

The crowd went berserk,

"LUN-TEE! LUN-TEE! LUN-TEE! LUN-TEE! LUN-TEE!"

Asticot offered up his hand like a priest at Communion, "There, Lunty. That ought to whet your appetite. Make things a little more palatable. Now... it's snack time!"

Without warning, Asticot's free hand shot out and seized young-Brandon by the back of his head so violently that clumps of hair came free. Yet despite his distress, Lunt offered no retaliation. Asticot easily forced his victim's head down towards his palm. The cigarette-butt drifted up at Lunt through a kaleidoscope of tears. Gripped by terror, the frightened student let out the faintest of shrieks...

The crowd went berserk. With cold air racing through hot lungs they demanded blood.

Yet at that moment events took an unexpected turn.

Inky decided that enough was enough. Brandon Lunt had already suffered too much. It was time to intervene...

The detective, having watched the drama play out from a safe distance, stepped into the centre of the arena. Fast as a whip-crack, he raised his arm. Then, with the flat of his palm extended, he knocked the tab-end out of Asticot's hand sending it tumbling to the ground like a spent bullet case. Before the French-teen could react, the detective's hand had changed direction and clamped down onto Asticot's wrist so tightly that the French-teen winced in pain. Inky then pivoted, a move which allowed him to twist his opponent's arm high up behind his body. Stopping just short of breaking it, Inky then heaved the bully's arm into a half-nelson. With the crowd silent, the eerie *popping* sound that Jacques' shoulder made could be heard echoing off the bike-sheds walls. Asticot shrieked in agony. All thoughts of Brandon Lunt had evaporated. Jacques Asticot's features twisted into an expression of agonised torment.

Brandon Lunt didn't need a second chance. No longer the focus of attention, he melted away through the crowd to seek the protection of the

Reflection Room. Competing against such astounding entertainment, his departure went completely unnoticed...

In full control, Inky renewed his attack. Maintaining his grip, he shoved Asticot forward then, once the young-Frenchman had reached the limit of his trajectory, the detective reeled him back with a sudden *snap* of his arm. Like the upswing of a yoyo, Asticot found himself winding back into the detective's grasp.

Limp and helpless. Sunglasses flying.

To maximise his advantage, Inky suddenly let go of Asticot's arm then clamped his hands onto the sides of the youngster's head, and squeezed.

Hard. Very hard.

Burrowing beneath tufts of glossy hair, Inky established a vice-like grip onto Asticot's ears. He squeezed firmly, nails digging into Asticot's flesh. Anguished, Jacques managed to clamp his hands over Inky's but, wearing gloves, his grip was ineffective. And still the detective continued to squeeze, forcefully pressing the sides of Asticot's skull. A walnut trapped in a nutcracker.

Asticot sank to his knees, teeth clenched against the building pressure. Lacking all dignity, a stream of saliva dribbled from his mouth and his trousers slipped down exposing bright orange underpants.

Inky, having immobilised his foe, loomed over him like the angel of death. By angling Asticot's ears, he was able to manoeuvre his opponent to look up at him. The bully cowered beneath the intensity of Inky's stare. He caught a glimpse of what lurked inside the detective's soul, and what he saw scared him. Immensely. His eyes opened so wide that the full circles of his irises appeared.

Inky then forced his victim to stand by lifting hands which were still locked on to the sides of Asticot's head. Inky's legs were planted firmly onto solid ice whereas Jacques' wobbled unsteadily like those of a marionette. Now nose to nose, the detective spoke in a whisper, the menace behind his words inescapable,

"To victimise one weaker than yourself is the action of a coward, Asticot. You possess many attributes yet to misuse them in this way is unacceptable. Am I making myself clear?"

Inky could feel Jacques' nod beneath his hands.

"Should you ever treat Brandon Lunt, or anyone else, with such contempt, you'll have me to answer to. And I promise you that next time I'll not be nearly as tolerant as I'm being now. I will exact upon you terrors the like of which you have reason be scared. I will hunt you down," he paused, "and I will finish you. There'll be no escape. Vous comprennez dont je parle, n'est-ce pas?"

Asticot's nod was more of a tremble, "Mais, bien sur, je connais, ce que vous voulez dire."

"Bon. Then we understand one another. If you fail me between now and the time you depart these shores you will not escape my vengeance. However far you travel. Do not think you can cheat me and do not think I don't mean what I say. I will use my powers to take you down, then destroy you. Now," he added, "if you want to escape with some dignity I advise you to play along."

Inky opened his hands and Asticot fell to the ground clutching his ears.

"And that fellow students," Inky announced, "concludes this morning's introduction to wrestling. If you'd be so good, a warm round of applause for my accomplice, Monsieur Jacques Asticot!"

Despite the confusion, a ripple of applause emerged, one which Inky encouraged by gesturing towards the collapsed teen and clapping himself.

"Seriously," Inky declared, "I really must thank friend-Jacques for the challenge he threw me. Earlier this week he dared me to catch him off guard. He wanted to know whether the moves of a British wrestler could outdo the guile of the French warrior. And I'm pleased to say, or rather a little ashamed to admit, that on this occasion the ways of our country, helped greatly by Master Lunt's decoy, came up trumps." Inky felt the crowd soften. "Indeed, when I visit Mal-de-Mer, as my good friend Jacques has so kindly invited me to do, I suspect that our rematch at the Alain Bernard Arena, named after famous French boxer, will be quite different matter altogether. Isn't that so, Jacques?"

Asticot, who'd shuffled into a kneeling positon, nodded weakly, circling his shoulder.

"My friends," Inky continued, "it's my pleasure to congratulate the best sport that Blinkton School's ever welcomed, Jacques Asticot!" Inky grasped hold of his opponent's hand and pulled him up onto his feet. "What a sport. Formidable!"

Relieved to accept Inky's version of events, the circle closed in. Big-Sean Kennedy passed Jacques' sunglasses back to his fallen hero. As Asticot accepted them, a spattering of applause rang out once more, this time much louder. Inky then took Asticot's hand and raised it high into the air, gesturing towards him in appreciation. And while the school-bell sounded some-where far off in the distance, the gathering became engulfed by a surge of spontaneous celebration. Friends hugged. Hands were shaken. Backs patted. And, from the centre of the commotion, Inky retreated and shrank away unnoticed. While congratulatory arms were still being slung, Inky was no longer there.

He'd departed in less than a blink.

En-route to C2, Inky reflected on what had just happened. Mind alert, he could feel the pieces of his investigation slot into place. All of a sudden, everything was starting to make sense. And what was emerging was as incredible as it was terrifying...

'The truth had been there all along, it's just that no-one was brave enough to search for it. The bliss of ignorance. At least,' he reasoned, *'after facing Jacques Asticot, an encounter with Tommy Woggle ought to prove more straightforward...'*

13. Stirring the Pot:

Wednesday 21ᵗʰ December (Late-morning).

After leaving Jacques Asticot looking decidedly off-colour, Inky swept onwards to Home Economics. As he journeyed, he wiped his hands onto his trousers to remove a layer of hair gel from his palms. Inky knew that to complete his assignment he didn't actually need to speak to his remaining suspect. A single glance at Tommy Woggle ought to be sufficient...

From knowledge obtained from Bennett's computer, the investigator knew that Oggy had Cookery Period 3 with Miss Pinkerton. Pinkerton had a reputation for running a tight ship, so by the time Inky'd entered the Art Block, her lesson had already begun. He was careful not to compromise himself, discreetly shrinking into an alcove which housed a fire-extinguisher. From there, he had an uninterrupted view into C2 through a rectangular piece of glass set into its door. Inky watched Miss Pinkerton complete her register then instruct her class to don their aprons. Having done so, the excitable third-years scuffed their stools into position ready for the customary demonstration. As they did so, Inky scanned C2 for a certain sandy-haired student, with a kiss-curl at the front...

Marjorie Pinkerton knew that with Christmas so close every lesson was going to be tough. As a result, she tried to make her classes as interesting as possible. That morning she was making fresh pizzas from scratch. To add interest she allowed her class to flavour their creations with home-bought toppings. Though simple enough in theory, Pinkerton knew that her class would struggle to grasp the concept that pizzas actually had to be made, not just removed from cellophane and put in a hot oven for ten minutes. So, while her class gradually settled in readiness, Pinkerton geared herself up for the ordeal to come. Peering over her spectacles, she demanded,

"Eyes this way. Yes everybody. Good. Now that we're all here and reasonably calm, I'll begin. We're going to need the full lesson for our delicious pizza creations so we need a prompt start."

"Do we have to do all this cooking-pizza-stuff, miss?" shouted Geneve Smith. "It's Christmas. Couldn't we make something seasonal? Like Christmas cake. Or a chocolate log?"

"No we can't Geneve."

"Why not?"

"Because, Miss Smith, our esteemed Headmistress has decided that it's pizza on the menu this week, so pizza it is. That's why not!"

"Can't we watch a video instead?" asked Barrington Hall. "'Brycream' Mountjoy's shown all kinds of films this week. Period 2, I watched one about Africa, its geography, wildlife and culture."

Stuart Parkin added, "It was great, just not very Christmassy. There were men bungee jumping off trees with roots tied to their legs!"

"Boring," shouted Rita Harmer, "we played Christmas darts in Economics. It was fantastic. Well, it was fantastic until Barry Heeks accidentally..."

THWACK!

Marjorie Pinkerton slammed her rolling pin down onto a fresh lump of dough causing flour to puff out in all directions. Simon Duringer, a pasty looking boy sitting at the front, caught a faceful of white powder and immediately started coughing. Durringer's over-elaborate *hacks* and *wheezes* added to an already unsettled atmosphere. Heads bobbed and swivelled as everyone craned to find the source of the disturbance.

Nudging. Pointing. Sniggering.

Pinkerton reprimanded sternly, "Durringer, learn to control yourself. Now, that's enough year-three. All eyes on me." Then in a much calmer tone, she added, "If we're to complete our thin-crust masterpieces then we need to get a move on. So less of the prattle and pretend-coughing, and watch me very carefully. Now, firstly, here's how to roll out the perfect pizza-base..."

But Inky Stevens was no longer there. He'd seen everything that he needed to see. Satisfied, he'd eased out of concealment and was already journeying towards English. He knew that Mr Tate's lesson in Room 3 had already started but he'd made allowances for this. The person he was about to intercept would also be late...

* * *

Inky stepped out to greet the injury-prone youngster outside English.

"Inky?" said Carlos Orange, startled. "What's going on?"

"Not here," said the detective, leading Oz by his good arm, "it's time for a little walk."

"Where are we going?"

"Mr Bennett's office."

"Bennett's office!" Orange stopped dead. "Why?"

"Don't worry, he's not there. Come on," he said, coaxing Oz back into movement.

Checking that they weren't seen, Inky unlocked the Deputy-Head's office door knowing in advance that on Wednesdays Bennett would be staffing the school's Intervention Unit. Once inside, Inky re-locked the door and invited Orange to take a seat. Oz refused, voicing his concerns,

"What are we doing here, Inky? Why have you just locked me in Bennett's room? Am I in trouble?"

"Not if you tell me what I need to know. Now sit," he said, this time a command.

Carlos Orange did so, reluctantly. "What's this about?" he said, cradling his injured arm.

"All I need to know is the name of the person who threw the snowball at Miss Birkin last Friday. And you're about to tell me who it was."

"Am I? I didn't do it."

"I know you didn't do it," Inky responded, "but you were there when it happened and you know who did. So I'd like a name."

"But I..."

"Right, let's back up a little," said Inky. "You're not in trouble, Oz. Not yet. But I need a name and I haven't time to waste. Neither do you. You're already late to Mr Tate's lesson. Twelve minutes late to be precise..."

"But I've absolutely no idea what...?"

Inky held up a hand, "Carlos you're a likeable soul and I'd hate all that to change because of some silly stubbornness on your part. From this point on I don't want you to say anything. Just listen. You see," he continued, "I'm about to outline the rather tricky situation you happen to find yourself in..."

Oz shifted uneasily.

"You will then have just two options. The first is that you can continue being awkward, in which case things will very quickly turn sour. Positively hellish. Or, secondly," he said, "to avoid this distress, and there will be distress I can assure you, you could simply say two words to me... the name of the person who injured Miss Birkin. Then," Inky said, rubbing his hands together, "you can be on your way as if this little conversation had never happened. Clear?"

Oz nodded in a manner which suggested that he was clear but would be reluctant to co-operate anyway. As Inky sat down, the youngster sitting opposite started to rub his plaster-cast.

"Then I guess we have an understanding." Inky's tone was business-like,

"Last Friday, during all the chaos caused by the fire alarm, Miss Birkin was hospitalised. And although the attack happened in a secluded part of the school during a storm, the event was witnessed. You witnessed it, Carlos…"

Orange began to pick at the edges of his cast causing tiny white flakes to fall onto Bennett's carpet.

"… and I know this because your footprints are still set into the ice beside Broker's Archway. And how do I know they're yours and not someone else's?"

Orange looked up, then back down again.

"An outsider would think you've had an extraordinary run of bad luck," Inky paused, "but we both know the truth. At the start of term you had a false plaster cast on your leg. You confessed that you weren't really injured to Ross Berry last September, if you recall. But I imagine that hobbling along on crutches suited you fine. After all, it was only a harmless ruse designed to incite pity and enable you to coast through year-four at your own, desperately slow, pace. And that pot on your arm is another example of your *armless* trickery…"

Carlos made to protest, but Inky silenced him with a look, then snapped, "Don't even try, I'm two steps ahead and five times more intelligent. I believe," Inky continued, "that you're going to tell me that your broken arm is a legitimate injury. Well of course it is," he said plainly, "not even you'd try the same stunt twice. And no teacher's going to force you to write with a damaged hand. But," stated Inky, "it's just a shame that you've been a little selective with the truth. Unlike most of the world's population, you're not right-handed. No, Oz, your good arm, the left one, is actually injury free. Yet, strangely, you've chosen to withhold this rather crucial piece of information." Inky shook his head, "I saw you yesterday. Before German. Traditionally," he explained, "people wear their watches on the opposite hand to the one they write with. To protect an expensive item from harm. As, indeed, do you. Your watch isn't on your left wrist right now because that's not where you wear it. You normally wear it on your wrong hand, the right. And as that arm's in plaster, you now keep your watch in your pocket instead. I saw you take it out."

Oz flushed.

"No Carlos," said Inky, suddenly sinister, "you've deliberately manipulated this scenario to your own advantage. Another gift-wrapped opportunity to do as little work as possible and turn up to class perpetually late. When you broke your right arm you must have thought Christmas had come early?"

Oz shrugged his shoulders.

"Returning to my initial point, having a pot on your leg at the start of term meant that your right shoe wore down while your left shoe, the one displaced, remained pristine. Let's have a look shall we?"

Reluctantly, Carlos Orange slid both feet out from under his seat so that the soles of his shoes were exposed.

"There," said Inky, unmoved, "your right shoe is scuffed and worn whereas the left one still has a deep tread. No one else in school has footprints as mismatched as those, the exact ones still stamped all over the crime-scene. Along with Miss Birkin's stilettos and the footprints of the mystery attacker, of course. This, of course, is the person you're just about to reveal to me now. Feel free to check Broker's Archway for yourself. After English. You're a size nine, I believe? Or a ten at a push?"

Oz slid his feet back under his seat.

"It's OK Carlos, don't look so glum," said Inky, showing his palms, "there's no need to worry. Not yet. Your prints identify you as being present over by the Old School area but they don't suggest that you were in any way involved in the assault. Quite the opposite, in fact. They show that you were positioned in between the person who threw the snowball and Miss Birkin. And that you fell over. Probably ducking out of the way, knowing you. Now," said Inky, maintaining rhythm, "I've done my homework on him too, this mystery attacker. He also has size 9 feet and by the style of his shoe I'd guess he's most likely a fourth or fifth-year male. Someone who you're probably very familiar with. How am I doing?"

Orange failed to raise his head from the steadily growing pile of plaster peelings.

"I'll take that as *a yes*. So," Inky went on, "let's focus on this hit and run snowballer. I've reason to believe he's connected to the initials 'C.C.' I'm unsure about the first 'C', but I'm guessing that, at the very least, this boy's surname begins with the letter 'C', yes?"

Again Inky took Orange's silence as confirmation, "That's good, Carlos, we're nearly at the end now. You'll be back in English quicker than you can say *Ding Dong Merrily On High*. So," Inky rose and stood over the troubled fourth-year, "let me remind you of your position." His words emerged calm and clear, "As I've already said... although you didn't hurl the object which injured Miss Birkin you are in a position to tell me who did. You're just caught in the cross-fire, that's all, Carlos. I'd never reveal you as an informer, of course. If it's ever mentioned, we can say that one of the Languages staff saw what happened. Mr Deitz perhaps, your German teacher?" Inky circled

Bennett's desk and sat down in the Deputy's chair. Unable to resist, he swung his feet out and planted them solidly on the desk-top. "As you can see, Oz, I've established quite a productive working relationship with Mr Bennett. He'll also back us up if you co-operate, or prove quite a nuisance if you don't. So Carlos," Inky levelled, "I need a name. Should you choose to be un-coop-erative then your injury-scam will become common knowledge starting with Mr Bennett and ending up... who knows?" Inky's expression was one of mock-concern, "I don't think your teachers will see the funny side of that one, do you, Carlos? A whole term's work to catch up on at once, now that'll take some doing. So," Inky concluded, "I'll leave it up to you, Oz, but if you do intend to reveal the name of the rogue snowballer please hurry as I've a lot of thinking to do and, as usual, you're extremely late."

Carlos Orange, deliberately avoided Inky's stare. "What's... what... will happen to the person who..."

Inky shushed Orange by placing a finger to his lips, "Remember what we agreed, Carlos? Two words only," he said, "that's all. There'll be a price pay for the culprit, of course, there always is. But I may just surprise you. There's a chance his name will never be mentioned. I haven't made up my mind. Not yet. Well, Carlos," said Inky, sliding his boots back onto the floor and making to unlock the office door, "what's it to be...?"

* * *

Peering into Pinkerton's Cookery lesson Inky had initially struggled to locate Tommy Woggle. With the class all facing forwards, all the detective had to go on was the back of thirty unwashed heads. However, after careful scrutiny, he'd finally located who he assumed to be Oggy Woggle. The lad's mop of thick sandy-coloured hair had been the giveaway. The young third-year was seated right at the front of the room in between Annie Turnbull and Debbie McAndrew. Inky'd been able to fashion a perfect view of him, but in terms of his investigation, the back of his head was no good. He needed to see young-Tommy from the front. And quickly.

While he'd deliberated on how to cause enough of a commotion cause the whole class to turn around, fate had come to Inky's rescue. As Miss Pinkerton had begun to speak Geneve Smith led a series of objections and rude comments. In order to quell this disturbance, Marjorie Pinkerton had slammed her rolling-pin down onto her dough mixture. This in turn had sent clouds of flour billowing into the air giving Simon Duringer, sat at the front, the excuse to start coughing like a forty-a-day-smoker. Durninger, purely for devilment, started to gasp for air clutching at his throat. This, in turn, had resulted in several of his classmates joining in the disturbance.

Nudging. Pointing. Sniggering.

And one of these had been Thomas Woggle. While Duringer turned an unhealthy shade of purple, Oggy had turned around, a banana-shaped grin stretching across his freckled face... providing Inky with the all evidence he needed. Even through a grimy window at a distance of several feet, Inky had been able to identify Oggy Woggle. Stick-thin, sandy-haired Oggy. The timid-bird-of-a-boy with a rough sea of a haircut. And as he'd turned around to celebrate Duringer's antics, Inky saw exactly what he'd been expecting... that Oggy's willowy frame bore the marks of a recent altercation. Just one glance was all it took. There, running the length of Tommy's cheek, was a gouge. Faint, yet unmistakable. A single straight line down the left side of his face, slightly raised with bruising either side. The state of Woggle's uniform further supported the idea that he'd been involved in some form of scuffle. His shirt-collar revealed a slight tear. His shirt-pocket had also been ripped, its stitching loose and frayed.

Although Inky'd only glimpsed Oggy briefly, little more than a snapshot, that was all he needed. In that fraction of a second, the investigator knew for definite who'd set off the fire alarm. In that instant his investigation into the school-bell was solved. Everything had slid into place as naturally as ice over a lake in winter.

Several possibilities but, in the end, just one solution.

And even before Miss Pinkerton had regained control of her Cookery class the detective had vanished. Gone to intercept Carlos Orange before English, the sound of leather boots echoing along a deserted corridor...

* * *

Carlos Orange sat inside Mike Bennett's office fidgeting under the intensity of Inky's stare. Everything that the detective had levelled at him had been correct. Oz wondered how Inky could've possibly known so much about what had happened to Miss Birkin, and about him! Feeling uncomfortably hot, he loosened his tie with his *good* hand.

Oz wasn't someone who possessed a natural sense of honour. If there'd been a way to worm out of Inky's request he'd have found it. Yet, after viewing his predicament from many angles, he realised that the two options Inky had presented to him right at the start were the only viable ones...

And, in reality, Oz knew that he had only one.

Carlos Orange undid the top button of his shirt. Finally he rose to his feet and approached the office door. Conscious of avoiding Inky as he left, he mumbled two words almost inaudibly, then departed without looking around.

Alone in Bennett's office, Inky Stevens nodded to himself. Relocking the door, he allowed himself a momentary smile. Another victory. Within 24 hours of Bennett's request he'd managed to ascertain the names of both the snowballer and the alarm wrecker. Yet knowing these things didn't mean that his case was over. Far from it. In reality, Inky knew that his mission was only just beginning.

The Great School Detective settled back into Mike Bennett's chair. He steepled his fingers and began to focus on what lay ahead. The importance of his mission, he realised, had just escalated.

Wildly. Alarmingly.

Should he choose to act on what he'd just uncovered then the path ahead was fraught with danger. And not just restricted to school either. The whole of Blinkton, he realised, was now under threat. Yet, like Carlos Orange before him, although Inky recognised that he had two distinct choices, in reality he knew that he also had only one... The path ahead was strewn with peril, but it was one which he had to face.

That he needed to face.

An image of Peregrine Dukes flashed through his mind. Inky could visualise his History teacher standing at the front of the class announcing,

'In terms of History, significant actions bring about significant changes. Let's just say that an omelette was never made without cracking a few eggs.'

The Great School Detective realised that the time had come... to crack a few eggs!

Inky knew that he couldn't begin to put his startling theory to the test until around seven o'clock that evening. So, making use of Bennett's facilities, he used the remaining time for research. To formulate a strategy and tie-up loose ends.

Inky switched on Bennett's computer and while he waited for it to boot up, he lifted up the telephone. First he dialled the Mayor's office. It took awhile for Carey's secretary, Sandra Choudhury, to persuade her boss to come to the phone. But when he finally deigned to respond Solomon Carey was *all ears*. The subsequent conversation between schoolboy and Lord Mayor lasted a considerable amount of time. It was also one which was to have significant repercussions for Blinkton-on-Sea. And for Mayor Carey himself. What Inky revealed, and what he'd demanded in return, had Solomon Carey fighting for his political existence...

By the time Inky'd finished his call, Bennett's computer had long been up and running. After only a few clicks on the keyboard and just one press of the space-bar, the telephone number he needed, one with a very long prefix, flashed up on the screen. Inky scribbled this down onto a piece of paper then punched it into Bennett's desk-phone. As he waited for an answer, the teenage detective pondered on how dialling tones sounded different throughout Europe,

Finally, a muffled voice said, "Bonjour?"

"Ah, bonjour," came Inky's reply, "Je me demandais si vous pourriez m'aider..."

14. The Harbor Lites Guest House:
Wednesday 21ᵗʰ December (Evening).

Inky suspected that what he'd find at the Harbor Lites guest-house that evening would shock him. Yet he'd no idea just how much ...!

When Mike Bennett unlocked his office that Wednesday afternoon he'd found Inky hunched over his computer. Yet despite Bennett's plea for an update, the detective remained tight-lipped...

"My protocol remains exactly as it was, sir. You'll receive the two names you seek and a full explanation in due course. But for now, with all due respect, I'd like to be left alone."

The senior teacher, after being relieved of a ten pound note which Inky claimed was to cover *potential expenses*, had done as requested. Buoyed by Inky's news, he'd departed in search of some schoolkids to harass, leaving Inky to carry on his groundwork undisturbed...

That evening, the detective was the last person to leave Blinkton School. He let himself out using his personal set of keys knowing there was a possibility that he'd need to return later that night. For now, however, Inky's priority was to be at his destination by seven-thirty, yet he'd planned to arrive well in advance. Just to be on the safe side.

It was time to uncover what had really been going on in Blinkton-on-Sea.

The solstice that year had been bright and cloudless. Pleasant by day, the temperature had nevertheless plummeted significantly by nightfall. By the time Inky passed through the school gates, the cheery winter sunshine had been swallowed up by a sky pricked with stars.

Inky passed Higgison's shop, crossed through the estate, then descended towards the orange glow of the town below. His pace was brisk yet sure-footed, mindful of the frost. He turned up his collar and thrust his hands deep into warm pockets. Looking out at the sea, he watched the crescent moon tracing a silver pathway from horizon to shore. A thin layer of mist hung motionless above the water like a gauze.

Airy and mysterious.

Inky's only company on his journey was a bedraggled mongrel which padded along behind him. Lean and hungry-looking, the mutt scavenged in a variety of waste-bins along the way.

As Inky approached the town-centre the neon flashes and infantile tunes from the amusement-arcades disturbed his sense of tranquillity. A mechanised version of 'O Little Town of Bethlehem' drifted out from the Funshine Arcade, troubling the air with its garishness. Taking in his surroundings, Inky noted that Blinkton was completely deserted. On such a bitter night, those without a ticket for 'Babes in Boots' had clearly decided to take refuge indoors.

As the investigator neared his destination, he took time to pause outside the Codfather Fish and Chip Restaurant. Closed for the holidays, its interior was dark and lifeless. Through dirty glass, the investigator could see the brand new chairs and easy-wipe tables that Frank Parkinson was so proud of. The restaurant's double-doors still harboured evidence of the previous Friday's attack. A wooden board had been nailed over the spot where a rock had shattered its glass. Knowing Blinkton as he did, Inky guessed that the damage wouldn't be repaired until well into the New Year. The Codfather's other door, still intact, sported a poster showing Frank Parkinson dressed (somewhat inappropriately) as a stereotypical Frenchman. Onions around his neck, he was serving Jean-Pierre and Jacques Asticot heaped plates of fish and chips. Inky noted that their portion-sizes were substantially bigger than those he normally dispensed. Above the poster, scrawled in marker pen, was the claim...

'The World Famus Codfather Fish and Chip Restaurant.

Blinktons saviour. Endorsed by world-leeders.'

Inky contemplated which offended him the most... Parkinson's outfit, the unusually large portion sizes, the assertion that the Asticots were world-*leeders*, or the dreadful use of spelling and grammar.

Glancing up Babylon Lane, Inky noted that it was also a quiet night for Blinkton's emergency services. The doors to the Fire Station were closed and all of its engines garaged. The Police Station likewise was devoid of all activity. Just a single light in an upstairs room belied any presence. A small fleet of police-cars with frosted windows were parked up on the pavement giving the station the appearance of a car-sales forecourt.

Inky checked his watch.

Seven-fifteen.

He was early, although if everything had run according to plan, the individuals he was there to check up on ought to have left some time ago.

According to the Gazette, both would be spending their night at the theatre, courtesy of Mayor Carey. Nevertheless, Inky didn't like taking chances. As a precaution, he receded into the shadows and approached the Harbor Lites from the side.

Inky crept the length of Babylon Lane, watching the cottage-style building slowly reveal itself. Dark and still. Now that the mongrel had wandered off in search of richer pastures, the only movement came from the guest-house's misspelled sign which persisted in blinking on and off, informing no-one in particular it possessed three stars. All of its windows were dark with no tell-tale slithers of light seeping out from beneath the curtains.

Inky concealed himself behind the telephone-box on the corner of Babylon Lane and Grimeford Avenue to take stock. All he could hear was a lone car several streets away. Gears crunching, this vehicle was struggling to navigate roads which had not been effectively gritted due to council cutbacks. Inky couldn't help reflecting on the decline of the British seaside industry. Such an absence of life was dreadful for Blinkton... but excellent for his own purpose.

Seven-twenty.

Still early, but the Harbor Lites appeared completely desolate.

'Time to make a move.'

The detective stepped out of concealment... only to recoil in horror. He instantly darted back behind the phone-box in alarm.

Someone was there.

Waiting.

Inky, safe in the shadows, worked on slowing his breathing. Then, clinging on to the blackness, he leaned out the fraction needed to confirm what he he'd seen...

Sure enough, he saw the silhouette of a solitary figure sitting on the seawall outside the Harbor Lites. Directly across the road from its entrance. To Inky, it was no coincidence that someone *just happened* to be positioned outside the Asticots' residence while they enjoyed a night out. He was forced to assume that this person had to be some form of lookout, a very unsuitable one judging by his demeanour.

The mystery figure had made no attempt to conceal himself. Dressed in padded clothing, he fidgeted incessantly. He sat, he paced, he circled, he jumped up and down and then finally coughed and spat out what he'd dredged up straight into the wind. Backlit by the moon, his silhouette was clearly visible and, as luck would have it, Inky had no difficulty in discerning who was. Such an oversized shape could only belong to one person... Big-Sean Kennedy from year-five.

Big-Sean was a lummox of a lad, one of Jacques' henchmen who'd been present during the bike-shed scuffle earlier that day. As big as he was dense, Sean's fearsome appearance belied a manner that could only be described as *powder-puff*.

Inky remained exactly where he was. Watching. Wondering what Big-Sean was doing outside the Harbor Lites on such a desperately cold evening.

Seven twenty-five.

Prolonged observation revealed that Big-Sean was alone. As such, he posed no direct threat to Inky other than the fact that, being situated where he was, he was preventing the detective gaining entry into Ms Butterfield's guest-house.

'If Big-Sean is indeed some kind of lookout, then why's he there? What's inside the Harbor Lites that the Asticots feel is worth guarding?'

Stalemate.

Inky knew that he could prise open a window to the building's rear and enter that way. But he also knew that he needed to inspect the Citroën parked up in front of the guest-house first.

Time continued to slip away.

Seven-thirty.

And still Inky waited, desperately thinking of a means to enter the Harbor Lites undetected. 'Babes in Boots' was due to start. Time was moving on. Time was slipping away.

Big-Sean stood up and stretched. He then cleared his nose crudely by blowing down each nostril in turn. Then he sat back down again.

Seven-thirty-five.

Stumped, Inky was considering how he could create a diversion, or simply chance Daft-Sean not seeing him creeping across the road... when good-fortune came to his rescue.

Inky watched as Big-Sean took a cigarette lighter from his pocket. Removing his gloves, the daft teenager placed a cigarette to his lips and attempted to light it, but all that emerged from his lighter was an erratic spark. Over and over he tried. Each time the result was the same. A weak flash, but no flame. Swearing audibly, Sean tossed the plastic object over the seawall down on to the beach.

From that point, Inky knew that it was only a matter of time. He knew that

Sean's craving for nicotine would outweigh his duty to someone currently settling down into a plush seat for a cosy evening at the theatre.

Seven-forty.

Sure enough, Big-Sean lost the battle over his willpower. Cursing, he loped off in the direction of Wallbank's Newsagents to buy a replacement lighter.

Inky didn't think twice. He was instantly on the move.

The detective had darted out of concealment before Kennedy's sizeable frame had bowled out of view. Inky eased down the right-hand side of Asticot's Citroën and slid his hand under its handle. He tugged up sharply but the driver's door was locked. Frozen solid. Walking around the vehicle Inky tried each door in turn, then the boot, with the same result. The car was locked up tight (and painfully cold to the touch). A thick layer of ice had spidered its way across all the windows so Inky needed to be creative in order to see into the car's interior. Ignoring the cold, he placed the flat of his palm directly onto the driver's window. Moving clockwise in tight circles, Inky's body-heat slowly melted a hole the size of a saucer. Then, reassuring himself that he was still alone, the detective shone his torch through the gap. The car's interior lit up immediately, sickly and white. Raising a hand against the glare, most of what Inky could make out was the garbage left behind after a long car journey... fast-food wrappers, cigarette-butts and a piece of spent chewing-gum stuck onto the dashboard. A map lay unfurled on the back seat and a looped rope lay in the footwell behind the driver's seat. Squinting, Inky could see that this rope rested on top of a car registration-plate. Though partially concealed, he noted that this was a British plate. The characters J-M-6 were clearly visible at the start of its sequence, followed by a C at the end. Nodding to himself, Inky turned off his torch then crunched up the gravel path towards its door. Beneath a bare metal frame, Inky tried the door handle. With Ms Butterfield refusing to lock her premises the door yielded and swung inwards, a fact for which Inky paid silent thanks. For a final time the teenager checked that that Big-Sean hadn't returned, then slipped into the cold darkness...

It was Inky's confrontation with Jacques Asticot that morning which had led him to Ms Butterfield's door, that and his glimpse of Oggy Woggle in Cookery. Suddenly everything floating around inside his mind since I'd first approached him, slotted-together. Solid and unbreakable.

Watertight.

Yet the theory which he'd arrived at the Harbor Lites to test was as shocking as it was dangerous...

That the Asticots were not who they said they were, was obvious. Such a 'supposedly' high profile figure would never conduct international business with such an obnoxious son in tow. Neither would a genuine Mayor drive around in such a battered vehicle. And where was Asticot's army of attendants and advisors? Big-Sean Kennedy was hardly one of the three Musketeers! So it had become obvious to Inky from the onset that the supposedly important foreign visitors were not actually 'important' or 'foreign' at all. Or if they were, they certainly weren't from France. Citroën is undoubtedly a French car manufacturer and Asticot's vehicle displayed a genuine French number plate. But with the steering-wheel positioned on the right, wherever the car was registered, it certainly wasn't France.

Inky used my office that afternoon to check things out with the relevant authorities. The French licensing office informed him that the number-plate on Asticot's vehicle, 1342-BS-13, was, in fact, stolen. It was removed from a Peugeot in Mal-de-Mer on Saturday 10th December (the day before the duo chugged into Blinkton). This meant that vehicle currently parked up in front of the Harbor Lites was doing so illegally.

Suspecting that Jacques Asticot was not French, Inky had then set about proving this. Knowing in advance that Mal-de-Mer didn't have a sports-centre, he simply made one up. The venue he'd mentioned to Jacques was supposedly named after the world-famous boxer, Alain Bernard. Despite Jacques acknowledging this fictitious stadium, Alain Bernard, though French, was no boxer. He was, in fact, a famous swimmer who'd won medals at two different Olympics. If Jacques Asticot really was French then he'd certainly have known this. Also the 'French' teen's accent and vocabulary, though impressive, were also suspect. His responses were muddled. 'Je connais' used instead of 'je sais'. 'Ma' petite histoire instead of 'mon'.

Tiny, tiny errors.

Miniscule.

But errors which would not have happened if the teenage bully really was who he claimed that he was. So the Great School Detective found himself asking...

'If the Asticots are not who they say they are (and they clearly aren't) then just who are they? What's their real interest in Blinkton-on-Sea? What are they after?'

Questions which had led him to the door of the Harbor Lites guest-house...

Inky had a theory, of course, which, if proved, would shake the sandy foundations of the sleepy seaside town. But in order to find evidence to support this he had to go on the offensive.

Take his bucket and spade and do some digging.

From reading the Gazette, Inky knew that the imposters would be watching 'Babes in Boots' that evening as the guests of Mayor Carey. With that in mind, Inky had used my desk-phone to contact Solomon Carey directly. Once Carey'd been persuaded that the call was genuine, he'd suddenly found himself incredibly attentive. If what 'Inky' revealed was true then Carey's political future was at stake. In all innocence, Blinkton's Mayor had welcomed a disease into town which threatened its very existence. Inky, revealing only what he thought relevant, instructed Carey to keep the Asticots occupied for as long as possible at St Hilda's church hall to enable him to conduct vital research. Carey was instructed not to let the Asticots leave the pantomime early under any circumstances...

Inky went about his business cautiously, mindful that Deidre Butterfield had not been seen out and about around town recently. Peering into the cold blackness of the hotel's reception, he called out,

"Hello?"

Hearing nothing but a faint echo, he tried a little louder,

"Hello?"

Nothing.

He shouted a final time,

"Hello, is anyone there?" But his words were swallowed up by the freezing darkness. The building appeared deserted and a smell of decay hung in the air...

Along with a heavy sense of foreboding.

Inky switched on his torch and tip-toed into the lounge. As his beam of light shot across the room a pair of eyes stared up at him from floor-level.

Sharp and focused. Black.

The creature's mouth was twisted into a fearsome snarl yet for all the leopard's ferocity, Deidre's rug was nothing more than that. Just a harmless floor-mat. Lifeless and long dead.

The detective made his way over to the fireplace by torchlight. Ignoring the leopard's fixed gaze, he placed his hand up against the fireguard. It was cold to the touch with a tell-tale mound of ash piled high in the grate. It hadn't been lit for some time.

Moving on, a search of the ground floor revealed no conclusive signs of a recent presence... just a half-finished drink standing on a table top in the bar area, the liquid stale and cloudy with a thin film across its surface.

The sea-creatures ensnared in the netting in the dining room sprang to life by the light of Inky's torch. Yet once he'd moved on they shrank back to their decorative positions.

Fish out of water.

* * *

At St Hilda's Church Hall the curtain rose to a round of applause. Derek Chambers, framed in the spotlight, stepped gracefully towards the audience. As 'Widow Winky' the long-distance lorry driver was dressed in knee-high boots with stiletto heels. His pink dress had puffed sleeves and a sequinned heart emblazoned across its front. His outfit was completed with a lavish pink wig in 'Marge Simpson' style. As Chambers raised a microphone to lips daubed with lipstick, his tattooed forearm was clearly visible. Hairy and muscular.

"Ladies and gentlemen," growled hardened smoker, Derek, "I'd like to welcome you to Fairyland. I'm about to take you on a magical journey accompanied by a bevy of beautiful babes. Only these babes will not be what you're expecting..."

The audience drew breath.

"... because these babes, will be wearing boots!"

A gasp.

"Oh, no, they, won't," yelled a heckler, full of Christmas cheer.

"Oh, yes, they, will," replied Chambers.

"Oh, no, they, won't!"

"Look pal," said Chambers, raising a fist, "I'm telling you that they will. And if you're going to continue to interrupt, I'll personally come down and give you a taste of fairy-dust!"

Silence.

"Right, we appear to have an understanding." In character once more, Chambers added, "Where was I? Oh yes... it's time, boys and girls, for our first glimpse of those babes in their boots!"

On cue, the chorus emerged dancing the can-can, both males and females dressed in tap-shoes and nappies.

Jean-Pierre Asticot, seated on the front row, leaned over to tap his son on the knee. Jacques raised his sunglasses in response,

"Come on, son," said the *Frenchman*, "it's time to go."

With a nod, both began to rise.

Solomon Carey was seated beside them, "What's going on?"

"Pardon Monsieur Carry," said Asticot, "but I'm feeling a little unwell. I think I need to have a little lie down. Back home. I'm not sure all of this... this..." he struggled to find the correct word, then gave up, "is for me."

Carey spluttered, "But it's the can-can. I'm sure it was put in the show for your benefit. Like at the Moulin Rouge? Paris? Give the panto a chance. It's received excellent reviews."

"I'm flattered by your insistence but if I don't have un peu de repos I won't be fit to visit the lighthouse tomorrow. I think my malaise must be something to do with the pie I ate at the railway station. The whole meal smelled of diesel."

"But you can't go," insisted Carey, "I've paid for your ticket."

Yet *the French delegation* shuffled to their feet nevertheless.

"No!" said Carey, seizing hold of *Asticot's* jacket and sparking off a chorus of *shushes*.

Asticot glowered, "Remove your grubby paw from my Parisienne tailoring right now, Carry. Unless you want to cause an international incident?"

Solomon Carey withdrew his hand.

"Good. I'll bid you adieu. If I'm feeling well enough, I may see you a demain. Compris?"

Carey battled on, "But what... what about Ms Butterfield?"

"What about her?"

"Well, I don't know. Look, how about I take you for a meal instead? A good one. Right now? Let's give Deidre a break, eh? Perhaps I could...?"

"Ms Butterfield is fine where she is. And I think we're capable of making our own decisions don't you, Carry?" *Asticot's* bloodshot eyes widened, "Well...?"

Solomon Carey looked away, "Yes, yes of course. I suppose... I suppose I'll see you tomorrow then. Bright and early?"

"Not too early, we don't start 'til ten." *Asticot* turned to his son, "Come on, Jacques, let's go."

"Of course, papa."

"What about a lift?" suggested Carey, "I could call a...?"

But his guests had already departed.

Solomon Carey cursed under his breath. He'd failed *Bennett's* phone request. He knew that if what *the Deputy-Head* had told him was true, then it was only a matter of time before his political house of cards came crashing down. Could he trust *Bennett* to put things right? Did he have any other choice? A knot formed in the pit of his stomach. Instinctively, he reached for an antacid, praying that his failure to detain *the Asticots* would not prove fatal. As he sank back into his chair, 'Widow Winky' turned around onstage, bent over, then hitched up his/her skirt to reveal a pair of stripy bloomers. To Carey's horror he noticed that a French flag had been stitched across Derek Chambers' backside.

The French delegation were unconcerned by the disturbance they'd caused. They left the church hall by a side door. Noisily. In the crisp air outside, *Asticot* looked across to the spire of St Hilda's Church in the distance. "Come on, Jack," he sighed. "We've quite a walk ahead, but business back home has to be our priority right now. Not some tattooed bloke mincing about in a frock. And," he continued, "I don't trust that kid you chose to be a lookout. Why did you do that without asking me? It wasn't part of our arrangement. What's his name, anyway?"

"Big-Sean."

"Looked like a Big-Nothing to me."

"He's just some daft kid who wants to impress me."

"But Big-Sean could turn out to be a big liability. We should've kept this between ourselves. The last thing we need is some numbskull kid finding out what's inside Room 13."

"We'll be gone long before then. Sean's just guarding our assets from unwelcome visitors. From the outside. He won't go into the Harbor Lites. He daren't," *Jacques* bragged, "'cause I told him not to. We'll have forgotten all about daft Sean by next week."

"You'd better be right, Jack. My patience with this shabby town is wearing painfully thin."

Sunglasses on, Jack wound his scarf around himself, hitched up his trousers, then followed his father down the ice-covered avenue. They passed St Hilda's Church then pressed on towards the harbour.

Back at the theatre, Solomon Carey found it impossible to concentrate on the show. As a chorus of adult-babies paraded across stage wearing loincloths a small bead of sweat trickled down his back.

* * *

Inky, having assured himself that there was nothing of interest on the ground floor of the Harbor Lites, made his way up through the guest-house. Slow and meticulous. Leaving nothing to chance. Floor by floor, room by room, every part of Deidre's premises was inspected. And each time the result was the same...

Nothing.

Nothing but the disconcerting sight of rooms set up to accommodate *the ghosts of tourists yet to come*. Guests who, as yet, did not exist. Each room's wardrobe was empty except for a collection of padded coat-hangers meticulously arranged in the same direction. Deidre had personally made every bed, arranged every towel and pointed the end of every toilet roll, her attention to detail driven by both aesthetic and financial considerations. Inky checked inside every drawer, under every bed and behind every shower curtain, but the result was always the same.

Nothing.

Nothing but the smell of stale pot-pourri.

Torch leading the way, Inky trudged the cold blackness of the premises until all that remained was the penthouse suite right at the top. From reading the Gazette, the detective understood this to be *the Asticots'* base. He knew all along that if a discovery was to be made, then Room 13 was where he'd make it.

Feet planted squarely onto thick carpet, Inky progressed upwards. One step at a time.

Slow and steady.

The final flight of stairs doubled back on itself yet as Inky swung his flashlight around, he saw nothing unusual up above. Just a plain white door the same as every other throughout the guest-house. He trained his flashlight on the number '13' at its centre, watching the circle of light contract as he slowly made his way towards it.

At the top, Inky switched off his torch and reached out for the handle. Cold to the touch, he turned it slowly and felt the door yield with the faintest of *clicks*. He pushed against it gently, holding his breath as the door swung open.

Inky peered into the silent blackness of an empty room, his nostrils immediately assaulted by the smell of rotten food and stale nicotine. Through the gloom he could recognise various furniture items by their silhouettes. Content that nothing posed an immediate threat, he stepped into the lifeless space and lit his torch... to be confronted by an alarming scene of devastation. The room had been wrecked. Completely trashed. Wallpaper ripped. Carpet torn. Armchairs upended. An ashtray had been emptied out and its cigarette-butts strewn across the floor. A suit jacket and trousers had been tossed over the back of the sofa while an assortment of ties were clumped together on the hearth like a tangle of used bandages. Cushions competed for floor-space with dirty socks, unseemly underwear and fast-food cartons. Uneaten pizza crusts lay on the sofa like fossilised slugs. A variety of decaying foodstuffs stained the carpet... mouldy bread, furry sausages and what looked like the remains of eggs and bacon.

All festering. All rotten.

The detective stepped over the devastation towards the balcony doors trying to work out why *the Asticots* were living in such squalor. Through iced glass, the roof-terrace outside looked bare and uninviting. Frozen.

And that was when he heard it...

Scrape.

Inky held his breath and remained deathly still.

Concentrating. Listening.

Very slowly, he turned to face where the sound had originated...

Scrape.

Listening intently, Inky focused on the bedroom door to his left. Checking that no light was seeping out from underneath, he brought his torch to bear on the door. At first glance it looked no different to any other within the guest-house... white paint, wooden panelling, brass handle. A single key protruding from the lock.

Inky slowly reached down and removed a poker from the rack beside the fire. He clutched hold of it firmly, assessing its weight. He then crept the remaining paces towards the door.

Stooping, he placed an ear against its surface...

Silence.

Then the noise came again, longer, more irregular...

Scrape. Scrape. Whimper...

Inky placed a hand onto the door handle simultaneously raising the poker aloft. Keeping the door pulled towards him, he slowly turned the handle, then ever so delicately pushed forwards...

Nothing.

It was locked.

Scrape. Mmmpf. Scrape. Mmmpf.

Wary of losing his advantage, Inky acted on instinct. In a single move-ment he unlocked the door, kicked it open then surged into the room, torch angled to dazzle anyone lurking inside...

Silence.

What he saw framed in the circle of his torch-beam was far more alarming than anything he could have predicted...

* * *

Jacques and Jean-Pierre Asticot finally reached the harbour. Tired and cold.

"How much further?" complained Jack, swerving around a concrete mooring bollard.

"Don't slip," warned his father. "The last thing I want is you holed up in Blinkton General. I was shown around there last week and it was dreadful. Plus," he added, "we can't afford to attract publicity. Not yet. And take those stupid sunglasses off. No-one's impressed, you know?"

"My mates are at school."

"My mates are at school," mimicked *Asticot*. "If Big-Sean's anything to go by I'll choose to remain unimpressed. I tell you one thing, Jack, if you're intent on making it in this line of work, you'll have to toughen up."

"I wouldn't have to toughen up if you'd let Carry book us a taxi. 'Cause then I wouldn't be freezing my..."

Asticot whirled around, gripped by rage. He roughly pulled *Jacques* towards him by his scarf, then clamped pudgy hands around his throat, "Look," he said backing his son towards the water's edge, "this isn't some kind of holiday that you can just invite your mates on. This is real, Jackie-boy. Things aren't going according to plan, admittedly, but in our line of work they never do."

"That's not my fault," wheezed Jack. "I did everything that I was expected to do. I did *my bit.*"

"No, you didn't do your bit. You have not done your bit!" Demonic, *Asticot* held Jack over the water's edge, "Your bit isn't finished until I say so. 'Til we're in that car and out of this God-forsaken town with what we came for. Understand?"

Jack could sense the freezing seawater slapping against the harbour wall below him. In terror, he shrieked, "Of course I understand."

"You don't sound convinced," yelled *Asticot*, "I repeat, do you understand?"

"Dad, I've said I understand. Yes. I *do* understand," he stressed. "I've always understood. Let me go. You're beginning to scare me. Let go!"

Asticot's anger subsided. Gradually he pulled his son back towards him, fists relaxing, "Then make sure you do exactly what I say. If we're going to get what we want you know that things are going to have to get nasty from now on."

"Yes."

"Good."

With a grunt, *Asticot* hauled his son away from the harbour edge and swung him down onto the frozen cobbles. As Jack hit the stones his sunglasses came free and skittered across the ground. The teenager watched in horror as they disappeared over the side. Moments later there was a faint *plop*.

The young man looked up in contempt.

"Don't even think about it," *Asticot* challenged, "I want no more whining. We're in Blinkton to do a job, not traipse around in some kind of fashion show. You can buy another pair when the money starts to roll in. And a new belt too. Right now its events back at the Harbor Lites which need our attention. So get up, pull yourself together and let's get home. My patience has all but run out."

Jean-Pierre Asticot set off along the deserted Promenade without looking back.

* * *

Inky's eyes widened.

Two figures sitting back-to-back were trapped within the circle of his torch-beam. Lengths of grey insulating-tape had been used to bind them to their seats. Legs taped on to the chair's legs, their arms had also been tied at the wrist then tucked behind them. The tape which restrained them had been expertly applied. Tight and secure. A final short strip had been stretched across their mouths to silence them meaning that all the pair could manage were terrified grunts and whimpers. Although both prisoners strained against their bindings, their resistance was half-hearted. More for show than with any real hope of escape. All they could do was blink into the torchlight and await what fate had in store...

Inky looked down in sympathy. The woman looked frail and drawn, her skin stretched tightly over old bones. By contrast, the man behind her retained a sense of dignity despite his predicament. He was wearing a fawn suit and white shirt. His hair had been dyed an unlikely shade of black then swept back into a ponytail which hung down over his collar like a piece of old rope.

The teen-detective remained motionless for several moments, torch in one hand, poker raised in the other. Finally, he relaxed, "Don't worry," he said, reassuringly, "I'm not here to hurt you. I'm here to help, if I can."

The detective unhooked his backpack and set it down. Having located a light switch, he ensured that the bedroom's curtains were closed before switching it on. Then, instead of attending to the prisoners, Inky completed a full search of the apartment. Poker in hand, his hunt revealed no further surprises. Satisfied, he returned to the individuals back in their bedroom cell. As he approached, the pair looked up uncertainly.

"I'm sorry for your plight," said Inky, setting the poker down. "My name is Inky Stevens. I'm here to help, but, sadly, not to untie you. Not yet. I need to explain everything first. Then we need to plan ahead, together. As time's not on our side, I need you to listen to me very carefully..."

The bedroom they found themselves in resembled a bedroom no longer. It had been re-fashioned into a makeshift prison-cell. The double-bed had been upended and stripped of its bedding. Its mattress was propped up against a side wall. Scattered across the carpet were an assortment of DIY tools... a spanner, nails, a chisel, wrench and, strangely, a blowtorch. Under the window lay a discarded golf-club, a five iron. The carpet was peeled back in the far corner and its floorboards exposed. Burn-marks revealed where cigarettes had been stubbed out onto the bedroom walls and the flooring. A full length mirror had been overturned, its glass smashed then strewn across the room.

To Inky, the willowy frame of Deidre Butterfield was instantly recognisable. Her hair was dishevelled and her clothes in disarray. From his research, he also recognised the smart, middle-aged man she'd been tethered to.

When Inky spoke his tone was level, "Although it may not appear so now, I can assure you that I have everything under control. I'm not here to harm you. I'm here to end your distress. But in order to do so, and ensure justice, I need your co-operation. I'll provide a means of escape for you in the hope that you'll agree to what I'm about to propose. I guarantee that if you follow my instructions you'll come to no further harm and that those who've caused your suffering will be punished." Inky elicited eye-contact, "Do you understand?"

Both figures nodded, mesmerised by the striking young-man towering above them.

He added, "I'm about to peel back the tape covering your mouths. Do not panic and do not, under any circumstances, make unnecessary noise.

I have reason to believe that your captors have placed a lookout outside. If this watchman suspects foul play then it's Game Over for all of us. We've only a small window of opportunity to lay our trap before your captors return."

In the ensuing silence, Inky picked at the edges of the masking-tape. He first peeled back the tape stretched over Deidre's mouth, mindful of leaving a slither still attached. Where it had been glued, the pensioner's skin was sore and angry-looking.

Mouth now free, Deidre gulped in stale air, "Thank goodness you're here Mr...?"

"Inky Stevens ma'am."

"Stevens, yes," she rasped, "you don't know... you don't know... how scared I've been." With her head she indicated the man behind her, "How scared we've both been. I don't know who you are but you must, must help us. These men they mean, they mean..."

"To do you harm," said Inky, "yes I know."

"They want, they want... information. But we don't have it. Neither of us. I keep telling them that we don't know the answer to their questions. But the more we protest, the angrier they become." The man behind Deidre nodded. "They keep threatening us. Threatening to hit us with... with that golf-club lying there. Or burn us with cigarettes, or... or even to use that blowtorch. Please forgive me, Stevens, but... but I have to confess that I'm very afraid..."

Deidre's head sank onto her chest and she began to shake. Tears trickled down her wrinkled cheeks like dew on an apple. Gone was the dignified pensioner so highly thought of around Blinkton.

Deidre Butterfield was beaten.

Inky removed a handkerchief and gently dabbed the sides of Deidre's face. He then crouched down to look her in the eye, "Listen carefully, miss. Now's not the time for weakness. If you can hold out for one more day all of this will be over. Can you try? For me? And for Blinkton? To show everyone that no-one's capable of beating Deidre Butterfield. Not now. Not ever."

"You know who I am?"

"Everyone knows you, miss. You represent Blinkton's heartbeat."

She returned Inky's look, "In that case, Stevens... for you, I'll try."

"Good," said the detective, firmly. "Forgive me," he added, circling towards Deidre's companion. "Unless I'm mistaken, sir," he said, freeing the gentleman's mouth, "you must be Jean-Pierre Asticot. The *real* Jean-Pierre Asticot, Mayor of Mal-de-Mer."

Ungagged, the man exercised his jaw as though chewing gum, "Oui, d'accord. Yes of course."

"Your office is worried about you, sir. Back in France. I spoke with your secretary on the telephone earlier. You've been missing almost two weeks. A lot of people are concerned for your welfare, monsieur. I assured them that you'd be home as soon as I'd found you." Inky checked himself, "My apologies, sir. Do you understand English? Parlez-vous Anglais?"

"Mais oui, naturellement," stuttered Asticot, "but not always perfect. I know enough to get by."

"That's all we'll need, sir."

The Mayor added, "This man and the horrible boy, they seized me and drove me all the way here in the boot of their car."

"I know, monsieur, and if time allows I'll explain why, and what all this," he gestured at the room, "is about."

Inky, suddenly distracted, switched off the main light and moved over to the window. Parting the curtains, he gazed down at the Promenade noting that Big-Sean had returned. The lummox's cigarette glowed bright every time he took a drag.

Satisfied, Inky closed the curtains, switched the light back on and returned to the tethered pair, "Hear me out. You have a choice, of course, but as our lookout out there could blow our cover sky high I'm hoping to use you as bait in an elaborate trap... one designed to catch two fat rats."

"We're not going anywhere," said genuine-Asticot, ignorant of the humour in his reply.

"The final decision will be yours, of course, only, if the kidnappers take flight there's a chance they could evade justice altogether. They could simply vanish into the deep midwinter, taking a significant piece of Blinkton's history with them. If that happens," said Inky, "then our town could face ruin. I'm assuming that the document your abductors stole has not yet given up its secret?"

Deidre nodded, "How did you know?"

"If your kidnappers had achieved their objective, they'd have left Blinkton last Friday when they took it."

Deidre's optimism started to return, "Everything's beginning to make sense now. Everything our captors do revolves around what's written on that piece of paper. *Asticot* keeps it in his jacket pocket. He talks of nothing else." She tilted her head, "We're in this mess right now because we can't tell him what it means. And we can't do that because... we don't know what it means either."

Inky continued, "Don't worry, miss, monsieur. Things will get better from now on. I'm here."

Asticot's shoulders relaxed, "Young man, you may just be le miracle we've prayed for. Tell us what we have to do, s'il vous plait."

"I'll try," said Inky, "but be mindful that I need time to collect enough evidence to send your abductors down. If you choose to co-operate, I promise that neither of you will come to harm. And I can say this because," he said, plainly, "we're going to give them exactly what they want and," he paused, "an awful lot more besides!"

Inky stooped to remove a penknife from his rucksack. He approached Asticot, "As a show of good faith, I'm providing a means of escape for you, sir. This knife," he said unfolding its blade, "is razor sharp."

Inky reached behind the genuine Mayor and, with great care, pulled the vent of Asticot's jacket to one side. He then tucked the weapon into the Frenchman's belt within easy reach of tethered hands.

Smoothing the jacket back down, Inky added, "My knife's now available to you. You can cut your restraints at any time you choose, but," he stressed, "I'd be grateful if you'd hear me out first."

"Tell us who these savages really are," demanded Deidre.

Asticot added, "And why they're bullying us."

"Monsieur et madame," said Inky, "I don't know their true identities. Not yet. That's one of the reasons I'm begging your co-operation. But I'm close to finding out. Very close. You must've realised that this man is pretending to be you, sir? Impersonating you."

Asticot was not surprised, "Of course, the similarity between us is inescapable." He added wryly, "Although I do not have a son, nor some silly coloured tooth at the front of my mouth. See?" He opened his mouth in explanation.

Deidre went on, "Both of them dressed the same. Same general appearance. It's spooky."

"Pourquoi?" asked Asticot "Why has he done this?"

"As time's precious," the super-sleuth stated, "I'll hurry. Then you must fill in the blanks for me." He sat cross-legged at the feet of the hostages. "Sir, you were kidnapped on the morning of Sunday 11th December. In your home town, Mal-de-Mer…"

"Oui. They hit me over the head outside my house, tied me up and, how you say, *bundled me into their car.*"

"I saw the rope they used in the back of their Citroën. And yet," Inky continued, "this was no random attack. It was your status as the Lord Mayor of Blinkton's twin-town that they were after. You see, by pretending to be on important Mayoral business, the imposters duped Mayor Carey, our own Mayor. Having fooled him, they then wormed their way right into the heart of our community. Carey was more concerned with *political standing* than checking out their story."

Deidre sneered, "Politicians, eh? Carey's just a maggot! At the Town Hall meeting he couldn't have fawned over the imposters any more if he'd tried. Just trying to win votes. Pathetic little weasel!"

Inky continued, "My Deputy-Head described everything that happened at that meeting to me. And because these fakers arranged to stay here at such short notice, they were able to catch everyone off guard. Just as they intended. Carey was just hypnotised by thoughts of re-election." Inky went on, "I spoke to him myself today, pretending to be Mr Bennett, my school's Deputy-Head. I explained the gist of *the Asticots'* corruption over the phone. To say he was horrified would be an understatement."

Genuine Asticot interrupted, "So he should be. He's completely ignored standard procedure."

"Undoubtedly," agreed Inky, raising a hand, "but I've given him a chance to make amends. At this very moment he'll be with them watching 'Babes in Boots' at St Hilda's Church Hall. That gives us plenty of time to plan our retaliation. Carey might still emerge from this fiasco with some dignity..."

"Huh!"

"But I've instructed him not to interfere. He's largely to blame for this mess and knows that trusting me, or rather Mike Bennett as he thinks I am, is his only way out."

"Mais pourquoi?" asked Asticot. "What's so important in Blinkton-on-Sea to justify kidnapping, impersonation and, how you call it, *subterfuge*? What is this document they keep questioning us about?"

"This whole scheme," said Inky leaning forwards, serious, "all this plotting, this violence and pretence, was designed to enable them to get their hands on the only item of value which Blinkton possesses..."

Deidre's face lit-up, "Of course," she said, "How could I have been so stupid? It's obvious. The document that's at the heart of all this, the one that these impersonators now have in their possession is..."

Inky and Deidre spoke in unison, "the Codfather's secret recipe!"

"Fish batter!" exclaimed Inky, rising, "that's what all this deception has been about. Pretend-Asticot's scheme was carefully devised to deprive Frank Parkinson of his great-grandfather's world-famous formula!?"

"Zut-alors!"

"*Jean-Pierre* stole it from the Codfather Fish and Chip Restaurant last Friday as part of an elaborate scheme. The Gazette reported the damage inflicted onto the restaurant's door yet, fooled by *Asticot's* elaborate smoke-screen, failed to recognise its significance." Inky placed a hand onto Jean-Pierre's shoulder, "And your kidnapping, monsieur, marked the start of their filthy scheme."

"C'est terrible!"

Inky continued, "Fast-tracked into Blinkton's elite, *the Asticots* found themselves in an ideal position to pinpoint the ultimate moment to stab us in the back."

Deidre's jaw clenched.

"They felt that the unrest caused by last Friday's blizzard would be the optimum time to strike. It was then that *Jacques*, having familiarised himself with Blinkton School's layout, set their plan in motion... at precisely ten minutes past one, just after lessons and an important Maths exam had begun. Everyone in school had somewhere to be at that point and the corridor he targeted ought to have been empty. It wasn't, of course. Not completely. But that explanation will have to wait 'til another time." Inky went on, "*Jacques*, being a visitor, was not on the school's official register thus free to operate undetected."

Deidre and Asticot listened to Inky in astonishment, "I know that it was *Jacques* who smashed the sensor because I found a tiny fragment from his glove snagged inside its casing. This tiny remnant matched the indentation I felt when I made a point of shaking his hand this morning. In that single moment, everything fell into place. Besides," he added, "it had to have been him who set it off. I was able to eliminate every other suspect one by one. But again, that account will also have to wait. What I can assure you of, however, is that the school's alarm was deliberately set off at that time. The diversion this caused created a smokescreen for *daddy* to undertake what the pair had really come to Blinkton for."

Responding to a disturbance outside, Inky once again pulled up short. Stock still, he gazed down from the bedroom window. Hearing nothing but Sean's over exaggerated coughs coupled with what sounded like a bout of extreme flatulence, he re-shut the curtains and turned his attention back to the two adults, "Last Friday *Jean-Pierre* cut short his visit to 'the Age of Aquarium' and waited back here for the storm to hit. In both senses. The disturbance up at school was *Asticot's* cue to start *Phase 2*. After watching

Blinkton's fire-brigade race up to school to put out an imaginary fire, he ensured that they were joined, minutes after, by the police. He did this by phoning them up from the public telephone box on the street-corner just outside. He probably invented a cock-and-bull account of *some pressing emergency* or other up at school. No-one in Blinkton would have recognised *Asticot's* real voice and the call couldn't be traced from that box. So," said Inky, "all he had to do was sit tight and watch the boys and girls in blue join in the wild goose chase up the hill. Lights flashing and sirens wailing. Everyone headed towards the commotion his son had intentionally caused."

"Quelle folie!"

Inky added, "The ambulance service zooming up there to attend to an injured teacher was an unexpected bonus."

Asticot shook his head, "Quite a circus."

"Indeed," said Inky, wryly. "I was there myself. It was chaos. The alarm. The snow. Friday afternoon... and schoolkids. Bedlam! And," he added, "all orchestrated by *Jean-Pierre* from just outside this room. You see, this location," Inky stated, "is at the heart of a small area covering your guest-house, the police and fire stations, a phone box and, most importantly, the Codfather Fish and Chip Restaurant."

Deidre Butterfield released a pained groan, "Oh, I see it all so clearly now. What fools we've been. All *Asticot* had to do was wait for the emergency services to rush off, then just stroll over to the Codfather unchallenged. No police. No fire service. All gone. It was too easy."

"With the blizzard providing cover too," Inky confirmed. "So while Blinkton took refuge, *Asticot* was able to throw a rock through the Codfather's door and slip inside unseen. And he was able to do this just after midday on a Friday because..."

"... he knew in advance that it had closed for Christmas the day before."

"Exactly, miss, a fact mentioned at the Town Hall meeting. In fact, as plans go, everything ran like clockwork. It was perfect. And once inside, it was simple for our fake-Mayor to remove the picture-frame that Frank Parkinson had so recently made such a feature of..."

Deidre reasoned, "From the very spot they'd eaten the night before."

"As evidenced in Saturday's Gazette."

"Quelle horreur! They are nothing but, how you say... *slugs*!"

Deidre's sense of injustice erupted, "I thought that their visit might enhance my hotel's reputation and bring in some much-needed revenue for me. And Blinkton too, of course. But they weren't interested in the Harbor

Lites at all, were they? All they wanted was to book-in as near to the Codfather as possible. The quality of my hospitality was irrelevant as were all the activities my friends in Blinkton planned for them." The piece of masking-tape flapped at Deidre's jaw as she spoke, "And to think that dear Frank Parkinson invited them into his establishment for free. Double portions for the double-crossers. They've taken us all for fools!"

Inky sprang to his feet, "*Asticot* stole the Codfather's secret recipe from the picture-frame then returned the empty envelope to its frame, re-hung it, and then left through the door he'd just smashed. Back out into the anonymity of the storm. He was back in here before the snow had caused his hair-dye to run."

"C'est vrai," said Asticot, in disgust. "I recall hearing him myself. He was singing to himself that afternoon. I was tied up in here and he was singing. Celebrating. He's a vile monster. A cochon!"

Beneath her bindings, Deidre's fists tightened, "All his flattery. All his pompous talk of *community* and *integration* were just nothing but lip-service. Hot air." She looked up at Inky, "Thank you, young-man, you've helped me to see everything clearly. For someone so young, you possess such wisdom."

Inky replied, "Sadly, your guest-house just happened to suit their purpose. It was safe and private. Somewhere where they could," Inky looked down at Asticot, "stow-away their contraband. They've been here before, you know? Blinkton."

The hostages looked up in astonishment.

Inky confirmed, "They're not strangers here. This isn't an international operation at all. It's something *much* closer to home."

Deidre's anger continued to simmer, "But this *Asticot-fake* didn't know that my front door is always kept unlocked though, did he? He went pale when I told him about that on his arrival. Thank goodness I stick to my principles. And thank goodness you could get in, young-man. You're an angel!"

"Now here's where I need your co-operation," said Inky, purposeful, "their plan was a good one. A very good one. After all, it worked! *Jacques* created the distraction. *Jean-Pierre* stole the recipe. So far so good. But," he stressed, "*had they been successful* then last Friday would have seen them flying out of Blinkton faster than Saint Nick on the 25th. But the fact that they're still here," he paused, "suggests that that something went wrong. Badly wrong. And I'm guessing that everything began to turn sour when you, Deidre, stumbled upon on the real French Mayor in here. Last Thursday, was it?"

"Friday morning," spluttered Deidre. "I mean, *the Asticots* told me not to disturb them during their stay..."

"Of course they did."

"... but that's not how I operate. I decided to interfere anyway." Deidre's voice trembled, "I like to serve people, build up a rapport, plus," she added, "I'd also become concerned about some strange noises coming from this apartment. *Bumps*, and *bangs*, and what-not."

"C'était moi."

"I know that now, Jean-Pierre, but last Friday morning I didn't. So," she continued in a whisper, "rather than waiting in the dining room for them to fail to appear as usual, I decided to take matters into my own hands. I cooked two of my finest breakfasts, all served up with a fresh pot of black coffee like they like it in," she hesitated, "France. And then I carried them up here. Three flights of stairs. Everything on a single tray. But when I arrived I couldn't knock 'cause my hands were full, so I shouted ahead, just to be polite. Only," she paused, "only when I... elbowed the door open... I saw... I saw..."

Asticot continued out of politeness, "Cette dame charmante saw me being fed from a tin, like a baby. Hands tied behind my back. Those dogs tried to bundle me out of the way but they weren't quick enough. Deidre'd caught sight of me," Butterfield nodded, visibly moved, "so they had to react. All of a sudden they became very violent. The man grabbed her and put a hand across her mouth. The boy picked up her legs, and together they carried her into here."

Inky said, "I saw rotten food all over the carpet."

"That's what's left of their top-notch breakfasts," Deidre explained, fighting her emotion. "They plonked me on this chair, sat Jean-Pierre behind me, then wound tape around us both. Then they started to ask us questions. In English and French. Never-ending."

"Sans arrêt!"

Inky said, "I noticed that they share the bedroom opposite. Their room is nowhere near as untidy as..."

Sensing danger, Inky rushed to put out the main light once more. Peering down towards the Promenade, the young-sleuth was relieved to see that Sean was still at his post. Alone. The investigator watched the daft youth as he paced the pavement trying to keep warm, cigarette balanced between chattering lips. Then, suddenly, Inky's attention was caught by a rapid movement. Squinting into the darkness, he located its source... just a carrier-bag carried on the wind. The crumpled piece of litter swept past Big-Sean then tumbled over the seawall and disappeared into the silver darkness.

Satisfied, the detective turned his attention back to the hostages...

... missing *the Asticots'* return by a matter of seconds.

* * *

Two figures rounded the corner of Babylon Lane. They approached Big-Sean who was sitting on the seawall scanning the horizon for a carrier-bag which had just swept past. The dopey lad was relieved to see that *the Asticots* had returned much earlier than expected. He stood up, massaging life back into his backside.

Jack thanked him for his vigilance, "Merci Sean. You're free to leave now."

"Thanks, Jacques," replied Sean, shivering, "anything to help out. You're a gem, you know, 'Asti'."

Jean-Pierre interrupted, "I trust that everything's been quiet this evening, Sean?"

"Oh yes, nothing's stirred at all."

"And you've been here all evening?"

"Never moved once." He gazed along the Prom., "This place is a bit dead, isn't it?"

Jack smirked, "Yeah, it is. Thanks Sean, I owe you one. You're a true friend. See you tomorrow at school."

"Anytime, Asti," said Sean, setting off. "It's been a pleasure, a real pleasure. Au revoir!"

Asticot could not stop himself smiling at the sight of Daft-Sean staggering off, legs frozen stiff.

Jack turned to his father, grinning himself, "Told you not to worry, dad. Better than a guard dog is Sean. I said no-one would come sniffing round here, but it's best to know for sure, I suppose."

Asticot's mood turned sharply, "You've needlessly involved someone else. I'm still not happy about that, *Asti*."

The teenager defended himself, "There were always going to be others..."

"Shut it, would you, I'm beginning to lose patience!" He span around to face the Harbor Lites, the moonlight catching the evil glint in his eye, "All this is going to end, right now. One way or another. Get inside!"

* * *

"Time's paramount," said Inky, returning to the captives. "To ensure justice, we need to plan ahead." After a few moments of contemplation, he went on, "What our *foreign-friends* found inside the Codfather's envelope was not what they expected. Not fully. That's why everything's suddenly become very messy. Your abductors don't know what to do. They're making it up as they go along. Floundering. One hostage has become two, civic-duties are being undertaken half-heartedly and *Jacques'* behaviour at school has deteriorated. Their plan's hit the buffers, yet," Inky raised a finger, "the fact that they're still here suggests that they still feel that they can salvage the situation. They must have found something useful inside that envelope. Something relevant. And, Ms Butterfield...?"

Deidre looked up.

"Monsieur Asticot..."

"Oui?"

"I need you to tell me what that was."

* * *

Jean-Pierre Asticot shoved the guest-house door open so violently that it slammed back and dislodged the plasterwork inside. He kicked his shoes into the darkness then disappeared, leaving Jack to follow. Shoulders hunched, the young man closed the door, unlooped his scarf and flung it over the reception desk,

"Why can't we have the heating on in here dad, it's freezing? Or at least a light or two? Can't we get *Mother Theresa* up there to stoke the fire? What's the point in us taking over this place if...?"

Asticot whirled around, face cut by a slither of moonlight, "Because this isn't some kind of holiday camp, Jackie-boy. We're here to make life as diffi-cult as possible for them. Besides, once they start blabbing, and they *will* start blabbing," he added, "we'll be able to relocate somewhere hot."

"Spain? Jamaica? South America?"

"As far as you like once we've made our fortune. That recipe's our golden ticket."

"Sounds good," said Jack, feeling his way towards the staircase. Instinctively he raised a finger to push his sunglasses up his nose, cursing at finding them missing. Distracted, he'd failed to notice that his father had stopped walking. The teenager ploughed straight into the back of him.

"Oaf," cried *Asticot*, pushing him away, "learn to concentrate, would you?"

He ran the flat of his hand down his wiry sideburns, "Our time here's almost over and I'm running out of patience. With you and with them. It's time for our little sparrows to start singing…"

"But dad," Jack ventured, "I really don't think that they know what that sheet of paper means. If they do I'm sure they'd have told us by now."

"One thing's for sure," said *Asticot*, "they're going to spit something out. Whatever it is." He added, "We've come too far and been too nice for too long. This is it, Jackie-boy, I'm about to present them with a very simple choice, tell us what that stupid rhyme means, or suffer the consequences."

Jack's brow furrowed, "What consequences?"

"Let's just say that we're about to see how good you are at metalwork."

"Metalwork?"

"That's right."

"Why?"

"Because it's you who's going to be using the blow-torch! Come on," he snarled, "you were complaining about the cold. Let's go warm ourselves up!"

* * *

Deidre spoke in a hurry, "*Asticot's* spoken of nothing but that blasted paper for the past few days. He's read it to me over and over. That rhyme will be forever burned into my memory. But there's a problem. According to its wording, the secret recipe…"

"… is not actually a recipe at all," genuine-Asticot added.

"Quite the opposite, in fact. It's a *non-recipe*. Just an old-fashioned piece of advice made into a silly verse."

"Recite it," Inky demanded. "Quickly. That *bump*, I believe, was your front door."

While the prisoners opened their eyes in alarm, the detective flipped the light off and pulled back the curtain. Eyeing the empty seascape below, he muttered, "Big-Sean's gone. I'm guessing that Mayor Carey's failed to detain *the Asticots* at the theatre, and now," he asserted, "they're back." Inky's voice emerged out of the darkness, "Tell me what's written on that paper…"

Deidre's voice was laden with tension…

"*Multitude have asked of my pop-lar fish preparation*", she began,
"*Yet it be a secret I'll take to my grave,*
For what I do needeth no explanation,
No ethos, no learning… save…

A pinch of prayer to great God above,
To ask for a spoonful of kindness and love.

Then at the bottom," she added, "it was signed, *Geoffrey William Parkinson.*"

A silence settled upon the room. The sound of intense thought. Of mental wheels slowly turning.

Cloaked in darkness, the room momentarily seemed to exist outside time. No past. No future. Just three entities locked inside the workings of a complex riddle.

Asticot, whispered, "Monsieur Stevens, are you still...?"

"It's done," Inky announced, "here are your instructions. The ones which will save you... and condemn them." As he spoke, Inky hurriedly reapplied the tape to Asticot's mouth, "To begin with you must withhold this information for as long as possible." With the Mayor's tape re-attached, Inky turned his attention to Deidre, "Be brave. Be evasive. But finally, reluctantly, *pretend* to give in. At that point you must offer-up the following, very specific, information..."

Inky returned to Asticot.

"Monsieur, in a blinding moment of clarity you must relay that the patron saint of *learning*, the word mentioned in the rhyme, is of course, *St Hilda*." He repeated, "Learning links to St Hilda, d'accord?"

Asticot grunted his acknowledgement.

"Then," said Inky, circling back to Deidre, "it's over to you, miss. After Jean-Pierre's sudden realisation, *as if by coincidence* you must remember that Geoffrey Parkinson, Frank's great-grandfather, is buried inside St Hilda's Church. You must see where this is leading...?"

Taped up once more, Deidre snorted.

"Our plan relies on those two very simple pieces of information. You see," Inky explained, "as you may already know, Geoffrey Parkinson's *grave*, the one mentioned in the rhyme, is located inside St Hilda's Church. It's set into the floor in the north transept. Tell *Asticot* that on top of Geoffrey's gravestone there's a commemorative plaque. That much is actually true," he admitted. "Then say that, as a guess, the Codfather's rhyme must be some kind of coded message directing the reader towards the real secret recipe which *must be* concealed beneath that plaque." Inky summarised his instruction, "*St Hilda's. The patron saint of learning. Geoffrey Parkinson's grave.* We know that all this is nonsense, of course. There won't be anything beneath that plaque. But the key thing is that you make *the Asticots* believe that there might be. They're desperate enough, and stupid enough, not to be able to resist checking it out... which is where I come in."

* * *

Jack watched the number 13 appear through the gloom, "Why's it me who has to use the blow-torch?"

"Because, my son," said *Asticot*, forcefully, "it's time for you to come of age. To prove your worth. Besides," he paused, catching his breath, "if we get caught you'll get off far more lightly than I will because you're a teenager. Now less talk, Jackie-boy, and get a move on. We've work to do!"

Jack gripped hold of the banister-rail aware that his hand had started to tremble...

* * *

Inky went on, "My trap will be set for tomorrow evening. With this in mind I need you to urge *the Asticots* to be patient." The investigator placed a hand onto Deidre's shoulder, "Miss," he whispered, "as you're local, this information has to come from you. You must impress upon them that they'll be unable to respond until tomorrow evening. Tell them that St Hilda Church is locked up 'til then. Protected by an impregnable alarm system. Then intrigue the pair of them. Say that the church is unlocked at 5pm every Thursday. For bell-ringing practice. Tell them that it's your good friend Maude Perkins who opens up the church. Regular as clockwork. Say that Maude's so conscientious that she arrives well ahead of the bell-ringers, who won't drift in 'til about five thirty."

In the semi-dark Inky could sense Deidre's uncertainty.

"Yes I know it's all lies, miss. I know that the bell-ringers meet up on Mondays and that your friend Maude has nothing to do with them. But," he stated, "the important thing is that the kidnappers don't know this. Just make sure you relay exactly what I've told you. Maude Perkins. Tomorrow. Five o'clock. OK?"

Deidre nodded.

"Now this is important," said Inky, silhouette black as pitch, "once they've left here tomorrow you'll be able to free yourselves with my knife. But I'm asking that you wait until a quarter past five before leaving the Harbor Lites yourselves. At five-fifteen precisely I need both of you to enter the Police

Station across from here and tell the duty-sergeant everything that's been going on. *The Asticots* being frauds. The theft of the recipe. The kidnapping. The hostage-taking. Bullying. Torture. Absolutely everything," he stressed. "Then tell them to go to St Hilda's immediately. 'Cause that's where they'll be found. Where I'll have them. Strung up like French onions!" Inky's voice dropped, "A quarter past five tomorrow. Not a second more. Not a second less. Understand?"

Both Asticot and Butterfield nodded.

"*The Asticots* won't be able to help themselves. Greed will drive them there," Inky's mouth twisted into a cruel smile, "and when they arrive, I'll be there waiting. Waiting to squeeze enough evidence out of them to send them to the bottom of the stagnant pool from which they came."

Inky squeezed Deidre's shoulder reassuringly, then withdrew his hand, "Miss, you could add that Maude can be forgetful at times and that if she fails to show up, for whatever reason, you'll happily call on her yourself on Friday morning for the key. That way they'll not risk harming you. They've come too far to jeopardise everything in one moment of rashness. Oh," he added as an afterthought, "the Gazette's reporting of what's about to occur may be a little different to the truth. Don't be alarmed. I just think there's someone who deserves a lucky break, that's all. Don't let on, it'll be our secret. Those are my wishes. Please honour them. So, mes amis," he concluded, "it's over to you. You still have a choice, of course. My knife gives you control over your destiny. But if you're prepared to trust me, and want justice badly enough, then you'll find the strength to manipulate the *fake-Asticots* for a few hours longer. It'll all be worth it, I promise. Tomorrow at five I'll be waiting for them at St Hilda's Church," Inky's voice dwindled to a whisper, "and I promise you they won't know what's hit them. Au revoir...!"

* * *

As Jack barged into the penthouse, he stepped onto a slice of toast. "Urrggh," he grunted, scraping it from the underside of his boot.

Asticot followed, panting. He flicked on the light, tutting at the disarray, "This place is a pig-sty."

"Good job we're leaving soon." Jack removed his gloves and tossed them onto the sofa. Pulling up his jeans, he added, "These things just won't stay up."

"You'll get no pity from me. It was you who lost your belt."

"I didn't lose it. I was forced to use it in the line of duty."

Asticot smirked, "Well it serves you right for not retrieving it. We're not here to go clothes shopping. We're here to make money." Distracted by a noise, he said, "*Shush*, can you hear something?"

A pause.

Jack broke the silence, "Must be those two in there, or your imagination?"

"I don't imagine things, imbecile. Look," said *Asticot*, pointing, "the balcony door's ajar. What've you been up to? It's freezing in here."

"I've not done nothing. I didn't leave it like that."

"Don't lie," said *Asticot*, "you must've done 'cause it wasn't me. Go and shut it. And check outside while you're about it."

"What's the point in checking outside? There's no-one out there. Sean said...?"

"I don't care what Dumbo said. Do it!"

Jack did as instructed. Muttering.

* * *

Inky had acted on instinct. He'd used the remaining seconds to slip through the lounge then pass out onto the roof-terrace through the balcony-doors. Fearful of making unnecessary noise, he'd opted to leave the door slightly ajar. Thus, when *the Asticots* had returned, Inky'd found himself outside, several storeys up, facing out to sea.

Stranded.

Inky'd crouched down behind the garden furniture feeling the sharp air pull at his coat. Carey's failure to detain the imposters had cut short his planning time with Butterfield and Asticot. The scheme they'd cobbled together was good. Very good. It might even work. But it was also a plan which had been put together all too hastily.

Whether too hastily, time would tell?

When Room 13's light had come on, Inky's shadow had been thrown across frosty gravel all the way up to, then over, the metal railings. Yet with the penthouse window acting as a two-way mirror, the detective was able to remain hidden. Confident, he'd even stood up to eye his adversaries with distain. He'd watched Jack throw his gloves across the room. He'd even been able to listen to *Asticot's* empty boasts.

In steely silence, Inky's eyes burned with hatred. He vowed to derail the imposters who were standing only feet away from him, yet completely ignorant of his presence. Then, realising that Jack was about to search the roof-terrace, the Great School Detective made to leave...

* * *

"Done," said Jack, re-entering the room.

"Nothing unusual out there?"

"What did you think I was going to find? Lord Lucan? The Abominable Snowman? The Loch Ness Monster? We're three storeys up. It's the middle of winter. Sean told us he'd not seen nothing."

"But you checked nevertheless?"

"Relax," said Jack, locking the balcony-door, "and put our fire on, would you? It's perishing in here and snow's forecast for tomorrow."

"This scuzzy little town makes me feel sick," grunted *Asticot*. He unfastened his tie and disappeared into their own bedroom, voice raised accordingly, "I'll be glad to wipe its sand from the soles of my shoes. Bootlickers, the lot of 'em. Mention money and everyone goes weak at the knees. Right," he said, returning, "our electric fire's on. It's time for business. Time for our little piggies to start squealing!"

"Or become bacon," Jack added, with a sneer.

Asticot removed a yellowing sheet of paper from his jacket pocket then unlocked his hostages' improvised cell, "Get a move on, Jack. I've already witnessed one dreadful pantomime this evening. Let's make sure this one's much more agreeable. A blow-torch ought to warm up a few dormant brain cells. It's showtime!"

Bound to wooden chairs inside the shell-of-a-bedroom, two individuals sat bolt upright in alarm.

* * *

Inky'd held on to the guest-house's drainpipe as if his life had depended on it.

While Jack had fruitlessly scraped garden furniture around, the investigator had clung on with all his strength. Stubbornly rigid against weathered brick.

The tenacity of the wolverine.

And he'd remained this way for some time. Pain creasing his face. Arms cold and heavy. Mind blocking out the pain.

Finally, at the sound of the door closing up above, Inky'd been able to continue his descent.

Mindful of ice, he'd slithered down the drainpipe cautiously. Inch by inch. Hand over labouring hand.

Minutes later, the detective's boots made contact with the ice-coated ground. He peeled his hands from the drainpipe and attempted to blow life back into stiff fingers. Wary of being discovered, he flexed aching muscles as he shrank away into the night.

It wasn't until he'd crossed the Promenade that he turned back to see what was happening up above at the Harbor Lites. From a tight angle, all he could see was a muted glow seeping through the penthouse windows. To a passer-by everything would look completely normal, yet Inky wondered what was really going on inside Room 13. He consoled himself with the thought that he'd done all he could in the time available.

But had he done enough?

The trap was sprung, but would *the Asticots* take the bait?

Turning up his collar the detective manoeuvred along the deserted Promenade, hands clasped around the bunch of keys in his pocket. Despite the hour, instead of heading home Inky prepared to make the long trek back up to school. Mike Bennett's computer was beckoning. The young-investigator's nocturnal visit had revealed crucial information which needed immediate processing.

The Great School Detective could feel it. He was close, so close... to unmasking the true identity of *the Asticots*...

As Inky paced back uphill, a scruffy mongrel emerged from behind a bus shelter and fell into step with him. Inky gazed down at the creature in sympathy, "Come on, boy," he said, "how'd you fancy another walk?"

15. 1 Cornflower Close:
Wednesday 21ᵗʰ December (Night).

Scott Cunliffe was lying on the sofa watching television with his family. From a Christmas tree in the corner a set of fairly-lights flashed on and off bathing the room in a kaleidoscope of colour. Young-Scott was gazing at the decorations half-heartedly, slowly drifting off to sleep, when his mother announced, "Scotty, there's someone from school on the doorstep."

"Someone from school?" enquired Cunliffe, suddenly awake. "At this time? "Who?"

"Didn't say," replied Jill Cunliffe. "Spooky-looking lad with a long, leather coat. Black hair. Deep-set eyes." Scott looked hesitant. "Well go on," she added, "go and see what he wants, it's freezing out there."

Scott Cunliffe made his way out into the hallway feeling troubled, "Oh no," he exclaimed on seeing who was on his doorstep.

"Aren't you going to invite me in?" asked Inky.

"No I'm not," replied Cunliffe, grabbing his parka from the hallway and joining his fellow fourth-year outside. "What are you doing here?"

Inky noted that Cunliffe wasn't wearing any shoes, "Can't you guess? It took me awhile to work it all out. But I've caught up with you eventually."

"It wasn't me," blurted Cunliffe, bunching fists into the sleeves of his coat.

"Who did what?"

"Who..." Cunliffe checked himself, "ah, you can't catch me that easily!"

"Look, I've had quite a tough evening, Scott, so I'll make this as painless as possible. Miss Birkin's coming out of hospital soon. She's recovered from her concussion and won't experience any permanent damage after you attacked her. You must be relieved."

"Must I?"

Inky removed a golfball from his pocket and held it up. Cunliffe could clearly see the initials *'C.C.'* embossed on its surface. "This object was found at the centre of your rather nasty little weapon. I checked the school records. Your dad's a *Christopher*. Is he in? Perhaps he'd like to return it to his stack of *Drivesure* golfballs...?"

"He's actually out right now, so why don't you just push off, Stevens? Besides, I don't know what it is you think you know...?"

"What I know," Inky stated, taking a pace forward, "is that you injured an innocent young-lady and that an awful lot of people are unhappy about this."

"It wasn't me."

"Look, Scott I haven't time for this..."

"Me neither," said Cunliffe, turning around and stepping back into the warmth. As he made to shut the front door, he found Inky's foot blocking its path.

Jill Cunliffe's voice drifted out of the sitting room, "What are you playing at out there, Scotty? Shut that door, all the heat's going out. Either invite your friend in, or say goodnight and come back in here with me and your dad."

Inky raised an eyebrow, "Come to think of it, *Scotty*, I could do with a nice cup of tea and a cosy chat. Chris and I could talk about handicaps, and green-fees, and backswings, if you get my drift?" Inky's tone softened, "Come on, Scott. It's not very warm out here and you're being uncivil. You do know I'm not going to go away, don't you?"

Cunliffe scowled, then stepped back outside, closing the front door behind, "Look, Stevens," he whispered, "what's all this about? What is it that you think you know? Say your piece then clear off."

"In that case," replied Inky, "I'll be brief. Last week you injured Miss Birkin with a snowball thrown at Carlos Orange..."

"Oz, so it was him who...?"

"No it wasn't, Carlos was incredibly tight-lipped about the whole affair," Inky lied, "but there were others who did see exactly what happened. Nothing goes unnoticed in a school. Plus, your footprints are still all over the yard by Broker's Archway. Your assault's immortalised in ice. Let's face it, Scotty," Inky paused, "it's only a matter of time before the Snake finds out what you did."

Cunliffe's face drained of colour.

Inky continued, "I'm more than happy to leave things to follow their natural course but, if I do, you'll be looking over your shoulder for the rest of the week. Imagine it Scotty, your name being called out in assembly, or strange notes arriving in the register. Being banned from the Christmas disco. Flashing blue lights illuminating Cornflower Close, and I don't mean pretty, festive ones either." Inky paused to let his words take effect, "Or if all that doesn't bother you, perhaps I could have a word with Chris while teeing off at the thirteenth...?"

"Why are you doing this, Stevens? What's in it for you?"

"Justice," he stated simply.

Silence.

Cunliffe's shoulders slumped, "Alright, Stevens. Let's suppose I did throw that snowball at Miss Birkin. Suppose I couldn't see her properly 'cause of the blizzard. Suppose it was all just some prank to get Oz back because he'd defaced my Biology book and when he fell over miss just happened to be in the way?"

"Then perhaps you deserve a second chance. You're only small-fry anyway, Scotty. You do know that, don't you?"

Cunliffe folded his arms, "So what are you going to do? Snitch on me? Run me into the Snake's office, dead or alive?"

"You misunderstand the situation. I'm not here for revenge. I'm here to protect you," Inky's expression hardened, "but we all know that protection comes at a price." He shot Cunliffe a knowing look, "How'd you fancy a day off school?"

"What?"

"No catch, I'll sort it all out. Mr Bennett and I have struck up quite a *flexible* arrangement. In return for a day of leisure all I require are two favours. The first will involve you taking the train to Plumpton Sands. It leaves tomorrow morning at eight-fifteen..."

"But I haven't any..."

"Here's ten pounds," he said, holding out Bennett's note, "that'll more than cover it. You'll even have enough left over to buy a can of Irn-Bru from the kiosk. I need you to conduct some fieldwork for me, that's all. You'll not be in trouble, I promise."

Scott rubbed his chin, "You mentioned two things?"

"Well," confessed Inky, hesitant, "my second favour's a little more tricky. You'll need to have your wits about you. Think on your feet. And you'll also need to wear something distinctive. Let's call it *a costume*, of sorts. I'll provide it."

"Dressing up," said Cunliffe with a frown, "no way!"

"Then you give me little alternative." Inky snatched back the ten pound note. "Have you seen the inside of the Snake's office? There's a coffee machine in there. Brand new. It's all very *swish*. Very civilised. So after She's finished playing with you like a cat with a bird, She might offer you a freshly ground cup of...?"

Scott was clearly panicked, "Why don't you get Ross or Rose to do your dirty work? You normally do?"

"Because this assignment carries a certain amount of risk. Risk that I'd be unwilling to subject two innocents to. Whereas you, on the other hand... are far from innocent!"

"Would I miss all of school tomorrow?"

"Yes."

"And I won't get in trouble?"

"No."

"Promise?"

"Promise!"

"And if I do what you ask, then me lobbing that snowball at Oz will be forgotten?"

"You have my word."

"OK," Cunliffe consented, reluctantly, "I'll do it. Now give me that tenner and my dad's golfball, then tell me what I have to do." Brightening, he added, "I might even be able to afford a Curly Wurly too, if I decide not to travel first-class?"

"Trains leaving Blinkton don't have first-class. Aren't you going to ask me in to toast our partnership?"

"No!"

Mr Mike Bennett (Deputy-Head):

Everything was set. Inky had masterminded it so that Thursday the 22nd December was to be the climax of his investigation. This date, one which will be forever etched into my memory, coincided with the weather breaking. After what seemed like a month of Arctic temperatures, heavy clouds rolled in from the south and things finally started to warm up. Compacted ice began to loosen and thaw. By morning, Blinkton's playground was a soggy carpet of slush. Rather than slipping over, the new risk to the school community was from 'ice-bombs'. I thought that after what happened to Sally Birkin the kids would know better.

(On that count, I was sadly wrong.)

That morning Inky called at my office as agreed. I didn't bother to answer the door, he just surged past me in his usual fashion.

'Another sleepless night, sir?'

My reply was curt as I was indeed short of sleep, 'I need to know where we are, Inky, and I need to know right now. If I have to cancel the Christmas disco then arrangements have to be made. There are procedures to follow. People to be informed. Refreshments to be,' I struggled, 'unrefreshed!'

But my attempt at being assertive fell short. Assuming control, Inky looked down at me with a mixture of amusement and pity, 'Sir, I've told you that I'll supply the names of the culprits by tomorrow morning and that agreement still stands. Yet before I can reveal this information, there are still loose ends to tidy up. Evidence to collect. Debts to be paid. Just keep faith, sir.' He went on to explain, 'Today has the potential to be explosive. But that's my concern, not yours.' He added, 'If Mayor Carey's office tries to make contact, I'd be grateful if you'd wait 'til you've spoken to me tomorrow morning before responding. It will be in your interests. Trust me.'

'Mayor Carey's office? But why would he, would they...?'

Inky raised a hand, 'By dawn tomorrow everything will make sense. By then, my mission will have reached its conclusion. One way or another. All you have to do is carry on as normal.'

Inky placed his hands on the edge of my desk and leaned in, eyes hypnotic,

'It'll soon be Christmas, sir. The season of goodwill. You'll be able to forget everything and relax. Have a glass of sherry. Or two. But,' his tone sharpened, 'I need you to be strong for one day more. Now,' he snapped, 'I have a couple more requests. First, Scott Cunliffe must be excused from lessons. Just for today. It's

nearly Christmas. No-one will notice. He's running an errand for me, or rather,'
he corrected, 'for you. Right now he's on a train, all expenses paid.'

I protested, 'What do you mean 'on an errand for me'?' But Inky cut across,
'When I leave here, my first task is to confront Ray Day. He and I have unfin-
ished business. After this I'll need to use your office for the rest of the morning.
I'm expecting a phone call around lunchtime. After this I'll leave school early to
prepare for tonight, and believe me, I do have a lot of preparations to make. But
from tomorrow, sir, everything will be back to normal. Now,' he said, with a far-
away look, 'it's time! Sir, I need you to contact Day as you did before, via Miss
Cartwright. He's in the Humanities corridor again and needs to be diverted
away from there. You must tell him, and this is very important, that the heat-
ing's too hot for the Biology mock in the Hall. Tell him the controls on our new
boiler need adjusting. Immediately. Got that?'

I nodded.

'Well that's just about it...'

Without waiting for a response, Inky marched out of my office.

I tried my best to stop him, of course. I recall setting off after him with a
barrage of questions...

'How's Ray Day involved in all this?'

'Where's Scott Cunliffe headed?'

'What is it that you're making these preparations for?'

'What's all this got to do with Mayor Carey?'

'What about 'Health and Safety'!!?'

But as I set off in pursuit of the Great School Detective I ran straight into a
number of students loitering outside my office, late for class,

'Come on you lot, get a move on!' I snarled, just in time to see Inky melt into
the crowd.

He'd gone. Vanished. A bloodhound on the scent. On his way to honour a
promise he'd made only days before.

Had I been aware how perilous that that day was to prove I'd like to think
that I'd have tried a little bit harder to catch up with him...

But I didn't...

And what happened as a result has passed into Blinkton's folklore.

16. Loose Ends Tied and Untied:
Thursday 22nd December (Morning).

Inky used his key to let himself in to what used to be Frederick Varley's Maintenance Room. He knew that things had moved on since the previous September, but still felt uneasy nevertheless. Turning a full circle, he observed that little had changed since Varley's departure just three months previous. Despite Day having taken over as caretaker, the room was still as cluttered as he remembered it. Work-benches and shelving dominated the room holding all manner of hardware... tools, chargers, nails and screws, batteries, mothballs, mousetraps (one containing a mouse skeleton). Without a window, the room's only light came from a fluorescent strip-light up above. Two mismatching armchairs provided a choice of seating. Just one desk and computer were sufficient for all of Day's administrative tasks. A single door in the far wall allowed access to the school's boiler in the basement below.

At the centre of the right-hand wall was a metal locker. Its door was half-open, attached to the frame by a single hinge. Inky made his way over to this. For someone so tall he found it a tight fit, but in the end he nevertheless managed squeeze his way inside. From within, he took hold of the door and pulled it towards himself. Now hidden from view, Inky waited for Ray Day to appear clutching the Boiler Room's key in one hand and Day's own cordless screwdriver in the other. Resigned to wait for some time, the young-detective allowed his mission's odd cast of characters to float through his mind...

'Jacques Asticot and both Jean-Pierres. Deidre Butterfield and Maude Perkins. Mayor Carey. Crispin Merridew. Carlos Orange, Big-Sean and Scott Cunliffe. Amanda Blunt and Oggy Woggle, and, of course, Ray Day.'

The sound of a key being slotted into a lock brought Inky crashing back to reality. He heard Day grunting as he unlocked the door. Blinkton's caretaker then lugged his enormous frame into the centre of the room.

Through slats in the locker door Inky watched the oversized ogre bend to tie his bootlace. Day then stretched up to his full height, slapping meaty hands onto his domed-head. "Smarty-pants Bennett," he muttered to himself, "do this, do that, do the other. But not for much longer Mr Know-it-all. Not for much longer..."

Day struggled to remove his jacket. Having initially snagged on his thick wrists, he flung it across the room in disgust. Seeing it headed in his direction, Inky clutched hold of the locker door and braced himself for impact. He felt the inevitable shudder as the workcoat slammed into his hiding place then slid down onto the floor.

But his presence remained undetected.

Inky head Day mimicking Bennett, "Would you mind awfully altering the thermostat on the boiler, Mr Day?" Then answer his own question, "Of course, sir. Yes, sir. No, sir. Three bags full, sir. It's not as if I've got better things to do. Much better things!"

Cursing, Day loped over to the far side of the room then headed down to the Boiler Room. Down below, the Neanderthal lunk stood before the heating system's bank of buttons, dials and switches, scratching his head in annoyance.

Inky didn't need a second chance.

He unfolded himself from Day's locker then raced across the concrete floor. In no time he'd slammed the Boiler Room door, inserted its key, then locked it.

The egg-headed caretaker, sensing the disturbance, charged upwards four steps at a time.

He was quick...

But not nearly quick enough.

By the time Day's palm slammed against the door he was already locked in.

Inky, unwilling to rely on a single lock, first slid the metal locker up against the door. He then further imprisoned Day using the cordless screwdriver. Ignoring the caretaker's frenzied pummelling, Inky drove ten two-inch screws straight through the doorframe and into the door jamb. Sealing it tight.

"Let me out!" cried Day, his breathing heavy and laboured. "What is this? What's happening? Whoever's doing this better have a good reason. A damn good reason. 'Cause by the time I get my hands on...!"

Inky, leant back against the metal locker and placed his mouth as close to the door as possible, "We meet again Day-o!"

Silence.

"Stevens? Stevens is that you?" he asked, voice clouded with confusion. "Let me out. Let me out, you bat-faced oik!"

"I'm afraid that's not going to happen, Day-o."

Silence.

"If that's you, Stevens. If all this is one of your pathetic games designed to get back at me then..."

"Then what Day-o? What will you do? Take a photograph of me and hang it up on your *washing line of shame* in your darkroom, eh?"

The resulting silence stretched on. Inky could almost visualise Day's brain working overtime.

Eventually the teenager took charge, "Sounds like you're lost for words. Now that's a first, Day-Break. If I were you I'd listen very carefully to what I'm about to say. Mr Bennett," he began, "has just requested that you turn down the heating in the Hall. In reality, that request didn't originate from him, it came from me. But rest-assured Bennett's involved..."

"What is all this? What are you talking...?"

"I'm speaking," said Inky, flaring up. "I always thought it was rude to interrupt someone when they're speaking!" He waited for silence, "That's better. Now, I'm about to leave you to your own devices for about half an hour. An hour at most. What I'll be doing during this time is dismantling your secret photo-lab. The one in the Humanities store cupboard. Every print and every negative will be placed in my rucksack and this, in turn, will be deposited somewhere very safe," he paused. "That is unless you decide to be awkward. In which case my helpers have specific instructions to pass your material over to the nearest staff-member..."

"But...?"

"I've already warned you, Pay-Day, I'll not give you a second chance!" The steel in Inky's voice was unmistakeable, "After that I'll be searching this place. Your room. Your desk-computer and so forth. See what grisly secrets it'll cough up. Then, and only then, will I release you to inform you what's going to happen next." Inky's voice took on a sinister tone, "I warn you in all seriousness, Day-o, *do not attempt to escape.* First, because I've secured your door strongly enough to withstand anything you can throw at it. And second, because, as I've already explained, I will distribute your photographic misconduct everywhere from here to County Hall via the Snake's desk. So until I return, and believe me I will return, just sit back and relax. Take things easy. Think pleasant thoughts but don't overtax that huge potato-head of yours, I'd hate it to overheat!"

On hearing Inky lock the Maintenance Room door, Day gripped hold of the largest pipe inside the Boiler Room, intent on ripping it free of its moorings. His act of vandalism was cut short, however, as boiling hot metal burned into his paint-stained palms,

"AAARRRRGGGHHHH!!"

* * *

At exactly the same moment that Ray Day was screaming in pain, *fake-Asticot* loomed above his victims inside the Harbor Lites guest-house. The dishevelled pair looked up at their persecutor in terror. Yet *Asticot,* now in possession of the information he'd sought all along, was full of cheer,

"Well it looks like this will be our last encounter," he said, a golden grin cutting across his face. "St Hilda's Church, eh? You realise that if the pair of you are lying then this international exchange will end up with both of you becoming *French toast*!"

Deidre and Asticot nodded, eyes wide.

Asticot turned and hollered through into the lounge, "Have you finished packing yet, Jack?"

"Just about."

"Well hurry up, you're late for school."

"I can't do everything at once," he complained. Lighting a cigarette, he added, "Do I have to go back? You know that I left..."

"I don't care that you left school last year. You have to go back to Blinkton Comp. just one more time. Perhaps you'll pass your exams this time around?" he chuckled.

The imposter smoothed down the sides of his moustache with sausage-sized fingers, then gazed through the window at the slate-grey sea, "Fate's finally smiling down on us, Jack," he shouted, "now that your blowtorch finally managed to squeeze a response from Charles De Gaulle and Dame Edna, here. We're going to have a merry Christmas after all. It's amazing how effective a fierce flame can be in loosening a stiff tongue. Blinkton's fish recipe is so close I can practically smell it. So, Jackie-boy," he called out, "put that cigarette out and shut your suitcase. Our job here's almost done. Now," he said, turning to his prisoners, "you know that if you're telling *porkies* then things around here are going to become very messy. This room's untidy as it is, but I dread to think how much worse it'll be splattered with a few pints, sorry *litres,* of blood."

Asticot placed his hand inside his jacket pocket and removed a small pistol. Black handle, silver barrel.

Releasing its safety catch, the false-Mayor slid his finger onto its trigger, reassured by the gun's weight. He then dragged the gun's muzzle across the face of each prisoner in turn, grinning at their terrified reactions.

Finally, he conceded, "Forgive me. I couldn't help amusing myself one, last time. I have a dark sense of humour, you see? I've actually no intention of harming you *provided* what you've told me about St Hilda's is true. God bless Geoffrey Parkinson, eh? I only hope that Blinkton's dead serve up a feast more appetising than its living do. Because, if not," he levelled the pistol at Deidre's forehead and mimed its recoil, "*boom!*"

Deidre Butterfield stifled a cry.

"That's right, Miss Oddball. You know that I mean what I say. So," *Asticot's* voice shrank to a whisper, "you really do need to pray that Parkinson's grave surrenders its treasure!"

Asticot laughed as he re-pocketed his weapon. He then closed the bedroom curtains and straddled the assorted debris on his way back to the door, "Right," he said, "it's time for Jack to head off to school and me to visit Blinkton's dreary lighthouse. You don't know how glad I'll be to drive down that desolate road out of here. I still can't believe that Carry's been so gullible. That man wouldn't know a swindle if it jumped up and bit him on his staff-of-office. You know, my little turtle doves," he added, "five o'clock can't come soon enough." He turned, "Cases ready, Jack?"

"Yeah."

"Good. Let's get the car loaded up. I'll drop you off at school then pick you up later. We can travel on to St Hilda's straight from there. We need to be there nice and early to wait for Maude Perkins. If things go well, we'll be out of Blinkton by half past five and back home by six." He spoke with feigned regret, "Well, I guess this is it. I do hope someone comes to your rescue otherwise Christmas is going to be a bit of a turkey for you. Starvation can be such a lingering death," he smirked. "Well, as I hate farewells, I'll not say goodbye," the gold tooth emerged at the front of his grin, "I'll say, au revoir!"

Asticot flicked off the light then slammed the bedroom door.

Deidre Butterfield and Jean-Pierre Asticot found themselves alone in the room which had been their prison for some considerable time. The frightened pair listened to the sound of a key being turned in the lock followed, shortly after, by the noise of heavy suitcases *bumping* downstairs. Finally a Citroën's engine started up. The sound of its tired engine gradually receded as it trundled away in the direction of Blinkton School.

Back to back, the pair could sense each other's relief.

Asticot knew that this was the moment they'd prayed for. He immediately fumbled inside the band of his trousers for Inky's knife. With nimble fingers, he struggled to attain a firm grip. Deidre remained totally still so as not to impede his progress. Using only his fingertips, Asticot managed to prise his belt to one side and snatch hold of the concealed weapon. With tremendous care he slid the blade upwards, relishing the feel of the cold metal in his palm. Careful not to let it fall, Asticot manoeuvred the knife-blade to bear against his bindings. Then, with the tiniest of movements, he began to slice...

Forwards and backwards. Up and down. Side to side.

And gradually, the tape began to yield.

Minutes later, after nearly two weeks a hostage, Jean-Pierre Asticot could finally taste freedom. He inclined his head towards his companion as best he could, unable to suppress a smile. From the corner of his eye he could just about make out his Deidre's tears of joy...

* * *

"*Ddddddddrrrrrrrrrrr*!" Day's drill started up with a fearsome growl.

Inky clasped the cordless tool firmly in order to remove the screws he'd driven into the Boiler Room door. They gradually succumbed one by one. As the final one spiralled free, Ray Day launched himself against the door. With a single shunt, his shoulder splintered the doorframe and opened a jagged gap between wood and plaster. In turn, this caused the locker which Inky'd set against the door, to tumble. It landed hard on the concrete with an ear-splitting *crack*, contents scattering. Day then squeezed his bulk through the hole, his astronaut's-helmet-of-a-head emerging as if part of a grotesque birth ceremony. While Inky set the drill down, Day heaved the rest of himself through the gap. With a pained lunge, he finally flopped down onto the Boiler Room floor massaging elbows which he'd snagged on the splintered doorway,

"Think you're clever, don't you, Stevens?" he snorted, springing to his feet and lurching forward. He seized hold of the teenager by his coat and flung him into one of the room's armchairs. Inky landed in a heap but quickly manoeuvred into a sitting position. He proceeded to brush down the leather of his coat with affected composure. Ignoring Day's presence, Inky crossed his legs and mimed a yawn. His response, when it came, was deliberate and controlled,

"I'd like to say that I'm *considerably* more clever than you, Day-o, but I'm beginning to tire of my stock response to your childish question. All your macho posturing is a bit," he pretended to struggle for the expression, "*deja-vu*. Our constant battles to work out who's top dog have begun to bore me. So I'm afraid to say, Day-tona, that this will be our last. And before you turn all Neanderthal again, you need to know that I've just allowed you to blow off a little steam. But in reality, you really need to listen to me. Seriously listen, I mean." Inky's stare was unflinching, "What I'm about to tell you will have a significant effect on your future, so, without wasting any more of your precious time, I'll explain how things are going to pan out from here on. Unfortunately for you," he shot Day a look of mock sympathy, "things are about to develop much less well than your photographs. Please," he gestured towards the armchair opposite, "take a seat. And don't pretend to look all uncertain because we both know that you're going to do as I say. Eventually."

Day looked uncertain, then took a seat.

Eventually.

"Right," said Inky, "I said time was short, so I'll speed things up. I reckon you've about five minutes…"

"Before what?"

Inky wagged a finger, "There you go, interrupting again. Four minutes-fifty now and every second's vital. Now, where was I?" he paused, "Ah, yes. Your predicament." He established eye-contact, "I've just dismantled your little photographic laundry in Humanities." Inky's tone was deliberately patronising, "From the exhibits on display, exhibits now in my possession I hasten to add, it would appear that the theme of your portfolio was 'Blinkton School warts and all'… broken machinery, hazardous set-ups, teacher inadequacies, *Headteacher inadequacies*, that kind of thing. And obviously," he added, "I had to ask myself, why? Why are you so set on documenting us at our very worst? For whose benefit? I had my suspicions, of course, but I needed confirmation. That's why I forced you to sit a Boiler Room Detention."

Day shifted uneasily.

"Roger Rowlandson!" Inky crowed. "Does that name mean anything to you?"

"Should it?"

"Of course," Inky said, steepling his fingers. "Having now scanned your computer, it would appear that you and he have been in regular contact. And judging by the photograph-sized envelopes I found in your bottom drawer with St Derek's School's address on them, it would also appear you and Roger have become quite good pen-pals. In fact," he went on, "Miss Cartwright's postal records suggest that such packages have been dispatched to Krull with alarming regularity. Not only that," Inky continued, "in your desk drawer I also discovered your audio equipment..."

Day's eyes bulged in their sockets.

"It's exactly the type of hi-tech equipment I'd expect an *ex*-Science teacher to be obsessed by. An impressive piece of kit. It would appear you've also been bugging the school. Your recordings, the ones which you stowed in your drawer on disc, are also now in my possession. Several of them, as you already know, are recordings of what goes on inside the Snake's office. All neatly labelled in your own handwriting. Snooping on the Headmistress, eh?" Inky wagged a finger, "Tut-tut, I dread to think what would happen if She ever found out!"

Day gripped the handrests of his armchair. Sensing that he was about to launch a protest, Inky raised a finger, "No need to say anything Day-break, I have it all covered. You see, it would appear that following your demotion last September you've been harbouring thoughts of revenge. Such notions appear to have rotted away the last trace of goodness that even you must have possessed. Once. Working here at Blinkton, yet on Rowlandson's payroll, you've painted us all in an exceptionally poor light. On his part, I imagine Roger must have been delighted with your camera and audio work?"

Day opened his mouth to speak, but again Inky cut him short, "No need to speak. Anyone with a brain bigger than an amoeba would have recognised that that was a rhetorical question. Yet for some reason you didn't. So," Inky went on, enjoying himself, "it would appear that Rowlandson, buoyed by your *billets-doux*, has been telling tales to his band of bootlickers at County Hall. Hoping to humiliate us, perhaps? Close Blinkton School down?"

A shadow passed across Day's face.

"I bet a puddle of drool collects around Rowlandson's ankles every time one of your envelopes drops onto his doormat. But," Inky tutted, "setting off the alarm in the Humanities corridor just to ruin the Maths mock was an act of pure spite. Even for you that was quite a *nadir* which, in case you don't know, means *low-point*." Inky shook his head gravely, "An act of pre-meditated malevolence designed to cause maximum disruption. Very naughty Mr Day."

The caretaker shot to his feet. A vein like a strand of spaghetti pulsed at Day's temple.

"Relax great ape," said Inky casually, "we both know you didn't do it. But unfortunately I've an army of witnesses who can be persuaded otherwise. There's no smoke without fire, after all. And your recent activities have created so much smoke the fire-brigade could be involved, if you understand my mixed metaphor?" He went on, "And you were hidden away in your secret den at the time, right next to the damaged sensor so you can be placed at the crime-scene. I *do* have witnesses for that. The photographs you took of the resulting playground-chaos further implicates you." Inky extended his palms in mock-sympathy, "When you're caught in quicksand, Day-Glo, no-one's going to notice an extra bucket of grit being poured over that shiny head of yours. It's all going to suck you down anyway, kicking and screaming." Inky rubbed his chin, "Perhaps we could also implicate you in Miss Birkin's attack too, to round things off with a full-house. Let's face it, Rocket-man, I'm now in control of your fate. Feel free to sit back down whenever you choose, you're blocking out my light. And no," Inky stated, "that wasn't a request, it was a demand."

Inky waited for Day to shrink back into his armchair.

"There's a good boy," Inky patronised. "So, as a little recap, if you don't do exactly as I say, it'll be Game Over for you. Reputation. Career. Perhaps we can even throw a few criminal charges into the mix too? Prison?" Inky made a show of looking at his watch, "Mr Bennett will be arriving in about a minute with the rest of the posse. I'm only giving you the heads-up out of the kindness of my heart. Because I care, you see," Inky smiled, savouring every word of his revenge. "You'll thank me one *Day*. So, let me tell you what you're going to do now, Day-o. You have a choice of course... but then again, you don't. That's why I'm sitting here cool as a cucumber whereas you're shaking like King Kong on top of the Empire State."

Nostrils flaring, Day eyed Inky with pure vitriol. Yet instead of launching himself forwards, he remained seated.

Ray Day was terrified.

* * *

Free of his bindings, Jean-Pierre Asticot had wasted no time in releasing Deidre. Once he'd reassured himself of his companion's welfare, he'd immediately turned his attention to escape. Despite having an assortment of tools readily to hand, breaking out of their bedroom-cell hadn't proved easy. While Deidre recovered, Asticot had first chipped away at the door's lock with a screwdriver. Then, using the five-iron golf-club, he'd finally managed to prise the door from its frame. Both he and Deidre had then clambered through the wreckage into the lounge. Asticot had then opened up the balcony-doors and emerged out into bright daylight, drawing in deep lungfuls of fresh, winter air. On her part, Deidre was completely overcome. She'd sat on the settee massaging her wrists. Weary, yet relieved.

Now composed, Asticot strode back through the lounge, golf-club in hand.

"Where are you going?" Deidre croaked.

"Where do you think I'm going? I'm getting out of here. Now. First I'll telephone my office in Mal-de-Mer then I'm going to walk over the road to the Police Station and tell them what's really been going on in this miserable little town."

"No you're not!"

Jean-Pierre Asticot stopped. Stunned.

"I'm sorry but I simply cannot allow you to do that, sir," she continued. "We made a promise to that young man, Stevens. He's the only reason we're standing here now. He enabled us to escape and, now that we're free, it's only fair that we honour his request. He said that he was going to set a trap for that loathsome pair, one which would guarantee enough evidence to send both of them down for good. So that's exactly what we're going to let him do. It's only a few more hours, Jean-Pierre. When you're my age, what difference is a couple more hours going to make? Some people call me *a queer old bird* because of my silly ways, but that's who I am, monsieur," the steel in her voice was apparent, "that's what makes me, me. Sorry, sir, but leaving here before five-fifteen is not an option. This is my guest-house and those are my rules!"

Asticot leaned up against a wall to consider Deidre's outburst. Eventually he let the five-iron fall to the floor, "D'accord," he said plainly. "So what do you suggest we do?"

"This is a guest-house, monsieur. There are always lots of things to do. Especially in the light of," she paused to take in her surroundings, "in the light of what's happened. You, young man, are going get that fire going downstairs. But first... we are going to have ourselves a nice cup of tea."

Asticot smiled, "But of course, madame. We are in Britain, after all. How could I forget my manners? It will be my pleasure to serve..."

"Don't you dare, young man!" she said, slapping him playfully on the wrist. "After everything we've been through, that pleasure will be all mine!"

* * *

Ray Day sat opposite Inky.
Broken.

"Now, Day-o," said the teenager, calmly, "we've only about thirty seconds left so I'll wrap this up quickly. Right now you're going to leave this school forever. You will stand up, walk out of the school gates and never come back. Do Not Pass Go. Do not collect anything. All you'll take with you is what you're wearing. Nothing more. You will never set foot in this town, or indeed this county ever again. Because if you do I have all the evidence necessary to bring you down." Inky sneered, "And nothing would give me greater pleasure, believe me. The final clause in our arrangement is that you make contact with Mr Rowlandson one, final time. You will inform him that Blinkton Comprehensive School will finish above St Derek's in the forthcoming table of mock exam results. I don't care how Rowlandson achieves this, or to what lengths he has to go to fudge, swap, massage and manipulate the figures. He'll be able to find a way. People like him always do." Inky leaned forwards, "But it will happen or I'll bring him down and St Derek's with him. And you, of course. The bigger they are the harder they fall, eh Day-o? Right," Inky gestured towards the door, "that's about time-up by my reckoning. Give Roger a kiss from me…"

Day held his pumpkin-sized head in his hands. He remained motionless for several moments then, having reached a decision, stood up. Swaying slightly, he glared at Inky, face the colour of beetroot. He opened his mouth to speak but, unsure of what to say, closed it again.

In silence, Ray Day plodded towards the door. Stooped and clueless.

Then, finally realising what it was that he wanted to say, Day lurched back towards Inky. Exploding with fury, the beefcake caretaker slapped his hands on the armrests of Inky's chair. With the wood creaking in protest, Day lowered himself down, stopping only when his face was an inch away from Inky's. Top lip twitching, Day's voice was hoarse, "Think you've won, don't you, Stevens?"

Inky returned his opponent's stare, "I know I've won, Day-o. Time for an early bath, I'm afraid. And from this distance it smells like you need one."

"Oh yes I'll go, Stevens. I'm out of here. But I promise you, this isn't over. I'll wait. I'll wait until you think I must've tired of waiting. Then I'll wait some more. But just when you least expect it, I'll be back. You may have won the battle, Stevens, but you haven't won the war. If I was you," he whispered, "I wouldn't let my guard down. Not now. Not ever!" To emphasise his point Day shunted Inky's chair backwards in a single explosive movement. It squealed on the concrete then slammed back against solid brick. Then, sensing the chair's fragility, Day wrenched one of its armrests free of its fixings. The sound of splintering wood echoed around the room. Day hoisted the severed limb into the air then flung it down towards Inky's feet in fury.

Snorting.

Both caretaker and detective watched it disintegrate into kindling, the fractured wood scattering throughout the room. Then, with a savage grunt, Ray Day turned, stepped over the debris, and strode our into the December morning. Inky's last memory of Ray Day was of the reflection on the back of his head changing from the orange of the strip-light to the milky grey of the wintry cloud cover outside.

Ray Day was gone.

Relieved at his departure, Inky nevertheless pondered that somehow, for some reason, he didn't feel he'd seen the last of Ray Day.

'You may have won the battle, Stevens, but you haven't won the war.'

By mid-morning Inky found himself back at Mike Bennett's desk. At the agreed time his phone began to sound. On the third ring Inky picked up the receiver and placed it to his ear. The detective listened carefully to Scott Cunliffe's revelations,

"Even more interesting than expected," he said. "Just one task remaining for you now, Scotty. Then you're off the hook. I'll meet you at the railway station... No don't worry about that, I'll bring everything along with me. I have it all bagged up ready for you... Yes, of course I'll run through arrangements one more time. Don't panic, it'll be me in danger, not you. Just get a move on, your train back leaves at one twenty-four. Make sure you're on it. See you at three-seventeen."

Inky Stevens hung up the receiver.

The arrival of lunchtime saw the clouds which had been gathering all morning begin their discharge. Small flakes of snow floated down peacefully only to be snatched by packs of giddy schoolkids below. Rebecca Plant took particular delight in catching as many snowflakes as possible in the centre of her palm, then licking them off before they'd had time to melt. Lynn Smith and her friend Veronica Whiting reclined upon wet ground in a desperate attempt to make 'snow angels'.

Elsewhere, clusters of students huddled in doorways discussing arrangements for the following night's disco...

'Who're you going with?'

'What time you going?'

'What you gonna wear?'

And more importantly...

'Who're you going to ask to dance at the end of the night?'

Inky, aware of the mounting excitement, slipped underneath Broker's Arch, then out through the school gates. With so many distractions, his escape was effortless. Not one person saw him leave.

The Great School Detective strode down into town leaving distinct footprints in snow which was already beginning to settle underfoot.

A storm was brewing.

If everything went according to plan then the school disco would be a fitting celebration to work well done, both for Inky and for the rest of the student population.

If things failed to go according to plan, however...?

17. St Hilda's Church:

Thursday 22nd December (Evening).

The snowstorm had intensified during the afternoon trapping all of Blinkton within its icy jaws. Fierce squalls laden with thick flakes had blown in from over the sea so that, by evening, the landscape was carpeted in a vast blanket of white.

And still the snow continued to fall...

The Asticots, wary of leaving tell-tale footprints, had changed their plans accordingly. They'd opted not to approach St Hilda's Church from the front, but through Bluebell Wood to the rear instead. They'd thus reached the church's perimeter under the cover of both the wood and the storm's blurry darkness.

Jean-Pierre Asticot, sweating profusely, cradled his hands and set them down onto his knee. Son-Jack accepted the step up and clambered up onto the wall. From there, by pivoting on his stomach, the teenager manoeuvred around in order to stretch a hand down to his senior. Moments later both had scaled the wall then dropped down onto the graveyard's thick covering of snow. The duo quickly identified a suitable gravestone then crept up behind it to await the arrival of Maude Perkins. Their chosen headstone was one embedded so firmly into the ground that it could have been hurled down from the church tower way up above. It provided both excellent cover and an uninterrupted view of the church door, (far off and to the right). In this way, *the Asticots* were in position several minutes ahead of Deidre's five o'clock deadline. Exactly as intended.

The schemers began their vigil full of optimism. They scanned their surroundings intently while keeping one eye on the enormous church clock which slowly ticked away the seconds, beat by beat. If everything went according to plan they'd be back in their Citroën and out of Blinkton well before the bell ringers had arrived to foul the winter air at half-past five. Their car was already loaded up ready. Parked just the other side of Bluebell Wood.

Jean-Pierre whispered, "This Perkins-woman better be on time otherwise I'll personally give Butterfield what-for back at the guest-house!"

While father and son then settled to their respective thoughts, the snow continued to fall. And although their clothing soon became damp and cold, neither allowed personal discomfort to interrupt their concentration. Instead, they peered out from either side of the gravestone like sentries.

Eyes trained.

Waiting. Patiently waiting.

From concealment *the Asticots* were afforded a Christmas-card view of the magnificent church. St Hilda's was set at the centre of its grounds, encircled by a wide path. Of Norman design, the ancient place of worship was all about straight lines and strength. Its walls were heavy and thick, made from blocks of rough-hewn stone. Its windows were little more than open slits. From above, the church's cross-shape became apparent, its nave extending all the way towards the east-facing chancel. At its west an imposing tower rose up like a cliff-face. Square and solid, this was topped off with a two-tiered wall which gave it the appearance of battlements. From there, a steeple extended even further upwards like a giant splinter. This was crowned with a brass cross so high above the ground that it appeared to connect St Hilda's to the sky above.

Despite the winter dark, the snow's whiteness gave the structure's time-blackened stone an otherworldly appearance. St Hilda's was a tremendous feat of architecture.

And all the while the snow continued to settle all around, smooth as Christmas-cake icing... on gravestones, holly bushes and the tiled roof of the lichgate. Even the gargoyles clinging onto the church walls wore snow-wigs like macabre high court judges.

Jack studied the snowscape, alert to the slightest movement. Gazing up at the clock, he caught sight of a clump of snow falling from the top of the tower. Seconds later it landed heavily with an audible *thwump*.

And still *the Asticots* waited.

The giant church clock crawled its way towards five o'clock... then passed it. *Jean-Pierre* contemplated a return to the Harbor Lites to unleash his frustration on his prisoners. When he saw it...

Movement.

Unmistakeable. Far off in the distance.

From the bottom of Rectory Lane a decrepit figure approached. An old lady hobbled up the snow-filled avenue. Her duffel coat, crimplene skirt and wellington boots looked so big on her that they seemed to envelop the whole of her frail body.

After what seemed like an age, Maude Perkins passed under the lichgate. She paused to draw breath then trudged up the path towards the church. Because her boots shifted on the uneven snow, she moved with agonising slowness. Like *the poor man gath'ring winter fuel* in the popular song, she cut an abject figure battling the unforgiving elements.

The Asticots, frustrated by Perkins' sluggishness, were heartened by the fact that she'd appeared at all. From hiding, they squinted into the storm in order to monitor her approach. As she neared, *Jean-Pierre* attempted to catch a glimpse of her face, but he was impeded by the hood of a coat which she stubbornly held down for protection.

Reaching the church, Perkins produced a large key. She duly inserted this into the locked door with arthritic fingers made doubly-painful by the cold. Seconds later a loud *click* resonated all around the churchyard and Perkins disappeared inside.

Jack turned to his father, perplexed.

"Don't worry, son. She'll be turning the alarm system off. Once the old goat's done that and then turned the lights on, she'll clear off. If she knows what's good for her!" he sneered.

Sure enough, moments later, the church's lights lit up one bank at a time. The glow of the electric light on falling snow gave it a radiant aura.

Like a halo.

As Jack gazed through the church windows at the festive decorations within, Maude Perkins suddenly reappeared. Deidre's friend then closed the church door, thrust her hands deep into her coat pockets and retraced her way back along the path. Moving even slower than before, she shuffled back under the lichgate then made her way down Rectory Lane.

From their hiding place, *the Asticots* watched Maude's gaunt figure being swallowed within the whiteness of the storm.

"She was late," said Jack, no longer mindful lowering his voice. "The stupid old bat's cost us valuable minutes."

"Relax," came the reply, "we've still more than enough time to raid Parkinson's grave. Plus, I don't think the bell ringers'll be turning out in this weather, anyway. And the pantomime's not 'til much later, if that's still going ahead." *Asticot* produced a screwdriver from his pocket, "If this little thing won't unscrew Parkinson's plaque we could always use it to lever it clean off. We'll be in and out of there in a jiffy. Has she gone?"

"Can't see her."

"And there's no-one else around?"

"Don't think so."

"Good," said *Asticot*, with a grin. "Come on then, Jackie-boy, it's time for us to make some money...!"

And with that, father and son left the protection of their grave, grateful of the opportunity to stretch legs which had been cramped for too long. As they crept along they weaved in between headstones, monuments and snow-covered shrubs. They moved cautiously, constantly on the look out.

"Here goes, Jackie-boy," said *Asticot*, on reaching the church door. "As you know I'm not a religious man, but if I were, I'm guessing this could be the answer to all our prayers!"

As arranged, the stooped figure in the duffel coat continued to trudge *her* way down Rectory Lane. Then, as *Maude Perkins* came to a sycamore tree rendered skeletal by the season, *she* quickly darted behind its trunk.

'So far so good,' thought Scott Cunliffe checking his watch, *'bang on time.'* Ignoring the cold, Cunliffe dug beneath the snow to retrieve the holdall that he and Inky had buried there an hour before. He rummaged inside for his own clothes, quickly swapping them for Inky's grandma's clothes which he'd been forced to wear. As Cunliffe thrust his arms back into his own anorak he cursed at how stupid he must have looked, dressed up like a granny. At least the wellington boots were his.

Shivering, Cunliffe zipped up his coat and then the holdall. With fingers suddenly free of arthritis, he heaved the sports-bag up onto his shoulder.

'Inky owes me for this, big time. I don't care what I did to Miss Birkin, nothing in the world's worth this amount of humiliation. After all this is over, Inky and I are quits, and if he ever dares tells anyone...!?'

Cunliffe checked his watch again, mindful of Inky's very specific schedule. Satisfied, he stepped back out onto Rectory Lane. No longer hunched over, he retraced his tracks, tracks which were already being covered over by the snow. Fired up, his progress back to St Hilda's took him only about a quarter the time as previously...

The Asticots, having entered St Hilda's through by its west door, found themselves in the church's utility room. This specially adapted space housed the church's mechanics... banks of light switches, pipework, a sink, and a series of ropes connected to the church bells far up above. Pressing on, they travelled through a small wooden door and found themselves under a wooden canopy supporting the organ loft. From there, the main body of the church opened out in front of them. Cavernous and majestic. Momentarily awestruck, the pair were met by an unmistakeable smell. The sickly aroma of incense was inescapable, as if centuries of devotion had driven it into the very fabric of the building... into the stone pillars lining the central aisle, the raised pulpit, the wooden pews and the vaulted roof of interlocking beams. Even the font, around which the figures of the nativity were boldly displayed, seemed to be infused with the heavy scent of spirituality. Though not religious themselves, *the Asticots* couldn't help but be moved by St Hilda's atmosphere of soulful piety.

Yet awe-filled reflection was not going to make them rich.

Snapping out of their trance, the kidnappers set about their objective. *Jean-Pierre* paced up the central aisle, the echo of his footsteps filling the entire space. It was time to locate Geoffrey Parkinson's grave... then snatch its treasure.

As the thieving pair approached the altar they were confronted by an enormous stained-glass window. Stark and savage, its central image depicting the brutality of the crucifixion assaulted their senses. Christ's tortured form hung down from the cross, head bleeding and scarred. His agony was intensified by the boldness of the coloured glass. It was as if Jesus was staring down at those about to desecrate His house.

Expression pained and drawn.

Disapproving.

Reaching the sanctuary, the imposters were able to redirect their eyes. There, in the north transept, they were greeted by a patchwork of interlocking gravestones that made up the church floor. Although eroded over the centuries, the graves' original lettering was mostly intact. Words and phrases stood out with clarity...

In loving memory... Dearly cherished... Much missed... Sadly departed before his time.

But amongst such expressions of remembrance, the headstone of Geoffrey Parkinson was clearly identifiable. Right at the centre.

"Butterfield was right," said *Asticot*, pointing. "There he is."

"Parkinson's grave's the only one with a brass plaque on it," Jack confirmed. "Just as the stupid old dear said."

"Go on then, Jackie-boy," he brayed, "read it!"

Feeling uncomfortable, Jack knelt down and used his finger to trace out the individual words, "*Here lies Geoffrey William Parkinson, beloved husband of Agnes and father to Harry and Sam. Benefactor of Blinkton-on-Sea. Let those short on sustenance come to me for nourishment.*"

A broad smile spread across *the Frenchman's* features, "This is it, Jackie. This is what it's all been about." He began to recollect, "All those preliminary visits to Blinkton, ringing Carry to have him sort out our accommodation, abducting Monsieur le Mal-de-Mayor then dragging him halfway across Europe in a car with stolen plates..."

"Don't forget all my endless French classes," added Jack, with a sigh, "I thought I'd lost the will to live. All that conjugating of verbs and declining of nouns. Took me an age."

"My lessons too. Then, once we'd arrived in Blinkton, our manipulation of Carry and his army of lapdogs. Not to mention," he sneered, "us *immobilising* old-woman-Butterfield."

"'Til finally," said Jack, "in what was my finest hour... the setting off of the school-bell to create enough of a distraction..."

"... for me to break in to the Codfather and steal its treasures from under the noses of the emergency services." *Asticot* grinned, "There've been setbacks along the way, Jack, but we've made it now. Everything we've done has led us to this point. If the Codfather's secret recipe is beneath that brass inscription then it will transform our lives forever. Blinkton's had its own way for too long. Now it's our turn. Come on, let's get what we came for then leave this soulless town for ever..."

"For ever and ever, Amen!"

"Here's the screwdriver, Jackie-boy. Don't stand on ceremony. Just rip it straight off the floor!"

Jack took the implement and, for no reason he could explain, made the sign of the cross. Then, ever so carefully, he placed its blade underneath Geoffrey Parkinson's plaque.

At that moment, however, his act of vandalism was interrupted...

"I'll spare you the trouble, *Monsieur Parker*. There's nothing there!" boomed a voice that reverberated around the chamber. The lingering words seemed to emerge from nowhere yet everywhere at the same time.

Confused, Jack clambered to his feet while *Asticot* looked around wildly, both of them searching for the source of the disturbance.

"Carry on," urged the voice, "check for yourselves. Wrench Parkinson's plaque clean off if you like. I can wait. I have all the time in the world, *Parker*."

Inky Stevens stood statuesque up inside the organ loft. The outline of his silhouette was sharp and focused against the organ's pipework. He looked down from his perch, hands resting on its wooden rail.

The avenging angel.

"I'm up here."

Asticot's head jerked upwards. Seeing Inky for the first time, he cried out,

"Who are you?"

"I know who he is," blurted Jack, "he's just some know-it-all kid from school. Thinks he's something special. He had a go at me yesterday. Tried to humiliate me in front of my mates. Damn near broke my arm too. Thought it was funny to squeeze my head like it was a great big zit."

Inky countered, "About as funny as forcing a defenceless fourth-year lad to eat your spit-covered cigarette, eh? I warned you that if you crossed me, I'd be back. Well here I am, *Jackie-boy*. I don't make threats that I can't follow though. Unlucky for you sunshine, it's judgement day!"

Asticot whirled around, "What's he talking about, Jack? What have you done? You never mentioned anything about this to me. You said everything was fine with our scheme. You said..."

"Your *scheme*," Inky mocked, hands gripping the ancient wood like talons, "was designed to deprive Blinkton of its most valuable possession. And," he added, "you almost pulled it off. *Almost*," he repeated for effect, letting the word resonate. "Yet not factoring me into your equation was a *grave* mistake. Because I'm here now to put an end to your greed. And all to turn around the fortunes of a seedy Fish and Chip shop in Plumpton Sands, too."

"I don't know what you're...?

"Oh, come on," snapped Inky, "let's not play dumb, *Parker*. We all know what's really going on here. My assistant was outside your restaurant this morning, although," he paused, "I use the word *restaurant* loosely. 'I Believe I Can Fry', nice name by the way," he added, sarcastically, "credits both of you above its door, 'Harold Parker and Son'. That *son*, of course, being you Jack. I checked Plumpton's town records. You're actually seventeen. Bit too old to be playing pat-a-cake in a school playground, eh?"

Jack seethed, "What have you done, Stevens?"

"You appear to have dropped your accent all of a sudden, *Jacques Clouseau*! Perhaps it's something *we British* put in our tea, eh? And in response to your question, what I've done is to prevent your scheme of kidnapping, impersonation, vandalism and theft." Inky looked down with mock sympathy, "There never was any secret recipe for fish batter, Harold. It was all a myth. Just a heart-warming story that Geoffrey Parkinson, and every generation since, was happy to perpetuate in order to give the impression that their food contained something extra-special. Something that the real Jean-Pierre Asticot would call *je ne sais quoi*!"

Hot with anger, Harold Parker ventured up the central aisle leaving Jack behind, caught in two minds,

"What shall I do dad?"

Inky answered, "Do what you came to do, Jackie-boy. Lever that plaque off. You know you want to. But you'll find nothing underneath. All of this," Inky indicated the church, "was designed to ensnare you. You see, Deidre Butterfield and Jean-Pierre Asticot are working for me now. They've led you here based on some cock-and-bull story about Maude Perkins, bell ringers and the ghost of dear departed Geoffrey Parkinson. Maude Perkins has nothing to do with any bell ringers. It wasn't even her you've just seen. And did you seriously think that Big-Sean would scare me off? He couldn't have advertised his presence more obviously if he'd been wearing a sandwich-board proclaiming COME IN TO THE HARBOR LITES. I'LL BE HAVING A FAG SO FEEL FREE TO WAIT INSIDE AND HELP YOURSELF TO THE MINI-BAR!"

Parker glared at his son.

Inky scoffed, "That church door wasn't even locked. Just like the door at the Harbor Lites, it never is. But I don't suppose a pair of chancers like you even bothered to check?"

Harold Parker stared at Inky, eyes burning with hatred.

"Thought not. Bell ringing practice is actually on Mondays," Inky smirked. "You followed the paper trail I laid out for you like the simpletons you are. And," he added, "in case you're worried about the welfare of your hostages, I gave them a knife to free themselves. They'll be walking into Blinkton's Police Station right about now," Inky framed his words carefully, "if they've managed to contain themselves for this long. The *fishing net's* closing in, and," Inky lowered his voice, "you've much more than a hotel bill to settle before I'll let you leave."

"Dad," said Jack, impatient, "shall I check out this grave, or what?"

Parker spun around, "Just shut up, Jack," he yelled. "Can't you make a simple decision for once in your life?"

Jack Parker, after some hesitation, stepped back towards Parkinson's headstone and sank to his knees. While he toiled away with the screwdriver, all that was visible of him behind the front pew was his thick mane of hair. When he reappeared, he shrugged.

"Told you," crowed Inky. "There is no secret recipe. The only secret, just as the manuscript said, is to add *a pinch of a prayer* to your food. Prepare it with *kindness and love.*" Inky's tone changed, "I've researched your shop on the school's computer. It's on the seafront at Plumpton Sands. Judging by appearances, Parker, you've not adopted such principles yourself. 'I Believe

I Can Fry's' not fit for purpose. My assistant phoned back the results of this morning's fact-finding mission. He said that your building's dilapidated, your menu's limited, your prices are exorbitant and that your standard of hygiene, according to the locals, is questionable at best. There's a sign on your chip-shop door saying you'll be closed from Friday December 9th onwards. Co-incidentally," Inky championed, "that's the same weekend that your unholy crusade began in the south of France... with the theft of the car-registration plate that you've just confessed to."

As he spoke, Harold Parker's ponytail shook like a spaniel's tail, "Plumpton Sands? Sorry, I don't know what you're talking about, erm..."

Jack came to his father's assistance, "His name's Inky Stevens."

"Stevens, eh? Well, you see, Stevens, I've never even been to Plumpton..."

"Don't patronise me, Parker. Number plates, you imbecile!"

Uncertainty clouded the shop owner's features.

"You journeyed all the way to Mal-de-Mer in a battered Citroën to kidnap its Mayor, who," Inky added, "you then impersonated in an audacious attempt to infiltrate its twin-town, our town, Blinkton-on-Sea. This, you hoped, would provide you with an opportunity to steal our greatest asset, the Codfather's world-famous recipe. Your Golden Meal Ticket, or so you thought," Inky mocked. "Yet you made a fundamental error by leaving the Citroën's original plate in the footwell. I saw it behind the passenger seat last night. Although covered with rope, the 'JM6' at the beginning and 'C' at the end were plainly visible. And, of course, the first two letters of any British plate indicate where every car is registered. Thus, with only minimal research, I was able to link you to Plumpton Sands, a similar seaside town to ours less than twenty miles away." Inky explained, "You arriving in town expressing a *penchant* for fish and chips and then the Codfather's door being vandalised. It all seemed too co-incidental." The pace of Inky's delivery quickened, "And when I discovered that this crime took place during a blizzard at exactly the same time all our emergency services were distracted by a false alarm up at school, I began to smell something rather *fishy*. Especially when I subsequently discovered that the school-bell was actually set off by one of these supposed VIPs. Come on, Harold," Inky mocked, "I won't insult your intelligence. Joining the dots between that alarm, fish and chips, Plumpton Sands and then you was child's play. Yours is the only *chippie* in the vicinity of Plumpton's car-registration district that could do with a taste of the Codfather's success. Coincidence? Not a chance!" Inky scorned, "You make me sick. Both of you. All you were after was money. As if a magic seasoning formula would guarantee you the same success as the Codfather!" The detective shook his head, "What a jolly holiday you must've had here. Everyone scurrying around after the pair of you. Well," he added, bitterly, "you didn't fool me!"

Casting the screwdriver aside, Jack moved to his father's side, "It wasn't me who set that alarm off, Stevens," he whined. "You can't prove nothing. I wasn't the only one in the Humanities corridor that day..."

Inky raised his hand, "So you admit you were there?"

"Yes... well, no... no..."

"You're right," said Inky, hitting stride immediately, "about one thing at least. It's true that you weren't the only one in that corridor. But," he added, "of the five possible suspects each can be easily eliminated. Except you." He explained, "Amanda Blunt excused Tommy Woggle from Mr Henry's History lesson with a forged note because she needed to talk to him. As neither were seen leaving before the alarm went off they can both be placed at the scene." Inky went on, "Blunt's not one for subtlety. She has a crush on Oggy, you see, and was compelled to find out whether young-Tommy felt the same. Life hasn't been easy for Amanda and she was terrified of rejection. For her to pluck up enough courage to ask Oggy to the Christmas disco wasn't easy. So when you interrupted them in the corridor, she grabbed hold of Tommy and dragged him into the Girls' Toilet. Neither of them saw you arrive, but they both heard *someone*."

"I don't know what you're talking about."

"No," Inky raised his eyebrows, "then how come you locked them both in? You removed your belt and looped it around the toilet door handles. Trapping them left you alone to trigger the alarm. Had there been a real fire, Jackie-boy, they could both have been burned alive. But then fish-batter's much more important, isn't it?"

Jack Parker looked at the floor.

"Lucky Oggy's so skinny. He was able to wriggle out through the narrow toilet window to save the day. In the process he scratched his face on the metal catch and also ripped his shirt. Blunt boasted that, *'he came back for me'*. Tommy Woggle battled against the tide of fleeing students, re-entered the building, and undid the clasp on your belt to rescue her. It's been on the floor down there ever since. No wonder you're always hitching up your trousers. Nice underpants, by the way. Orange is so *de rigueur* these days," Inky mocked.

Harold Parker looked at his son with contempt. Instinctively Jack felt for his belt loops, then slid his hands down into his pockets.

"Young Crispin Merridew from the second-year was hosting a cake-sale upstairs when you struck. Merridew's information was crucial in helping me to ascertain exactly who was where, when. It couldn't have been him who set off the alarm. If he'd left his wares unattended, even for a second, they'd have been stolen or vandalised. The fact that they weren't proves he was at his station throughout. There were empty bun cases at the scene but no evidence of any food having being knocked over or vandalised. And that area clearly hasn't been cleaned all week. Besides," Inky explained, "wanton vandalism's not in Merridew's character. And as for Ray Day our school's *ex*-caretaker, well he had a different agenda altogether. Although present on the corridor, he was inside his maintenance cupboard and didn't make an appearance 'til afterwards. If *he'd* triggered the alarm he would have photographed the resulting chaos, not stopped to help Merridew pack away. Day wouldn't have missed out on another delicious opportunity to record Blinkton School at its very worst." Inky affirmed, "So although Day photographed the subsequent disruption in the yard, the fact that he wasn't so trigger-happy around the Hall tells me that he wasn't aware that anything disruptive was about to happen. Which," said Inky, plainly, "just leaves you, Jackie-boy. Working in partnership with daddy, you've a cast-iron motive. You gave Brandon Lunt the slip last Friday and instead of going to Woodwork, Merridew told me all about where you really were. Plus your French," said Inky with derision, "although impressive, does have minor flaws..." Inky spoke over Jack's intended protest, "and most important of all, you left a small fragment of your glove inside the sensor's casing. I felt its indentation when I made a point of taking you by the hand after your sickening display of bullying yesterday." Inky scowled, "You deserve everything that's coming to you, Jackie-boy. You're too old to be at school anyway." His voice assumed a tone of pained simplicity, "So," he paused, "are either of you still going to try to pretend that this charade's nothing to do with you?"

In the ensuing silence a savage gust of wind buffeted the church.

Harold Parker suddenly wheeled around. Before Jack knew what was happening his father had ripped the glove from his hand to inspect it. Finding a small hollow at the index finger Parker hurled it into the bank of pews, "You complete and utter fool," he yelled. He seized Jack by the throat and backed him up against the nearest pew. Consumed by rage, Parker pressed at Jack's windpipe, hard. Yet while Jack tried to loosen his father's grip, Parker continued to rebuke, "One thing, Jack," he yelled. "One simple, little thing you had to do..."

"Ugh... uugghh...."

"... but it was too difficult, wasn't it? I can't rely on you for anything..."

"Urgh... uurrgghh...."

"You're a waste of space. Instead of helping me out in the chip-shop all you do is sit on your backside at home..."

"Buutt..."

"... and you've been no different here. If you'd applied yourself in the first place then we might not be in this mess. Big-Sean? Don't insult my intelligence!"

"Buutt," Jack choked, fearful, "buutt... it... might...not..."

"Might not what?"

"Might... not be over," he gasped.

Parker's grip finally relaxed. He let his son drop to the floor.

Clutching his throat, Jack Parker squirmed, "It might not..." he wheezed, "It might not be over. Stevens is a loner... a freak. He has no friends... Everyone... everyone says he's a weirdo... He won't've told anyone. No-one would listen to him anyway. No-one would believe all this. Would you? Despite what he's said, I can't... can't hear the cavalry arriving. Can you, dad? He's no proof anyway. Not really."

Inky's voice rang out, triumphant, "But that's where you're wrong." From his coat pocket the super-sleuth removed a small, square box. A red light pulsed on its surface while a thin wire trailed off beneath. Inky held it aloft, "See this?" he asked, "it's a recording device. I took it from Ray Day's Maintenance Room this morning. And guess what?" he said, "I've just recorded everything you've just said. With acoustics as good as St Hilda's it'll have picked up everything that you've just said. Clear as an alarm bell. Your whole plan neatly summed up in your own words. I think that'll make pretty compelling evidence in court. Don't you, Parker?"

Flexing his hands, Harold Parker glared up at Inky's shadowy figure. Raging mad.

"Dad. What Stevens says changes nothing. Not so long as we can get our hands on that device and then take care of him. No-one else in Blinkton knows who we are. Who we really are. If Butterfield and Asticot really are free, then time's running out. But I can't hear the rescue party, can you? We do still have some time," he implored. "Our dream may have collapsed, for now, but it doesn't have to end. We can still shut him up and then clear off..."

"Shut him up, how?"

"I think you know how, dad!"

Parker's eyes sparkled with evil. He turned away from Inky and discreetly slid his hand beneath the thick material of his coat. Then, in a single movement, he withdrew his pistol and aimed it up into the organ loft...

Into thin air.

Inky had turned on his heels and vanished.

The young-investigator shot past the organ's pipework and out into the spiral staircase beyond. From there it was simply a case of running and running, turning and turning, following the direction of the stairs. Higher and higher, coat flapping out behind. Gone...

Like a bat to the belfry.

Jack Parker rose to his feet, frantic, "He's getting away, dad."

Parker looked at his son with derision, "Are you going to be a cretin all your life, Jack? This boy, Stevens, may have escaped, but there's nowhere for him to go. There's only one staircase up that bell tower. Just one way up. The same way down. So we can take our time. We're going to flush him out like a rat from the sewer. That kid's going nowhere." Parker brushed his moustache with a hand still clutching his pistol, "And once we've sorted him out, we can all disappear. Come on."

Parker led his son beneath the organ loft and out into the utility room, "There," he said, pointing towards a wooden door cut into the stone, "give that a try."

Jack placed his fingertips onto the door as if testing the heat of a dinner plate. Satisfied, he slowly pushed against it. The sound of creaking hinges immediately filled the cramped space. Parker, glimpsing the base of the staircase, shoved his son to one side and thrust his head into the darkened space, "This is it," he yelled, "we've got you now, Stevens. It's time to meet your maker!"

Flipping a light switch, the stairway was instantly bathed in electric light.

"Right Jackie-boy," said Parker, "it's time for us to squash a particularly troublesome cockroach."

Pistol leading the way, Harold Parker disappeared into the alcove then up the narrow staircase. Jack Parker followed a pace behind. Heavy boots were planted one at a time onto steps worn down over centuries. And as the pair slowly wound upwards, Parker remained vigilant. Left hand placed onto the wall's curvature, his other directed the pistol up the stairs.

Turning and turning. Higher and higher. Passing narrow windows which allowed the storm to cut in and slice the chalky air.

A number of small rooms led off the staircase at intervals. Firstly, not far above ground-level, was the organ loft. Directly above this was a storeroom containing ecclesiastical items... broken pews, vestments, a set of baskets for Harvest Festival and a wobbly lectern. Each time, the Parkers' procedure for examining such spaces was the same... father kicked open the door, simultaneously pointing his weapon inside. Once father'd reassured himself, he then ushered son-Jack in for a more thorough search. Pistol on standby.

Yet neither organ loft nor storeroom had revealed sight nor sound of a rogue detective. Which left just one remaining hiding place...

The belfry at the top of the tower.

After a steady climb, the imposters reached the place where the staircase ended. There, they were greeted by one, final door...

'And Stevens has to be behind it. There's nowhere else he can be.'

With a nod of his head, Harold Parker enquired whether Jack was ready. The teenager nodded back, a lump in his throat. Parker slowly raised his pistol. And then...

Everything went black.

Scott Cunliffe had stood outside the door to St Hilda's for a number of minutes with Inky's sports-bag slung over his shoulder. While the snow had settled all around him, he'd placed his ear up against the wood to listen. He'd initially heard raised voices, then a quite loud curse and the hurried sound of footsteps. But after that everything had gone quiet. At that point, as instructed, Cunliffe had timed two additional minutes. Satisfied that no-one was on the other side of the door, he'd then cautiously opened it and peered inside.

Silence.

Finding nothing out of place in the utility room, Cunliffe set about Inky's final request. Blowing on stiff hands, he dropped his holdall onto the floor and positioned himself in front of the staircase door. Reaching up, he found an iron bolt set into the doorframe. He heaved this across with some difficulty. The metal was rough to touch but, despite decades of use, remained strong. It slid into place with a sturdy *thud*. Squatting, Cunliffe then repeated the process with an identical bolt only inches off the ground. Then, with a grunt, he tugged at the door to make sure it didn't move. Satisfied, he unzipped Inky's sports-bag and removed a large, stainless steel padlock. Inky'd explained how he'd screwed an extra lock into the doorframe earlier *just to be on the safe side*. Cunliffe swung its clasp across then inserted the padlock into the hasp, squeezing it shut with a reassuring *clunk*. Once more he tugged on the door to double-check that it wouldn't budge. Reassured, he then placed the keys at the base of the door just as Inky had instructed. Finally, he stood back to admire his handiwork. Nothing short of industrial-strength explosives was going open the utility room door. Whoever it was who Inky had lured up the tower... they would be staying there.

Cunliffe, feeling strangely proud himself, scooped up the holdall. Although he hated how Inky'd been able to manipulate him, he had to admit that being involved in the detective's mission (costume aside) had been immensely exciting. Fighting the urge to pull on the bell ropes just to see what they sounded like, he made to leave, then remembered the detective's instructions,

'*This one's for you Inky,*' he thought, reaching up and flipping off the stair-case light.

Scott Cunliffe's debt to Inky Stevens had been paid.

Harold and Jack Parker were immediately engulfed by darkness.

Bodies tense. Eyes wide open.

Fight or flight?

They stood motionless, like waxworks. Parker's gun remained trained on the belfry door while Jack, several steps beneath, stayed poised and alert. As time slipped by, their eyes slowly become accustomed to the tower's grainy darkness.

Silence.

In the semi-blackness Parker took control once more. Gesturing with his pistol, he communicated that he was about to force open the remaining door. Jack gave him a nervy thumbs-up. Parker instigated a countdown with his free hand...

Three... two... one....

On *zero* the pair launched themselves into action. Father kicked open the door and leapt into position, pistol raised. Son darted past him, body tense, weight balanced.

Then, having gained entry, they stopped.

Dead.

While the storm continued to rage outside, a stillness descended over the belfry. From far away, the sound of the sea crashing against sheer cliffs could be heard.

The kidnappers assessed the room which confronted them...

The belfry, like the rooms below it, was incredibly cramped. A wooden

walkway extended round all four sides of the room acting as a crude platform. In the corner opposite, a hollow set of steps led up to a hatchway set
into the ceiling which, in turn, led out onto the roof. Four oversized, bronze
bells were stationed at the centre of the space. These hung down partially out
of sight, sunk directly into the floorboards and connected to the ground-
floor by a series of wheels, pulleys and ropes. Although the bells dominated
the space they were unsuitable as a hiding place.

The Great School Detective simply was not there.

The belfry possessed eight arched-windows, two on each of its four sides.
These allowed winter light to filter in, coating the room in shadow. Beneath
each window a small pile of snow had blown in, then gathered in a mini-
drift. Harold Parker noted that the one nearest to him, just down to his left,
contained a bootprint. Clearly defined, the print was only minutes old. He
swallowed hard.

They were not alone.

Suddenly a shape shot towards him out of the darkness.

On instinct, Parker raised his weapon and fired. In the tight space the
explosion was deafening. A smell of sulphur immediately filled the air. While
Jack clutched at his ears, a startled creature alighted its progress. Screeching
in fear, the raven beat a hasty retreat through the window it'd just flown
through. Within seconds the bird had gone, lost amid the stormy whiteness.
A single feather floated down onto the wooden floor, the only evidence that
it had ever been there.

Jack slowly removed his hands, "Well there goes the element of surprise."

"I didn't know it was only a stupid bird, did I?"

"Neither did I, but I wasn't the one acting all *gung-ho*."

"Shhsshh!"

"What's the point in being quiet? You've just fired a gun. I didn't even
know it was loaded."

"Do you think I was going to tell you everything? Of course it's loaded.
Only five bullets left. Now shut up," Parker aimed the pistol at his son, "and
do as you're told. This is my show and we're going to do things my way.
Understand?"

"Yeah, that's how we usually do things," said Jack, resigned, "with you
pushing me around."

"Less of the pettiness!"

"Just point that thing away from me, OK?"

Parker slowly trained his weapon back into the belfry, "Follow me," he said, softly, "this isn't over. Not by a long way!"

From the bottom of Rectory Lane Scott Cunliffe heard a gunshot roll out down the avenue. Around him, a clamour of rooks took flight. Cunliffe began to think that perhaps Inky's missions weren't quite so thrilling after all. Feeling unsettled, he deliberated on whether or not to call the police. As if his thoughts had been telegraphed, the sound of sirens sparked up somewhere far in the distance. Scott Cunliffe was suddenly desperate to be somewhere else. Anywhere else. He turned to his left and ran headlong into a densely wooded area.

'Whatever Inky's involved himself in,' he thought, *'I want nothing more to do with it!'*

Harold Parker geared himself up to take his search even higher. He looked up at the wooden beams supporting the steeple. Tilting his head, he indicated for Jack to follow him. First, Parker travelled the short distance around the walkway...

Step by step. Inch by inch. Taking nothing for granted.

Mindful of facing into the room, Parker kept his pistol in constant motion. The weapon swept back and forth ready to hone in on a target in an instant.

Arriving at the steps opposite the door, Parker paused, then placed a foot onto the bottom rung. Testing its weight, he nodded to himself. He then signalled that he was about to begin his ascent. Inky Stevens simply had to be on the roof somewhere up above. There was nowhere else he could be.

Father gestured to son to keep guard then, one foot at a time, began his climb. Keeping his pistol on the trapdoor overhead, his progress up the few remaining steps was trouble-free. The stairs, though creaky, held Parker's weight comfortably. Reaching the top, he paused to look down, alarmed to see son-Jack showing signs of nerves. The chip-shop owner silently cursed to himself. This wasn't the time for second thoughts, they'd both come too far for that. It was time to put an end to what they'd started...

Parker placed his free hand against the smooth wood of the trapdoor above. Though crouched, he was able to plant his feet firmly onto the stairs and ready himself for the exertion to come. Composed, he trained the pistol on the door with one hand while pushing slowly upwards with the other. He was surprised to feel the trapdoor yield under only the slightest pressure. Suddenly, from the darkness above, a sprinkling of snow fell through the gap and landed on top of his head. Caught off guard, Parker immediately let go of the door. It slammed shut above his head.

Silence.

Jack looked up, puzzled.

Harold Parker bared his teeth in annoyance then proceeded to brush the snow from his scalp and shoulders. Cursing.

Silence.

Having regained his composure, Parker readied himself for another attempt. He clasped his pistol firmly, took a deep breath, then pushed upwards once more.

This time the fake-Mayor was prepared for the dusting of snow which came cascading down at him. Ignoring the wind which suddenly clawed his face, Parker caught his first glimpse of the church roof through the crack he'd created. He held the trapdoor steady, scouring the semi-dark for his prey. The snow up on the roof was lying about two inches deep and peering out just over the top of this he saw... nothing. Only the base of the steeple to his right and the stone of the tower-walls to his left and up ahead.

But no detective.

Parker remained where he was for several moments considering his next course of action.

'Inky Stevens has to be up here somewhere. He simply has to be!'

Arm aching under the trapdoor's weight, Parker felt compelled to continue his journey of recklessness. The ponytailed villain found himself deliberating whether to proceed violently at speed, or more delicately with caution. Yet the distant sound of police sirens forced his hand. With an anguished grunt he heaved the trapdoor upwards. Once the wooden board had passed vertical it fell backwards on itself, snow cushioning its landing.

Harold Parker reacted on instinct. Gun leading the way, he leapt up the remaining steps and sprang out onto the snow-covered roof. Exposed to the ferocity of the storm, he braced himself against snow which swirled before his eyes like strokes on a Van Gough masterpiece.

He was poised.

Ready for action.

He frantically scanned the blizzard, desperate for a glimpse of his target. His eyes shot from the slant of the steeple to the craggy stone of the ramparts and then down to the footprints imprinted in the wintry floor. Gun in constant motion. Primed to shoot...

(Desperate to shoot.)

But nothing.

Pause.

Once more Parker settled to catch his breath aware that Inky was still nowhere in sight.

He signalled down into the belfry. In response, Jack made the short climb up onto the roof, wooden steps creaking as before. He too emerged out into the bitter evening, hair tossed every which way, eyes scrunched against snow which flew at him in bursts.

"What do we do now?" he asked, clearly unsettled.

"Stevens is up here somewhere," came the reply, "look at the floor."

Jack did so and saw a single track of footprints disappearing around to the far side of the steeple.

"Those prints don't return, Jackie. That weirdo kid's on the other side."

"Can't you hear the sirens? They're getting louder, shouldn't we go?"

"No," yelled Parker, face twisted and savage, "we can't leave it here. Not now. It's too late for that. Come on, Jackie, let's go shoot ourselves a sitting duck!"

While Jack hesitated, his father moved on, step by deliberate step. Frustrated at his son's reluctance, he barked, "Come on, Jack. This is our last chance. Shut that trapdoor so he can't escape. Let's end it right here and now!"

Jack Parker hauled the trapdoor vertically then let it fall back with a definitive *whumph*. Then he shuffled towards his father with the storm mercilessly clawing at his clothing. Having joined up, the pair began to circle the rooftop, keeping the spire to their right. As space was restricted and the blizzard severe, their progress was slow. But they didn't have far to travel. Parker was right...

There was nowhere else for Inky Stevens to go.

The Great School Detective was waiting for them on the far side of the tower. He drifted into focus out of the whiteness like an image on photography paper.

"What kept you?" he said, plainly.

Inky was standing on top of the tower wall, hands pressed together in front of himself as if in prayer. Unsupported, he nevertheless appeared untroubled by the squalls which gusted all around him. He looked composed and assertive.

Angelic.

"It's over," said Inky, his voice torn from his mouth by the storm.

Parker laughed, "Well at least we agree on one thing, Stevens." From a distance of less than fifteen feet he raised his pistol.

"They're on their way," said Inky, indicating the sirens. "There's no escape."

"From where I'm standing it's you who's facing the firing squad."

"You're trapped," countered Inky, "the door at the bottom of this tower's been bolted from the outside. And then locked. Stainless steel. Unbreakable. There's no way out. Rather like those pathetic creatures in the dining room at the Harbor Lites, the net's closing in. You're stranded," he sneered, "like a fish out of water."

Jack called out, "You don't know what life's been like for us, Stevens."

"No I don't," replied Inky, curtly, "but hardship's no excuse for criminality. In this world there is no easy way. Hard work reaps fair reward. If you'd spent more time trying to make your business work than infecting us with your poison, then maybe you'd have stood a chance. But as it is, by washing up here in search of some mythical fish recipe," though lost to shadow, Inky's tone belied his smile, "it's you who's ended up being *battered*!"

"Why you...?" yelled Parker, but his words were drowned out by the sound of his pistol being fired. Abrasive and harsh. The noise of the gunshot was carried out to sea on the back of the storm.

Jack Parker, despite lunging, had been too late to prevent his father from squeezing the trigger.

Inky's fall was serene.

Beautiful.

There was no pained scream. No rapid movement or flailing limbs. He simply leaned backwards and, almost in slow-motion, disappeared over the tower-edge.

Father and son surged forwards, faces drained of colour, just in time to see the detective disappear into the frenzied whiteness. Inky Stevens didn't so much fall... as *fade-away*.

Like he'd simply *tuned-out*.

Jack Parker raised a hand to shield his eyes, earnestly scouring below for signs of what had happened. As he did so, he saw several sets of blue lights racing towards them, staining the storm's paleness like splashes of ink on blotting paper...

Pretty as fairy-lights on a tree...

18. Mike Bennett's Office:

Friday 23rd December (Morning).

Mike Bennett arrived early to school that Friday knowing that something bad had happened the night before.

Something very bad.

The whole of Blinkton was in shock. Many of its townsfolk had seen the army of emergency vehicles skidding along its icy roads. Lights flashing, sirens blaring. Everyone, it seemed, had come to their own conclusion as to what had happened. The vehicles' destination, according to gossip, had been St Hilda's Church. That evening's performance of 'Babes in Boots' had been cancelled accordingly. Some locals claimed to have heard a gunshot. Others claimed to have heard *several* gunshots. Jasper Thickett said that he'd seen a cannon being fired out at sea at a mermaid, but then it was generally wise to ignore anything that Jasper Thickett said. One thing that seemed to be generally agreed upon, however, was that Jean-Pierre Asticot was somehow involved. News had filtered back of an armed stand-off followed by an arrest. Mayor Carey, it was reported, had led the charge to quell the disturbance. Tales of corruption, fraud and impersonation bounced around like marbles in a tumble-dryer. Asticot, it was rumoured, had turned out to be someone quite different to who he said he was. It was said that he wasn't even French at all. That he was local. A man called Harold Parker. A fish and chip shop owner from Blinkton's rival seaside town, Plumpton Sands. It was also alleged that Jacques Asticot wasn't who he claimed to be either, just this man's seventeen year old son. Apparently neither individual was anyone of any particular importance. Just a pair of life's also-rans.

Such news had not gone down well at Blinkton School. Teenage boys dragged themselves to registration with hangdog expressions. Big-Sean had been spotted in the Senior Boys' Toilets shedding a discreet tear and consoling himself with an illicit cigarette. Clusters of girls huddled together sniffing noisily into damp tissues. Of everyone, there was only Brandon Lunt who seemed to have an extra spring in his step that day.

Yet such gossip sat heavily on Mike Bennett's shoulders. Blinkton's Deputy could feel the noose tightening. If such rumours were true then awkward questions would be asked about Jacques Asticot, questions he was not sure he'd be able to answer. And as the *French* teen had been one of the suspects in Inky's investigation, then perhaps Inky was also involved, or worse still, perhaps he'd even caused the whole affair. This, Bennett realised to his horror, could result in a tangled trail of wrongdoing leading back to his own door.

Mike Bennett was fearful for his career.

Mike Bennett... was in a state.

Having woken up even earlier than usual, Bennett had come into school before dawn only to drift aimlessly through empty corridors towards his office. From six-thirty onwards he'd tried to work while simultaneously ignoring his desk-phone which had rung at regular, five minute intervals (a fact which had only added to his sense of dread). So far Bennett had been successful in not answering it, partly through the promise he'd made to Inky, but mostly through fear of who might be on the other end. Yet Bennett knew that he could only ignore it for so long...

In the meantime, Blinkton's Deputy haphazardly placed red crosses into exercise books, willing Inky to arrive... yet fearful of what might happen when, or if, he did...

At a quarter to nine there was a knock on the office door. Bennett looked up in alarm but before he could say, *'Enter'* it had burst open and Inky marched in. While Bennett sat rooted to his office chair, the detective set a large manila envelope down onto one of the padded seats and sat down next to it. The super-sleuth then gestured for his teacher to sit opposite. As Mike Bennett clambered over piles of exercise books to join the detective, Inky noted the clearly defined patches of sweat which had formed under each of his arms. Bennett immediately attempted to instigate a conversation, but Inky cut straight across him,

"I'll be brief, sir, as registration's about to begin. There are a number of things I need to explain in a very short space of time. Some of what I'm about to tell you may be quite difficult to take in. Other parts of my account, I imagine, will be much easier to understand. Whatever, you need to listen very closely as what I'm about to reveal affects you directly."

"But will I...?"

"Will you have to cancel the Christmas disco? No. I've told you all along that that won't be necessary."

"That wasn't what I was going to ask, but that's good news anyway. Are you? Will you? I'm sorry..." he said, spluttering to a halt.

"I've told you before, sir, try to get some sleep. Now," Inky elicited eye-contact, "the person who threw a snowball at Miss Birkin was Ray Day, our school caretaker."

Bennett mouthed Day's name in astonishment.

Inky went on, "But you don't need to worry yourself on that score, sir, I've taken care of him. Day's left Blinkton and won't be coming back. It was a nasty occurrence, but then he's a nasty man. On a brighter note, I feel congratulations are in order..."

Bennett's brow creased.

"... I think you'll find that our exam results are going to be absolutely magnificent this time around."

Again Bennett looked confused.

"Trust me on that one. January's grades will reflect a sustained period of improvement, just you wait and see. And it's all down to you, sir," said Inky, evenly. "You'll have to wait until after Christmas for confirmation, of course, but do have a celebratory glass of sherry over the New Year in anticipation. You deserve it, sir. All your hard work in arranging the smooth running of the mocks has paid off..."

"But it wasn't all that smooth, not really."

"Don't be modest, sir, the proof, as I think you'll find, will be in the Christmas pudding. And as for the other *matter*," he dropped the word casually, "that needs to be handled a little more delicately. It was *Jacques Asticot* who set off the school-bell, the one which disrupted our Maths mock."

"I'd heard... Local news, well gossip actually... caused me to wonder, whether Jacques was...? 'Cause there's been a lot of concern, you see..." stuttered Bennett, failing to make sense.

Inky rose, placed his hands behind his back, and moved over to the window, "That facet of my investigation took an unexpected twist. *Jacques Asticot* turned out to be seventeen year old Jack Parker from Plumpton Sands..."

"Erm, I'd heard something to that effect..."

"He deliberately set off our alarm so that his father, a fish and chip shop owner from Plumpton Sands, could steal the Codfather's secret recipe undetected."

"Did they succeed?" asked Bennett, alarmed.

Inky turned as if affronted, "No, sir. No they did not," he went on, eyes sparkling, "thanks to you, sir. Congratulations, you're a hero!"

"Me?" choked Blinkton's Deputy.

The resulting pause was interrupted by a knock at the door. All too quickly, Bennett yelled, "Go away I'm busy!" before urging, more softly, "Carry on Stevens, keep talking. What's all this about? Me a hero? I don't follow..."

Inky made Bennett wait, "It took me a short while but eventually I worked out what was happening. You see, appearances can be very deceptive. Just because you want to believe something doesn't necessarily make it true."

"I agree... of course, yes... but I still don't...?"

"And as soon as I'd worked it all out I phoned Mayor Carey to explain the predicament that he'd put us all in. Through his greed and arrogance. Yet despite Carey's failings, he was still the one best placed to make amends. Although he failed to detain *the Asticots* at the theatre as *you* requested, he came good with the second thing I, or rather *you*, asked of him. Owning Blinkton's only haulage firm, I managed to persuade him to drive his biggest soft-topped lorry up against the west door of St Hilda's Church..."

"You did what?"

"Last night. Stuffed full of mattresses."

"Mattresses?"

"Loads of them. Soft ones. Deep. Memory-foam. Thick enough to cushion my drop from the top of the tower. I had plenty of time hanging around up there waiting for the brain-dead pair to arrive in order to gauge my fall accurately. Timed to perfection. Just as the police arrived."

Mike Bennett rose to his feet, "You... you... fell. From the tower. At St Hilda's. Why that's... that's...?"

"Well, strictly speaking, "I didn't fall... you did! All part of my plan, you see. I hadn't counted on Asticot, or rather Harold Parker, having a pistol though..."

"A pistol?"

"But there were always going to be risks. That's one thing I've learned from Blinkton Comprehensive... you can't make an omelette without cracking eggs."

"Granted, but can we rewind a little? What did you mean when...?"

The telephone rang. Mid-sentence, Bennett lifted the receiver and dropped it back into its cradle.

"...what did you mean when you said that *I* fell off the church roof?"

The teenage detective moved back to join Bennet, enjoying his teacher's confusion, "Let's just say I'm not a great fan of publicity, sir," he said. "When I commandeered your office, I was able to borrow your identity too. I'm not the only one who's pretended to be someone else this week, you see. But I was forced to do it," he said, "Carey would never deal with a schoolkid. He wasn't particularly inclined to speak to a lowly Deputy-Head either. Not at first. Until he'd listened to what I, or rather you, had to tell him. Then he was suddenly very much more responsive. Alarmingly so, in fact. Well done, sir," said the detective, with a wink, "you were very persuasive."

"But?"

"Don't worry, Mayor Carey and I never met. We only spoke over the phone. He still thinks it was you who foiled *the Asticot's* plan and recovered Blinkton-on-Sea's most prized asset."

"But.... How... But... How...?" Bennett paused, took a breath, then tried again, "But... how could I fall onto a mattress-laden truck and not be spotted?"

"In a raging blizzard? With an army of police cars racing to the scene and gunshots being fired...?"

"Gunshots?"

"Just one or two."

"One or two!?"

"Well, two actually. But only one at me, or rather you. And it missed. By a mile. No," said Inky, "having executed a perfect fall I, *you*, simply brushed the snow from my, *your*, clothes, rolled off Carey's mattresses, then disappeared into the storm. Mayor Carey's cue was the bump he felt when I, *you*, crash-landed on top of his vehicle. But from then he was involved in a foot race with the police to see who could get inside St Hilda's first. I'd promised him that the imposters would be locked up and waiting for him. I also told him that the keys to release them would be placed on the floor of the utility room. Right in front of the staircase door. He knew that the only way to slither out of the mess he'd created was to catch the imposters himself. To *been seen* catching them too. Publicly. So he really was in a hurry. Congratulating you was the last thing on his mind. But," Inky added, knowingly, "I think you'll find that things will be a little different now that he's had time to come to his senses. I predict that Mayor Carey will be much more generous towards you from now on." Inky moved towards the door, "Right, sir, I think you're just about up to speed. I believe you've a Christmas disco to arrange while I have the pleasure of 'Chalky' Whittle for charades. And don't look so worried, sir," he reassured, "you've dealt with everything impeccably. It was Ray Day who injured Miss Birkin, and he's gone. It was Jack Parker who set off the school-bell, and you've unmasked him as a dangerous imposter in the process of foiling his father's scheme to bring Blinkton to its knees. The Snake will be in raptures. I'm sure She'd like to kiss you, if you could stomach such unpleasantness? Not a bad couple of weeks' work, sir. Even for a teacher."

As Inky reached for the door handle, Mike Bennett mumbled, "Inky?"

"Yes?"

"I... I've heard... you always require a token from your investigations." He shrugged. "I owe everything to you. I can't believe... can't believe that you've... I can't express how very, very... It's just..."

"No need to say anything, sir, not that you're saying very much as it is. It's simply what I do."

"But I've nothing for you... I'm not sure what... It's not that..."

"Relax, sir," said Inky, taking a step back into the room. He extended a hand. Bennett did likewise, but instead of the anticipated handshake, the teenager placed a number of coins into his palm.

"What's this?"

"One pound thirteen pence."

"One pound thirteen pence?"

"The change from your ten pound note."

"The change from my... what... I... how...but...?"

The telephone sparked up again silencing Bennett's gibbering. Ignoring its shrill persistence, Inky stated, "Sir, I've already acquired exactly what I wanted from this investigation. I have in my possession many, many photographs, recordings too, which document Blinkton School's failings..."

"But how...?"

"... some of which concern the Snake."

"The Snake...?"

"Who knows what the future will bring but, whatever happens," Inky took a step closer to Bennett, "She won't be opposing me. Not now. Not ever. Because you're going to have a discreet word with Her, sir. On my behalf. You're going to mention that I possess certain evidence. Concerning Her. Just make sure that She understands the situation. That if She leaves me alone, I'll leave Her alone..."

Mike Bennett stood aghast, "But I can't...?"

"Oh yes you can, sir, and you will." Inky made to leave once again, "It's probably not ethical, so you can choose to take this in whatever way you choose, but the envelope I've just placed onto your seating contains a couple such photographs. For your own use. Two of the more revealing ones I hasten to add. Mr Day took them..."

"Ray Day...?"

"Trust me, sir. He's a nasty man. He deserves everything that life's about to throw at him." Inky added, "You may choose to destroy them, of course, or," he paused, "you may choose to use them to your own advantage. As bargaining power, perhaps? As I say," he continued, "the choice is yours. Oh yes, there's also an edited voice recording of the Parkers' confession. The one you made at St Hilda's. You'll be highly thought of for passing it on to the relevant authorities. You have the power to ensure the pair of them get exactly what they deserve. Merry Christmas, sir. Enjoy your holidays when they come and take some time to rest. Oh," said Inky, departing, "I'd answer that phone if I were you. I think you've kept Mayor Carey waiting long enough!"

Mike Bennett was overcome. Unable to control himself, tears started to stream down his cheeks. Two weeks of pain and uncertainty all came flooding out in one go. He watched Inky's departure through a blur of tears. Left alone, he collapsed onto the seating, head in hands, sobbing uncontrollably. His teardrops fell down onto a small pile of plaster shavings which had strangely appeared on the floor of his office.

Minutes later, Bennett had regained a sense of control. Having wiped his face on his shirt sleeve, he shook his head to clear his thoughts. Grounded, he reached out to lift the phone from its cradle,

"Mayor Carey? Yes this is Mike Bennett?... What's that?... You want to thank me for my courage last night and you'd like to reward me? In person? Sorry, what's that? You want to know all about my involvement regarding the capture of Jean-Pierre and Jacques Asticot up at St Hilda's Church? Well, sir, now that you mention it, that's a long and very complicated story..."

MR MIKE BENNETT (DEPUTY-HEAD):

And I think you'll agree, it was a long and complicated story. One which left me with a dilemma...

I'd like to say that I owned up and told Mayor Carey the truth. That I gave Inky all the credit he deserved for his selfless bravery...

But I didn't.

I was weak. And to my shame, I played the situation to my advantage.

I'm aware that that's what Inky instructed me to do, of course, but every time I profited from his actions, a little pang of conscience reminded me that my gains were undeserved. And this heavy feeling dogged me for years.

'My' heroics were splashed all over the Gazette for three weeks running. I was hailed as THE DEPUTY WHO RAN THE OUTLAWS OUT OF TOWN. Blinkton treated me as its saviour. I became a celebrity. Mayor Carey, desperate to identify himself with 'the hero of the hour', was suddenly very amenable. To start with he invited me for slap-up meal at the Codfather Restaurant. And while Frank Parkinson served up mountains of cod and chips for us both, Simon Kench took even more photographs for that week's Gazette. Parkinson was delighted to reward me as 'I' was the one who'd defended the secrecy of his recipe. The scrap of paper containing his great-grandfather's rhyme was seized at St Hilda's and returned to its rightful owner. Parkinson had then re-hung his frame in 'pride of plaice' back in his restaurant while secretly keeping the genuine manuscript under lock and key at home. As luck would have it, that winter's scandal made the Codfather's food even more popular than ever. Turnover rocketed. Frank's business thrived (as did Blinkton's tourist industry as a whole). And Parkinson continued to treat me as a VIP whenever I chose to dine there.

(Free of charge, of course!)

The same was also true of the Harbor Lites. Eccentric Deidre went on to make a feature of her ordeal. She left her penthouse suite exactly as it had been when she and the real Jean-Pierre Asticot had made their escape. Thus her guest-house became a kind of macabre museum... severed bindings, DIY tools, ciga-rette burns, mouldy toast... all proudly on display. Deidre delighted in showing dumbfounded guests around the site of her harrowing ordeal. The Harbor Lites became Blinkton's very own 'Chamber of Horrors' and its popularity soared. From the threat of bankruptcy, her guest-house became a thriving business. The hotel's coffers swelled and Ms Butterfield became quite wealthy. But not for one moment did she consider retirement. Oh no. Her success meant that she could continue to do what she did best... serving people. And in recognition of her efforts, her guest-house was finally awarded that extra star she craved. The Harbor Lites '4' stars now adorns her frontage in letters which no longer blink on and off quite so haphazardly...

On the few occasions that Deidre and I ran into one another I could tell by her expression that she didn't approve of how I'd stolen Inky's glory. She knew the truth, of course. But she was a lady of principle and, to honour the detective's request, never revealed all the details about who really came to her rescue that bitterly cold December.

To her immense credit, and my immense shame.

The real Mayor Asticot, however, was less forgiving. Once his promise to Inky had been honoured he returned to Mal-de-Mer under a cloud of Gallic disapproval. He never returned to Britain again and instantly severed all links with Blinkton-on-Sea. (For some reason he preferred the sunshine of southern France to Britain's drizzly desolation.) Shortly afterwards, the sign welcoming visitors into Blinkton was mysteriously amended. It now reads,

YOU ARE NOW ENTERING BLINKTON-ON-SEA, HOME OF THE CODFATHER'S WORLD-FAMOUS FISH BATTER, ONCE SUBJECTED TO AN AUDATIOUS HIJACKING. ENJOY YOUR STAY AND WHEN YOU LEAVE, PLEASE COME BACK AGAIN SOON. PLEASE.

(BLINKTON-ON-SEA WAS FORMERLY TWINNED WITH 'MAL-DE-MER', FRANCE.)

And as for the criminals...

Jack Parker, being only seventeen, was seen as his father's accomplice and given a lesser punishment. He was forced to attend a young offenders' institution. While there, he took advantage of some of the training on offer. He now runs a highly successful hairdressing salon, 'Jack of all Fades', a 'French-style boutique' situated well away from Blinkton.

Harold Parker, however, escaped much less lightly. To this day he remains behind bars. A surly, awkward prisoner, he makes a point of going on hunger strike every time fish and chips are served up on the prison menu. He no longer possesses a gold tooth either. His expensive dental work was removed in strange circumstances after lights-out during a particularly rowdy evening.

Solomon Carey, despite his unpopularity, somehow managed to be re-elected the following summer and I guess that I was partly responsible for this. Carey, the master manipulator, used me as part of his charm offensive. Although it was convenient for him to overlook his part in the Asticots' arrival, he was more than eager to celebrate his part in their downfall. He laid on a lavish celebration at the Town Hall so he could boast all about his courageous exploits. I was forced to deliver a short speech at the event myself. With reluctance, I explained 'my' role in the plot to foil the Asticots/Parkers. Carey then followed this up with a much longer account of how he'd teamed up with me in order to bring the armed-siege to a conclusion. You'd think we were Batman and Robin the way he spoke (he being Batman, of course). With outrageous pomp he boasted about how he'd brushed off all concerns for his own safety to drive an unstable, soft-topped van through perilous, snow-laden streets in order to save 'my' life. Then he went on to explain how he'd helped the police tackle the scheming duo as they were forcefully removed from St Hilda's. And as I stood beside him listening to his exaggerated bluster, my thoughts returned to Inky Stevens. The fanciful tale I delivered so willingly ought to have stuck in my throat, just like the words in the terrible nightmare that I'd had.

But it didn't.

I was just as bad as Solomon Carey. I also exploited the detective's exploits and I continued to do so over and over again. I even started to enjoy my celebrity status. To believe that I'd really done all those things Inky told me about. And worse was to follow...

(Or better?)

That January, when Blinkton's exam results were announced, they were every bit as good as Inky'd predicted. Better in fact. Miraculous. So good that they caused a seismic shock at County Hall. The Snake was beside Herself with delight. She simply could not smile wide enough (and it was not a pretty sight I can assure you!) As far as She was concerned both guilty parties had been smoked out and dealt with accordingly. And after all the stress She'd been subjected to I noted that visits to an aromatherapist, herbalist and a reflexologist were added to Her 'busy' schedule during the Spring Term.

On my part, when Blinkton emerged as the highest achieving school in the district I was hailed as a motivational genius. Suddenly I was in demand. Everyone wanted to know my secret. Everyone wanted a taste of my success. Especially over at St Derek's at Krull where their worst results in its history led to the sacking of Headteacher, Roger Rowlandson. So...

I took over!

I seized my opportunity and hurriedly applied for the vacant Headship. My appointment was a foregone conclusion. I was employed with immediate effect and by Easter I'd left Blinkton altogether. The Snake tried to prevent me going, of course. With fangs bared. She refused to write me a reference and demanded that I honour my contract with Her. But this resistance soon dissolved when I showed Her what Inky'd provided for me in that manila envelope. All of a sudden She became uncharacteristically charitable.

Eerily pleasant.

And in that way, Inky Stevens changed my life. Within a few months of my nervous visit to his shed I was earning significantly more money, had unparalleled status, and found myself in an establishment where hard work brought fair rewards. I even rediscovered my love of education. I was bulletproof... No more Sparkle Group. No more Isolation Unit. No more Big-Sean threatening to let my tyres down after school. And, most important of all, no more Snake. After years of torment, I was finally able to sleep at night.

All night, every night as I have done ever since.

But the shadow of my deception, like that of the Great School Detective himself, has haunted me ever since.

Poisoning my conscience. Suffocating my pride. Gnawing away at my integrity.

So I always knew that the truth would surface one day. That I'd finally give Inky the recognition he deserved all along. I took from Inky Stevens... and I never gave back. And that was very wrong. And seeing Dukes' book in my local bookshop that Saturday afternoon, I knew right there and then that the time had come to make amends...

And finally, belatedly, 'Inky Stevens. For Whom the School-Bell Tolls' came into being.

Every word of what you've just read is completely true. Throughout my career I've always striven to bring out the best in others, it's just a shame that it's taken so long for me to bring out the best in myself. Inky Stevens, I owe everything that I am to you...

Thank you!

19. BLINKTON SCHOOL HALL:

Friday 23ᵗʰ December (Evening).

The lights blinked on inside the school Hall shattering the intimate atmosphere. A roomful of students immediately stopped dancing and shielded their eyes against the glare. Mr Morris, at the music desk, faded out the senseless chirps of 'the Birdie Song'...

"Boys and girls of Blinkton Comprehensive," he said, fighting against a sudden burst of static that caused everyone to wince, "as we bring tonight to a close there are a few thank-yous to make. The Christmas disco would not have been the success it has been without the many, many dedicated people behind the scenes, all of whom deserve a quick mention now..."

Morris proceeded to name everyone connected with the event, however remotely, in order of importance. Such individuals included Crispin Merridew who arranged the refreshments, Moira Carr who designed the poster and printed off all the tickets, and Victor Toogood who donated the Christmas tree and made all the paper-chain decorations (his tongue was dry for a week).

"But," continued Morris, noticing that several students had sat down on the parquet flooring, bored, "I think there's one person who deserves an extra-special mention. This person has not only overseen tonight's event but we've also learned today that he's single-handedly saved Blinkton-on-Sea from an evil which has threatened to destroy us all. Boys and girls, please give a very warm round of applause for our beloved Deputy-Head, the extra-special, extra-heroic, Mr Michael Bennett."

While Bennett smiled coyly from the back of the Hall, the room erupted in heartfelt applause. The ovation swelled, quickly rising to a chorus of sustained cheers. Joan Ambrose, swept up in the moment, grabbed hold of Bennett and locked him in a tight clinch. This, it seemed, was the cue for several others to do likewise. Immediately Bennett was submerged beneath a mass of ecstatic well-wishers.

Mr Morris, watching on from the stage, felt a lump in his throat. What he saw reaffirmed his love of the teaching profession. He'd never seen such a spontaneous outpouring of affection in school before,

'Although they don't often show it,' he thought, *'our schoolkids really are grateful for what we do for them.'*

"And finally," continued the Textiles teacher, voice trembling, "if you could all unhand Mr Bennett and allow him the break he deserves, the biggest thank you of all has to go to... all of you. For attending tonight. For working so hard throughout the term and, despite your many, many faults," he laughed, "for being a splendid bunch of individuals. We'll see you all back here in January ready to start the whole process over again." Morris fought against the good-natured jeers, "And now, it's the final record of the evening. Have a safe journey home everyone. See you all in the New Year..."

All too quickly, the hall lights flicked off and the glitterball on the ceiling whirred into life. The room was immediately drenched in a silver shower of confetti-light. And as the introduction to Wham's 'Last Christmas' pumped into the darkened Hall, Blinkton's students began to couple up. Awkwardly.

(Or run off and hide.)

It was then that Tommy Woggle made the move he'd been planning.

Tommy, having deliberately ignored Amanda Blunt all evening, now began to thread his way through the darkness. He weaved around couples who were clumsily working out how to hold one another, and where. Amanda, sitting alone beneath the exit door, scowled at Oggy's approach.

"I was wondering," stuttered Woggle.

"Yeah?"

"I was just wondering if...?"

"Come on spit it out!"

"If you wouldn't mind... wouldn't mind sharing a dance? With me?"

Mandy cupped a hand to her ear, "You're gonna have to speak up, the music's too loud."

"Do you want a dance?" he shouted, red in the face.

Amanda eyed him warily, then held out her hand, "Of course, Tom, I'd love to."

"What?" he replied, cupping a hand to his ear, "I can't hear you?"

Instead of repeating herself, Amanda lifted Thomas Woggle of the ground and carried him to the centre of the dancefloor. She plonked him down then wrapped her arms around his neck a little too tightly. Finding himself enveloped in a bear-like squeeze, young-Tom placed his hands onto Mandy's waist. Gingerly. The unlikely pair then began to spin around clockwise in the same manner as so many others were doing all around them... like confused zombies.

Inky Stevens, concealed where the shadows were deepest, watched on as Tom and Mandy gazed into one another's eyes. Content, the detective allowed the faintest trace of a smile to appear. He then stooped to reach underneath a pile of stacked exam desks. Knowing exactly where Scott Cunliffe had left the sports-bag, he quickly located it and tugged it free. Ada Stevens would be needing her clothes back for the Christmas Day church service at St Hilda's. Slinging the bag over his shoulder, Inky slipped invisibly through the Hall, then out through a side-door and away.

No one saw Inky Stevens leave. No-one had properly been aware that he'd been there in the first place.

Not really.

Leaving the syrupy music and the haplessly embracing students behind, the Great School Detective became as one with the chill winter evening.

His job was done... for now...!

CASE CLOSED.

AUTHOR

Chris Martin lives in Adlington, Lancashire with wife, June. Chris began teaching in 1990. As Head of Drama, the majority of his career was spent in two secondary schools... the first in Bridlington, East Yorkshire, and then in Bolton, Greater Manchester. During this period, writing as a hobby, Chris established himself as Britain's foremost author of fundraising murder-mystery plays.

Inspired by this success, Chris retired from teaching in 2013 to concentrate on writing full-time. Combining his experience in education with his love of writing mystery stories the character Inky Stevens was born. *Inky Stevens., For Whom the School-Bell Tolls* is the second novel in the *Great School Detective* series.

Lightning Source UK Ltd.
Milton Keynes UK
UKOW06f1919211115

263246UK00002B/17/P